PRESS DIONYSUS

2021

First published in 2021 by PRESS DIONYSUS LTD in the UK, 167, Portland Road, N15 4SZ, London.

www.pressdionysus.com

Paperback

ISBN: 978-1-913961-00-8

Tottenham Boys

Dursaliye Şahan

Translated by Andrew Penny

PRESS DIONYSUS

Press Dionysus •

ISBN- 978-1-913961-00-8

© 2021 Press Dionysus

First Edition, November 2021, London

Translated by Andrew Penny

Cover design: S.Deniz Akıncı

Press Dionysus LTD, 167, Portland Road, N15 4SZ,
London

• e-mail: info@pressdionysus.com

• web: www.pressdionysus.com

About the Author

Born in a small village in Turkey, Dursaliye Şahan immigrated to Istanbul with her family at the age of four and then to London. Graduated from Anadolu University, Department of Radio and Television, the author continues her literary life, which she started at a young age, with stories, theatre plays, novels and cartoons.

Six stories, three novels, a cartoon and two children's books by her have been published so far.

Her short story "Güvercin" (The Pigeon) has been made into a television series twice. She received scriptwriting funding from the Republic of Turkey Ministry of Culture with her works "Hacı Murad and Ali Haydar".

The author, whose many stories have been translated into English and met with readers in various magazines and anonymous books, has various short story and literature awards from Turkey and abroad.

Dursaliye Şahan continues to organize story and writing workshops for children, disabled and adults, and to be a jury member in story competitions.

Chapter One

NOBLE WHORE

"The PKK[1] forced a dancer off the stage"

This was the total of the information, but the Boss was excited.

"Fantastic! Fantastic!"

If the information was high value – meaning more readers – this would be the first word we would hear. Until the article was finished he couldn't sit still. When we handed it over with the final full-stop we would relax, but he would go up a level. "Which page? How much to cut? How many photos to use? And if the news item was political its fate, as well as that of its writer, was a real mystery.

The "dancer forced off the stage" incident might well turn into a headline such as "Ban on Turkish dancers working in Britain".

As reporters we were in the category of ineffective employees at the mercy of the editors.

Facing these secret dictators in a media that had turned into

---

1 *PKK: The Kurdistan Workers' Party or **PKK** is a Kurdish militant and political organization based in Turkey and Iraq.*

a barrel of gunpowder through overwork we were ready to accept anything, because for us it was more important to see our names on the front page than to get two months' salary as a bonus. We assumed that everyone in the world read every sentence we wrote, including indigenous people living in the Amazon jungle. Whereas in reality, 90% of the population didn't even know the name of the most famous journalist in the country. Besides, journalism is a 24-hour job. The day you give up your pen means your press card falls from your neck.

Our news editor, as always, had begun to endorse the Boss, rubbing his hands gleefully.

I would usually be the one left carrying the can in such cases, but I was still feeling bleary-eyed and was amusing myself looking through readers' letters. It was one of our usual weekly diversions to read ads sent in out loud. Erdem had read out one in an eastern accent: "I'm seeking a woman," after which he had found a photo on the web browser that resembled Hannibal Lecter, enlarged it and pinned it on the wall. Mehtap had then printed out the words: "He's mine. No one else can have him" in large capital letters and pinned the note underneath the photo.

While we were still laughing, this shocking news dampened the mood.

Erdem swore, saying: "Even terror has its limits! What's this? What have they got to do with dancers?"

The Boss was already daydreaming. "They'll see! We'll give the headline seven columns."

The news editor gulped down some coffee, smacked his lips and said: "Out you go."

I put my camera in my bag and went out. Half an hour later I was sitting opposite my old roommate Habibe on the bus watching the crowds outside. Although we seemed to be very different, after Neriman, Habibe was the first person I would call if I was in trouble. She put the bubble gum she occasionally chewed under her tongue and refreshed her lipstick. Then she pushed the curls that had fallen onto her shoulders back onto her head.

I was certain the news was not true. What were they thinking? How could a dancer and that association have any connection?

Like lots of things in my life, the work I did was foolish. I said to Habibe, who was sitting looking at me impishly: "Do you think such a thing is possible?"

She scratched her cheek with her varnished nails as if caressing it. She put her hand on her neck and tossed her blond hair. Her overpowering perfume wafted towards my lungs. She puckered her newly-rouged lips and said: "Why not, dear?"

"Phoney Marilyn! I was wrong to ask."

She rattled her bracelets and pointed outside. "Look. Where are we?"

"In the middle of London," I replied.

She waved her middle finger, adorned with a large ring containing a large red stone, to left and right, saying: "No, you're wrong, this is not just London."

I was already fed up at going off after false news first thing in the morning, and with Habibe's ramblings I felt even more down.

"This is the Republic of Kurdistan."

She was right. Hackney, Britain's migrant paradise, was our ghetto. We had named it the Republic of Kurdistan between ourselves. Hackney, with its kebab shops, 24-hour grocery stores, tea houses and cheap restaurants was like a small satellite of Turkey.

As the bus passed Dalston market it stopped. Amongst those who got on the bus were two black youths. They stood diagonally across from us. Habibe began to eye up the tall, broad-shouldered one. We had found it hard to get used to her slightly wanton behaviour. She loved to make men fall in love with her and then treat the poor dears who had fallen into her trap like slaves. What was strange was that a woman like that was able to exist in a mainly Trotskyist group. Although we would pretend not to notice her absence at meetings she did not attend, our eyes searched for her. We were in awe of her unconcerned behaviour in not being embarrassed by anything that we found strange.

It was as if she was breaking all the rules single-handedly on our behalf.

"Love is my field of expertise. Love and men. You could say I'm an expert on men."

She would engage in the most banter with Neriman, who had abandoned her three-year-old son and her career as a nurse and not even told her parents when leaving the country during the military coup of 1980. Neriman would take every opportunity to needle Habibe.

"Stupid bourgeois! Is there such a sector as love and men?"

"Ignoramus! Of course there is!"

"Ah, I forgot, they're called brothels, aren't they?"

"Ooooh! How rude! You've made me feel sick. I'm talking about something else."

"What's the difference?"

"I'm bringing nobility to the profession of prostitution."

"Nobility and that profession… You're crazy!"

"How would a noble whore look, have you never thought about that?"

We looked at each other as if to say: "what is this maniac going on about?" but still none of us told her to drop the subject.

Her flirty conversation did not vulgarise her, rather in a strange way it made her stronger and more attractive. Her secret and hopeless lover Doctor Tahir smiled, trying not to make clear his anger. "Why don't you tell about this noble thing. I mean this noble whore, what nonsense is it?"

"What's up. Are you going to try it too?"

In fact, Tahir wanted to be sure whether or not she was a prostitute. Habibe narrowed her eyes and stared at him. "You know, it's a professional secret."

She then turned to me and told me anxiously: "Don't tell anyone, or I'll cut out your tongue," as if there was something to tell.

If you wanted to be a noble whore, you would show and show but not give anything.

While thinking about this, Habibe waved excitedly at a young man amongst those who had just got on the bus, saying: "come over here, it's so good that I saw you."

She embraced and kissed the man I did not know, then brought him over to us holding his hand.

"Look. The cure for a patient who will recover comes to him."

How was this person whose name I didn't know going to help us. Especially if it involved that organisation…

Habibe swiftly explained the incident of the PKK forcing a dancer off the stage. Then without drawing breath she turned to me.

"Zekai is a waiter at the kcbab restaurant where we celebrated Reyhan's birthday. Ah, you didn't come. Anyway, Zekai was very helpful to me. He is a sweet boy."

I suddenly revived. At last there was hope to rid myself of this nonsensical news. Zekai signalled to us to wait and moved towards the stairs on the bus. As he went up the stairs Habibe and I looked at each other. She put another piece of gum in her mouth and began to chew it. I was fed up with being stuck in a traffic jam. I resumed looking at the crowds outside. If Istanbul has 72 and a half nationalities. London must have a thousand. Wherever you look you see a riot of colour. Dealing with a news item concerning a handful of migrants from Turkey was like starting a storm in a teacup.

Habibe and the black youth had moved on from eyeing each other up to laughing. I would not have been surprised if at that moment she had got up and got off the bus hand in hand with the man whose name she didn't even know. Her past was full of men she had met in public places and driven mad.

I closed my eyes and tried to relax. If they heard I was spreading baseless stories, they would raid the newspaper, as they had before. While thinking about this, Zekai came downstairs and approached us.

Habibe said, excitedly: "As you are smiling you must have learned something."

"Now, it apparently happened like this. They said that 'a Kurdish dancer is performing in a night club,' so they went and raided the place. They gave the boss of the place, who is from Nigde, a good beating, and removed the half-naked girls from the stage."

"So you're saying it's true."

"It's true, it's true! Look, I'm explaining, listen. Then they gave the girls table cloths, for shawls, and took them to the association."

"You're talking about members of the organisation, aren't you?"

"Hey, don't interrupt! The girls began to cry. As they talked the girls apparently shook their heads. And then, do you know what happened?"

"Look, don't tell me something bad. It will upset me. Did they do something to do with traditions?"

"No, no!"

"So what happened?"

"They realised that the girls didn't speak Turkish or Kurdish. Why, do you know?"

"Because they were deaf and dumb!?"

"You couldn't guess in a thousand years. One of them was Romanian and the other Spanish."

"No way!"

"Yes!"

"But why did they say that a Romanian and a Spanish girl were Kurdish?"

"Why, it was the boss's cunning. By saying: 'I've brought these girls from Şırnak. Both village girls and Kurdish girls!' he increased the number of customers."

"Yah!"

We started to laugh as Zekai and his friends got off the bus.

Habibe began to act like a spoilt child, saying: "If it wasn't for me you wouldn't be able to do this news. Who cares?"

"Be quiet, yeah! Who's going to believe this? How can it be written?"

"Big deal. I want my present."

She wanted a kiss. She was full of life and unabashedly demanding of affection.

Two stops later Habibe, mincing on her 15-centimetre high heels, her bottom the centre of attention, got off the bus. She then turned round and blew a kiss to me or to the black youth, it was not clear which. He raised an eyebrow as if to say "why did you get off?" but she continued on her way without a backwards glance.

My mood had improved somewhat. It was a news item like an anecdote. The Boss, who was dreaming of winning the news of the year award, would be disappointed.

It would be stupid to go straight back to the newspaper office. The traffic had almost come to a complete halt. More passengers were boarding the bus. An Indian woman in a sari was having difficulty getting on the bus with a pushchair, as she had put three full shopping bags on the pushchair. The young man behind her picked up the pushchair and placed it in the vacant space in front of the window before sitting down in the seat Habibe had vacated. He was Turkish, without a doubt. He was wearing an old pair of jeans and a blue and white t-shirt. With his jet black eyebrows, long thick eyelashes surrounding large black eyes and wavy dark hair he looked like a typical Anatolian. He was followed immediately by a plump Moroccan who sat down next to me. They began to converse in English.

"Keko, don't do this to me!"

Keko was silent.

"Think of me."

They were at most 17 or 18 years old.

"Keko, you know Aziz. He will definitely do what he says."

Keko didn't seem to hear.

"And I didn't tell you."

The Moroccan lowered his voice and leaned towards Keko.

"He apparently said: 'take his mother'".

Keko shrunk back as if a needle had been stuck into him. He then leaned towards the other boy as if he was going to hit him. He was glaring at him. He didn't lower his voice, saying: "Whose mother, damn you?"

The Moroccan looked scared and shrank back.

"I'm not pleading with you for nothing. They told me: 'We'll kill you before them'. I have to hand over the goods."

"Have I got it, have I got the shit? And what's it got to do with my mother?"

The Moroccan looked around him worrying someone would hear and whispered:

"I know, Keko, that you don't have it, but you can find it."

"What's it got to do with me?"

The Moroccan's voice began to tremble.

"They think that if they take your mother you will agree to do the job."

Keko's dark cheeks had reddened. For a moment he didn't know what to say. Then he shook his head and said: "Tell them to come, in that case."

The Moroccan's eyes shone with delight. "Thank you, brother. I knew you would help me."

He stretched out his hand but Keko wasn't looking. He was shaking his head. The Moroccan seemed to be embarrassed. At the first stop he got off.

Keko looked confused. He was clenching his fists and stamping on the floor.

Two beads of sweat dripped from his head.

I couldn't bear it so said quietly: "Keko."

He was surprised to hear his name.

"I heard your name just now. Didn't your friend call you Keko?"

Instead of answering he grimaced and shrugged his shoulders.

"Are you ok?"

He nodded, as if to say yes.

"I think there's a problem."

"No."

I hesitated, then said: "I may be able to help you."

The beads of sweat on his face increased.

I was trying not to scare him, but he had no intention of talking to me.

"Sister, leave me alone!"

He swept his hair back with his fingers and looked around him. When we got to the stop he

was up like a flash and off the bus. I wanted to shout after him or get off myself. He had disappeared.

I didn't feel like going anywhere. At the second stop I got off the 149 bus and took a 243. It was best to return to the office.

This is how I met Keko, who in that tumult had impinged himself on my mind like a drop of water. He was just one of the hundreds of mainly dark migrants with beautiful eyes from my dear country that I saw every day.

Chapter Two

SUICIDE

Journalists die young, as they work 24/7. In reality, there is little difference between a kebab shop and a newspaper when it comes to running a business. Both provide a service according to the wishes of the customer. Consequently, I was just one of an army of reporters covering the most meaningless news on the treadmill.

That morning it was beautiful outside, like a summer's day. I turned my back on the sunlight filtering through the window and started to prepare the weekly magazine supplement on my perpetually dusty desk. Clichéd captions for a pile of photos.

"The happiness of the newly-married couple can be seen on their faces."

"Can Eyup entered manhood with a magnificent celebration [a circumcision feast]"

"London's Emel Sayin, Askim, at a charity night…"

"The esteemed Turkish Ambassador welcomed guests…"

Mehtap came in, looking agitated.

"A report of a suicide has come in. The Boss is not here. What shall we do?"

"Another one?"

"It's like an epidemic."

"Has anyone else heard?"

"No, it came direct to me."

"Leave it, don't tell anyone!"

It would be stupid to start something with only 2 hours of the working day left.

On finishing the magazine page I went downstairs. The news editor, taking advantage of the Boss's absence, had shot off early. Distributor Hasan arrived. He also looked agitated. He ordered a tea from the café next door and we sat down. I had concealed the news but I wasn't comfortable about it.

It was as if Mehtap had read my mind.

"This time two young people."

"Lovers?" I asked.

"No, they were both male."

It was never nice writing about deaths, even if you didn't know the people concerned, especially when it was suicide. As I picked up my bag and prepared to leave I turned to Erdem and said: "Don't forget to tour the tavernas. We still need material for the London magazine page. Advertisers are complaining."

In the cool of the evening I began to walk down Green Lanes. In fact, a file on the young people committing suicide would be a big story for Istanbul. I entered a Turkish grocer to do some shopping. As I didn't know what to get I just had a look around and left. I walked down Stoke Newington Road and went into the Halkevi. The air was thick with cigarette smoke. Young people were busy preparing banners for a protest against the Immigration Act in Trafalgar Square in two days' time.

Neriman came over, rolling her cigarette in her hand to soften it.

"Do you know, there's been another suicide, and this time, if it's true, two at once, they're saying."

"Perhaps it's not true."

If the Boss heard we had deliberately ignored the story he would have a fit.

It was as if they had a secret agreement between them, as nearly all of them ended their lives by hanging themselves. I bought teas for Neriman and myself. I didn't want to spend the evening thinking about the suicide case. "Let's go to the cinema. It will help us relax."

"I really don't feel like it. I'm very tired today."

"Afterwards I'll buy you tripe soup."

"Alright…"

"We got our stuff together and left the crowds and smoke of the Halkevi. We just made it to the last showing at the Rio. The film was *Les Amants du Pont-Neuf*, starring Juliette Binoche. I couldn't concentrate on the film, but it would not have been right to leave the sobbing Neriman.

As we left the cinema we ran into Neriman's cousin. I was not in the mood to have tripe soup so I left them and walked quickly up to the Halkevi. Although it was late it was still open as people were still preparing banners.

"No, mate, no! The police say it was gang related."

"Comrade, I'm telling you that the one from Siirt was engaged, but they'd broken up."

"Have the police made a statement?"

The news was true. Two young people had hanged themselves in front of their houses. What we had to do was learn the details. Names, surnames, home towns, short life stories. And if we could find a photo, it would be great.

A good journalist never misses out on a story. They get the story together, write it and send it in. The rule that they never let on to anyone else, is, in my opinion, a rule made up by editors to fire up their reporters. It has nothing to do with professional ethics.

An epidemic of suicides had begun, like a grotesque infectious disease. But there was nothing one could do about it. If I didn't drop off to sleep while reading my book I wouldn't have the energy to work the next day. And wasn't working like a slave a kind of suicide? Either this way or that way…. One day we will all die. If some people wanted to depart early that was up to them.

I left the book and got out of bed. There was nothing in the fridge but a carton of milk and half a pizza from the previous week that did not look edible. I made white coffee in a big mug and mixed in some crystallised honey from the bottom of the jar. Then I cut up some stale bread. It seemed to help the unhappiness in my stomach.

The doorbell rang. I wasn't expecting anybody. I hesitated. It rang again and again so I got up. It was Neriman.

"Were you asleep?"

"And…"

"Can I stay here?"

"Has your cousin brought his girlfriend round again?"

"No, no. This is something different. They're going to have an organising meeting for the demo."

We began to drink our coffee at the round wooden table. When I finished it I got up to go to the bathroom.

Neriman called after me: "Do you know, the mother of one of those who committed suicide is one of the people I interpreted for."

I stopped. Why couldn't I get away from these people committing suicide? What was it to me, these problem-ridden boys who kept intruding into my unhappy life?

Isn't it always like this? Life resists your attempts to plan your life. Your fate sucks you into maelstroms you don't want by tricking you. And sometimes it surprises you by offering you a stick to help you out of the pit in which you're floundering.

I turned to Neriman in despair. "Eh, what happened?"

"Nothing happened. The woman's life was dramatic. And a bit comic, so tragicomic."

"But aren't all the people's lives you translate for full of tragic stories?"

"This one is really comic. Both painful and comic."

I went into the bathroom, muttering to myself "So it's comic…"

I would have been happier if Neriman, who was scraping the last of the honey out of the jar, hadn't come. I longed for the nights I used to spend alone in my little flat when I slept really soundly. I wasn't that happy then, but I wasn't as edgy as I was now.

When I came out of the bathroom Neriman got up, smacking her lips, and took a file out of her bag.

"The woman's statement is here. Read it for heaven's sake. I didn't know how to translate what she said. If you tell a British person these things they will think you're mad. So to help her I wrote in a language they would understand."

I don't know why, but I didn't feel like reading the file.

"Isn't what I've read all day enough? And now you want me to read this?"

Two young people commit suicide and no one knows the reason."

"How do you know they don't know?"

"Maybe it was a homosexual relationship and of course they couldn't tell anyone."

"Gay?"

"Not everyone can commit suicide. It takes courage. Are imbeciles who put up with everything or those who dance on the edge and refuse to submit to their fate braver?"

I cleaned my teeth and stretched out on my bed. Did this Neriman never tire of talking?

I don't know how much time passed. I managed to drop off then woke up in the middle of the night. I felt as if I was choking. I didn't remember having a nightmare but I felt very uneasy. My doctor linked my insomnia to adverse events in my life and would always send me away as if to say: "don't come back."

I got up and walked over to the window. An empty train was rolling along the line 50 metres away.

I went into the living room. Neriman was snoring on the sofa. The file she had shown me before going to bed was peeking from her bag. I quietly took the file and returned to my bed. I switched on the bedside lamp. Underneath the English translation was Neriman's handwriting in Turkish.

"… I was born in Heredile in… I had eight siblings. When I turned 16 I married my husband, Ajar, who was my aunt's grandson…"

Always the same stories.

"… then soldiers came to the village. They said we were feeding those in the mountains. If only they'd known that our bread was not sufficient to feed us. We were pleased when a school was opened in the village. Those who had primary school diplomas were made sergeants when they did their national service. We said: 'now our children won't be beaten…'"

So those who are sergeants are not beaten. Who would have thought it!

"When I sent my son to school I didn't believe he would even be able to read letters written by those doing national service, but the teacher said: 'Your son is very clever. Send him to a boarding school.' His father, my late husband Ajar, didn't want him to go…"

Her husband has died.

"My son really wanted to go. His grandfather was very fond of him. He was going to Istanbul and wanted to take him with him. His father said: 'first he should be betrothed.' When he was engaged my son was fourteen. I put the ring on his finger and it fell off. I tightened it with thread. All the mothers in the village tighten rings with thread."

Huh! Morons! As if underage brides were not bad enough, now we have underage grooms!

"My son went to Istanbul with his grandfather. All the crops were burnt. We don't know who set them alight. The commander gave my husband a gun, saying: 'This land is entrusted to you. Now you are one of us.' My late husband liked guns…"

They cling to their primitiveness.

"I had no alternative but to leave. I started out intending to go to Istanbul. I got on a bus, then a truck. It lasted for days. When we got out, they said: 'this is London!'"

There you go! The people smugglers brought the woman bound for Istanbul all the way to London. Who knows why they did it.

"Then I gather that my son heard about it and came to London to find me. He apparently looked for me for a month."

Why was he unable to find her, I wonder. Don't these people all know each other?

"My son Keko…"

I couldn't read the rest of the statement. Keko. I thought of Keko. I felt a pain cut me to the quick, as if I had just met him on the bus. Could this Keko be the one on the bus? I ran into the side room and prodded Neriman, waking her up. Showing her the file I said: "Is this the mother of the children who committed suicide?"

She rubbed her eyes and sat up.

"Yes, what's happened? Why did you wake me up?"

There was an indescribable pain inside me.

Ah Keko! Why did you do such a thing? If only I had got off the bus behind you. If only I had run after you and made you listen to me. If only I'd said: "You're not alone. These gangs are ruthless. Come tell me. There must be something that can be done."

Keko… please, but please let you not be that Keko!

Chapter Three

DIPLOMA CEREMONY

As the sun rose we edged closer to the spindly willow tree. Those at the back had sweat dripping off them. As if that wasn't enough, we had to make sure we didn't touch the girls. In a small village we were like two groups banned from each other: girls and boys. As boys we were luckier. If my name had been Kerime instead of Keko and I had looked at a boy by mistake, or if I'd been seen to touch him, it could have been the end.

The impatient barking of Bera, who was waiting for us to disperse, for a moment suppressed the buzz of the flies around our heads. From the smell of fresh bread wafting from the oven it was clear that the women had already begun to prepare the food for the fields. Every now and then I made eye contact with Hamdo, who was surreptitiously scraping his backside against the tree. Whatever Aunt Yeter had tried she had been unable to get rid of her son's threadworm. Hamdo said when he scratched it helped, but his father had said: "If I see you do that again, I'll break your hands." A man couldn't play with his backside. It was both unbecoming and wrong.

Hamdo was constantly fidgeting in the class on account of the threadworms, which he said were increasing. Sometimes he would moan, saying: "When I feel them crawling on my ass I go mad. Oh my god, I'm going to put DDT on the bastards, I swear!"

Cafer believed him.

"You're an idiot! Are you going to make a hole in your ass with pesticide?"

In Heredile small boys would grow up to be first men and then fathers, while girls would grow up to first be brides, then mothers. The purpose of our existence was only to be mothers and fathers. The fate of those who thought otherwise in the other world was clear, but Heredile did not leave that to the other world.

I should have been the happiest person at that ceremony. However, I didn't give a hoot about being top of the class. The carefully written white card with the red ribbon coiled around it was my ticket to Ankara. For two years my only aim had been to escape from Heredile. In only three weeks it would all be behind me.

Although the route in my secret plan changed from time to time the destination was always the same. I don't recall exactly when I decided to go.

In those first days when I was introduced to fables I began to love words such as road, travel, go and escape. I was the hero of all the stories and legends. Whereas Pinocchio only had one nose, I had dozens of wonderful noses that I used according to the situation and did everything I wanted. When I got involved, Hansel and Gretel, who were held hostage by the witch in the woods, didn't come back. They went from adventure to adventure, until all witches were cleansed from the surface of the earth. The evil witches on their brooms fled to another planet. And it was me who caught the Forty Thieves and distributed all their treasure to the poor in a single night.

It was as if the feelings that germinated within me along with my dreams had taken over my soul and my mind. In the silence of the night I took wing and left the village. I would fall asleep while fighting evil people in the streets of a city I didn't know. When I awoke in the same adobe house sleeping on the floor I would sometimes feel depressed. What if just for once my dreams would come true?

Mt grandfather used to say: "Neither Kaf mountain is unique, nor the giant bird behind it." We were not at an age to understand what he meant. When years later I understood that the giant bird was inside us I realised that the Kaf mountain in everyone's dreams varied.

At that diploma ceremony it was not possible for me, as a thirteen-year-old, to make sense of how I felt. I was a little angry and resentful of Heredile, the village where I'd been born and grown up. My mother, father, relatives, brothers, Bera, in short, everyone who made me who I was, existed around me. I no longer wanted them or the village. While my mind and my dreams had gone far away it was unbearable that I was physically still in the village. My silent screams were of no use.

"Let me go!!! I'm saying to you. I'm going to leave. I have to go away from here."

Wanting, but not being able to shout, was a torture.

The school where I'd spent 5 years, my friends, even the teacher who had patiently used special programmes to prepare me for the exam, had lost their importance for me. I wanted to put even the good things in the village behind me. Although I was in fact indebted to the teacher who had rescued me from the well in those dark days and opened a new window for me every day, creating a new Keko who was straining at the leash. School teacher Fatih had introduced great dreams to my small world, sending me to the depths of the universe with all his power. I was running with all my might like the only dervish of that huge map that had opened under my feet.

I was heading for Ankara. I had full confidence in myself.

My father's little world sickened me. I didn't like the other fathers, either. If the old men who were as strong as lions when no one was in the village and then quaked when the gendarme turned up were to die, what would Heredile lose?

All the dreams that virtually intoxicated me were outside Heredile.

Sometimes, when I was between sleep and wakefulness at night, I wanted to jump into a crack that would suddenly open up in the ground and disappear. If they couldn't find me in my bed in the morning or if they didn't remember me, if a child called Keko had never been born in this village, how wonderful that would have been. My brothers and sisters were more than enough for my mother and father.

And if I could just go somewhere in this world like a wind that goes everywhere and be free. If only no one would know where I had gone and could not ask…

No one had yet noticed the revolt building up inside me, for there was even a tradition of revolt in Heredile. The only address rebels could go to was Kato mountain. However, in order not to look at the old, weary and wounded Kato I did not even look up at the sky. Even wandering around its foothills was boring, let alone enduring the legendary climb that took days. I couldn't have cared less either about the Peshmerga around the summit or the healing air.

There was no one in the village to whom I could explain my dreams. If I explained, they would say: "Keko has gone mad." The best thing to do was to keep quiet and leave without any fuss. No trace should be left behind.

In fact, the architect of the escape plan in my head was my teacher. He would start every lesson by saying: "the sky and the depths of the ocean are similar", and turn every lesson into a captivating fable. With him we would lose ourselves in completely different worlds and unwillingly awaken in the last lesson and go home.

With my dreams adding to those fables my wings grew new feathers.

Years later I realised that teacher Fatih was the one who experienced the real disappointment at that diploma ceremony. He was offended both by the fact none of our parents came to the ceremony and because none of us showed the slightest sign of joy. He couldn't understand our lack of enthusiasm. He was probably expecting us to be excited like city children.

"You've succeeded children! You've succeeded! Look, your parents who had no faith in you weren't able to come to the ceremony. Why? Because they eventually realised they had wronged you and were embarrassed. Isn't that right?"

As always we couldn't say: "No, my teacher, it isn't like that. Once again you are mistaken about Heredile." For some reason, we villagers found it difficult to explain even the most common realities of our lives to urbanites.

Mothers and fathers didn't even glance in the direction of the school. Most of the time it would even be forgotten that there was a school, a teacher and children who went there. Conversations that included the words school, exercise book, pen, book, teacher and diploma were rare.

"You're coming to the fields, not the school."

"If you go to school, who will look after your brothers and sisters?"

"What is this thing called school?"

"The devil's work!"

"You shouldn't educate girls."

"If girls learn to read and write they will also learn how to write letters to their sweetheart."

"Don't waste your time going to school. You haven't got the brains for it."

"Does school fill your belly?"

"Will you study and become an anarchist?"

"Children who go to school don't respect their elders."

"Those who go to school go off the rails."

With the situation like this, to expect parents to go to a diploma ceremony in the middle of June was something reserved for outsiders like teacher Fatih.

If adults came to the school there had to be an important

reason for it. Maho and Cemal had had a fight. One had a cut eyebrow, the other a cut on his head. Maho's father came to the school, but he didn't even look at the children's faces.

"These things happen, teacher. Don't worry. They are children of the same clan." And off he went.

He was right. When children from the same clan had fights, no one could interfere. If they were from different clans, then things might change. Fathers and uncles would get involved. Guns could be drawn, even blood feuds could start.

According to our teacher, even if our parents hadn't turned up, we, as children, should have been jumping in the air with excitement. He didn't know that for us long summer holidays were not a prize, rather they meant getting up with the sun and being worked to death until the evening *azan*.

Every child who could earn his bread had to help his parents in looking after the animals and doing all kinds of work in the fields and orchards. When it snowed we were trapped in our homes. Those who wanted to live to see the spring had to stock up in summer.

Perhaps for this reason village children had no right to be spoiled or get bored. We all knew when to be quiet. Even for babies to cry was like a crime. My granny, who told stories of the baby whose nose was eaten by rats when his mother went to the fields, would say: "If it weren't for angels, who would protect these little ones?" I don't remember a season when there were not babies taken to the cemetery. It was a sin to question fate.

When harvest season began I would set out with my father and uncle before daybreak, and walk to the mill two kilometres away that my great grandfather had built.

The sacks of wheat carried by ox carts would be emptied one by one onto the mill stone and either my father or uncle would supervise the slowly turning threshing stone.

My grandfather would say: "Not everyone is fortunate enough to work with flour and bread. Appreciate the value of your destiny," and at every opportunity he would pray for the souls of his father and ancestors.

Our life was dependent on those sacks of flour. I would spend the whole summer under sacks that got heavier every year, looking forward to the day that school opened. While city kids would feel joyful over escaping from lessons, we village kids would feel joyful at being free from work at the end of summer.

As I felt Niyaz's gaze upon me I began once again to listen to our teacher. Niyaz was a good friend of mine. In recent days he had been vexed at all of us. He guessed that I knew who had played that dirty trick on him and was angry that I didn't tell him their names.

"My way is clear," he had said. "I know. You will see. I will kill whoever did it and go to prison. Who cares? If I don't do it, I will be dishonourable! If I don't kill that bastard I will put on a skirt and walk around the village!"

Niyaz used the singular, but there were more than one involved in the prank. It was his brother Remzi who was the leader of the three pranksters. He wasn't wrong. They had gone too far. They probably hadn't realised that Niyaz would be affected that much. They regretted what they had done, but it was too late.

A week before, when we first went into class we had found Karakaçan in the middle of the classroom with a bridal veil on it. It its bag was an embroidered bundle, inside of which was a small straw. On the blackboard in large letters were the words:

"MY NIYAZI. I HAVE FLED FROM THE STABLE WITH MY BUNDLE TO YOU!"

We all knew Karakaçan. While only two weeks old its mother had died been killed by a mine during a smuggling trip. After that Niyaz raised Karakaçan.

If when bringing wood from the mountains his father put too much on Karakaçan, Niyaz would grumble and take some of it himself. And whenever Karakaçan saw Niyaz it would sidle up to him. This innocent and compassionate familiarity was the butt of remorseless gibes; sometimes it even angered Niyaz's father.

"Niyaz, your son has arrived. See, he is looking for you."

""Niyaz, your friend from national service has arrived."

"Niyaz, where is your foster brother?"

Niyaz had laughed at all our jokes about Karakaçan, but when it came to an insult to his honour, like all men in Heredile, he flared up. He had beaten Cemal, who said: "Niyaz, your sweetheart has arrived."

The beating suffered by Cemal had not discouraged the others, on the contrary it incited them.

When his father heard he swore he would sell it, but Niyaz cried so much he relented.

After all that, when Niyaz saw his donkey wearing a veil in the classroom he started to shout at the top of his voice. It was the last straw. Everything could be said in Heredile, except for matters concerning honour.

After the teacher had calmed Niyaz down with difficulty, he explained animals, animal rights and friendship with animals to us for the whole day. Then he repeated the famous sentence he had used often over five years: "Children, first you will believe in science. All mysteries are hidden in it. And know that serving nature is the most ancient worship."

Niyaz, who listened while snuffling, grew redder and redder while not uttering a word. On leaving school he ran home. He took a copy of the Quran and went in front of the tea house in the middle of the village, where he shouted: "I swear on the book! If I don't find who did it and kill him, no one should think I'm a man!"

Niyaz's uncle Seydo had just returned from doing his national service. He jumped off the chair where he had been sitting with the village headman, went over to his nephew, took the Quran, kissed it slowly three times, placed it to his head, then gave it to the headman, who also kissed the book three times before placing it on the table. As for Seydo, with a sudden movement he turned and grabbed Niyaz's hair, then with the other hand slapped him hard around the face. "Do you think swearing an oath is a game, you wretch!"

Although Niyaz was shaken he managed to free himself from

his uncle's grip and run off. As he ran he swore. "You will see, you assholes! I will fuck you all!"

After that day Niyaz cornered all of us on many occasions, but was unable to get anything out of us. We all knew that he was so angry that he might try to kill those who had carried out the practical joke.

Niyaz had given up on the others, but he trusted me.

"So be it, Keko, mate!. But we were meant to be bosom buddies? Why don't you tell me the bastards who did this?"

Those who had put the veil on Karakaçan regretted what they had done, but didn't know how they could atone for it. Niyaz needed to retract his oath. His uncle Seydo and his father had subjected Niyaz to *falaka* [beating the soles of his feet] that evening, but he had refused: "I won't retract it, no I won't retract my oath! I'll find the bastard and kill him!"

So I was going to leave all this behind. My anger was such that I could not see the underlying layers of affection.

Cemal, who was immediately in front of me, squashed a fly that landed on his neck with a swift slap. As he wiped away the blood with a dirty handkerchief the red stain dispersed.

Teacher Fatih, losing patience with the lack of reaction on our faces, shouted:

"What did we say five years ago?"

We had been amazed by many things we had heard in our one-classroom school made of adobe bricks with overhanging eaves. Until the arrival of our teacher we had assumed the rest of the world was just a larger version of Heredile. We had heard about Ankara and Istanbul far away, but for us they were like two planets beyond the world.

The harshest reality of our lives was the soldiers. The commanders who often came to our village and didn't leave without hurting us…

The day teacher Fatih told us freedom was a right the first thing that came to my mind was those commanders. I began to look at that road that we perceived as forbidden, that snaked away towards the city. Why shouldn't I go? Perhaps, as our teacher said, the hardest prison was the place we imprisoned ourselves. Those of us who lived in Heredile had also played a part in this. Since we feared those who came from outside, we locked ourselves in. They could open the doors we had locked whenever they wanted, but we resisted opening our own locks.

As top of the class I had earned the right to be the free traveller on that road.

That was the first decision that I made with my child's mind.

"So 9 out of 10 kids starting primary school in this village weren't going to get to the fifth year? So children in this village couldn't learn to read and write?"

Teacher Fatih was shouting louder than ever, as if he was calling somebody to account. It was as if he was speaking to our parents who weren't there.

"So this village was meant to be cursed?" Where is that curse?"

That was true actually. Our village was cursed. There was not a single house that had not suffered.

"How many pupils were there when we started the first class?"

On the first day of school there had been twenty one of us. Our teacher saw we didn't have enough seats and asked for chairs. The village headman, looking at us sitting three to a bench, laughed, and said:

"Don't hurry, teacher! In less than two weeks half of them will have gone. Towards spring there may only be ten. Only two or three will make the final year. You'll give one or two diplomas, of course, so that Ankara will not regret sending you your salary."

Our teacher, who had just begun his career, took a step towards the headman, his eyes blazing.

"Listen to me, headman. All these pupils will get their diplomas! Do you understand me?"

The headman was taken aback.

"Okay, thank you. Did we say we wouldn't accept them? Those who go to do national service with a primary school diploma have an easier time. It's not as if nobody has ever got a diploma without learning to read and write."

Our teacher was getting increasingly angry.

"Headman! It's not possible for a child to attend my class and not learn to read and write! If it happens I'll give up teaching!"

The headman looked at the teacher as if to say: "Is this guy for real?" and left without saying a word.

By the end of the year the number of pupils in our class, rather than falling, had risen to thirty six, for teacher Fatih went from house to house badgering those who didn't send their children to school. The youngest was eight and the oldest sixteen. I was exactly nine years old when I started school. On the day I received my diploma it was two weeks after my thirteenth birthday.

Teacher Fatih attempted things that had not been done before in Heredile. In the evening he would visit our houses and remind us of our homework. His notebook, to which villagers became accustomed, would be in his hand. He always carried pens, rubbers, pencil sharpeners and crayons in his pocket and offer them to those who said: "I've lost it. I can't find it. I left it at school." The fact he was different was to some a positive, and to others a negative.

When I started school at the age of nine I had only one dream: to be able to read and write the names of footballers. Anything more was unnecessary for me. Those far off footballers, who I'd never seen, were the most unattainable heroes in my heart. The chance of my meeting them was equivalent to the chance of my going to the moon. If I could learn by heart the names of the teams they played for, and if I could even read and write them, I would feel as if the distance between them and me was less.

When I learnt to read and write a football still dominated my dreams. But I had also slowly begun to change with the excitement of my developing hopes. Some nights when I pulled the blanket over me I didn't know with which fantasy I would drop off to sleep.

By the time I got to class four I still loved to play football, but famous players didn't interest me so much anymore.

The Keko in my dreams had begun to move away from the real-life Keko. The skinny, helpless me I saw in the mirror was becoming alienated from the strong, self-confident Keko of my dreams. The imaginary Keko frequently got angry with the real Keko, but most of the time gave him hope and courage. I enjoyed being alone with the Keko of my dreams. The daytime Keko, especially if he was with his father, was rather unpleasant.

I could not have guessed then, that the aim that began with a small dream, a small secret, would go on to embroider my entire destiny. Adults assume that children cannot keep secrets. However, even babies have secrets they keep to themselves. The most innocent, beautiful and meaningful secrets belong to children.

Every roof in Heredile has its own unwritten history. The family secrets in those seemingly insignificant past times are maintained by being passed on from generation to generation. I was surprised years later when I didn't see the same respect for secrets in the city as there was in the village tradition. In Heredile, even if the person was from a family with which your family had a blood feud, revealing their secret was a crime. Everyone knew by name those who had gone to Kato, but they would never tell. Soldiers in particular would never be told.

We used to learn our traditions mainly from my grandfather and my paternal grandmother.

"A secret that is not kept will return as a curse and rain down on you as damnation. There are some secrets which will only be revealed on the day of judgement."

This was a summary of our philosophy of life: to remain silent in all circumstances.

I never liked this silence. To remain silent really wore me down. Years later I understood that this silence was despair and a slow death.

Who made up the rules governing our lives? Even if soldiers killed us we weren't to talk. We mustn't talk so that those remaining wouldn't suffer. For this reason even the stupidest of us knew that when we went to see the bodies that troops dumped in the village square we had to remain as silent and emotionless as stone. Whatever the commander said and however close a relative the body might be, no one must say anything. The commanders would be most enraged by this silent attitude of ours.

One winter day the soldiers returned suddenly several hours after leaving some bodies. The commander first checked the men's faces one by one, then the women's, separating the ones who had cried. The cunning commander who came that day taught the villagers not to cry even after soldiers had departed.

Our secrets, mysteries and traditions, which teacher Fatih had difficulty understanding, were the fundamental realities which shaped our lives. It was difficult to change those traditions that were like shackles on our feet.

Although I was only a child I could see my future. If I stayed in the village I would marry, as soon as the harvest was over, the first girl I had taken a fancy to in the short spring, with drum and pipe, then go off to do military service in the autumn. I would then hold my first baby when taking my first leave, before beginning a lifetime of working in the fields, and becoming one of the men of Heredile. Such a life was no different to death for me.

On that day, at that ceremony, if I hadn't been scared I could have gone to the middle of the village and shouted at the top of my voice: "Daaad! You won't be able to hold me! You won't be able to stop me! I'm off! I don't care about Heredile, the clan. I'm not frightened of you or the soldiers. And I won't go to Kato mountain!"

In those years to attempt a different life in Heredile with its 41 houses simply meant suicide. Those who brought new customs to an old village were not at all popular; they were even punished.

There was only one way for those who wanted to leave Heredile: to go to Kato mountain. Old Kato, with permanent snow on its summit, which looked like a scary giant bride when mist shrouded it, was like a waiting room between life and death. No one wanted to send their child to Kato, but there was a silent respect for those who went there. To go up to Kato was actually to run boldly to death.

To be a "guest" of the soldiers was what Heredile disliked most. Whatever happened, collaboration with the soldiers was unforgivable. While the punishment for girls who ran off with the one they loved was death without questions asked, no one could touch girls who went to the mountains and no one would say anything behind their backs. Mothers whose children went to the mountains or were captured by soldiers would from the first day wail as if they had received news of their death.

Don't you know, Kato?

You have taken my daughter as a bride

And taken her under your skirts

I could not even sacrifice one hair

You let her be crushed by boots

You have torn my heart out, Kato

May there always be mist around your summit

May you yearn for the sun

You killed my spring

You stole the salt from my hearth

May your nightingales flee

May you burn like kindling

Kato was not the only angel of death. Drought was like a sworn enemy waiting to ambush us. In summers where there was little rain we would often pray for rain. As for avalanches, that roared at least once every winter, they were a white monster on our slope.

To those from the mountains who came into the village at night regardless of the season our hands, arms and tongues were tied.

"So the flour in the store is only enough for you, is that right?"

"Say my son. Ah, look! Can children put up with hunger like adults?"

"You're right. Those who go up to the mountains don't feel hunger!"

The worst were the merciless commanders. They were the two-legged versions of the disasters such as avalanche, earth-quake, drought or flood that were not questioned. It was as if every time they came they stabbed the soul of all of us, even babies.

Sometimes they would take men, women or even children, and after giving them a good shaking, as they put it, and putting the fear of god into them, would bring them back.

"This is the first warning! The second time you are taken tell your mothers to get your shrouds ready!"

Perhaps that is why it was easier to accept in advance that those who climbed Kato mountain or fell into the hands of the soldiers were dead. Sometimes mothers who received confirmation of their children's death felt relieved. They knew what torture was. There were hardly any who returned from the clutches of death. When someone did return they would be met with a heavy heart and without questions. They would not be asked what had happened. We used to watch them from a distance as if they had returned from the other world.

My paternal grandmother would cry every time she told the story of the legendary Hamit. 12-year-old Hamit had hanged himself in his cell rather than divulge his father's hiding place in the orchard. Some said when he had died under torture they had made it look like suicide. The old women would from time to time wail the lament wailed by his mother, who put henna on his broken fingers when she received his body black and blue from beating, at his funeral.

I have lost my gold

Has anyone seen him?

My little one has gone and not come back

Has anyone heard his voice?

He silenced his tongue

He has handed his body to the grim reaper

It has become a sapling in heaven

They took my little hero from my arms

When I got angry I wanted to suddenly become a giant like in the fairy tales and turn Heredile inside out.

As soon as the threshing season was past I would be gone.

While thinking all this, teacher Fatih, who was by himself both the teacher and headmaster, and caretaker of our school, came over and proudly embraced me.

"Keko, I owe you a debt of thanks for not leaving my labours unreciprocated."

In fact teacher Fatih was unaware that Allah had sent him for me. Our teacher, who had squeezed five classes into one room, had tirelessly taken an interest in all of us and taught all the children in the village to read and write, including Abdurrahman, who had to pause to think even when saying his name. He had also attempted to do something for illiterate adults. Initially he had separated volunteers into groups of three or five and organised classes after school. After dealing with the volunteers he turned to the others, playing a virtual game of tag in the village. Teacher Fatih found whoever was illiterate one by one and forced them to attend class. He left women to the very end, as he understood that the men of Heredile were not keen on the idea.

In contrast to his short, skinny build he had a resounding voice. With his always carefully combed hair, his huge glasses and his ever-smiling face he was our sorcerer.

"There is nothing in the world that is impossible. When the day comes you will all get your diplomas. For this you will first learn Turkish, then reading and writing. The primary school diploma will be your first step. The real business starts after that. Everything will begin after that diploma," he would say.

Before our teacher came to the village the number of Turkish speakers was no more than the number of fingers on a hand. People had received diplomas without learning to read and write. For this reason many had been beaten by their commanders while doing military service. Some said that despite being illiterate they had been comfortable on account of their diplomas.

My grandfather compared teacher Fatih to previous ones:

"They would apply to be reassigned and head straight for town. They wanted to be in a city. It was as if Allah had not created this place. Those who weren't reassigned would resign. But this teacher Fatih is different. It's as if he was one of us, went to study and came back."

My grandfather's words: "one of us" stuck with me. Could the one who went away to study and came back have been Keko? I mean, could I have been a teacher Fatih?

I was teacher Fatih's biggest project. He would say: "You will change the view of Ankara."

What was Ankara's view? How did they see us? How did people live in Ankara? Did children there like playing football as we did?

Most of what I knew, like every child of that age, originated from my feelings, rather than what I had learnt. What you learn from your feelings is engraved not just on your brain, but also on your heart. In those days with my child's mind I had learnt that Ankara was close to the commanders and distant from us. The people of Ankara were not like us. They were the ruthless people who came to our village to shout orders, look down on us and sharpen our despair and sense of guilt.

Just as their use of arms was justified, our use of arms was something to be shocked and ashamed of. It could never be left unpunished. They were the authority after God. As for us, we were a handful of helpless people whose crime was not completely explained. They looked at our faces as if we were surplus to the world. Perhaps that was why the idea of leaving the village frightened everyone. If we had no rights in the village in which we were born, outside how would things be? Soldiers, officials and politicians didn't know what to do with us and did not refrain from expressing their frustration and anger frequently.

One day a commander spat in the face of Granddad Rüstem in the village square as he denied knowing the body there was his son.

"You're even frightened to claim ownership of your dead! And you think you are citizens! Shame on you!"

We all knew that if Granddad Rüstem identified the body of his son most of the clan's youth and children, even me, would be arrested and some would not return. Those who didn't return would spend months inside being tortured, beaten and subjected to all manner of suffering, and perhaps there would be deaths.

Granddad Rüstem was like a statue facing the commander, looking at the foothills of Kato without saying a word. At that moment I wanted to fire a stone at the forehead of the commander with a catapult… It was fortunate that I didn't have a catapult in my hand.

The commander threw the body in the back of the jeep like a sack and spat again. None of the soldiers sitting facing each other were looking at us.

When the jeeps left hoarse laments began. Granddad Rüstem did not shed a tear, neither that day nor in the following days. Two months later he was found dead in his bed.

Now my teacher was saying: "You will change Ankara's viewpoint." How could Ankara be different to this? I was trying to imagine them behaving in a friendly way towards us. I, who could even imagine various things happening from a couple of pebbles, could not manage to achieve this. Could a commander or someone from Ankara smile at someone from Heredile? Our memories of them were all interwoven with pain.

Despite this, the first stop on that road map was Ankara. My goal was far from Ankara.

Eventually I found some concrete information. So if they didn't know me they would like me.

In the final year I sat right at the back on my own. Teacher Fatih would put the test papers he had prepared the previous evening on my desk and put cotton wool in my ears. He put a stopwatch on the desk and as soon as he gave the signal to start I picked up my pen.

"Now think of the Olympic stadium I told you about. You're running. You know how to run, but knowledge is not enough. The important thing is to be fast. There are other athletes next to you. You have to be fast and pass them. Keep running until you hear the bell!"

Every day the bar in front of me got higher.

"You're going to fly! You're going to fly just like a bird. You will surprise everyone."

By now I recognised the questions from previous years' free boarding exams as soon as I saw them. I had memorised both the questions and the answers. In the previous six months I had answered all the questions countless times without a mistake. There was absolutely no doubt I would pass. Teacher Fatih even thought I should be amongst the frontrunners. This would have the effect of an atom bomb at the Ministry of National Education; the whole country would know my name.

When teacher Fatih went to town to get his salary and returned with the examination forms it was like treasure for me. Even knowing that they had come just for me was a fantastic feeling. We carefully filled in the treasured forms the same day. By the light of a gas lamp I read them again with great delight.

A week later my teacher went to town just for me to submit the forms. No one knew but it was as if I was in a dream. Although the idea of going to a big city to study at a boarding school might not please my father, I was sure he would be persuaded and even feel a secret pride.

Maybe he would smile, say: "Good God!" and look at me in a pleasant way, something I rarely witnessed.

"What? Boarding school? Are you taking the mickey? Or is this teacher conning us?"

While in the second year he heard I was reading letters sent by those doing military service it was as if he smiled.

The same evening teacher Fatih visited us. His surprise at my father's objections and his reluctance to listen did not last long. He pulled himself together and smiled. He explained to my father at length the Ministry of National Education, boarding schools, famous schools in the city and what use a diploma would be. He went on to explain middle schools, high schools, universities and why free boarding schools had been established, giving examples without tiring. He kept saying that I had made supreme efforts in the last year, that I was very intelligent, that it would be a great loss if I left the school, obstinately resisting the increasingly tense frown on my father's face.

Nothing teacher Fatih said pleased my father. I really hated that attitude of his. It had not occurred to me that he would stop me, even if he wasn't proud of me.

Once teacher Fatih had left no one could calm my father down as he raged with spit dripping from his mouth. The fear in my mother's anxious and sad eyes after a while spread to me.

"I can't give 5 *kuruş*!. I'm waiting for the school to end and look what you've done to me! My son has become an enemy to me and I didn't know! Damn the milk you sucked!"

My father's insults were getting harsher. Every time I wanted to curl up and die. Teacher Fatih did not take a step back. After that day he continued to come every day. My father no longer greeted him; when he saw him he turned his head away. In Heredile to not greet a guest was a great insult. My teacher didn't care about this behaviour that could lead to years of offence. He would encounter my father at the most unexpected times and try to persuade him.

"Have you got nothing better to do, teacher? Haven't you got fed up every day like this?"

"Look, Ajar uncle. Keko is your son. Don't you want him to study and become something?"

"Teacher! Teacher! Doesn't your ear hear what comes out of your mouth? Aren't we something?"

My teacher's patience didn't run out.

A week later my father said: "Okay, whatever happens, if I give you any money I'm a coward!"

"You're behaving shamefully, Ajar uncle. Is anyone asking you for money?"

"Eh, what's the problem?"

"What's the problem? I am trying because Ankara may say: 'Haven't you been able to find one child from the whole village?' I mean for me it's also a matter of my bread and butter."

Teacher Fatih assumed that in this way he was flattering my father's pride. We were to go together and come back together. He swore many times that, just as he would take me, he would bring me back and hand me over to my father

When my father got angry from time to time and said: "I've abandoned the idea," my world caved in. I had nightmares.

My father threw the bus going to Ankara over a precipice and waited on the side of the road.

My mother pleaded with him and he softened, but it didn't last long.

"So who is going to work at the mill? Why have I got these children? If these dogs are going to leave like girls who will do all the work? With your woman's mind you never think of these things, do you?"

My misfortune was partly to do with me being the first. I

was the first child in the clan to want to study. I wanted middle school, high school and university education. This was the whole of my huge dream that looking from Heredile was too big for the universe.

My father and the others didn't know, but I actually intended to return to Heredile. Perhaps I would return as a commander. If I had been a commander the first thing I would have done is bring electricity to Heredile. Just electricity? I would have issued an order and after electricity I would have sorted out water and the road. A clinic was also needed. Of course the school was more urgent than all of them. It needed to be repaired and a few more classrooms added. As the number of classrooms increased the number of teachers would also rise. When the other teachers came teacher Fatih should be the headmaster. Just like an official everyone would listen to me and believe me. When my father saw me like that he would pray five times a day to our teacher Fatih. And there was also the issue of radios. Perhaps the first thing I would do is ask for the return of the radios the soldiers had seized. And I would say: "Bring them immediately!" I would distribute them one by one to the houses. With my first pay cheque I would even buy two radios and hand them over to the headman. I would say: "Let those whose radio is broken use these radios until they mend them." Children whose fathers were listening to the news could use these spare radios when wanting to listen to a match. My cousin Yusuf had once let us listen to a match. All the village children got together and split into two. It was a Beşiktaş-Fenerbahçe match. Those who supported Beşiktaş were on the right and those who supported Fenerbahçe were on the left. I was still very young. It was the first time I had heard the names of the teams. Yusuf explained Fenerbahçe, Beşiktaş and Galatasaray. To all of us. There were others too, but they were not very important. That day the word "Beşiktaş" emerged from my mouth. I was thus to remain a Beşiktaş supporter for the rest of my life.

I came out of my daydreams and went up to the stage with

my diploma. According to our teacher this was done every year in the big cities.

"Come on Keko! Why are you lost in thought? We're all waiting for your speech, can't you see?"

Speeches made by the first in the school was a tradition in the big cities. Three days before my teacher had told me: "You will speak at the diploma ceremony on Friday. Make sure you are ready!" But what could I say?

"As you know, we are like a tribe living in a jungle like in the fairy story. We've never had electricity, water, a road or clinic. As far as my father is concerned, electricity is not necessary for the village, and is even the devil's work as it makes people used to comfort. But my grandfather is not like my father. He loves to listen to the radio. Again, as you know, our radios were confiscated. It is necessary to write a petition in Turkish to Ankara to ask the reason why. Our teacher taught us how to write a petition."

I didn't say anything and gulped.

There were now people in the village who wrote and read Turkish. No one was pleading for soldiers' letters. I answered most of the letters. Reading and writing them was entertaining, but martyrs' letters were hard. Their letters would be in yellow envelopes. When the headman received those letters his brow would be furrowed.

Cafer's cousin Kamil was martyred during his military service and his body was sent to the village. Three days after his funeral the last letter he had written arrived. His mother, aunt Sabriye, made me read the letter numerous times and cried her eyes out. She kissed and smelt the two-page letter so fervently it became crumpled and some of the writing was erased. The whole village knows that aunt Sabriye still carries that letter in her bosom. Out of respect, no one in the village asked for the hand of Kamil's fiancee, Makbule. Her father gave her hand in marriage to a lame shepherd in the nearby village.

Why do fathers not love their daughters? Why are they unwanted children whereas male babies please everyone? Why is it shameful to love someone? Why is it unbecoming to cry, laugh, want, have dreams or try new things? Why is it bad to be a villager facing a soldier? Why are city people superior to us? Without Ankara how would Heredile be?

My grandfather used to say: "He who says hell is on the other side is blind. Don't the fires of hell descend to places where there is fratricide?"

Looking far away was not an indication of better things. The furthest places in our eyes were Ankara and Istanbul. Ankara meant soldiers and punishment; Istanbul was a fairy tale, in other words, money. Both were virtually prohibited to us. Although as I dared to dream of going far away I began to feel pride in myself. I was going to go. I was going to go to the farthest corner of the world and say: "I've arrived." I knew, I was as sure of that as I was of my name. And when they got to know me they would love me, too.

I enjoyed reading the life stories of famous men. Without knowing it I was putting myself in their place.

Bedri Baykam began to paint when he was two years old. Mozart began to play the piano when he was three. Mehmet the Fourth became sultan at the age of seven. Mustafa Kemal Atatürk took the second name of Kemal in addition to Mustafa when he was twelve. Pascal began to draw geometric triangles when he was twelve. Sikorsky constructed a helicopter when he was twelve.

Teacher Fatih used to say: "All children, all of you, are as powerful as atom bombs." I wanted to be one of those atom bombs, even if I knew I would explode and be destroyed. For that reason I had to go far away.

At that time no one from Heredile had ever become a civil servant, although it needed a merciful and fair official.

Sometimes at the evening meal while sitting on the floor next to the stove I would suddenly want to say: "You will see, I will save this village!" Then I would glance at my father and abandon the idea, for the grandson of Ali Kemal Karadağ, of the Şemsegil tribe, the first son of Ajar, Ali Kemal, that is, Keko could not entertain such thoughts.

A Kurd should first think of his clan, then himself. He should not humiliate his tribe nor himself in front of foreigners.

Teacher Fatih seemed to be a little offended by my silence.

"Come on Keko. Look, your friends are getting impatient. Didn't I tell you yesterday to prepare?"

"Won't it do if I don't speak?" I stuttered.

"No, Keko! You can at least tell us about the preparation for the free boarding school exams."

I knew that the teacher wanted to encourage pupils who would come after me.

"It was very easy, teacher. It is not at all difficult to prepare for exams."

"What was it like at the beginning? Were you able to easily work out the questions?"

"No. At first I didn't understand the questions at all, but later..."

"Yes, later?"

"As I learned it got easier."

"And then?"

"Then, you see, now..."

"Today when you get your diploma is that the end of school, Keko?"

"Nooo."

"That's understood, Keko. You're not going to speak. What shall we do?"

As first in the school I also had a prize. A grey watch. It was the first time I'd owned a watch. I didn't know what to say. If I were to show my joy everyone would say I was 'greedy'. My cheeks were red, I opened my mouth to say thank you, but my tongue was dry from the excitement.

"My teacher, you shouldn't have got it. You've been to a lot of trouble," I mumbled as I attempted to leave the stage.

"Wait a minute, Keko! There's no hurry! It's not over yet."

Now my teacher gave me a large envelope. Inside was the latest edition of the monthly newspaper we posted on the wall.

"You have done more work than anyone on the wall newspaper. So I thought it appropriate to give it to you. You can keep it as a memento."

In order not to show my joy and pride I did my utmost to look solemn. I always had to remember that I was a Kurd, that I was from the Şemsegil clan, that I was a man, moreover that I was a Kurdish man.

The other editions of the wall newspaper that I had greatly enjoyed preparing from the second year onwards had also been put in envelopes. Lots had been drawn between the students who wanted them. Cemal, who was amongst those who lost, was trying to conceal his eyes that were misting over.

The amount of tears we kept inside ourselves in those years. What did those childhood tears, that later when we were adults came back to take revenge like a cannonball, not make us do?

That day there, although inside me there were storms raging that were bigger than me, I was still a young child. I rigidly accepted my diploma, present and wall newspaper. I only managed to say: "thank you, my teacher", in a husky tone, to the most important person in my life, who had opened the way to my dreams, who had ensured I flowed like a waterfall.

There were also six friends who came from surrounding villages. Teacher Fatih looked at them and in a wry voice said: "Come on, children, embrace each other! Maybe you won't be able to see each other until the autumn."

We looked at each other.

Teacher Fatih raised his voice a little. "Come on!"

Bekir laughed: "My teacher, boys don't hug each other like girls."

Teacher Fatih sighed and shook his head.

"I've still got lots of work to do with you."

Our teacher, who was unable to realise the magnificent ceremony he had planned, was looking tired. But he still smiled and hugged each of us one by one and gave us advice.

"Don't forget what I've said, Niyaz!"Let that prank stay in your memories. Don't let it create a bad turning point in your life. Foolish acts of revenge result in regret."

"Cemal, don't forget to read the books I've given you. We will meet again."

"Hasan, come here! You know, don't you, that what Keko did this year you will do next."

"In education there is no boy or girl. Even if you can't go to middle school you know how to read and write. You will never abandon books. Every day you will learn something new. When you go to bed, when you put your head on the pillow you will ask yourselves: 'what have I learned today?'"

"You are very talented at maths. You must develop this. In summer I want you to finish the tests I've given you."

Our teacher did not know that we all really, really loved him. We were just reluctant to demonstrate it. To expect and show affection was both shameful and difficult. If only I hadn't suppressed my desire to hug in those years. In particular while crying secretly I couldn't tell anyone I wanted to lean on my teacher's shoulder.

When I went to the threshing floor my mother was spinning wool. I showed her my diploma with a red ribbon, then my watch and wall newspaper.

My mother's hazel eyes shone on her sunburnt face and she smiled wryly. Then she bent down again as if I hadn't arrived or as if she hadn't seen me.

"I'm going indoors. I'm going to study," I said, as I walked towards the stairs. My mother called out from behind me:

"Keko, I've made you some molasses *bulamaç*."

"Good, I'll eat it as I study,"

When I heard my father's voice coming into the threshing floor in the evening I closed my book and ran down. He had returned from the mill with Bahoz. As soon as June arrived the mill would begin to turn. Until the crops were harvested and the grain threshed there would be people bringing last year's wheat.

My father's temples were covered in sweat. I helped him down the steps. Then I took Bahoz to the barn. I gave him water and fed him. I turned and pulled my father's boots from his outstretched feet. While in the barn he had spoken to my mother.

"You've got a diploma?" It was as if he was calling me to account. "Of course, you will get one. You're as big as a donkey."

"In fact, in Ankara..."

"What about Ankara?"

I was going to say; "Wait until you see me enter the exam in Ankara", but as always I was unable to complete my sentence when faced by my father.

His voice suddenly rose. It wasn't so much what he said, but the tone of his voice which frightened me. I was resisting, but my father was so terrifying at that moment that his anger struck my face and I whispered:

"Dad, but the teacher.."

"What, the teacher, who does he think he is?"

"But..."

"Of course, he is well off, the bastard."

"Dad", I whispered.

"That's great! They've given him the village's children and you'd think he was playing a game."

I couldn't speak. There was no point in replying or pleading with my father. I knew he wouldn't let me finish a sentence. If I wanted to continue I would be silenced by heavy slaps on the face. Added to the growing fear inside me was a panic. I looked in despair at my mother. My mother, whose neck was visible under her undone thin headscarf, was also in despair. As she wept silently she turned her head away. But she was my only hope at that moment. I continued to look at her stubbornly. I heard her mumble as if my father wasn't there.

"You've got your diploma, son. What else do you want?"

What she meant was: "That's it, it's over. Accept it. If your father doesn't want you to study, to take that exam, don't resist any more. Forget the school!"

That was my father and mother's first reaction to my outstanding report and diploma.

Chapter Four

MY FATHER AND ME

However much I tried, I hadn't heard a single positive word from my father in praise of me. This really upset me, for I had not realised that all the fathers in Heredile resembled each other.

I was determined to go to boarding school in spite of my father. There would be new teachers there who would support me, take me by the hand, appreciate me, praise what I did and show me the way. Who knew what I would discover amongst new books? All my bad memories of Heredile, including my father's anger and aggression, would be in the past.

"I don't want to hear the words boarding school! That teacher won't come, either. He can piss off, the asshole. Am I a village idiot? Give birth, nourish, raise, then let him stroll off shaking his balls!"

When my father spoke like this my ears started to hum and my eyes would swell up. I would feel an unstoppable heat surging through my body.

I went out to the threshing floor. My mother followed me as if she felt something was going to happen. I waited for my father in front of the door, standing bolt upright. Coming out of the barn he saw me and walked straight towards me, As always his eyes were flashing. I didn't move and looked straight at my father. I took a deep breath and said: "I must take that exam."

"What? What did you say?"

"I'm going to take the free boarding school exam!"

Suddenly my father's huge, gnarled hand hit me in the face. My feet left the ground.

Until the day he died my father was thin, but he was powerful. It was as if there was a monster that emerged from within him when he got angry and lived with him. In particular when he faced my mother and me he became like a giant demon.

My nose was bleeding and my head was throbbing. I found it difficult to breathe. A burning feeling was rising from my stomach. Despite the pain the only thing on my mind was the exam.

As I tried to stand up straight I looked again at my father. For the first time in my life I wasn't frightened of him. The blood trickling from my nose mingled with the tears running down my cheeks.

My father leaned over me frowning, as if he was disgusted. "And are you crying like a woman?" he said as he hit me again.

It was shameful for a man, especially a Kurdish man, to cry, but I didn't care. If I was not going to be able to go the boarding school, nothing else mattered. I started crying more. I knew that the more I cried the more embarrassed my father would become and even get into a flap. I was bawling my head off.

"I'm going to go to that school, see!"

"Look, look! You rude, shameless boy! Are you sobbing like a woman? This is what comes of going to school, see! If you study so much this is the result! So that they'll say: 'Ajar's son is crying like a woman without a man'. I'll kill you! I'll spit on you! You've dishonoured me!"

I wiped my nose and the tears with the back of my hand. I was no longer fleeing from my father. Either I was going to die or I was going to take the exam. There was no middle way. As a child facing up to death it was as if I had aged by ten years. Whatever happened we had to respect our fathers without question. However, that day my father was just an enemy wanting me dead.

Two years previously my cousin Ali, on his way to the mountain, said: "I'm going. Give this letter to Nevin." I saw despair in the look on his face as if he had no other choice. Months later when I saw him amongst the bodies the gendarme left in the village square, Nevin, who was newly married, was opposite me. She was in shock. She was looking at Ali lying lifeless on the ground.

The commander shouted: "You can't fool me! Everyone will claim their bodies! If you don't I know what I will do!"

Perhaps the most fearless person there that day was Nevin. Despite her husband being next to her, she could not hide the pain of her old sweetheart. The commander had not noticed the two tears trickling down her cheeks. No one apart from me knew they were lovers. I suddenly felt nauseous and began to gag. The commander turned and looked at me. As my mother hurriedly came over and tried to usher me away, I walked over and tugged at Nevin's hand.

That day in the village square, as always, no one claimed the bodies. When the commander gave the signal the soldiers began to beat the men. The women turned their backs so as not to embarrass their menfolk.

My wish to take the free boarding school exam had angered my father. In fact, what enraged him was my challenging him. As long as he continued to prevent me studying I was determined not to be the son he wanted. Perhaps because he sensed this he came up to me and kicked me as hard as he could. On receiving the kick to the stomach I fell and slid backwards.

"Spawn of the devil! Are you opposing me? I will feed you to the wolves! I will throw your parts to the carrion crows!"

I was struggling to breathe, curled up in a ball. My mother came and fell on me. "Light of my eye!" she said, embracing me.

Mother and son we were crying in each other's arms. As a boy I should have been closer to my father and more distant from my mother. My father pulled my mother by the hair and separated us. She freed her hair and hugged me again. Like a thick, live blanket she shielded me from my father's blows.

"Ajar, don't hit your son! For God's sake, hit me, not him! Don't send him to school, but don't hit him!"

Wherever my father wanted to hit me, my mother reacted quicker and extended her arm, leg or head there. As she took the blows aimed at me I was devastated. It was as if my father had gone berserk. After a while mother and son competed to protect each other. At that moment I had forgotten all my masculinity. I was just little Keko on my mother's lap.

In later years whenever I remembered that painful beating I took with my mother I also felt a bit of pleasure. That day when my mother protected me desperately I was the Keko that was not allowed to be a child in his mother's lap. I was a loved, protected small boy.

"Woman! Zöhre! You're the one who spoiled him! I'll divorce you, I'm telling you!"

When my father left the threshing floor I began to tremble out of anger in my mother's arms. As I trembled my mother, in tears, stroked my neck and head. Our blood and tears had mingled and we were black and blue. The more I cried the more she sobbed.

"My Keko! Part of my liver! Don't break my heart! He's your father. If he's not sending you, don't go. There's nothing we can do. Don't beat yourself up. Salt of my food, most treasured of my hearth. Don't do it!"

The shock I had suffered was so devastating that at that moment I wanted to curse all the rules in the world. Even if I'd died I surely wouldn't have felt such pain. Dying, even going to hell couldn't be as agonising as this.

Sometimes I was frightened by my crying fits. If I was a man, why did I frequently want to cry? Or was I one of those men who, as my paternal grandmother said, lost their way when they grew up? I wasn't in fact frightened of this. If such a thing were to happen I would take my own life. Allah would not be angry with me for this. Killing was a sin, but as this situation counted as a sin there would not be a problem. I would say: "I did it so that I could leave this world, to which I came as a man, as a man."

I wanted to tear up my diploma, report and certificate of excellence and throw the pieces in the faces of everyone in the village. Then I wanted to kick, break, dump, crush scatter and destroy everything. Let Heredile disappear. Let those living in it burn and become ash.

The more people entered the house, spoke, wiped the blood off my face and wanted to put ointment on my aching places, it was as if I was distancing myself from the place. I didn't hear or see any of them. At one time I saw teacher Fatih leaning over me. He was saying something, but I couldn't understand him. He was shaking his head from side to side. His eyes were moist. Teacher Fatih was able to cry. No one would reproach him, for he was not from our village. If Ali Kemal Karadağ from Heredile's grandson, Ajar's first son, Keko, cried in public there was no way he could avoid the nickname of 'girl'. Thirteen-year-old Keko would in a moment become 'Girl Keko' and the name of the entire clan would be dishonoured. The only way to save the clan's honour would be to remove the reason for the slurs. That day I felt I didn't fear either my clan or my father. I wanted them to see me whatever I was. The good- for-nothing child Keko who wants to study.

My teacher held my shoulder and shook me gently. My vacant look must have scared him. Stammering, he attempted to console me. "Keko, please don't let yourself go. We'll sort it out together."

What could I say? He didn't know my father. When he embraced me I felt a pang of sorrow in my heart. At that moment I wanted to shrink to the size of my sister Sumra's rag doll and get in teacher Fatih's pocket. If he took me and left me in the garden of one of the schools in that big city and nobody noticed my absence how great it would be. In particular I wanted my father to never remember me. And if I forgot him how great would my life be?

There were undoubtedly other ways of leaving the village but in those years even an adult found it difficult to survive outside the village. As for me, I was a child. For me to freely hit the road was more difficult than escaping by digging a tunnel.

I don't know how many days had passed. My mother had removed my diploma, certificate of excellence, watch and the old nylon bag given to me to keep the wall newspaper as a memento. She assumed I had forgotten and would remember the exam if these things were visible.

My school life was over. After teacher Fatih had gone out the door I realised that he was the only teacher I would see. My whole education was up to my primary school diploma ceremony. The rest consisted of my dreams. As my father said, I had inappropriate dreams that for us were *haram* [forbidden by religion].

Dreams and fantasies were also subject to religious rules of *haram* and *halal*. I should have had dreams and fantasies that could be *halal*, that is, appropriate for Heredile. Although it didn't make me happy, I should as soon as possible be dreaming of marriage.

I didn't want to leave my room. There was still anger and despair within me that I hadn't been able to suppress. I felt that I was on the verge of beginning a life imposed on me that I didn't want. A fear, the cause of which I didn't know, was growing bigger inside me.

I had long since returned to the destiny prepared for me. I was to be a miller. It was not permitted for me to be anything else but a master miller, like my father, grandfather and his father before me.

And was it as if everyone had the chance to be a miller? If someone had a mill like that could he just leave it and go away? Only a good-for-nothing, shameless son could reject such a job. May Allah grant working with flour and bread.

Those who opposed their mother and father were to burn in hell in the same pot as anti-Christs. If I were to continue like this all curses would rain down upon my head. And when curses rained down on me they would also rain down on my house. I couldn't dare to break the chain of miller Maho, miller Ali Kemal, miller Ajar and miller Keko. We were like stones laid on the path to heaven. Besides, there was a separate place in heaven for all millers. The idea that I would even sit next to my father in heaven was both nonsense and frightening.

But really, how did these clans come together in heaven, I wondered. Since millers all gathered together the place of clans must also be certain.

Allah did not love rebellious creatures. The Creator was not fond of those who showed ingratitude to blessings, peace and order. If I could be not a Kurdish man befitting my clan, it was better if I died. And what did they say: A dead man cries one day, a mad man every day.

And I was not just to become a miller. I would take a personal interest in the honour of my children, my wife, my sisters and everyone in the clan, and would, if necessary, not hesitate to give up my own life or take another's. When needed, I would know when to suppress my pain. If one day they were to lay out the body of one of my children in the middle of the village I would be strong enough to look at it expressionlessly as if looking at someone I'd never me or at a handful of earth. When necessary I would remain silent to protect my children and the tribe. I would not see the lifeless body of my son even if it remaining hanging in front of me for the rest of my life. If a tactless person were to ask me I would reply: "The sword of justice does not hurt."

I would also be careful towards those who came down from the mountains. I would take possession of my family. I would hand over winter provisions to them while ensuring I didn't condemn my dependents to hunger.

Of course, I wouldn't always remain silent. If my daughter, sister, wife, one of my nieces, even my mother, were to besmirch our honour, I would roar like a lion to punish them and without hesitating take the life of anyone who had ill intentions towards our honour. Everything could have a shadow, but honour could not tolerate a shadow.

Was I the only intelligent one? Why had no one before me had the idea to study? It would have been good, others would have wanted to. As no one had that intention, it means it was not deemed an auspicious thing. What good had city people brought to villagers that I should now want to become a city person? A person who studied was semi-urban. Which city person did I want to emulate? Teacher Fatih? Who was this person who had infiltrated the village like a communist infidel?

Who knows, maybe he got a rise in his salary in this way. He had given me a couple of pieces of paper and said: "You are the most successful student in the school." Who knew the truth? Perhaps he was conning me. Did Ankara come to check up on pupils in village schools?

He had given everyone a diploma. Even to the stupidest one. It was obvious that this teacher had conned the whole village. Why hadn't the previous ones given them out? Because they were honest. Should a complaint be made to the district governor? But would a dog eat a dog? Would the governor take sides with villagers against a fellow townsman? Let this teacher depart and not come back.

It was as if I had just awoken from a deep sleep. The most difficult thing was to distance myself from my dreams. It took me a night to say goodbye to each of my dreams written down one after the other. I took leave of them one by one. I was saying goodbye to that huge building with dozens of classrooms, where dozens of teachers worked, and the hundreds of students with whom I was to play football in the yard.

Hey school! I was unable to come to you, but I know there are schools like you. Be happy with your hundreds and thousands of students. Allah is fair. He must definitely have a reason for not considering my dreams worthy of me. I cannot fathom His works.

The more I tried to abandon my dreams it was as if they were going deeper into my brain. I was tired. I withdrew into myself as if I was hibernating. I didn't want anyone, even my mother, coming to me.

Without realising it I had accumulated so many dreams that it was as if they wanted to revive me and they would come and go. Childhood is a little like swimming amidst dreams. My dreams, that made me what I was and determined my path, were my only reality.

Whenever I tried to break away from my dreams, first the roots of my hair would heat up, then my ears and finally I would sweat. I would hide in corners when I had the occasional trembling fits so that no one would see me. After dinner I would go straight to bed.

I would not be able to see my teacher, who I loved even more than my father, again. I would not be able to enter that school, where I had found such tranquillity. I would not have other teachers, friends, books or diplomas which I had dreamt about the whole night. I would not be able to see the far away towns, big cities, countries and different people teacher Fatih had told us about. I would not hear about the incredible discoveries made in the world. I would not have a profession I loved. The centre of the world, that no one had seen, was far from me and it would stay that way for ever.

Those places were just for city folk, for they were in the majority there and they wouldn't accept villagers. With my child's mind I couldn't know this, and as I didn't know I was behaving in this shameless way. If my father was angry, it was for my own good. I was his son. I was rebellious towards him, none of my work would go well. I should pull myself together.

I should go with my father to the mill every day and carry sacks of wheat and flour until late. Then when the sun went down we should come back along the same route. In the evening we should sit down to eat and be thankful for what we had. Wolves will get those who leave the flock. Opposing your father was ingratitude, shamelessness and impudence.

I knew all this, but I could not prevent my hatred for my father. If I had heard he'd died, even if I'd seen him, not a single tear would have come from my eyes.

That wall newspaper I had brought home as a memento no longer had any meaning. My mother was right. To look at them, to remember the old days, would bring nothing but gloom. The best thing to do was to tear up the wall newspaper, and the certificate of excellence. If I was to rip them up, what about the primary school diploma and report? I should destroy them, too.

I didn't get out of bed until the darkness of the evening. Then I sat up on hearing my mother's voice and went to the old chest. As I had guessed, the torn nylon bag was behind the chest. Everyone was waiting at the floor table for my mother to bring lentils and bulgur. My grandfather thumped the vacant cushion next to him and beckoned me over. Since I was little I had become accustomed to sitting next to my grandfather. Distant from my father, close to my grandfather, my childhood had been a flood of affection on the one hand and on the other, pain and violence.

However aggressive my father was, my grandfather was to the same degree calm. His slow and serene speech calmed those listening to him. A pocket watch inherited from his father he carried in the pocket of a grey jacket and a seed pouch he kept in an inner pocket were possessions unique to him. He would collect the pips of fruit the taste of which he liked and plant them on the verge of the orchard, then monitor those that put forth shoots. Not just on our own land, but the mountain where we went to collect wood, in the meadow and even on the path to the mill there were saplings and trees he watered. He even used to visit the poplar cuttings he had planted on the other side of Kato and weed around them. I have never met anyone who knew better how much water each kind of tree needed. For my grandfather sun, water and soil were sacred. Serving the soil was the most flawless worship.

"Look Keko, this sapling will in a couple of years produce great apricots. Get a dry branch and put it over it to stop the birds eating them."

According to my grandfather, not only sun, water and soil, but fire, too, was sacred. Fire was another form of death; if death and fire hadn't existed, this world would have disappeared long ago. "No one loves the grim reaper, but he is a lifesaver for humankind. Thank God, before he created us he bestowed death on us."

It was enjoyable for us grandchildren to spend time with our grandfather. None of us were frightened of him. I don't remember him threatening me or any of us. He loved all of us, but he loved me above all. In his eyes my place was different. Whenever he saw me looking sad his warm look would descend on me like a cool shadow. When he said: "What's up, Keko?" I would relax and snuggle up to him. He would hug me with his huge arms and make me forget everything. After my grandfather, my second refuge was my mother. Although she did not have as much sway as my grandfather, her unconditional love was the remedy for all the wounds in my heart.

I stopped by the fire and opened the nylon bag. I threw first the wall newspaper, then the certificate of excellence, then my report, then my diploma one by one into the fire.

No one was talking. When my mother saw my report falling into the fire, she left the tray she was holding and jumped up. She took the diploma out of the flames and put it out by blowing on it. "Keko, have you lost your mind?" she said.

This unexpected behaviour of mine pleased my father. He scolded my mother, as if he didn't care about me or hadn't seen what I did, the joyful tone of his voice was obvious: "Woman! You deserve a beating! You have ruined a tray of *pilav* for the sake of a piece of paper!"

As for my mother, she was tearful. She ignored my father and knelt down in front of me holding the charred diploma in her hand. "You will need this when you go to do your military service, son. You will be a sergeant. Your father knows how those without a diploma are treated..."

My father was preparing to hit my mother and me when my grandfather's stentorian voice resounded:

"Ajar!"

I went back into my room. I had an increasing bloating in my stomach as if I had eaten all the meals in the world. If I had eaten a morsel I would have thrown up.

I got up before dawn and dressed. As my father was about to go out the door I took the bag of provisions my mother extended. I didn't see my father's face at that moment, but from the way my mother looked at him I realised he was smiling. My mother shook her head with a meaningful expression on her face. My father must have been both pleased and surprised. My dreams had died, but my father had got his wish. His eldest son Keko was finally going with him to the mill. This was the way it should be. What more could my father have wanted?

I was now going to work like a robot in my new life and be my father's slave. In fact this was not enough, more was needed. In order for the children to be born to become a miller after me I should embark on the road to marriage as soon as possible.

Our village was full of brides of thirteen and grooms of fourteen and fifteen. So why shouldn't miller Keko be a groom in the village of Heredile where cousins were betrothed while still in the cradle?

Heredile's rules functioned smoothly. Keko was, although belatedly, fulfilling the rule of unconditional obedience to his father. A father's reputation was tied first of all to his children, in particular his sons.

All day I bustled about in the mill like a loose cannon, trying to help my father and uncle. I did not differentiate between the different tasks I did. When we returned home I realised I was aching all over as I wasn't used to it, but I didn't care. To forget what I was going through pain, aches and weariness were like medication. I wanted to go to bed and fall into a deep sleep as soon as possible. I went to my room without eating. I undressed and got under the quilt. My grandfather put his head round the creaking door and said:

"Keko, come and sit with me, my lion."

When I heard my grandfather's voice my eyes welled up. I quickly wiped the tears welling up in my eyes with the back of my hand and blew my nose.

"I'm going to my room. Why don't you come?"

I went into my grandfather's room and closed the door. He indicated for me to sit next to him. I sat down and he put his arm round my neck and kissed my head.

"Don't underrate the primary school. More than half of this village are illiterate, Keko."

It was as if that was the first time that day I had heard the word school and something inside me broke. I hugged my grandfather and buried my face in his chest to hide the sound of my sobbing. I was choking. If it had been my father he would probably have panicked and beaten me for crying like a girl, who knows. My grandfather stroked and kissed my head. I don't know how much time passed. It was good to be freed of the tears I had tried to hold back for days. I looked around me and at my grandfather as if I had just woken up. I still felt like crying.

"Granddad, I can't bear it."

Apart from my grandfather and mother I was angry with everyone. My siblings, uncles, aunts, cousins, neighbours… They were all against me. I only trusted my grandfather and only loved him. I was aware of my mother's helplessness, but sometimes I blamed her, too.

My grandfather hugged me tightly and stroked my face. He kissed my head many times. His eyes had also welled up.

"It's a shame about your tears, Keko. Don't waste yourself!"

"But granddad, a man keeps his word?"

Granddad sighed deeply.

"Ah, my boy!"

"My father tricked me."

"Before the day breaks what things may happen, Keko. Just be patient."

"What's that to me, I want to go to school! Even if I'm patient, will school wait? Everyone will start school, but I haven't even been able to take the exam."

"Ah, my brave boy! If only I was able to have you educated in the best schools in the big cities by the best teachers. Is learning and receiving science ever a bad thing?"

There was not a middle school in either our village or in the surrounding villages. The few village schools there were all consisted of one class, like ours. Five years all in the one class. What passed for education in most of them in small classrooms with no heating, was a single teacher giving superficial lessons.

"Keko, even if there are no costs to the free boarding school, when you go there will be no one to help your father."

I had calmed down on my grandfather's neck when we heard the village headman and my father's voices coming from the threshing floor. I cocked my ear to listen. The governor had apparently sent word to the headman that he wanted pupils to take the free boarding exam.

"If anyone would pass the exam, your son would."

"Headman, I was happy when the teacher went. And now you've started?"

"I gather your son always has his head in books."

"If only I hadn't sent him to school!"

"Whoever else I send will disgrace the village."

"Huh, the one who is disgraceful is our headman! If only his mother had had a daughter instead of this tiresome cur!"

"Ajar, please!" It won't do to offend the governor."

"What do I care about the governor, headman!"

"Don't be crazy, Ajar! Are you opposing the governor himself?"

"How would he have heard about my son?"

"From where, for sure the teacher would have told him."

"As if I didn't know, who else?"

"He didn't do it with ill intentions. He's the state's teacher!"

"That's okay, but he should know his place. Is the bastard bringing new customs to an old village? Look, at my age I'm stooped. What is the teacher doing? He is taking my grown up son away from me. What shall I do, give my walking stick to them? Don't drive me mad. I don't recognise any such governor. Do they supply my daily bread?"

"Don't say that, Ajar! You promised the teacher. He then told the authorities. This is government business. It's no laughing matter."

"What are you saying, headman? Just because the governor sent someone you're praising schools? Isn't this boy mine? If I want I'll send him, if not, I won't. Is this military service or what?"

"Alright Ajar, alright. I'm off, but the governor wants to see Keko."

"Why? Is he going to give him a salary? Headman, be on your way. Oh My God!"

The governor's order had not changed my father even a little. When my teacher came the following day I was exhausted from thinking. He had also realised he would not be able to persuade my father.

In Heredile surprises were not well received or understood. It was not possible for things that were disliked and not understood to occur. At the slightest deviation all rules of logic would be cast to one side and traditional merciless laws, that it was not clear who had introduced, would come into play.

My father was not talking to the headman who brought the order from the governor. Some days I didn't go to the mill and stayed at home. On such days my father didn't pressure me. I would stay in my room and not come out until the evening. My mother, who would begin preparations for the evening meal with the sound of the *azan*, would come and try to persuade me to emerge.

"Come on, part of my liver, come to eat! Without you the morsels stick in my throat. If I eat honey it flows like poison into me."

I wasn't going to eat. My father couldn't beat me when my grandfather was there. My mother came into my room again.

"My son Keko. How can you not come to the meal! Your grandfather, uncles, father are all there. What happened? Is it because your father hit you? You didn't go to school, but who from this village has, Keko?"

I looked at my mother and shook my head. I was determined.

"Mum, I'm not going to school but if my father hits me again I will flee the village. Just so you know."

My mother turned hurriedly and looked at the door as if she feared my father would hear.

"What do you mean, my son? Heaven forbid!"

I shook my head.

"You will see, mum. I will flee!"

A look of fear spread over my mother's prematurely creased face.

"What about me? Don't you ever think about me, my son?

"Have you ever thought about me?"

In actual fact I was not thinking about fleeing. However it happened I just suddenly blurted it out. After my mother had left the room a feeling of relief came over me. Why hadn't I thought of that before? I had two legs. Two legs that were stronger than most in the village. To escape was a good idea.

I must find Celil and tell him about my plan. This was the only solution. I was going to flee somewhere, find a school and continue my education. Suddenly I felt hungry. My mother had roasted potatoes and taken out pickles.

As my mother and aunt collected the plates I sneaked out. I went to Celil's family threshing floor and whistled. He looked at me in amazement. "Are you mad?"

In a moment we had gathered all the children. The idea of escape excited all of us, especially Niyaz, but he was still too upset to show his pleasure.

"And where can you go without money?"

"I will go as far as I can, then work where my money runs out, then when I earn the fare hit the road again."

"What work will you do?"

"Whatever there is."

"Your father will find you straight away."

"He can't come looking for me now. It's the mill season. If he leaves the mill and chases me the whole village will starve."

"What if the gendarme find you?"

"What if you run into those in the mountains?"

"I won't head towards the mountains."

"Which way will you go?"

"Towards Istanbul."

Sülo wasn't saying anything. He was always quiet, but this was something different. When he saw that I was looking at him he came to my side.

"You can't escape."

"Why?"

"Because you're not an adult."

"Adult?"

"Yes, adult. Until you're at least eighteen you can't be an adult."

"What does that mean?"

Until you're eighteen your father owns you. For instance, if you escape, they will catch you in the big city and bring you back here and leave you at your father's feet."

"And he will beat you again."

"No, not beat, in my opinion he will kill you."

But despite this I was still not frightened of escaping.

"If he finds me let him beat me, let him kill me."

I had decided once and for all to flee.

"I'll flee! If they bring me back and hand me over to my father I'll escape again and again! I won't stay in this village!" I shouted.

Remzi was also excited.

"Don't be selfish, Keko," he said.

All heads turned towards him.

"You're going to escape, what about us? When you go, why are we staying in this village?"

I had not expected my escape plan to gain such broad acceptance. For a moment I was nonplussed and didn't know what to say.

The idea also pleased Bekir.

"Ehh? So when you go will I be left here alone to play with the girls?"

We put our hands up and swore our habitual oath.

"One for all, all for one!"

We had learned this oath from teacher Fatih.

Only Sülo was standing apart, head lowered, looking at us with a sheepish look on his face.

From that day on we began to make a plan. We talked for a long time. How were we to get out of the village? How would we reach the tarmacked road without being seen by soldiers or those in the mountains? How would we get in the back of one of the trucks secretly, moreover, how would we travel without being seen by the driver? It obviously wouldn't be easy to jump on a truck while it was moving. But there was no other way.

Sülo said: "You need something to make the truck slow down and stop."

Sülo wasn't coming but he joined in our plans. He also produced the most incisive solutions. Remzi tried to persuade Sülo to come along, but it was no use. He said: "Consider me dead."

"Sülo, don't be coy like a girl! Come with us. What happened to 'for better for worse'?".

"I can't come. If I do, there will be no one to look after the flock."

We laughed. He was very serious.

"I know them, they know me. I know the character of all of them. Some will always find grass to eat, others have to be fed by hand and even then are not enthusiastic. I've also learned how to make them better when they fall ill. Now if someone who doesn't know the job comes along, they will perish. No, I can't come. I would be thinking of them. I can't leave them."

When Sülo was still a baby his father had gone up the mountain. Two years later his body had arrived. His grandfather in a distant village came and took Sülo's mother away. Sülo grew up with his uncle. When those in the mountains wounded his uncle, who was a village guard, he suddenly went to Istanbul. Sülo, who didn't even have an identity card, was left alone in the house. Our teacher made great efforts to get Sülo an identity card. Teacher Fatih would visit Sülo, who lived alone from the age of ten onwards, every evening. Sometimes he would eat his meal together with him. Sülo began to work as the village shepherd when he was nine, and slept most nights with the animals in the barn. Those who saw Sülo unexpectedly on the threshing floor knew he had come to look after the animals in the barn. He could have given his life for his flock without hesitation.

One day he jumped on a bear that plunged into the flock. If it hadn't been for the dogs he might have died between the bear's paws. While the dogs, the bear and Sülo grappled, the sheep started such a bleating that it was heard in the village. When the headman and his retinue went to the scene they found Sülo semi-conscious, and the bear escaped with difficulty. However it came to be injured, no one saw the bear, which had lost a lot of blood, again.

With every passing day our escape plan and the number of escapees got larger. Remzi said: "If it goes on like this, there won't be any children left in the village. There will be a lament in every house."

Cemal was intending to find a job straight away. Then he would marry one of the Istanbul girls. What was the attraction of village girls? Bekir was going to be a footballer. But, then again, perhaps he would be a singer. Baha was going to be a night watchman, but he didn't know how he was going to free himself from his cradle betrothal. When he became a night watchman he was also going to do other work during the day, in this way he would become wealthy. Celil was going to work in a restaurant and both earn money and be able to eat a variety of free food. Diyar was going to be a driver. Once he'd finished work he was going to go sightseeing in Istanbul every day.

Sometimes we had no time to talk over our escape plan on account of talking about our constantly changing dreams. At such times I got annoyed with them. They were like that in school, too. Once they started to talk about footballers they forgot their homework and on every occasion were told off by the teacher.

A few days before we were due to escape our plan became known. Baha's big sister had hit him on the head and called him "ham-fisted!" He had got angry with her and replied: "When I go to Istanbul you will see what I manage to do."

Baha's father came to our house and said: "Ajar, look after your son. I hope families are not going to have trouble. This idea came from your son."

When my father walked towards the clay oven and picked up a thin stick I understood what he was going to do, but I didn't feel like fleeing.

"You can go as far as hell! Since you're fucking off, why are you leading other children astray? Their fathers are coming to my door," he said as he started to lash out with the stick. My hands, arms, face, shoulder, back… The stick was going up and down. I was getting a real beating from my father for the second time. He had beaten me before, but nothing like on the last two occasions. My mother again came and jumped on me to protect me. My father hit my mother so hard she cried out and shrank back.

Kibar, Sumra and Hatun were watching, crying. From time to time Sumra said: "Dad, don't hit my brother," but he didn't even hear her. Then suddenly Kibar shouted: "Dad, granddad's coming!"

Who knows, perhaps that was Kibar's first lie. My grandfather was not coming, but Kibar, with her little mind, knew that if our grandfather came he would be very angry with my father for beating me. For a moment my father stopped and glanced towards the entrance to the threshing floor. With all my strength I ran and jumped over the wall. I was running through the village and crying. Remzi was the first one to see me. His face was also puffy. It was obvious that he had, like the other village boys, been beaten by his father.

My father was most resentful of my idea to flee. He didn't speak to me anymore. I was forbidden to see the other children. Not just me, all the children had been punished. It was forbidden for us to speak to each other or be seen together. When Sülo came to get the sheep he whispered in my ear:

"Remzi says: let's wait for now. Let them forget it then we'll have another look."

I couldn't wait. As the exams could not wait for me, I couldn't wait for them, either. There must be a way for me to take that exam. I could have found teacher Fatih's address and written to him, but I would be very late. And what could I write? Was I going to write: "Abduct me and force me to take the exam."? And anyway, there were some papers that my father had to sign and that was impossible.

I was looking for a solution. Perhaps the way to get my father to sign for the exam was via the mill.

Before sunrise I was setting off with my father and uncle. Carrying our provisions we walked to the mill in an hour and a half. My father behaved as if I wasn't there on the way and at the mill. As his elder brother wasn't speaking to me, my uncle was also reluctant to do so. By the time we got to the mill the sun had risen. While the tea was brewing I left Sürmeli to graze at the back. We ate our cheese and flat bread with tea. As they started work I would take the tea glasses down to the stream to wash them. After washing the glasses I began to carry the sacks of flour and wheat. I don't know what my weight was in those days or how heavy the sacks were. One day my uncle compared me to the weight of one of the sacks I carried.

"This sack is at most one and a half times your weight. Not too much," he said.

My cousin Gülistan brought our midday meal. My uncle was not pleased about this.

"Gülistan, you're a big girl now, is there no one else to bring it?" said my uncle, to which Gülistan responded by shaking her head despairingly. "Who can I send, dad? They would drop it and be late. If you were hungry, how would you work?"

One day Gülistan arrived looking weepy with red-rimmed eyes. I don't know who she had been angry with, but she wasn't someone who would easily let people get the better of her.

My paternal grandmother said she was the most shameless woman in the family. That day as we ate our lunch, Gülistan took out a small knife from her waist and gathered up her apron. She was going to go up the back slope to gather thyme.

My uncle said: "Don't go too far away, just in case."

Gülistan left. Before 5 minutes had passed my father pointed at me and indicated my uncle, who said: "Keko, go with Gülistan so that she's not alone."

I hadn't yet finished my soup. I took my bread and dashed to the back. Gülistan was nowhere to be seen. I climbed the slope. I was tired and sat down. I heard a voice from behind the rose hip bushes. As I walked in that direction Gülistan emerged from under the bushes.

"Keko, did I give you a fright?"

"Who were you talking to?"

"No one. Who could it be? I made my voice deeper to frighten you. Well done. You weren't scared."

She looked agitated and her cheeks had gone red. One of the buttons on her blouse was undone.

That evening my mother had made a meat and bulgur dish. She brought some fresh butter and red peppers she had fried on the oven and poured it over a tray of the food. We all stuck in our spoons and began to eat with gusto. For a moment Salıha looked at me and pulled a face. Gülistan, who saw it, laughed, turned towards me and winked.

Chapter Five

WAKE UP KEKO

Advertising was not even paying the basic bills and the London Magazine supplement of the newspaper for which we worked was on the verge of closing. Mehtap and Boncuk were relying on her uncle. As for me, I didn't care. I was working from morning to night for peanuts producing news for the magazine, and preparing the sports page, even though I didn't know anything about football, which was a kind of torture. And Jaklin had become manager of the Plaza in Oxford Street and had told me:

"Whenever you want come and work as a waitress."

In fact the Boss was expecting us to beg.

"Am I the Central Bank? Every week I'm paying you out of my pocket. No one cares. Everyone who gets their weekly money dashes off home. That's enough! Put it on the front page: this is the last edition. One should respect the readers."

In that turmoil Şükriye had somehow managed to cream off some of the distributors' wages. Hasan said: "It's not the money, but it's not on."

"Hasan, she wouldn't do that."

"It's not just mine that's short. You can ask the others."

I sat down in the chair by the window and began to observe Green Lanes. I thought of Vedat Türkali. His council flat was two streets away from the office. He was busy with his latest novel. I wanted to go and tell him about the latest developments, but what use would that be?

Keko was still in intensive care and there was nothing to do but wait for him to wake up. As soon as the sports page was done I grabbed my bag and went out. Just as I was about to go out the door the Boss called out:

"They say that first rats leave a sinking ship."

I turned in surprise. Our eyes met.

"Which ship?"

"How many ships are there?"

"In that case, am I the rat that's leaving?"

The news editor butted in with his usual false bonhomie.

"Maybe the girl's going to meet her boyfriend. How do you know?"

"No no, if she was loyal she would look for advertising rather than go looking for another job. She would look to save the newspaper that pays her wages."

I leaned forward and said in a voice only he could hear: "When have I ever gone out looking for advertising?"

He got very annoyed. "That's it! Why do I bother? Why am I doling out money from my pocket? Let it close down, then I'll be rid of it. I'll go and do some proper stories."

"That's just what I'm saying. Is a magazine supplement worthy of you? It's an insult to your signature."

As I left he was still shouting behind me.

"Look! Such a gob on her! Ungrateful!"

As he was talking so much it meant London Magazine was

not going to close. So slavery was to continue. As I saw the 141 bus coming round the corner I began to run towards the stop. I sat down on the bus, out of breath. It was good to be out of the office. I began to think about the photocopies of Keko's journal that, thanks to Habibe, we had taken from the police file. It was sunny and cold outside. A voice inside me said: "Keko will recover and we will sit down and have a long chat." And even Habibe should be with us.

When I went into the garden of Homerton hospital my heart was beating fast. How wonderful it would be if has woken up when I go in and the doctor says: "He is out of danger."

While talking to nurses outside the intensive care ward his mother arrived. Her eyes were like Keko's. She opened her hands with long fingers and prayed with her lips twitching. Two tears ran down her cheeks. I didn't know what to say or how I could console her.

"The nurse says 'he is the same'. But that is a good thing. At least he is not deteriorating."

She was about to speak, but her voice came out as a croak. She wiped away her tears and sat down. We sat side by side without speaking for a while. She was crying constantly.

"What did they want from my son? If they had come I would have given my life gladly. Why didn't they leave my son alone? Don't they feel any mercy for youth?"

Just at that moment two young men appeared at the end of the corridor. They looked at us and then began to have a conversation. I got up slowly and began to walk towards them. When our eyes met they turned hurriedly and ran off. I was about to call out, but abandoned the idea.

I returned to the office in the afternoon. Sezen Aksu was on the radio.

Sleep Memik my son sleep
Grow up in the other nights

When Mehtap saw me she ran over. She was smiling and whispered: "Guess what? The Boss says it won't close down. He apparently said if we tidy things up in three weeks it will continue."

My ear was still listening to the song. Even if Memik sleeps I wanted Keko to wake up, and to wake up immediately a long way from where he was born. Let him run towards the bus stop again. Just before getting on the bus let him pick up the push chair of a woman he didn't know and fly like a bird. Let him bring it and put it down by the window. Let him comb back his wavy hair with his fingers and his long eyelashes and this time may his dark eyes laugh.

And also, just for the sake of talking, perhaps I would say something like: "How are you?" If he wanted to he would flee from me. But don't let him die.

Whenever I thought of Keko my heart would swell up. The Boss came over. In a semi-sarcastic voice, as if he expected me to apologise, he said: "Ah ah, lady, have you realised that it's not so easy to find a job out there?"

I was not in the mood to talk or argue. I was so tense that if I had let myself go I could have cried noisily. The Boss thought we were all scared of losing our jobs, and he wasn't wrong, to be fair. It was difficult to survive in London without working. In order to reply to him I mumbled a couple of meaningless sentences.

"You're right. It's difficult to find a job. It's even difficult to live."

He was exuberant. There was no better time for him to start one of his sermons.

"You see, that's why I can't close the paper down. I ask you, who else would put their hand in their pocket and bring out a newspaper? But I can't help it. Why? Because I love you. I love everyone in this office."

He was right. That office was his whole world. His obsessive love was the icing on the cake of his life.

Hasan brought in baklava and Mehtap ordered tea. We celebrated the non-closure of the paper together.

Şükriye was unhappy as she had once again failed to get the paper closed down. She glared at us. She hated all of us. According to her, all the money being spent on the newspaper should be going into her pocket. Everyone's money, even, should be going into her account, as far as she was concerned.

Chapter Six

CHILD BRIDEGROOM

After eating I went into the room and sat down on my grandfather's bed. As I had become the kind of child they wanted, they couldn't pressurise me too much. I didn't want to speak to any of them, or even see them. Civan and Kibar came into the room one after the other.

"Keko, have you heard?"

"What?"

"Dad is going to marry you off."

"Shut up! Get out!"

Neither had any intention of leaving the room. When my mother came in to get my grandfather's prayer mat I was pushing Civan.

"Keko, what are you saying?"

"They're dirty!"

"What's happened?"

Kibar sidled up to my mother and said: "Mum, Keko is annoyed because he's getting married." My mother got the two of them out of the room and sat down next to me. I was so sure that Civan had made up such a thing that I couldn't fathom the serious look on my mother's face.

"Wait a minute, son. Don't fly off the handle."

"Didn't you hear me, mum? They're talking nonsense"

My mother gulped as if she didn't know what to say.

"If not this year, then next. If not next year, then the year after. What do you say? It's the right way, son."

"What?"

"Don't oppose your father, son."

I was looking for an opportunity to let off steam. With my mother's words it was as if a cork had shot out of my brain. I was shouting at the top of my voice:

"Who says I'm going to get married? I'm not getting married! You get married! Leave me alone! God damn you! You've already taken my school away!"

I recall my father opening the door as if he was breaking it and coming over to me. When he moved to hit me my grandfather's voice was heard: " Ajaaar!"

My father's hand was suspended in mid-air. His cheeks turned bright red.

"Ajar, don't touch the boy!"

My father stormed angrily out of the room, muttering: "Oh My God…"

I was walking up and down in the room. I could not bear my father, uncle and mother ignoring me, taking decisions on my behalf and behaving as if I was their slave. And now they wanted me to get married. As he saw it my father was being cunning. He thought he could attach irons to my feet by getting me engaged.

In Heredile, boys who reached 13 or 14 were engaged to girls chosen by their parents who were almost all cousins of the same age. It would not be thought strange for me to be engaged to one of my 13-year-old paternal cousins. It was expected that in this way I would be swept up in the excitement of engagement and marriage and forget the world.

I had only just heard, but my father, paternal uncle, mother and maternal uncles had discussed it for weeks. All the girls had been reviewed one by one.

My mother had apparently said: "Perhaps we'll take Saliha." Saliha had said: "I won't marry Keko," hence saving me from her. Her making a face at me at the meal had been a message: "I don't want you". If only the others would say: "We won't accept Keko as a husband," then I would be free of all of them.

From that day on, whenever Beyaz and Kiraz saw me they would giggle. God knows, maybe they were thinking: "I wonder which of the two of us will have Keko for a husband?"

There was no alternative for girls. Some of them married joyfully, but almost all of them realised on the morning of the wedding what a hell they had entered. For those who married boys of the same age, that was one thing. But there was a strange look on the faces of those who married men much older that never left them. They looked surprised, stupid, frozen. You could find an excuse for everything in the village, but not for getting married. In Heredile, having offspring was still more important than anything.

A week later Gülistan came over to me in the barn, looking around her.

"Psst! Come here, you!"

"What's up, Gülistan?"

"Listen to me well."

There was no one else there but for the two of us. I was already listening to her.

"Keko, you will ask for me."

"What?"

"I'll go with you to the big city. Once we're married, no one can interfere."

"What marriage, Gülistan?"

"If they mention others, don't accept."

Without waiting for my answer she kissed me on the cheek and shot off.

I had understood why my uncle beat Gülistan frequently. Her intention, like mine, was to leave the village. But why did she want to leave? Gülistan had left primary school in the second year. She had only just about learned to read and write. As she didn't want to study what was pushing her to go to the city? There was a sudden flash of lightning in my brain. I ran to my grandfather.

"Granddad, can married people go to middle school?"

He laughed and stroked my hair.

"Where did that come from, Keko?"

I needed to find out about this. Although only small, a beacon of hope had been lit inside me, but the first thing to do was to go to my mother secretly and ask her to get me engaged to Gülistan. If someone asked for her before me my plans could be scuppered.

Until that day I thought I would be able to say anything to my mother, but when it came to marriage I felt embarrassed. And if I told my mother, how would she tell my father? Would she be able to say: "Keko wants Gülistan"? Even if my father didn't have any money owing to him he wouldn't ask for Gülistan for me. If my uncle said no, what would happen? If he said: "Keko is fine, but he's not only younger than her, but he's confused. He's thinking of studying. I can't give my daughter to someone like that."

While spooning up lentil and flour soup at the evening meal, I was thinking about these things. As children, none of us had any control over our lives. We were children. It was not possible for us to have wishes, dreams, desires or decisions. We were the slaves, or even the victims, of first our parents and then our clans.

Gülistan was silent, but looked thoughtful. My aunt glared at her from time to time. If she noticed something missing on the table she held her responsible.

"Where's the salt, girl?"

Gülistan immediately got up and brought whatever was requested. After the meal was over my grandfather held his hands up to recite the prayer of thanks, as always. We repeated every sentence after him.

"Oh God, may we be truly thankful for what you have given us. Please protect us and ensure we stay on the straight and narrow..."

He had still not finished the prayer when the door shook as if it had been kicked. My grandfather's hands were still held out in front of him. My grandmother said: "Bismillah!"and looked around. My mother and aunt straightened their headscarves and sent Gülistan and her sister Yeter inside. My father jumped up and grabbed the poker we stirred the fire with. The new arrivals were neither soldiers nor those in the mountains, as we had feared. It was Şakir's grandfather, Uncle Cemo, who had knocked the door as if he was breaking it, with his son, who limped, behind him. Uncle Cemo, who was red in the face with rage, stood in the middle of the room and looked at my grandfather. My grandfather looked bashful, as if he knew what Uncle Cemo was going to say.

"Ali Kemal, I gave you that girl, and at the first time of asking! I said: 'this girl is no one's, she is yours'!"

My grandfather was listening without raising his head.

"I gave you a fresh bride, Ali Kemal. Is this how you behave?"

We thought granddad was just married to grandma. There were lots of co-wives in the village, but grandma didn't have one. Which aunt of Şakir had granddad married? Why had we never seen this bride? The more Uncle Cemo shouted the quieter our elders became.

At one stage my father said: "Uncle, don't get angry. Come and sit down."

As if he had not heard, the old man took another pace towards my granddad, stamped his foot on the ground and said: "Don't worry, Ali Kemal. I know how to get the girl back. And may the stain on your honour be lasting."

Uncle Cemo left. My grandmother was crying silently. My grandfather's head was still down and he looked preoccupied. When my father left I went over to my grandma. In that house I most loved my grandfather and least loved my father. After my grandfather, in order, came my mother, grandmother, brothers and sisters. In fact, my friends were somewhere between my grandfather and my family. I was frightened to even tell myself that I didn't love my father, but that was the case. And it was as if my father didn't care whether his children loved him or not. I said to my grandmother, who was quietly wiping away her tears:

"Grandma, when did granddad marry after you?"

She began to sob more, hitting her knees and keening: "Ah, if only this calamity had not befallen us and your granddad had married two other women! Ah, Rahmi, Rahmi!!! You've lost your home, haven't you come to your senses yet? As if the longing wasn't enough, you're making us fret as well."

My grandfather, who had not spoken until then, suddenly roared:

"Didn't I tell you not to mention the name of that accursed one, woman? And didn't you swear not to?"

"My insides are aching. So what if I mention his name, as he hasn't left my head?"

No one was explaining anything to us children. While my mother was doing the washing up I collected the spoons and joined her.

"Mum, who is Rahmi?"

"Quiet, your granddad might hear!"

"What shouldn't he hear?"

"Don't mention Rahmi. And don't ask anyone. Your grandfather will get very angry."

"You say then, mum. Who is he?"

She whispered: "Your uncle."

"So do I have another uncle?"

"If only you didn't."

Since Uncle Cemo had visited our adults were disgruntled. And I was unable to pluck up enough courage to ask my mother to ask for Gülistan. In any case, before we had been born like everything else who we would marry was written on our foreheads. For just this reason to oppose our parents was tantamount to opposing the Creator. And anyway, what was a woman?

With every passing day I was getting into more of a flap. Sometimes I felt I was walking in a tunnel of fear. My father was at both ends. I was becoming short of breath, but I couldn't get out. They were saying: "You were born in this tunnel and you will die in it." I wanted to blow the tunnel up with a bomb and escape. The explosion was taking me so far away that those left behind immediately forgot me and didn't come after me. How wonderful it would be to be forgotten in this way.

Seven days a week we were going to the mill. In the evenings we were so tired that all night I slept semi-conscious as if the sacks of flour I had carried were still on my back. I had dragged my bed under the window. Every night before sleeping I would watch the stars and recall what our teacher had told us. Closing my eyes and listening to the crickets, I thought about life on other planets. Who knows, perhaps among those billions of stars there was a tiny little village like ours in a small country on a small star. And even a small child just like me. Did they not send him to school either, I wondered?

Then my dreams got bigger. I produced answers to my own questions. Perhaps in the universe there was a duplicate, or even several duplicates, of our world. Our teacher Fatih had said: "There are so many unknown things. If we knew them it would be necessary to include today in the Stone Age." Once my grandfather had said: "Every human being has a soulmate." Perhaps my soulmate was on one of those distant stars, not in this world. Could I not have two, three or even four soulmates? I was frightened and wanted to be a crowd. If there were three Kekos, would my father still be able to beat me? If the Creator was omnipotent, why didn't he do such interesting things? If I was the Creator, I wouldn't allow humans to get down. I would have cocked an ear to all the wishes of children. If God accepted the wishes of children, what an entertaining place the world would be. Children were not loved in this world, but perhaps in the world on those stars they lived happily like in the fairy stories.

Some nights I wanted to put on wings and fly. Would it be possible to soar, get lost in the depths of the sky and fly high above the clouds?

If only Heredile would accept me as dead. Then if I returned to the world and landed in a place I wanted. And if I didn't like it I would fly off. If only I was a bird no one could hold. More predatory than an eagle, faster than a hawk. If only I could flap my wings and fly around the world…

I had cleaned out the small unused depot behind the mill and turned it into a den. In rare moments when I wasn't needed I would take refuge there. Sometimes I would spend hours praying, hoping Allah would hear me. I promised that if I left the village and took the exams I would be the most honest child in this world. I was even content to pray not five times a day, but twenty five.

One morning I awoke to the sound of screams. My mother and aunt were standing in front of my uncle trying to protect Gülistan, who had already been beaten and looked dishevelled, from further blows. My mother had gripped the club in my uncle's hand and was not letting it go. He was hitting my aunt and his daughter, but seemed to be taking care not to hit my mother.

"Let go, I say! Let go, or I'll hit you too, sister-in-law!"

"I won't let go. May I be your slave, but don't hit them so hard! You'll cause permanent damage and regret it. Is that what you want?"

"Let her die, spawn of the devil! Better to have no child at all than one like this. She will make it impossible for me to show my face in the village!"

My aunt was crying.

"My God. Take me away. What is this suffering?"

My uncle hit my aunt again with his free hand. "Shut up, Şemse! That's as much as I'd expect from a daughter of yours!"

"So now she's my daughter, Ekber?"

My mother suddenly grabbed the club from my uncle. Then she unexpectedly stood up to him. It was the first time I had seen her like this.

"When they're good they're yours and when they're bad they're our children. Did we bring them from our father's house?"

My mother had gone too far. My uncle walked towards her in a determined way. Meanwhile, my grandfather came out of his room. From the way he was moving his lips his prayers had just ended. My uncle's hand, about to strike, remained suspended in mid-air as my grandfather shouted:

"Ekbeeer!"

My uncle turned round. He didn't know what to say. Blood from Gülistan's nose was mixing with her tears.

"Dad, leave me alone. I'm going to break their bones…"

"Why aren't you at the mill, Ekber?"

Like my father, my uncle could not oppose my grandfather. He left the house muttering. As my aunt straightened her headscarf she was crying while gingerly feeling her eyebrow. My mother was wiping the blood from Gülistan's nose with a damp cloth. Then she turned to my sister.

"Şerbet, take her and put her to bed."

My sister was very stubborn. "I'm cross with her," she said.

My mother turned and looked at my grandfather. He had returned to his prayers. She took off one of her sandals and threw it as hard as she could. It hit Şerbet on the back as she went out the door.

I took Gülistan by the arm and led her to her room. While sitting on her bed she held her aching places. Her sobbing increased. She lay down with difficulty. It was obvious that my uncle's blows were hurting. I covered her. I couldn't even guess what was upsetting her and had led to her being beaten.

From that day on Kibar and Veli began to bring our food. At their pace this meant lunch arrived towards evening.

Two weeks later my grandfather also came to the mill with lunch. I was white like a snowman between the sacks of flour. I was happy to see my grandfather. As he had come my father would take a break.

"Congratulations!" said my grandfather.

I thought: "He must have understood what I'm thinking."

My grandfather said to himself: "They didn't say in vain that every cloud has a silver lining."

My father was surprised to see my grandfather.

"Dad, did they send you with the food?"

"No, when work is over come and see me."

My grandfather said: "There was no other way."

My father looked depressed. "It's up to you, dad. It's not for me to offer you advice, but don't tire yourself at your age."

Then the village headman arrived. They all looked thoughtful. When my father made a signal I prepared *ayran* and took it to the headman.

The headman took a mouthful, then breathed deeply.

"Such a great taste. Can someone who has not tasted mountain water say he has drunk water, I wonder?"

My father was thoughtful.

"You're right, headman," he said, but seemed to be suggesting something else.

"Granddad, shall I put thyme in the *ayran*?"

He was out of sorts and shook his head.

"Let's hope for the best, Uncle Ali Kemal. Doesn't Uncle Cemo know? You don't seem to be happy with it, but there is no one else who can go."

My grandfather didn't reply to the headman. He indicated with his hand that they should get up and they walked towards the village together. As they left my father and uncle returned to the mill. Then my father sat down and began to watch the mountains. As I collected the empty *ayran* glasses my eyes met my father's. It was as if he was trying to tell me something. While washing the glasses in the stream I heard him grumbling. "Ah Rahmi, you're shaking us all up."

When I returned home wearily, there was an odd look on everyone's face.

My mother embraced me and said: "Keko, part of my liver."

Serbet saw I was surprised and didn't miss the opportunity.

She leaned down and whispered in my ear: "Good news, Keko."

In those bad days I couldn't think of anything that could be good news for me. Perhaps teacher Fatih had come. Even if I wasn't taking the exam I had really missed talking to him.

"Has teacher Fatih come?"

"What teacher! I said good news."

I didn't even want to listen to them.

"If you go to the big city..."

"Are you making fun of me now?"

"Keko, you're going."

"Who?"

"Ah, I'm not saying. I'm keeping quiet."

Veli came running over to me.

"Keko, are you also going with granddad?"

I didn't know where my granddad was going.

Gülistan was putting plates on the shelf. She turned and laughed at us.

"I was saying to you: 'this boy is a simpleton', but none of you believed me. You see, he doesn't even understand what is being said. I wonder what that city teacher saw in him."

Even if we actually hear words and sentences which we're not sure of, we can't understand them.

Veli, Sumra, Kibar and Serbet were all telling me one by one that I was going to the big city, but I thought they were taking the mickey out of me.

My grandfather and I were going to Istanbul to see Uncle Rahmi, whose existence I had only learned of 3 days previously. Could this be true? How had my father given permission for me to leave the village? No one could oppose my grandfather, but still my father would not have wanted to let me go.

"This is honour, it's like nothing else!" my uncle was saying.

My grandmother was crying constantly, saying: "Ah, Rahmi, ah!"

My father was not at all happy. "Whatever the blokes say, they are right. What he got up to here was not enough, now he's not behaving himself in Istanbul. If I could go there I would give him a good thrashing."

"It's work time, you can't go."

"You don't say. Yes, it's appropriate for my father to go."

Going to Istanbul with my grandfather was beyond my wildest dreams. Only that morning I had rebuked Allah as if he was facing me:

"I thought prayers didn't go unanswered. You didn't see me as worthy of taking the boarding school exam. If you wanted to you could naturally fill my father with goodness. Aren't I one of your creatures?"

That evening the village suddenly seemed to have changed. Everyone around me, even my father, seemed to be more pleasant. I was finally to leave the village.

An exciting wait began. I was counting the days, hours, minutes and seconds. What they called fate was sometimes capable of playing tricks. My grandfather was determined. I didn't know what my uncle had done, but whatever it was, my grandfather was going to correct it. He should go. In fact let us go now.

That evening a great closeness and gratitude grew inside me towards the uncle I didn't know. Thanks to him I was going to the big city. Whatever anyone said he must be a very good human being.

The idea of taking me was entirely my grandfather's idea. I didn't know what my grandfather had said to my father and how he had persuaded him. In any case, my father had not liked the idea. There was no one apart from my grandfather who could have prised me away from my father's hands. It was just as well my grandfather was not like my father. If he had been like my father, life would have been unbearable.

I thought: now let no one tell my grandfather not to go. Let them not even open their mouths. If anyone was to say to my grandfather "don't take your grandson," let them vanish. May everyone keep quiet and get out of our way. I was going to that big city I didn't even dare to dream about. For someone from Heredile to go to Istanbul was a miracle. Now I was sure that Allah loved me very much. I was embarrassed because I had rebuked Him. He had accepted my greatest prayer. And by giving me more than I wanted. From now on I was going to fulfil all my duties towards Him, as He had granted me more than I had wished for.

Gülistan kept saying: "Where is Istanbul, where are we..?" She was right. Who would have thought of Istanbul? What had I wanted? When it was impossible to go to one of the free boarding schools, and just when I was so unhappy and despairing as to want to die, suddenly the way had opened to the Sultan's palace. Ankara was just a small town compared to Istanbul. My mother said: "you are going to the city of saints." Ali Kemal Karadağ, that is, Keko, was going to study in Istanbul. No child from Heredile had ever been so blessed. Full stop....

"A blind man asked for an eye, Allah gave him two…."

"You're really jammy, Keko!"

"Istanbul, huh?"

The ban had been lifted. I could now meet my friends. Neither their parents nor mine said anything. It was as if my grandfather and I were not from the village, we were like guests, being treated with more respect. Everyone already loved and respected my grandfather, but for a child to be respected in Heredile was not something we were used to.

"Keko, eat some pastry with butter."

"I won't eat it, Aunt Takdir."

"Keko, you'll soon forget Heredile. When you are a resident of Istanbul you won't even look out here. Especially when you study and if you get a good job?"

"No, Hajji, never!"

The excitement of the journey had gripped all my friends like a wave. Istanbul was the one subject of conversation. That Istanbul, which none of us had seen and regarding which we knew very little except for legends. We were meeting almost every evening. Everyone had something different to say. Nearly all of them wanted something. Eventually I decided to make a list. I was to send my blood brother Remzi a Fenerbahçe shirt. Although he was upset I was going, I knew he would be saying: "Just as well he went". Sülo wanted a whistle. He'd seen one with the commander the previous year. The commander blew it once and the sound resonated around the whole village. Such a whistle would be very useful to gather the flock when it dispersed. The only one who was silent was Niyazi. I was waiting to see what he wanted, but whenever I looked at his face he appeared preoccupied and thoughtful.

One evening when there was no one else around, I sidled up to him and said: "Niyaz". He didn't even look at me.

"Niyaz, tell me what you want! I'll send it to you with all the others'. If you like I'll send you a ball."

He shrugged his shoulders. "I don't want one. It would be of no use to me."

"Why are you behaving like this, Niyaz?"

"What am I supposed to be doing?"

"What's your problem?"

"Don't pretend you don't know my problem. You got together and made me a husband of Karakaçan."

"It was a joke. Have you still not understood?"

"It was a joke, huh?"

"Anyone who heard would assume they had forced you into bed with Karakaçan."

He laughed. We hugged. He began to cry.

My cousin Talip was going to paint his wall and prepare it for a large Beşiktaş poster. For Celil I should find a football, even if it was old. I was surprised at Halil. He wanted books from those that the teacher read to us. He came to see me at the mill looking distressed and downhearted. It seemed that he had also been sad to leave school, but had not let on.

"If only I was in your shoes. When you said you wanted to go to boarding school I thought to myself: 'he's lost his mind.' Sometimes we made fun of you behind your back. Now you're going. Maybe we won't meet again but you're doing the right thing."

"Halo, shall I tell you a secret?"

"What secret?"

"I'm going to come back."

"You're going to come back? But you said you were going to leave this village and never return."

"Because I didn't believe I would be able to go, I got angry. But really I want to go, come back and then go again. I can't do without seeing my mother, grandfather and siblings"

"Haven't you had enough of them? And what is there here for you to return to?"

"I know what I'm going to do."

"If I was in your shoes I wouldn't return to this village."

"It's necessary to return, Halo. If you ask why, I don't know, but I feel it."

Eventually our departure date was fixed. I couldn't contain myself. The headman who was to take us to town in a tractor had come late one evening and said: "Be ready on Wednesday morning." In exactly four days' time we were to leave the village.

My father stroked my head for the first time that evening. When he stretched out his hand my hair stood on end as for a moment I thought he was going to hit me. The fact I was going had saddened him, or he was unhappy because he was losing a worker.

Sometimes I would be scared as if someone was going to prevent us going.

The calamities that might befall us in the village were different to those in the city. For instance, in the middle of the night while you were fast asleep an avalanche could envelop your house or a village raid take place. Those in the mountains who came to collect young people who couldn't go to the mountain because they feared their parents, soldiers raiding the village, or village guards acting more forcefully than commanders. One night your crops could go up in flames. Your livestock could be stolen or disappear. All these would fling you up into the air and bring you crashing down again like an atom bomb falling on your house. Because these all meant pain, poverty and despair. The previous year those in the mountains had come and had a fight with the men of the village. It couldn't really be called a fight, it was more like a shouting match. When they left, the village divided into two camps. Half thought they were right, while the other half were angry with them. The disagreement spiralled, then Uncle Cemo went into the village square and called the villagers every name in the book:

"Only another one in the mountains and Allah know the one

in the mountain. And the commander doesn't know what the soldier is thinking. Only a soldier sent to the mountain knows that. If you are going to have a shouting match go outside the village. Some of you join the mountain, some join the soldiers. An empty pot makes no noise."

If those in the mountains came would they take me? They wouldn't as I was too young, I would have to be fifteen, but there wasn't long to go. In a year's time one night they could summon me above. I really didn't want that. If soldiers came, would they arrest me, saying I was helping those in the mountains? Why shouldn't they? Once they had arrested Şakir. He was only ten. Şakir started crying in front of the commander, who summoned Şakir's father. His father cuffed him because he had cried in front of the commander.

The question, could our departure be prevented, was nagging at me. It was like a nightmare. I couldn't have endured my dreams being wrecked again. In that case I would really have fled. I would have gone on foot to the town and then let whatever would happen to me, happen. What if Uncle Rahmi were to suddenly return to the village? After all, he had been born in the village. It was really strange that he hadn't come for years and years. For instance, if there should be a knock on the door one night, and if there should be someone there we didn't know.

"Yes, who are you?"

"I'm Rahmi. You're a kid, move to one side. Dad, I'm back. Or to be precise, I heard you were coming and came so you wouldn't tire yourself."

In such a situation would there be a need for grandfather to go? Of course not. Consequently, I wouldn't go either. This was the biggest calamity. But according to what my mother said, for Uncle Rahmi to come back, the sun would have to rise from where it set. All my worries were baseless.

My grandmother was talking to herself:

"Who would have believed that Rahmi would go to Istanbul?

It was his destiny. God blew him away like a dry leaf. He put all the thorns of Kato mountain into my heart. There hasn't been a day when I haven't watched the road. Now he's dragging his father after him. Is it so much if you go too, grandson? Neither one or the other, it's all destiny."

I went to bed. Out of happiness I couldn't contain myself. Two tears trickled from my eyes. I was angry with myself. "Keko, when you're upset you cry, and when you're happy you cry. Boy, be a man! Don't bawl like a woman at the drop of a hat. You're going to the big city. Are you going to let the people in the city laugh at you?"

There was an irrepressible joy in my heart. I pulled the quilt up to my head. I was laughing at myself. I don't know how long passed or when I dropped off. I woke up choking. A hand had covered my mouth and nose, preventing me breathing. I began to struggle for dear life.

"Quiet, damn you! Don't make a noise!"

I released myself with difficulty and sat up in bed. There was a woman in a black shawl at the head of my bed. As I rubbed my eyes she sat on the side of the bed. Her face was not visible. My tongue was dry out of fear. With difficulty I said: "Who are you?"

She lowered the veil over her face. She was the last person I could have expected.

"Gülistan, what's going on?"

"Quiet!"

"Are you crazy? I almost choked."

She put her finger to her mouth and listened. No sound came from outside. Everyone was in a deep sleep.

"Gülistan, why are you wearing such clothes?"

"Why do you think, you idiot! So I won't be recognised."

"What's happened?"

"You were going to marry me?"

"Have you gone mad, Gülistan? What marriage? And I'm going to Istanbul."

"God damn you, Keko!"

"Gülistan, if someone sees you here they'll think I called you."

"As if I care. Look, if you don't get up in the morning and say you want to marry me, I'll have you done over."

"How will you have me done over?"

"I'll say you kissed me forcibly in the barn."

"Gülistan, no one would believe that. You're both older and bigger than me."

Gülistan's shoulders slumped and she looked at me in the face despairingly for a while. She also wanted to go to the big city and be free of the village, like me, but I didn't know what it was that was driving her away.

"Gülistan, if you really want to, plead with my grandfather and come with us."

Her eyes filled with tears.

"Don't talk nonsense. Who would let me go to Istanbul?"

She was right. As a young girl Gülistan's chances of leaving the village were a lot less than a boy of my age.

She shook her head angrily.

"Either I'll leave this village and go away or I'll kill myself."

"Gülistan, or do you want to study, too."

She turned and slapped me on the head.

"I'm worried about my life and you talk about school."

I didn't understand anything she was saying. When she left I put my head back on the pillow. I dropped off to sleep while praying: "My God, as you can see, all the children in Heredile are unhappy. You know the rest. I don't want to die in this village. At least I don't want to die before school is over."

My grandmother had sewn a new quilt for Uncle Rahmi. My mother wrapped it up carefully and put it in a sack. My aunt also prepared a pot of molasses. Our nights in the village were nearly over. In three nights' time we would be at Uncle Rahmi's house in Istanbul. Who knew what a nice place was waiting for us in Istanbul. It might be in one of the high buildings we'd seen in photographs. It must be pleasant to live somewhere where you could look down from on high.

As the time when we were to travel got closer I thought I was dreaming, and that when I woke up the dream would end so would secretly pinch myself.

A tradition was being broken. For Heredile I had shattered the saying that goes: "The village in which you are born is the place you will be buried." According to some I was abandoning it, for others I was escaping. I didn't care about any of them. However far away I went, I was part of them, their pains were mine and their joy was mine. It was not possible for me to break away from them.

There were also promises I had made to myself. One day when a stranger showed me respect, I was not going to make them quake with fear. I was going to behave however was necessary towards both my own people and strangers. I was not going to oppress strangers. In brief, I had been born in Heredile but I was going to choose the place I was going to die. The place I wrote and completed the story of my life would be my grave. I didn't know by what road that story would take me or how that story would end. The dreams inside me nourished my instincts and influenced my decisions. However large my targets may have been, I was still a child and I wanted what was in my heart, rather than what was in my mind. That was it. Perhaps teacher Fatih was responsible for this, as he had opened the valve. And it was he who had taught us there was no shame in having dreams. According to him, all children knew how to dream. Children were even born with dreams. As for the adults banning children's dreams, in fact they were dangerous. We should pay attention to them. It was true. Until he had come I had thought having dreams was madness and even that it was not seemly for men.

Years later when a drunk at a nearby table said: "Death in the place you want to die is good," my childhood memories came back to me. I had felt this when I was only a child and understood that I needed to be in the place I wanted to die, not to die in the place I was forced to be.

That night, after Gülistan had turned up in a sheet, I had a strange nightmare. The village road leading to the town had disappeared. I was running around the village in a panic trying to find the road. My grandfather said: "Is it possible for there to be a traveller without a road? We can't go out of the village." Meanwhile, my father was shouting at the top of his voice from the mill: "Kekoooo!" When I woke up in the morning it was as if I was suffocating. I felt bad when I woke up on account of the nightmare.

My mother was cooking me my favourite food at every meal. No one could take food from my plate. That morning buttered pastry had been prepared. When she spread honey on it and gave it to me I would have hugged and kissed her hands if I hadn't been embarrassed. Why hadn't my mother and father always loved me? Why hadn't they been close to me like my grandfather? Whereas I had always loved them. Some nights I had felt an irresistible desire to go to my mother's bed and sleep with her. But in Heredile after the age of seven it was not considered proper for a boy to even embrace his mother too enthusiastically. And for a thirteen-year-old boy to sleep with his mother was completely unacceptable. However, I was a child who slept every night embracing a dream of his mother.

My grandfather was looking silent. My father stood up and went to the threshing floor. As he left my grandmother hugged me.

"My grandson is intelligent; he won't say no."

My heart missed a beat. What would I not say no to? I looked at Gülistan. She shook her head as if to say: "I told you so." The buttered pastry for a moment stuck in my throat. I looked at my mother. Her eyes were full of tears.

My uncle suddenly snapped. "What's wrong with you, sister-in-law? You should be pleased that your son is happy, instead you are bawling."

Two tears trickled from my mother's eyes. She wiped them away with the edge of her muslin headscarf and got up from the floor spread. My grandfather's head was down and he didn't say anything. My uncle turned to me.

"Keko, my nephew, now look..."

I turned to my uncle, suppressing my fear, and stared at him. There was silence. My ears were humming. I was still waiting and no one was talking. Had my grandfather abandoned the idea of taking me? In a husky voice I said: "What's happened now?"

No one answered. Everyone was laughing with scornful looks on their faces.

"I understand, uncle. I understand."

"If you've understood, nephew, why are you getting annoyed?"

"Was I meant to be pleased?"

"Of course you'll be pleased. Isn't a man happy when he hears he is to be married?"

"What?"

It was as if my uncle was joking, but in our house adults didn't joke with children.

"Nephew, we're getting you married."

"Me?"

"Yes, you."

"You're marrying me off..."

"For God's sake, nephew, you don't seem to understand the simplest things. How will you manage in the big city?" There was a derisory look on my uncle's face.

"How?"

"Are you deaf, son?"

"Uncle, look..."

"You're getting married, see! The person giving away their daughter doesn't have much sense, but..."

What did this mean? I turned to my mother.

"Don't worry, son, you're going to Istanbul."

If I was going to Istanbul the rest was of no importance, but where had marriage come from?

What I had feared had not materialised. Our journey to Istanbul had not been postponed, but I was facing another disaster. It was something that hadn't been on the list of potential calamities I'd been thinking about for days. Getting married hadn't crossed my mind. What marriage could take place at the last minute? I didn't know how Gülistan had managed it. At that moment I was probably the last person in the world who wanted to get married. And the idea of going to bed with one of the girls in the family in which I'd grown up always made me feel sick.

Me and a girl next to me, a ring on each of our fingers, our children who would begin to be born a year later, the fields we would sow in the summer, the little house with an earthen roof in which we would be imprisoned during the winter... This was an unbelievable nightmare. No, I couldn't be content with that. No one would be able to sit me in front of the imam and marry me.

After days of thinking my father had found a way to take revenge, I was going to be shackled to Heredile with a chain. If I wanted to go to Istanbul I was expected to submit to the condition of being engaged. Of course, the girl would be chosen by them. As if I would have been happy if they had said: "You pick one". I was looking for the opportunity to complain to Gülistan. Ah Gülistan, what a stubborn girl you are! If only my uncle had beaten you more.

She was milking the sheep in the fold with Hatun. I went in and took the sheep's head from Hatun and said: "Mum is calling you."

Hatun ran out without saying a word, as usual. As soon as she had left I went up to Gülistan and said: "Gülistan, what do you want from me?"

"What's up?"

"Gülistan, could I ever be a husband to you?"

"What husband?"

"Why don't you find someone else?"

"Keko, I'll belt you and you'll bite the dust!"

"Oh, Gülistan, what kind of human being are you? Are you going both to marry me by force and then beat me?"

"Shove off! You brazen boy!"

"Gülistan, I would rather kill myself than marry you."

Just then my mother came in. She had heard our voices from the threshing floor and wondered what was going on.

"What's up, Gülistan?"

"Do you know what Keko's saying, auntie?"

"What's he saying, my dear?"

"He says: 'What if my fiancee came with me to Istanbul?'"

My mother was startled and looked at me as if to say: 'Is she telling the truth?'

"No Mum, I didn't say anything like that."

"Ah Keko, didn't you just say to me: 'Either I'll go with my fiancee or not at all'?"

"I swear to God that I didn't say anything like that."

My mother knew both me and Gülistan very well.

"Gülistan, why are you annoying the boy at the last minute?"

"By God, I'll tell uncle Ajar as well."

I really panicked when I heard my father's name. I could get engaged to Gülistan but I didn't want my father to find a new way to prevent me leaving.

"Gülistan, if you tell my father I won't speak to you for the rest of my life."

"What's the difference, if you speak to me or don't speak to me?"

"Gülistan, look..."

"You don't even know who you're getting engaged to."

I stopped suddenly and looked at my mother. Who else could it be apart from Gülistan? I thought of all my uncle's daughters one by one. For me none of them were any different to the others. Let them all be well but far away from me. In particular if it was Gülistan, let her stay even further away.

"Keko, by God, when you get married tomorrow or another day, you wouldn't notice if they took your wife from under you."

My mother confronted Gülistan, saying:

"What do you mean by that, Gülistan?"

"But Aunt, just now his fiancee passed in front of him, then he says: 'Who is the girl I'm getting engaged to? Or is it you?' Shame on him."

My mother was startled, as she didn't know the past of this matter.

"What does that mean, my son? Why should Gülistan be your fiancee? Don't be impertinent!"

Gülistan carried on amusing herself at my expense. "Okay, let me be the one to give you the good news."

"What good news?"

"Your fiancee, Hatun."

"What?"

"Hatun, Hatun! She's the unlucky girl. How was she to know she would end up with a jerk like you?"

Me and Hatun. Perhaps it was better it was Hatun than the others, as she was the quietest girl in the clan. According to my grandfather, she took after her mother. We had studied at school together for 2 years, but I didn't recall speaking to her even once. But what difference would it have made if I had recalled speaking to her? She had downcast eyes and freckles.

After learning we were to be engaged I took care not to look in her direction. Those who had decided on our marriage were thinking about everything on our behalf and taking decisions.

My father had said: "If he doesn't put that ring on his finger I won't let him go." Hatun had probably not been consulted at all.

Two days later in the morning my grandmother began to roast the *halva* that was to be eaten with the sherbet. The headman had brought two rings from the town. They put one on my finger to see if it would fit. As my mother had guessed it was a little large. As other mothers did she wrapped thread around it to narrow it.

My mother was cross with Gülistan for bringing white thread.

"Gülistan, won't white thread jar on this ring? Isn't there any yellow thread in the house?"

"Auntie, do you really think your son is going to wear this ring in Istanbul?"

My mother's eyes were full of tears.

"My lion! Don't worry, when you grow up this ring will be tight on your finger."

I didn't say anything in reply. I wanted it all to be over as soon as possible, either with or without my grandfather. I wanted to leave the village and stay in the first big city I saw. I was alone in the room with my mother. My joyless, tense state was upsetting her. I went up to her and whispered: "Wouldn't another girl do instead of Hatun?"

Her eyes flashed.

"My lion! I'll get whomever you want? As long as you're happy."

"Mum, Gülistan..." I hesitated. "I want Gülistan."

The joy in my mother's eyes vanished. She looked at me curiously and lowered her voice further.

"My son, where did you get that idea from? Gülistan is two years older than you."

"So be it."

"My son, are you mad? She talks to you like she talks to a dog! What do you like about that floozy?"

My eyes lowered, I said: "I want her."

"My son, whichever girl you want is okay, but not Gülistan. Don't mention her to anyone else. I don't know what will become of her."

At the sound of my father's voice my mother left the room. Children then filled the room. There was the same look on all their faces. They thought I was excited to be engaged and embarrassed about my joy.

"Keko, are you going to leave your fiancee and go?"

"Keko, when you marry Hatun, which room will you stay in?"

"Keko's not going to stay in the village."

"In that case he'll take his fiancee to Istanbul."

As nonsensical questions followed one after another, my heart sank. Once again I hated my father. My aunt came in and pointed at the children. They left laughing together. A short while later Gülistan came in virtually dragging Hatun by the hand. Hatun came in bashfully, not looking me in the face. She began to wait by the door as if she was going to flee at any moment. My aunt was careful towards me but stern with Hatun.

"What's up, girl? Are you playing hard to get?"

Hatun was looking down at her feet. She wasn't saying anything. When my aunt left there were Gülistan, Hatun and me left. The bruises on Gülistan's face were still visible. As much as I was angry with her, I was also sorry for her. We had something in common, but I couldn't give it an exact name. I didn't want her to resent me.

"Gülistan,,,"

"What is it?"

"You remember you said something to me..."

She looked at me as if to say: "Where did this come from now?"

"I told my mother, but she didn't accept it."

Gülistan continued to stare at my face with disbelieving looks. Assuming she was sceptical, I continued. "My mother said it wasn't possible."

"She said what wasn't possible?"

"I mean, I did what you said. Whatever you said, that."

"Ehh?"

"My mother said, 'It's uncertain what will become of her.'"

The sarcastic smile on Gülistan's face was replaced by sorrow and anger. Her cheeks turned bright red and her eyes moistened. She shook her head as if to say: "I'll show them."

"I know what they think. I know what I'll do to them!"

I felt that a bad end awaited Gülistan. I didn't know if she would be able to escape this bad end. She had a crazy side. My grandmother always said about her that: "while an intelligent one is still thinking, our mad Gülistan has already jumped over the stream."

A downcast Gülistan slammed the door on her way out. I was alone with Hatun, with whom I had grown up in the same house. For whatever reason it was as though I had noticed her existence for the first time. Who knows, perhaps she was also reluctant about the marriage business. And why should she want it?

"Hatun, you know, I didn't want this."

She remained silent and didn't even raise her head. She was still looking at her feet.

"If I hadn't accepted, they weren't going to allow me to go to Istanbul."

She was motionless, like a statue. I couldn't understand whether she was striking an attitude towards me or was really embarrassed.

"If you don't want it, I'll oppose it despite everything. I mean, I don't want to upset you just to go to Istanbul."

She suddenly raised her head. In an agitated voice she said: "No, don't do something like that!"

At that moment I was surprised, but later I learned that Hatun had been asked for her cousin who was ten years younger than her. I was surprised. There was a pleading look on her face. I lost my temper. Had it perhaps been her idea? I stood up, went over to her, gripped her shoulders and began to shake her.

"Or did you ask for me, girl?"

She tried to free herself out of fear.

"No, I swear I didn't. You never even crossed my mind."

I felt confused. Since she hadn't asked for me, why was she now so keen to be engaged to me?

"You know, I'm going to Istanbul to study. Who knows when I'll come back."

"Yes, you're going."

"It might be years."

"That's alright, I'll wait."

"Do you know how long you're going to wait?"

"I'll wait, I'll wait until the end of my life."

"That's to say, without marrying, as a fiancee?"

She was almost kneeling before me.

"Yes, Keko. Please don't say no. I'll wait. You study there. Godspeed."

She fell silent and began to stare at her feet again.

"Okay, in that case. Don't say in the future that I didn't say it. I agree to be engaged to you to be able to go to Istanbul. Be aware of this."

She replied without raising her head. "I knew. I mean, I know, don't worry."

"Is there anything you want from me?"

"Yes, there is!"

She said it in such a loud voice I was startled.

"What do you want?"

"Promise me that whatever happens you won't break off our engagement."

What things did Hatun, who didn't speak, want from me?

"I'm going all the way to Istanbul. How do I know what's going to happen there, Hatun?"

"Marriage is not important. It's the engagement that's important."

"Hatun, look, you and me are going to be in different places. At the moment I'm not thinking of getting married at all, but if one day there something happens, what will you do? Who knows, perhaps I'll want to stay there permanently."

"So be it. Do whatever you want, but don't break off this engagement."

"Are you crazy, Hatun?"

She shrugged her shoulders. "So be it. If you love someone else, even if you marry her, we can still stay engaged."

"And then what will happen?"

"Let everyone know that Hatun is Keko's fiancee. Let no one ask for Hatun's hand."

I had begun to lose my temper, but when two tears fell on her feet I stopped. I didn't know what to say. I couldn't know at that moment what Hatun was after. And I had no time to think about it.

"Perhaps it's better like this," she said. I nodded.

"It's up to you, Hatun."

She stopped. Looking downcast, she nodded.

"And this ring will stay on your finger. You'll never take it off."

What kind of agreement was this? Unable to help it I raised my voice.

"Okay, and I'll hang a sign round my neck."

She had a hopeless, despairing but determined look on her face.

"Alright, Hatun. We will remain engaged for life and this ring will always stay on my finger. But I'm not promising marriage. Okay? Do you want anything else?"

I knew that what was happening was not her fault, but there was no one else I could raise my voice to. She shook her head from side to side silently to indicate she had no other wishes.

I left her in the room and went out. For some reason I felt more relaxed. I finally believed I was to go. I was escaping from this marriage business with an only-for-show engagement. I felt a kind of chilling happiness inside me. If I hadn't controlled myself I would have gone and hugged my mother and smothered her in kisses. My grandfather was sitting by the hearth. Alongside him was my grandmother waiting for the coffee pot she had put on the hearth. There was an impish look on my aunt's face.

"Did you talk?"

I nodded.

My aunt laughed, saying to my mother who was laying the floor spread, "Look at the one who didn't want it. They didn't know how to leave the room."

Who knows, perhaps they were wondering what we had talked about in there. If my father had heard what I'd said to Hatun, he would probably not have allowed me to go to Istanbul. He would have taken me by the ear and dragged me to the mill, then he would have done everything he could to ensure I worked there all my life and left it in working order for his grandchildren.

My first miracle was my grandfather, the second was teacher Fatih, and the third, it seemed, was going to be Uncle Rahmi.

After giving me a meaningful look, Gülistan began to speak as if she was saying whatever came into her head.

"Ask him, did he promise to return to Hatun? A promise is not enough. Did he swear, I wonder?"

I went over to her and in a whisper said: ""God damn you, Gülistan! Leave me alone!"

My angry glances seemed to further incite Gülistan.

"There should be both promises and an oath. I wouldn't accept it if I was in Hatun's place, by God. Let him swear on the book."

Promises made in Heredile are still the most reliable document in the world. In those years I assumed that all over the world promises were kept like those in Heredile. Promises were never forgotten. As for oaths, they were the guarantor of those promises in the next world. No one born in Heredile, in particular men, would easily repudiate a promise or an oath. When promises were not kept, they were inherited by sons or even grandsons. City dwellers think us villagers only pursue blood feuds, but we feel we have to honour all promises, good and bad.

Hatun left the room. I knew she had heard what was being said. First she looked at her mother, then at me. My aunt wasn't saying anything.

Hatun answered Gülistan with a barely audible voice.

"Keko both promised and swore an oath. And he will never remove his ring."

My grandfather, grandmother, mother and uncle all smiled, their faces lighting up. The doubt on my Aunt Tahire's face had vanished. Gülistan was flabbergasted. She must have been surprised at how easily I had promised and sworn an oath.

"Now, did you promise Hatun? Did you say: 'Whatever happens I will come back and marry you'? Did you say: 'I swear on my good name, honour and religion'?"

"Gülistan, what's up with you? What are you trying to say? Why are you interfering?"

"I understood you. You didn't promise. You are deceiving Hatun. Wait, let me call my uncle and say: 'We will celebrate in vain'. 'Keko has lied to us all'. Let this business end here. You go your way and Hatun hers."

I didn't know what to do or say. Gülistan was always like this.

She liked to interfere and ruin things. As if it wasn't enough for her to get herself in trouble, she enjoyed causing trouble for others.

As I pondered what to do and what to say, a sandal flew through the air. It passed me and landed on Gülistan's ear. My aunt could not put up with Gülistan's loud-mouthed antics.

"You've absolved yourself, now you want to mess up someone else's engagement. You're shameless!"

In the evening my paternal aunts, maternal uncles and maternal aunts visited us. The headman was with them. Mother had ironed a shirt left by Riza. I washed and performed ablutions, as my mother wished. I put on the white shirt with my clean clothes. My mother cried as she combed my hair. Hatun wore a dress with a flowery design. Her mother's eyes were dewy. Although my father tried to disguise it, the pleasure and happiness on his face was evident. For the first time I saw some pride on my father's face as he looked at me. Who knows, perhaps rather than me getting married, the hope that I would return and work with him at the mill was making him happy. They put two wooden chairs side by side in the middle of the room. I sat on one and Hatun sat on the other. Neither of us looked at the other, as if we were cross with each other. I was thirteen, whereas Hatun was twelve. Uncle Hasan was reading the Quran. The children were looking forward to the sherbet and *halva* that would soon be distributed. In my mother's eyes it was as if joy, longing and sorrow were all mixed together. My grandfather looked thoughtful. They were saying things, we got up, they said more things, we kissed the hands of the adults one by one.

When I woke up the next morning I thought I had dreamt what had happened the previous evening. Then when I saw the ring that had been tightened with thread on my finger, I recalled everything in detail. Istanbul was the only way to free myself from this calamity. For me Istanbul was not just a big city where I could continue to study, at the same time it was one haven where I could take refuge from marriage. Hatun had already accepted this. We were to remain engaged, but this was not a promise of marriage. We might not get married. And she wouldn't object even if I loved another girl. Her only condition was that we remain engaged. This couldn't harm me. I didn't know what Hatun's dilemma was, or what she was after. And I wasn't desperate to find out. But again, the ring put on my finger at the last minute was a heavy load to carry. So be it, once I had started school it would all be in the past. If I wasn't about to go, no one could have made me accept marriage, but in order to leave the village I had to do it.

Chapter Seven

JOURNEY

I had completed my thirteenth year two months previously. Birthdays were not celebrated in Heredile, and no one was curious about the day they had come into the world. Babies born in the winter were considered fortunate. Women would say: "He got his fill of milk and his mother's embrace." Babies born in the harvest season would be alone. I still wonder how babies waiting for their mothers to breastfeed them, lying under frames by the side of fields listening to the cicadas, perceive the world in their swaddling clothes. Our mothers weren't as frightened of scorpions, rats and snakes as they were of djinns. As soon as babies were born a pair of scissors would be placed next to the baby for forty days. In this way fever, that is, possession by a djinn, would be prevented.

A male child who began to walk was thus ready for circumcision. In mass circumcisions the same scissors would sometimes be used to quickly cut the penises of thirty or forty boys. Those who didn't cry were praised, while those who did were thrust onto their mothers' laps as if they were guilty of a crime.

Our first examination was circumcision, the second was military service, the third was marriage and the fourth was fatherhood. Circumcision and military service were unavoidable. Marriage was almost the same. A man who didn't want to get married or who delayed a little would be viewed with suspicion. Marriage was essential. A man who didn't have a child would remarry again and again and when he had proved his fatherhood ability he would be deemed to have passed this exam. How he raised the child was for him to decide. It was sufficient for him to have children and to supervise the honour of his daughters. For Heredile fathers, the feeling and saying "My poor child!" was not possible.

Kurdish men, who could not easily forget their military service or their commanders, when it came to matters of the heart were much more reticent. For love and the like was more appropriate for women.

There were various ways of expressing feelings that could not be talked about. The names of those who died during military service and on Kato mountain would be given to the first babies to be born. Those who died before their time were like lumps that never dissolved in the throats of those left behind.

It was rare for women to go up to Kato. My grandmother didn't like this new generation of girls.

"There used to be bandits. They wouldn't want women with them. What business do women have in the mountains?"

While mothers whose sons went up the mountain began mourning with laments, those whose daughters went up would keep their tears to themselves. That unease they were reluctant to name was a fear concerning honour. Although the honour of those who risked death by going to the mountains was not questioned, their mothers and fathers would be uneasy. The practice of going to the mountains had damaged the existing order.

Men who had received their call-up papers and girls who had started their periods were ready for marriage.

"The first period in the father's house, the second in the husband's house."

"Once a girl is sixteen, she'll either be with her man or in the earth."

In recent years the rebellious girls who preferred Kato mountain to a husband or a grave had confused the minds of Heredile.

In fact, I was no different to a girl. Only two months into my fourteenth year I had been engaged against my will. I did not even want to think about how me and my cousin Hatun, who was no different to my sisters, would be husband and wife.

My father had got his way, but he didn't know about the agreement between Hatun and myself. I didn't care if he learned about it once I had gone to Istanbul.

The moment I had been looking forward to as I counted the days, hours and minutes had arrived. At dawn we gathered on the threshing floor. Everyone in the house was there to see us off. My mother's eyes were red-rimmed from crying and she had not been able to sleep all night. I began to kiss the hands of the adults one by one and kiss the cheeks of the children. Instead of the usual sarcastic look on Gülistan's face there was sadness. It was as if she was apologising to me. I wanted to take her hand and kiss it, but she hugged me around the neck.

"Keko, you were my sympathetic ear."

Which of her problems had I been able to share?

Hatun was right at the back, waiting a little bashfully. For a moment our eyes met. She lowered her head. I kissed my father's hand. He leaned down and kissed me on the cheeks. This was a first. Until then my father had not even kissed me at religious festivals. That timid touch on my cheeks could now not awaken anything. He had withheld his affection from all his children. He was not even aware of it, but how we needed his compassion, love and appreciation. As his son I had not even once put my head on his chest and gone to sleep. What use had that affection he had withheld been? These feelings were burning my insides.

Years later when I realised I was not the only child who had been deprived of fatherly love in the village I was a little relieved.

My mother could not speak from crying. My aunt's eyes were also moist.

The only person I didn't say goodbye to was Hatun, as we were engaged. It was shameful for us to look at, speak or touch each other. We were to act as if we didn't exist and ignore each other. To do the opposite would be immodest and disrespectful to the adults.

On the way out of the threshing room I saw Sülo. He was waiting for us with a small bag of hawthorn berries. "You can eat them on the way," he said.

My heart sank. I gulped and said: "Sülo, don't forget to write!"

A wry smile spread over his face. "And don't you forget. What am I going to write? You already know everything here."

If only my friends could have come with me to Istanbul. If only we could have gone to the same school. If we had said: "We've arrived." Sülo's appearance had also touched my grand-father.

"Sülo, my boy. May God grant your every wish."

Sülo was finding it difficult to hold back the tears.

"Have a good trip, granddad."

In one way, Sülo was more mature than all of us. Living by himself without mother or father amongst animals had it seemed matured him before us.

As the years passed Sülo's place in my heart grew. Whenever I hit rock bottom, the taste of the hawthorn berries he gave us that day returned to my tongue. I've never had a friend as honest as him.

We left the village like in a dream, with the headman and my grandfather at the front of the trailer and me at the back. It was as if the earthen road in front of us led to heaven. I felt an indescribable elation inside me. I wanted to jump off the trailer and run along the earthen road skipping as I went. I looked back. Şerbet and the other children were waving handkerchiefs. Everyone gradually got smaller. The trailer began to go faster. At that moment I wasn't just leaving the village where I was born, I was running towards freedom and my dreams.

The sun was slowly rising behind two hills and I was greeting the day by flying. I shut my mouth firmly to suppress the laughter coming from inside me. I felt more at peace with God than at any time before, as I was as sure as I was that I drew breath that the future would be bright.

It was the first time I had seen a bus garage. There were so many buses there. We said goodbye to the headman and boarded an old bus. My grandfather cautioned the headman firmly.

"God knows the work of he who travels. Tell Cemal to give me his blessing."

I sat down in a window seat. It was a great feeling to travel looking around. I felt a pleasant tiredness. I wanted to laugh. If I hadn't been shy of the other passengers I could have laughed out loud, but it wouldn't have been appropriate. Who had invented the bus, I wondered? What a great discovery? When I grew up I must definitely learn to use a car.

When I woke up I found myself alone in a vast stretch of water. I'd had a bad dream. "The nightmare is continuing," I thought.

The previous winter, all the children of the village were sledging on the hill. Despite the low temperatures we didn't feel the cold. We were racing and shouting. Suddenly a faint hum filled our ears. It was a sound that came from far away that we had never heard before or could not compare to anything. We all stopped where we were and listened. The hum gradually turned into a rising roar. Yes, we were not mistaken. What we had feared was happening. The same question came to our minds:

"On which roof would the avalanche fall and who was in the house?"

We were children. We didn't care about the houses, but we didn't want our grandfathers, siblings and mothers to die.

It was always what we hated that determined our wishes, prayers and dreams. Our desires and prayers would not easily be granted. We would be saved from wearying of life by taking refuge in destiny.

The white giant had for days been thickening its mantle. It had been waiting sneakily. Then it slowly stirred and slid in a moment down the slope and fell on the roofs of three houses.

Ibrahim's scream rent the sky and remained suspended in the air:

"Muuummmm!"

Throwing down the sledge he was holding, Ibrahim ran towards the avalanche that had struck a second or two before, shouting: "mum! Mum!" Men ran over and saved him at the last moment.

In my recent dream I had again been on that slope, but alone. I couldn't stop myself. As I slid down at top speed the avalanche that had swallowed the roofs that day was before me. Stretching out one of its arms resembling a wing that had enveloped houses, it was saying: "come." "I'm going to take you under me. You won't be able to breathe again."

Now looking at this vast expanse of water I assumed I had woken up, but in reality I had still not awoken. On diving into the water who knows what demon I would encounter? As I was dreaming there was no need to be frightened, but my fingers were quivering. Could this blue water be real|? In that case, was I going to my death or could I have jumped into that deep pit which I always imagined?

I was trying to remember the bus journey, but everything was disjointed.

As I left the village I felt weary, but I kept quiet, thinking the journey would be delayed if I said anything. On the bus I suddenly felt cold. My grandfather had closed one of the windows. My temperature slowly rose and I began to shiver. Meanwhile, he had said I was talking in my sleep.

I slowly straightened up and looked around me with bated breath. As I wondered whether what I was seeing was a dream or reality, I thought my imagination was playing tricks on me. In a vast lake there was no one I could ask for help. How had I got here? The land had gone, trees, mountains, hills and everything I knew had disappeared. This must be the doomsday my grandfather talked about. But I had assumed that doomsday would come with fire.

"The land and the sky will mingle and disappear. Then, when humans say they are burnt, water will come; when they say they are frozen, fire will come."

When had I said I was burnt? Could this fizzing water be the cold water of doomsday? I looked at the sky. It was bluer than ever and calmer. On hearing my grandfather's voice I turned round.

"Have you woken up, Keko?"

"Yes, Granddad, where were you?"

He put his hand on my forehead and smiled. "Thank God," he said.

"You were burning like an oven in a bakery. I prodded you, but you didn't wake up. You were like an empty sack. Thankfully, your temperature has dropped."

"Granddad, what is this water?"

"We are passing Izmit. We are in the sea. They call it the Sea of Marmara.

Mouth open, I looked at the water around me. What a magnificent, fascinating sight it was. My grandfather had explained numerous times the sea he had seen when he went to do his military service.

Three thousand years ago Moses had gone as far as the Red

Sea during his unrelenting war with the Pharoah. He was caught between two fires: in front of him was the sea that swallowed those who entered it, behind him was the Pharoah, who was determined to put Moses and his army to the sword. Moses thrust his staff into the sea and it divided into two. In this way the army marched between the waters and safely reached the other side. Seeing this, the Pharoah and his army followed them without hesitation, but God then demonstrated his miracle by returning the sea to its original state. In a moment the Pharoah and his army were submerged. As he drowned, the Pharoah said: "I am also of the Moslems."

"Granddad, how many people has this water swallowed?"

"Only the Creator knows."

"What if it swallows us?"

"Don't be frightened!"

"Granddad, aren't you frightened of anything?"

"Grandson, trust in God. If you take refuge in him he will protect you."

My grandfather always instilled us grandchildren with courage.

Being frightened or frightening others was not becoming for men. If someone was to hit us in the back we were to try to stand up even straighter. If we were to allow what the Creator had left in trust with us to be damaged, we would have to account for it in the next world. Our body, our soul, our name and everything Allah had given us in this world was in trust. We had to protect them, look after them and use them in beneficial ways.

"Keko, look at this blessing. Won't someone who sees this believe in God's mercy? He who has created this, what a blessing he has granted to his creatures. Only the unaware would fear this blessing."

My grandfather was my only hero in this world and the only place I felt no fear was his lap. I had grown up. It was not appropriate to hug my grandfather constantly like a baby, but hugging my grandfather always gave me tranquillity and confidence.

We began to wait with the suitcase, quilt, pillow, small sack of bulgur and pot of molasses my mother had carefully wrapped that we took off the old cargo ship. My grandfather was looking for the scrap of paper on which he had written my uncle's address. One of the quay workers who saw us waiting came over and took us, muttering as he did, to the watchmen's hut. When my temperature rose again my grandfather let me lie on the quilt and made his jacket a pillow, putting it under my head. When he found my uncle's telephone number he gave it to the man who helped us. The man phoned my uncle's workplace. We began to wait again. As my eyes closed Bera, who I had left behind, came and sat opposite me on his four legs. While leaving when my mother repeatedly hugged me and cried, I was crying too. But my tears were more for my dog, horse and friends. For me Bera was more of a loyal friend than a dog. From the moment he felt I was leaving he followed me everywhere. Sometimes we went to the vegetable garden together. There I would explain to him why I had to go to the big city. I enjoyed talking comfortably to Bera as if there were lots of people, even my father, there.

"Bera, you know there is no middle school here. And there's no football and no electricity. You might say go to the school in the town, but in winter it would take three days to get there in deep snow. I would freeze and even you, Bera, couldn't find me until the snow melted. Anyway, the hungry wolves wouldn't leave even my bones behind. Isn't that true? For instance, Ismail, from the neighbouring village. He was coming to school in our village. What happened? If he hadn't fallen in the water last winter perhaps he wouldn't have suffered a seizure, would he? And if he hadn't suffered a seizure he wouldn't have got meningitis. And if he hadn't caught meningitis now his ears would hear, like yours and mine. Isn't that right? And you know, when I go there I will both study and become a footballer. And I won't stay like this, I'll get bigger. And no one, not even my father, will be able to say anything to me. And then I promise, Bera, that I will have you brought to Istanbul. Why not? Are dogs banned from entering Istanbul?"

While I explained all this he would look at me dolefully.

I woke up on hearing Uncle Rahmi's voice. A short, fat man was explaining that he took us in because he felt sorry for us, and that his boss would be angry if he saw us. While my uncle took money from his pocket and stuffed it into the man's pocket he patted him on the back. My grandfather was annoyed.

"If this boy hadn't been ill I wouldn't have come into this hut, even if I thought I was going to die. Isn't your boss a human being, too? What harm have we done that he should sack you?"

"Granddad, I'm just doing my job."

"Yes, and it's obvious you're doing it slavishly."

"Yah granddad, why are you saying this? We've helped you and now you've all but cursed me."

Uncle Rahmi resembled Uncle Baki, but he had a paunch. He was dressed somewhere between a soldier and a policeman and had a brand new minibus. We carried our stuff to the minibus. My uncle was worried about the minibus getting dirty.

"Oh, nephew, don't put anything on the seats!"

"Okay, uncle, I won't."

"Stop, stop! Don't pull the door like that. It's an automatic door. They brought it from Europe."

"Will it stay open?"

"I'll shut it from here. This is the latest system. They say they've got the same at the ministry."

I was expecting my uncle to say 'welcome' to me. As soon as he said "welcome nephew" I was going to leap and kiss his hand, but he seemed to have forgotten out of excitement. From looking at his ironed clothes and his minibus he must be very rich. I had a rich uncle in Istanbul and I had come to stay with him. What was I to do but study and become a footballer? Everything was going well. It was even better than well, it was great. My uncle even had a vehicle. Who knew where he would take us?

My uncle sat my grandfather next to him. I went to the soft leather seats at the back. For some reason my grandfather was frowning. I was looking around, being careful not to harm the seats. My grandfather looked back. He had realised I was anxious.

"What's up Keko? Have you dropped something?"

"No, Granddad. I was just making sure nothing happened to the seats."

"What could happen to the seats? Is there a thorn in your bum?"

My uncle didn't say anything. As for me, I didn't know what to say. The minibus began to slide along the wide asphalt road like oil. Roads in the big city were superb, like their names. They were all wide and asphalted. I began to count the vehicles that passed us, all different colours. They were endless and I gave up. High buildings, large grocers', traffic lights that we'd read about in books… I had already seen a lot of things to tell my friends in the village.

My mother had come to my bed on the last night.

"My son, how many people are fortunate enough to go to the big city? Don't take any notice of me crying. Most of them are tears of joy. You study, I don't want anything else. If I see you come back to this village as a public servant I will sell everything I have and sacrifice an animal. Let this be my offering. I'm not saying this in front of your father, but I always pray for you to study."

Leaving the wide asphalt road we turned off onto narrower, small roads. The houses were smaller, but most of the grocers' were still large. Then we went onto an earthen road. As my uncle's vehicle went into potholes we were bounced out of our seats. My uncle slowed down as we went into each hole.

We went into a slightly narrower road where there were single storey houses. The houses were neither city not village houses. They were something in between. Most of them were not plastered. Most of the women's heads were covered. Then we saw a small mosque, with a small grocer's next to it. A man wearing a cloth cap was sitting on a wooden chair in front of the shop. He was facing the sun. That grocer I didn't know warmed the cockles of my heart. He reminded me of the only grocer in Heredile, Cerçi Bekir.

My uncle drove a little further on and stopped in front of a small house. When he opened the door and got out I was surprised. As we hadn't yet reached the multi-storey luxury apartment in my dreams, why had we stopped?

Chapter Eight

A "WELCOME" BEATING

From the top of the luxurious apartment building I had descended to the little house in the '*gecekondu*' neighbourhood. Whereas I was expecting to watch Istanbul from my rich uncle's house high up in the towers like in fairy stories. And I was even going to make a paper plane and hurl it from a window. That paper plane was going to fall in front of an Istanbul boy I'd never met. The boy was to pick up the paper plane and read the words written on it. "Hey Istanbul boy! Congratulations, Keko has arrived!"

The boy was then to look up into the sky, but would not be able to see me. I was going to wave to him, knowing full well he couldn't see me. In this way we were to get to know each other.

While thinking all this, my aunt emerged from the door of the old house that opened with a creaking noise. She ran over, first kissing my grandfather's head in respect, then placing it on her head. She then hugged me and kissed me on the cheeks. This was my first nice surprise in Istanbul. The warm welcome I had expected from my uncle I received from my aunt.

For some reason, the old two-room house in a garden and the reality that my uncle was poor, like his brothers, and not the rich man I had imagined, a dream that had been maintained by the vehicle we had seen on first meeting, was a slap in the face.

My aunt approached me and put an arm around my shoulder as she wiped away her tears. At that moment the disappointment of the old house turned into a warm feeling I could not describe. At last someone in this enormous city had said "Welcome" to me. While the joy on my aunt's face drove away my inner troubles, I was tense on account of the discontented look on my uncle's face that I was unable to figure out.

While my uncle and aunt carried the loads together, I carried the pillows. We went into the house. Instead of the seats like thrones that Gülistan had described, there were couches with coverlets on them. Since they were old, we would be able to sit on them and get up in comfort. My uncle would presumably not say, like he had in the minibus, "Be careful!".

The real surprise was the radio on the nightstand. I went over joyously to my grandfather.

"Granddad, good news!"

My grandfather looked at me as if to say: "What's up?" There was an uneasy, sad look on his face due to strain.

"Guess what's inside?"

He stroked my head with a wry smile.

"Have you brought the village to Istanbul in your pocket, grandson? What good news have you found in this foreign place?"

I was not in a position to understand what a great sacrifice it was for my grandfather to leave the village and come to Istanbul.

"A radio, granddad, a radio. You will be able to listen to all the stations."

My grandfather chuckled.

My uncle, who had heard the last thing my grandfather had said, intervened. There was pride in his voice.

"What's a radio, nephew, when there's a television in the house?"

When my uncle began to speak my grandfather's laugh vanished. When uncle Rahmi saw the serious look on his father's face he fell silent. My grandfather went inside without saying a word and sat on the end of a couch. I noticed that he wasn't even looking at the radio. I was trying to understand the tension between my grandfather and uncle, but in vain. Whereas in the village whenever the radio was mentioned my grandfather would have something to say.

"Look Keko, don't underestimate the radio. Whoever invented it, may he not lie on the ground, but rest in peace. It changed the world. For instance, if there was a flood on the other side of the world in a country we've never been to, I would hear about it here. This America, has it said something to us? If I turn it on I too will learn about it out here in the mountains, like the gentlemen of Ankara."

One day soldiers suddenly came to the village and confiscated the radios one by one.

"Do you think we don't know that you don't listen to folk songs on these radios? By God, if you had Qurans, perish the thought, you would even turn them into weapons."

After the commander had gone my grandfather's eyes were moist.

"It is as if they cut off my ear and took it away. A black curtain has descended before my eyes. Is it better to live in such a blind well?"

Once the soldiers had gone I thought: "If only I was an inventor and could cheer up my grandfather." I asked our teacher how a radio worked and what it was made of. He explained to us at length the radio system, how it was used by the military and how it could, if needed, be turned into a kind of two-way radio.

Surfacing from my village memories, I returned to Istanbul and my uncle's house. We were a long way from Kato mountain and Heredile. As the headman saw us off he had said: "You are going as far away from home as possible."

What was it like to be a migrant? Was it only villagers that did this? Didn't commanders, teachers, soldiers and public servants who came to the village from Istanbul and Ankara count as migrants?

My mother started to wail laments and sing folk songs before we had even left the village.

Being away from home has happened to me
Don't cry my eyes, God is kind
While looking for strength
Don't cry my eyes, God is kind
The bird that never alights fell in the water but didn't die
The world has not been left to Sultan Suleiman
I said may I go to my love, it didn't happen
Don't cry my eyes, God is kind

On the other side of the road there was a small piece of land. At one end there was a fig tree, at the other a ramshackle building and in between children were playing. The children playing football with a small plastic ball suddenly looked like a huge team to me. If I'd thought that my grandfather and uncle wouldn't be angry I could have gone and watched them straight away. I thought about my friends in the village. I replaced every child there with a friend. Last of all, I joined them like a whirlwind. We had a fantastic match that could only take place in the imagination. We weren't running, we were flying. We were shooting from one goal to the other.

Although most of the children in the 19 May *gecekondu* neighbourhood had been born in Istanbul, nearly all of them were villagers. They were still eating from a cloth spread on the floor.

My aunt hurriedly made my grandfather a coffee after his long journey. While he drank the coffee Tahir arrived. He looked more like my aunt than my uncle. He was wearing jeans and an old vest. He kissed my grandfather's hand like his mother, and nodded to me. He then went and sat quietly by the window. He didn't raise his head. Then Berivan and Hazal kissed my grandfather's hand and said, shyly, "Welcome" to me.

My uncle had tried to get Tahir educated, but his head was no different to a piece of marble. So his father had sent him to work with a repair man. He now had a trade and spent all day mending the cars of smart men, serving them. He deserved this.

My cousin Tahir, who was two years older than me, listened to his father's accusations and insults as if they had nothing to do with him. It was as if uncle Rahmi was trying to get my grandfather to talk and to approve of what he was saying. As for my grandfather, he didn't seem to hear his son.

My uncle got up and turned on the television. I was seeing a television for the first time. If I hadn't been shy, I could have let out a yell. It was like a radio, but it showed people. What teacher Fatih had told us about televisions didn't begin to explain it. I began to watch with my mouth open. Such a thing would not even have oc-curred to magicians.

A blond-haired women in a long dress was in front of a group of men and women and they were singing a song together.

Now you are far away, my heart is full of sorrow

While saying I could not leave, coming together is a dream

All the roses in the garden of love have withered.

As the song ended a photo of a huge packet of biscuits appeared on the screen.

"When the word biscuit is mentioned, that is the name that comes to mind: Eti! Eti! Eti!"

Then another:

Your clothes will be super clean with Persil,   Sparkling with Persil!"

It was as if I had been mesmerised by what I had seen on the screen. Then men, women and children I didn't know came into the room and then left. None of them knocked on the door. They went as they had come, as soon as they had left they were replaced by others. They were very quick and didn't express surprise.

My grandfather was still silent and calm. It was as if he had seen a television numerous times but never mentioned it to us. He rolled up his sleeves and said to my aunt: "I'm going to perform my ablutions."

When my grandfather left the room, my uncle's face took on an even more anxious look. He looked bothered. He was drumming his fingers on the table in an irritated way. He had knitted his brow and looked unhappy. My uncle was not pleased to see my grandfather and me. He didn't like his father and it was as if he didn't see his nephew, i.e. me.

As soon as my grandfather entered the room my uncle leapt to his feet and picked up the towel behind the door, extending it to him. My grandfather took the towel without looking at his son, then, while drying his face, arms and hands, he also recited a prayer. "Tahir, get up and take me to the mosque."

My uncle leapt to his feet before Tahir got up.

"I'll take you, Dad."

After they'd left, my aunt went to the kitchen to prepare the evening meal. The girls, too, went to the kitchen to help their mother. I was left alone in the room with Tahir.

Tahir took a cigarette out of his pocket and lit it. He asked me if I wanted one. I shook my head and drew back.

"Is the school nearby?"

"There's one near and one far."

"Is it difficult?"

He thought for a moment, then nodded. Tahir had started school here. Why had it been difficult, I wondered. In those days I assumed all schools were made for pupils and that all teachers were self-sacrificing, like teacher Fatih. I had easily convinced myself that teacher-pupil relationships were always like they had been in our village.

"Which lessons were more difficult?"

"Ah… lessons, I don't know."

"Just now you said they were difficult."

"I didn't say it was difficult for classes."

"So what did you say difficult for?"

He smiled vaguely. Just at that moment my uncle came into the room. Tahir threw his cigarette out of the window. As my uncle smelt the air his eyes slowly bulged. He squared up to Tahir and dealt him such a blow he went red. I tried to intervene in a timid way to calm my uncle down. I regretted it immediately.

"So you were smoking with him, too? Let me beat you in advance so that you don't smoke again."

Blows started hitting me everywhere, first to the right cheek, then the left, then punches and kicks to every part of my body. I almost fainted, but my uncle was hitting me so hard I was coming round again. While my uncle, who I'd only met that day, was crazily hitting both his son and me, he was shouting: "You won't change your ways. You're an animal. I'll kill you, you bastard! No one deserves children like you. As if one wasn't enough, now there are two of you. I can be a murderer!"

My aunt, on hearing voices, came dashing into the room. As soon as she came in she tried to get me away from my uncle's grasp.

"Rahmi, Rahmi! The boy has only just arrived. Have you gone mad?"

My uncle left us and turned to my aunt. She was both crying and pleading.

"Enough, Rahmi, enough. As if beating your own son every day was not enough, now you're beating a guest's child."

"You gave birth to this demon!"

"Rahmi, if you don't fear humans, at least fear Allah!"

While my aunt was being beaten Tahir was staring at his father. I was looking towards the door. I would have fled, but I was frightened of my uncle catching me and beating me even more. I was in shock. I didn't know where to go, but I couldn't stay in this house.

My aunt's headscarf had slipped from her head. My uncle was dragging her by the hair and slamming her head against the walls. The girls were crying and saying: "Dad, don't!"

My uncle turned to us and said:

"So, are you going to do it again?"

I couldn't speak. I didn't know what state Tahir was in. My ear was throbbing terribly. Blood began to trickle from my nose.

On seeing the blood my aunt said: "Look what you've done to the boy!" as she tried to wipe away the blood with her headscarf.

As my uncle straightened his clothes he shouted angrily: "It's good, let him be beaten on the first day so that he learns who I am. I'm not like the sleepy men of Heredile!"

My uncle turned to go out the door. Just as he did so he came face to face with my grandfather, who was looking into the room. My uncle shrank back. It was as if he had turned into a guilty child who didn't know what to do facing my grandfather. His voice that had been roaring like a lion had wasted away like the voice of a thin, sick person.

"Dad, I caught the two of them smoking."

My grandfather looked at me. My ear was throbbing painfully. At that moment I wanted to hug him and say: "Granddad, let's go away from here."

My grandfather came over to me and said in a slow voice: "Keko."

At that moment all my fear vanished. It had always been like this. My grandfather had always been a fortress I had taken refuge in, trusted and hadn't wanted to leave. While he was alongside me I could have jumped into a volcano without fear. For my grandfather would burn himself but not surrender me to the flames.

My grandfather laid me down on the couch. He put a pillow under my head. While wiping the blood from my nose he looked at my forehead. He rubbed my throbbing ear softly with his hand. When I felt my grandfather's warm hands on my face I released my tears.

"Granddad, my ear really hurts."

He nodded, as if to say: "I can see."

My uncle had stopped like a small child by the door. He was looking at Tahir and clenching his fists. From time to time he shook his head and ground his teeth, as if to say: "It's all your fault."

My aunt brought ice and put it on my cheek and neck. My nosebleed had stopped but my aunt said: "It would be good if he went to a doctor, he's a guest, let nothing happen to him."

My grandfather didn't say anything. Tahir was also silent. He was sat on the couch, again looking at his feet. His unhappiness was plain to see. Seeing him like this frightened me. What went on in this house? What if my uncle often exploded like an atom bomb? Tahir didn't seem to be that affected by the beating. Had his father beaten him like that before? If that was the case then my grandfather's arrival must have greatly pleased him. My grandfather would never allow his grandchildren to be beaten and humiliated. But if my grandfather and I moved somewhere else, Tahir would be alone. The best thing was to take him with us. Just at that moment there was a knock at the door.

My aunt stuck her head out of the window to see who it was. "What's up, Ziya?" she asked.

A child's voice: "Auntie Güler, my dad says to move the minibus, our car is going out." Then my uncle said: "Dad, if you will permit it, may I go and move the vehicle?"

My uncle, who only a short time ago had given us a good kicking, was asking permission from my grandfather like a child. It was as if it was not him who had beaten us black and blue. My grandfather moved the ice on my neck and did not reply. He also checked my ear.

My uncle turned around in the room, straightening his jacket. Then he blinked and looked at my grandfather and me. When he left the room my aunt was crying quietly on the couch. The girls had snuggled up to her.

My dreams had taken their first tumble. When I woke up in the middle of the water I felt I was in the middle of a nightmare, but I hadn't been able to understand it. The fear in my heart had not evaporated during the journey, on the contrary it had got deeper. It was as if that water and my uncle were the forerunners of the hard life waiting for me in Istanbul. The beating I had received as soon as I entered the house was like a bomb thrown into all the dreams I trusted. It was not possible for me to live in such a house. Despite everything I did not want to return to the village. The joy inside me that was full of hope had been smashed to smithereens like a slender glass falling onto concrete and splintering into a thousand pieces.

Why was my uncle so angry? Why was he frightened of my grandfather? Why didn't my grandfather speak to uncle Rahmi? Why was my aunt always crying? Why was Tahir so quiet and unhappy?

In the big city I was supposed to stay in my uncle's house and go to school, and at weekends play for a football team. Now that I was going to leave my uncle's house where could I go? Where could I stay with my grandfather without money?

After everyone had gone to bed I went to my grandfather's side. He wasn't asleep. He lifted the quilt. As always I lay down beside him and put my arms round his neck. He put my head on his chest and stroked my hair.

"Granddad, where will we stay?"

My grandfather continued to stroke my hair without replying.

It was as if he was not surprised at what my uncle had done.

"Granddad, uncle Rahmi doesn't want us, does he?"

My grandfather did not reply, but I had no intention of being silent.

"Granddad, if we go to another place, will my uncle Rahmi continue to beat Tahir and my aunt?"

My grandfather didn't reply for a while. Then, he said: "Do you remember the fable of the Blind Witch I told you before?" He then began to tell the tale of the woodman and his son again.

One day the elderly woodman comes home to find his son crying. "Hey son, what has made you cry?" He says.

The son looks despairingly at his father and says: "I'm crying because I can't do anything that

you do. If something happens to you, what will I do? Where will I go? I'm frightened about what will happen to me, poor and alone."

The woodman strokes his son's head. "My son, don't forget that the greatest wealth is a wealth of intelligence. And the greatest poverty is stupidity."

The woodman's son is not convinced. "Father, in this wild forest we have no one. If I die you will be alone and if you die I will be alone. Once we are alone, what difference will it make if we have intelligence or not?"

The woodman laughs again. "My son, the greatest loneliness is to be vain. God does not leave his creatures in despair. It is sufficient for you to see what He has given you and to be thankful to Him."

For whatever reason I had convinced myself that my uncle was a good man, and so what I had experienced had suddenly made me pessimistic.

My grandfather, sensing my despair, once more embraced me with affection.

"Have you forgotten what I taught you, grandson? Or has Istanbul distracted you? Haven't I taught you to be patient? Never forget that you must know how to be patient. You mustn't be frightened. You must take refuge in the Creator and await his help. He will not abandon those who trust in Him."

***

We had been in Istanbul for a month. I was alone in the house with my aunt. There was a knock at the door. My aunt said: "Keko, I'm washing up. Open the door."

Facing me was a man wearing a cap, jacket and trousers all the same colour. He had a bag on his shoulder and envelopes in his hand... I had never seen a real postman before, but I had read about them in books. In our village, to which no postman ever came, our whole class had sung the song "Look, the postman is coming, he is greeting us" dozens of times all together. We had also learned how to write letters to official offices and how to put them in envelopes and send them.

"There is a letter for Ali Kemal Karadağ."

"My grandfather has gone to the mosque, he'll be back soon."

The postman said nothing, put the letter into my hand and left. Feeling elated I quickly returned to the room. Bera, my friends, my siblings, my mother... Who knew how much they'd missed me? If I opened the envelope would my grandfather be angry? He wouldn't. I was going to read it in any case. My aunt Güler called out:

"Keko, who was it?"

"Good news, aunt! A letter has arrived from the village."

She ran into the room.

"I wonder if my mother's family wrote it."

"I don't know, it's addressed to my grandfather."

The excitement on my aunt's face suddenly vanished.

"I thought it was from our side. Good, when he comes you'll give it to him."

I was feeling elated and was impatient to read the letter. Just at that moment my grandfather came in from the garden gate.

"Granddad, there's a letter from the village."

My grandfather smiled warmly.

"Read it grandson and let's listen."

As soon as I opened it I recognised Kibar's writing. Letters like pearls, all the same size.

"In this letter which I begin with the name of Allah the compassionate and the merciful, I first kiss my father's hands and wish benedictions. May Allah not deprive us of these. I ask after you all and kiss the hands of those who are older and the eyes of the young ones.

My dear father and his grandson, we have missed you after your departure. Thankfully autumn has been abundant, with the yellow cow having a calf.

May you know that you are always in our thoughts. You are our only concern. May you not come to harm in foreign places..."

In the letter, that went on for two pages, everyone sent their greetings, kissing the hands of their elders and the eyes of the younger ones. Amongst the sentences there was no mention of Bera or my friends. The letter ended with a meaningful sentence:

"I kiss the two hands of my grandfather, the hands of the other adults, kiss the eyes of my siblings and ask after the other."

On the back of the second page a hand had been drawn with outstretched fingers and thumb. There was a small inscription inside the fingers, like an *ant prayer*. Despite looking very closely I couldn't read it. Nor could Berivan and Hazal.

When Tahir arrived in the evening I asked him. He said: "What is this?" He went outside and came back with Ziya's grandmother's glasses. We used them as a magnifying glass to enlarge the letters. It was one word of five letters: Hatun.

It was Hatun who had written the letter and drawn the hand shape like a seal. Her handwriting resembled Kibar's but was more careful. And her g's had long tails. Did she think that I missed her? In fact, she hadn't crossed my mind since leaving the village.

Tahir punched me and smiled.

"Keko, are you excited?"

How could I explain to Tahir that I was, on the contrary, tense? Even if I didn't think about Hatun she was reminding me of her. The engagement ring that had been narrowed, and that I had tried to conceal, was still on my finger.

My mother had said: "Keep what you eat and drink to yourself and tell us about what you see."

What was I to write? That I had been beaten on my first day in Istanbul, where I had come as an engaged person, by my uncle? That no one had mentioned the word school? That I still didn't have a friend? That I was ashamed of my patched trousers when I went out? Was I to say: "Tell my friends that here nothing is like teacher Fatih explained."? Again, don't let them think I had forgotten them. I was going to explain what had happened to my friends in detail. If I said: "A ball has not touched my foot even once," perhaps they would not believe me. My mother must be talking about me frequently. And my father was probably saying things like: "Ooh, may Sir Keko go from school to school while Ajar breathes through his arse. Who cares?"

Let my father think I was happy. On the first day my aunt Güler had warned me. Her father's uncle Cemo should not hear about what had happened. "Keko! My father heard about what this madman had done, I denied it. May he not hear it from you."

I couldn't say: "I don't know what uncle Cemo shouldn't hear from me." All I knew was that my grandfather had come on account of my aunt. And that he was protecting his daughter-in-law and grandchildren from his son Rahmi, who he had driven from the village years before and whose name he didn't want to hear.

Uncle Rahmi could still not accept the fact he had been driven from the village, despite the years that had passed. He would say from time to time: "Bloody village. As if it was a holy place. What if I see it or not? It can go to hell…, " before turning his moist eyes to the window and watching the sky.

At these moments my aunt would not reply, but look askance at my uncle. After the beating of the first day he did not dare to lift a hand again towards me, but often reacted angrily to my aunt. When he got angry one day, he said: "My father will certainly leave, then I know how I will break your bones." At such moments I would feel my bones ache as if I was going to be beaten.

I was sleeping in the sitting room with my grandfather. He would determine our bedtime. Once he had performed the night prayer he would take out his pocket watch and put it next to his head. This was the first signal. My uncle, aunt and the children would immediately get up. Even if the turning off of a programme they were watching on TV didn't please them, they would say nothing.

When I woke up, Tahir and my uncle had already left for work long before. Although the scars of the first day beating had healed, the fear was still inside me. I only felt comfortable when my uncle wasn't at home. When he was due to come home I didn't leave my grandfather's side, even going to the mosque with him.

My grandfather seemed to be determined not to speak to my uncle. As for my uncle, he would hover around my grandfather like a small child. He didn't know what he had to do to earn forgiveness.

One evening neighbour auntie Hacer was chatting to my aunt.

"Thank God, we've had a rest. His father witnessed it on the first day. He saw with his own eyes what we were suffering. Since then Rahmi hasn't laid a hand on us. He knows what would happen to him, for sure."

"Your husband doesn't look like someone who would fear his father, but…"

"By God, he is frightened like of a fierce dog. If only he had come before."

I also could not understand why uncle Rahmi was frightened of my grandfather. My father and uncles in the village were very respectful of my grandfather, but I had never felt they feared him.

Every evening I wrote a letter to my friends in the village, but as I didn't know how to post them I saved them. I was also worried that if I posted them my father or uncles would get them. It wouldn't be right for them to learn about what went on here. I wanted everyone, including myself, to forget the beating I had received on the first day.

Two weeks later a second letter arrived. My grandfather said: "Daughter-in-law, make me a coffee so that I can drink it while listening to the letter being read out." When my aunt brought the coffee my grandfather handed me the envelope. It was like a copy of the first letter. There was a bit more longing. My mother had written: "For summer or winter, whatever you want, we will send it." My aunt listened quietly, smiling sadly while wiping her moist eyes with the corner of her headscarf. What a cry baby my aunt was. At every opportunity she would shed tears.

Tahir, Berivan and Hazal had not been forgotten. They also received greetings from the adults, children and everyone in the village. There was not a single sentence about my uncle in the second letter.

The letter once again reminded us of the events we knew about in the village. It was nearly the end of the threshing. The wheat crop was better than the previous year. The mill was working night and day. My father was going to sleep at the mill until the autumn. They had asked for the hand of Gülisten for her cousin Fevzi who had returned from doing military service. They were leaving the decision to my grandfather.

At the end of the letter everyone once more sent greetings to my grandfather and kissed both his hands. My father said: "Dad, may you not depart leaving something unaccomplished. I will deal with everything here with God's help. It is sufficient for you to be well. Keko, may you also not fear. Istanbul is a big city, may it not swallow you up. They will think you are a naive village boy and take advantage of you. Be careful."

For the first time my father was expressing concern for me. He was telling me: "Don't be frightened of Istanbul!" I was not frightened of Istanbul. I was only frightened of uncle Rahmi, but anyway my grandfather was with me.

My grandmother used to say that we all had angels on our shoulders, but that we couldn't see them. When listening to my grandmother I used to think that my grandfather was one of those angels. If he was alongside me, there was nothing I couldn't face in this world, and nowhere I couldn't stay.

Chapter Nine

AT SCHOOL

The heat had been replaced by the cool autumn breezes. Inside I felt joy mixed with fear. I was to start school (?) Children my age who I didn't know passed in front of the window. They were wearing their newly-bought school uniforms and going behind, alongside and in front of their mothers, sometimes hopping, sometimes running and sometimes crying. Berivan was in the fourth class. Hazal had been enrolled in the same school. The two sisters were going to go to the same school together.

I had realised I was a child after I'd started school. I know that such an idea is funny, but before I started school I didn't know who I was. When my father got angry he would start by saying: "You're as big as a donkey, but you are still..." then accuse me of something I didn't know whether I deserved or not, but giving me the feeling that I had to accept it whatever the circumstances. Sometimes we were reminded that we weren't adults by being told: "Do you think you are a man without cleaning the shit off your bum?" We grew up confused. We were actually no different from the house cat. We were not to object to what was put on our plates.

Teacher Fatih, on the first day we met, said: "It is the first day of your careers." What was a career? Then he had us memorise the World Declaration on the Rights of the Child. It was really difficult to memorise such a foreign document when not having learned a single letter. Then he had told us about children who lived differently to us. Very few children in the world lived in better conditions than us. Knowing this had somehow made me feel better. According to teacher Fatih, what we should not forget was this: most of the world's children lived in bad conditions that they did not deserve. Therefore we should one day in a small way do something to change these conditions. What could we children of Heredile, who didn't speak proper Turkish, do? What was this teacher telling us? Weren't we first meant to learn letters, then syllables, then words?

Without realising it, we were learning to feel pride. To know, understand, read, write and think made us feel pride and was a pleasant feeling. We began to produce the affection and respect that we were deprived of for ourselves. When I went in front of the mirror I smiled at myself and, sometimes when there was no one else in the room, I said: "Well done, Keko!"

Kurdish boy Keko from Heredile had received his primary school diploma in five years, learned Turkish after his mother tongue of Kurdish, memorised his times tables off pat and become a child who loved books and was determined to obtain more diplomas. He had earned his 'Well done'. If no one said it to him, he would say it to himself. Our teacher had told us:

"Protect, respect and love yourselves."

One morning, as the cool winds began to blow, I saw children passing in front of the window with hurried steps. This time their mothers were not with them. They were on their way to school, and I had yet to be enrolled.

It was as if everything had gone dark that day. Everything around me seemed to have gone grey.

I was in the queue outside the bakery with my grandfather. "Granddad, when will I go to school?" I said.

He stopped, leaned on his stick and turned towards me.

"I have been thinking about this for a few days, grandson. We need to ask and find out."

My uncle drove for a nursery and a private school. The minibus he parked carefully outside the house every day was not his. There was an emblem resembling a king's crown on it. Immediately underneath was written: Ilim College, we produce strong leaders.

Who ran the world? How did Ilim College educate children? Did those leaders know Heredile?

The next day while eating on the floor spread, my uncle poured water into my grandfather's glass. Then he started to speak as if the words had just come into his head.

"Ah dad, I was going to say. Keko… Keko is going to start school. Schools have now opened, yeah… I didn't say anything, thinking perhaps they wouldn't take him."

My grandfather continued to eat without replying. My uncle reached over and stroked my head. I suddenly felt frozen inside. Smiling, he said: "Nephew, uncle means half a father. Would I want something bad for you? Why do you go asking in the tea house? Ask me."

I shrank back a little.

"I didn't know."

When the meal was over my grandfather lifted his hands as always for the prayer of thanks. We put down our spoons and began to listen. After laying both his hands on his face he got up and sat on the couch. Then he picked up his Quran and put on his broken glasses.

As my uncle got up before dawn he went to bed early.

Just as he was about to leave the room, he said to my aunt: "Ah, before I forget, the headmistress asked for you. Her cleaner is ill. Go tomorrow, if you like." My aunt nodded in assent, without replying.

When my uncle left the house it was filled with a strange and pleasant feeling of relief, and Tahir and myself, in particular, relaxed.

Even when my uncle was at his calmest he made those around him feel uncomfortable. Years later I was to understand that my uncle was not alone, and that there were lots of humourless people who spread gloom and anxiety to every place they entered, and that most of them did not like people.

I didn't know who was responsible for my uncle's moodiness, his tendency for violence and his argumentative nature, but it was harmful for all of us. His aggression only dissolved when facing my grandfather, who he hadn't seen for years. His knees would knock together when facing his father and sometimes he would stutter.

In the evenings I would sit next to Tahir and we would look at pictures of footballers in magazines and chat. Tahir also loved to play football, but he was a Fenerbahçe supporter, whereas I followed Beşiktaş. We were now more like good friends than cousins, and we watched out for each other.

One day I said: "Tahir, why have you never come to the village?" He shrugged his shoulders, meaning he didn't know. I had been telling him about the village and my friends there for a long time. He usually listened wide-eyed. For whatever reason he didn't have many friends. One day he said: "My father talked about the village in a different way."

"How?"

"Like it was a really bad place. Arid. Its people like the earth, very dirty. A place where there were lots of bad people, doing wrong things, traitors, where innocent people like my father were even oppressed by their brothers."

I was shocked. I didn't know what to say. Until that day I hadn't thought about how many people in the village were good and how many were bad. I was angry with them for preventing me studying, but I was thinking in what way my uncle was innocent.

"And..."

"What?"

"He said they didn't understand love at all. He said they were even enemies of love."

I had not thought about this, but it was true that people in the village didn't understand much about love. Perhaps what was true was that traditions and customs were more important than love. According to traditions and customs feelings such as love were not really considered acceptable. Or at least they should be kept secret.

"They played a trick on my father because they were jealous of him. Then they caused him to be thrown out of the village. My father swore that one day he would return to the village and get his revenge."

After breakfast the next day my grandfather called me over. We went out of the garden gate. It was still early for the noon prayers. My grandfather was walking a bit faster than usual.

"Where are we going?"

"When we get there you'll see."

The owner of the small grocer's next to the mosque was sitting outside his shop, watching passers-by. When he saw us he uttered a greeting.

"Good morning Ali Kemal uncle."

"All together. All together…"

At the end of the dirt road we turned right. There was an old, wooden house in a garden. An elderly woman was cleaning withered roses with shears by the fence. A song could be heard from a small radio on the verge:

"The dear one has come

Fill the jug that we may drink

Save me from gloom

Hey vay hey hey

Fill the jug that we may drink

Fill it immediately

Flowers bloom in the garden

The robins begin to sing

They call this mortal

After the wooden house we saw a huge building. On the other side of an iron gate there were the children in uniforms who passed in front of the house every day. At last I was in front of one of the big schools in the city that teacher Fatih had told us about. Was that school that I had dreamt about so close to us? I was angry with myself for not having seen it before, if only from a distance. But my aunt had constantly warned me against straying far from the house, saying: "This is Istanbul, Keko, it's not like the village."

However, at that moment I was sure I would be joining those children who were playing. Who knew how many friends I would have? With such a wide choice people would probably be confused as to who to be friends with. And there were lots of teachers. I would be able to ask them anything that occurred to me, and certainly get an answer, too. If there were only one teacher, like in the village, sometimes our questions unavoidably would have to wait until the next day so as not to bore the teacher.

My grandfather knocked the iron gate insistently. A man in a long grey shirt ran up and opened it.

"Yes, uncle?"

"Show me the teacher's room."

"Which teacher's?"

"Whichever one is in charge of the school, that one."

"Uncle, why are you here?"

"What's it to you, young man? Take me there, I know how to explain myself."

"I'd better take you to the deputy head."

This man must have been the school janitor. Teacher Fatih had explained to us how employees called janitors carried out cleaning at schools in the cities.

Above the entrance in large letters were written the words Mustafa Kemal Atatürk Primary School. As we walked towards the building a bell rang. The sound was unlike the broken bell that teacher Fatih had used. The children left their games and began to go in through the main entrance.

We walked slowly behind the janitor following the children heading for their classes. There were two toilets, separate ones had been made for girls and boys. We passed a door bearing the words Headmaster Burak Yağız. We stopped in front of a door bearing the words Deputy Head Ali Dizdar. The janitor knocked the door and went in. Then he came out and called us inside.

As the deputy head spoke to my grandfather my eyes alighted on the radiators. I wondered what they were for. I was seeing them for the first time. When I recalled what teacher Fatih had told us I guessed they were for heating. They were heating that didn't have smoke and flames, instead of our open fires. Teacher Fatih had told us: "In the future there will be greater discoveries. Even coal-fired central heating will be consigned to history. Gas heating is a system that is both healthier and less harmful to nature. And one day ways will be found to use solar energy for heating. Maybe they have already been found, but it takes time to implement."

Who knew what lessons were like in this school?

The deputy head was telling my grandfather that the head was on leave for a week and that he did not have much authority.

My grandfather, who was bored, began to huff and puff.

"My son, can school wait?"

"It can wait, uncle. Thanks to the head, who doesn't allow anyone else to wield authority."

My grandfather said, as he stood up: "Okay, we have waited this long. Another week will pass. We'll come back."

Once again the wind had been taken out of my sails. And I had been so sure when we passed through the iron gate that my grandfather would have me enrolled and that the next day I would start school, or even that he would return home alone. I had even imagined playing a match with the children playing in the yard.

My aunt returned from her cleaning job in the evening with half a chocolate cake. And she brought some news.

"Good news, Keko! They say a doctor comes to see a patient who will get better."

"What's happened, Auntie?"

"I explained your situation to the headmistress. It seems they are looking for someone like you."

"Why?"

"Apparently they are going to take pupils without charging."

"What does that mean?"

"I hadn't heard of it before, either. It means having a scholarship. I mean, going to school without paying."

"Why, do you have to pay to go to school?"

My aunt laughed.

"Ah, Keko. If only you knew. Everything costs money here. Especially these private schools."

"Private schools?"

"And what money. Not for you or me. For rich and very rich people."

"But we're not rich, Auntie."

"Of course we're not. They even come to school by car. If you saw them you would think they were MPs, not pupils."

"So what's going to happen now?"

"They will accept you without money."

"Is the neighbourhood school also fee-paying?"

"No, that's a state school."

"So why don't I go there? I'll go there, it'll be better."

"Kekoooo, ah Keko! You're right. As you don't know, you want to go there. But you should know that you are very lucky."

I didn't understand anything.

"These schools charge fees, but they provide an excellent education. Once you've been there all doors open. Especially this school. The children of actors and factory owners go there. The teachers are cherry-picked. And it is so clean you could eat your dinner from the floor. State schools find it difficult to get a janitor. Are private schools like that? Extra janitors, watchmen, tea boys… they have everything."

I was both happy and confused.

When in the evening my uncle heard the news he hesitated, then a smile spread across his face. "It'll be good actually. I apparently have to have a hostess [assistant]. Keko can manage it. Then I'll be free of that ugly woman at the nursery's tongue."

My aunt exclaimed: "Will Keko be an assistant?"

It was the first time I'd heard the word 'hostess'. I was going to attend school. I had understood this, but not about being an assistant.

My uncle looked daggers at my aunt, and, with one eye on my grandfather sitting inside, began to explain:

"Now, don't I go out early and pick up those kids? They're small, the oldest is five. Someone needs to get them in and out of the vehicle. If I go with Keko early and drop the kids at the nursery, then we'll pick up the college kids, won't we? With Keko alongside me. On the way back we'll drop off the college kids then head for the nursery."

My aunt began to mutter to herself.

"If one day they hear you are also running the service to the nursery secretly, think what will happen to you."

My uncle replied to my aunt with the grimace of an eyebrow to which we were accustomed, sending the message "If my father wasn't here, you would suffer."

In any case, I was to go to school. Either free or paying. Both were schools. The next day my uncle stopped In front of my grandfather like a child expecting to be praised.

"Dad, the headmistress has asked for Keko."

My grandfather turned to me without looking at my uncle and indicated with his head that I could go. The idea of being alone with my uncle frightened me. I looked at my grandfather.

In a strong voice he said: "Don't be afraid! You are firstly in the safe custody of Allah, then of me. You, my daughter-in-law and my grandchildren are all my responsibility. If anything happens to you, first Allah and then I am responsible!"

My uncle, who was expecting praise, but had received a warning, was upset and took offence. Without saying anything he went out the door. My tearful aunt ran over and kissed my grandfather's hands.

"May Allah not deprive us of you, Dad. Before you came it was hellish every day for us. The pain of where he hit us has still not passed."

My grandfather seemed pensive. He looked out of the window. My uncle revved the engine, as if wanting to take out his anger on the minibus, and sped away.

My aunt brought out Tahir's old clothes that were now too small for him. She chose a pair of trousers and a shirt. Then she began to iron them. While watching my aunt the iron I had seen for the first time reminded me of what teacher Fatih had said. Without realising it what a lot of things I had learned.

"The iron was invented about three hundred years ago. Today most of them work with electricity. But it was invented before electricity. At the beginning heavy stones were used, then iron plates. In time incisions were made in the iron plates, which were filled with embers. The tool was over time developed by inventors. In 1888 American Henry Seely invented the electric iron. Although the iron appears to only be used to remove creases, it has another significant effect. It also kills parasites on garments, thereby ensuring hygiene. This is very important. Electric irons were mass produced in 1905 and became an indispensable household implement and part of modernisation."

There were still no irons in Heredile. Most of the villagers had also not heard of the iron. While I was thinking this my aunt looked at me and smiled.

"What's up, Keko? Why do you look so confused?"

"In the village no one irons their clothes."

"Here no one wears clothes that have not been ironed."

It was not going to be easy to adapt to city life.

"And especially in the school you'll be going to, you'll see. The children's outfits are razor-sharp. They're not like pupils, you would think they were governors, each one of them."

My aunt hung the clothes she ironed behind the door and wiped my old shoes. Then she polished them thoroughly with my uncle's shoe polish. With my aunt I felt both comfortable and well.

"Look Keko! From now on you'll polish your shoes. Your bloody uncle won't go to work if his shoes have not been polished. The gentleman's shoes must be polished every day, his shirt changed and his trousers ironed. You would think he was a school inspector, not a service driver."

"I will polish my uncle's shoes from now on, Aunt, as I've learned how to do it."

My aunt was pleased.

"Will you really do it, Keko? Hooray! Sometimes I'm busy and I plead with Tahir. He refuses to do it."

After the beating from my uncle I also didn't want to do anything for him, but I would do it for my aunt. She was very affectionate to me. She also loved my grandfather like her own father.

"And his vehicle has to be washed every day. Thank God he does that himself. You would think he was washing a tiny baby, he does it so tenderly. He is so scared that the vehicle will be scratched. But when he hits us he doesn't care where the blows land. Compared to that pile of metal I am worthless. Is it just me? He has beaten my son and driven him mad. The girls have no value, anyway."

"Is Tahir mad?"

"Don't you see, he is just sitting there in silence. You can't make his peers sit still."

"Auntie, were you forced to marry my uncle?"

My aunt stopped and her eyes moistened. She shook her

head and wiped her eyes with the edge of her muslin headscarf.

"Aiee, neither you ask nor I will tell. It was my destiny."

At that moment I felt more sorry for Tahir than my aunt, as although I felt pain when my father beat me, he didn't beat me as much as my uncle. What would it be like if he constantly beat me in this way? After seeing my uncle it was as if I had changed a little towards my father. My father was a good man, or at least he was better than my uncle.

The shoe polishing was over. My aunt was putting the tins of polish back in the box.

"Get ready, it's your turn to be washed."

My aunt made me sit in a bowl in the small stone bathroom. Despite my insistence she would not allow me to bathe by myself.

"Let me scrub your hair and scour your back with a bath-glove. Then you can wash the other places. If your mother is not here I am."

I had not taken off my pants, but I was still embarrassed at being washed by my aunt.

With every passing minute my excitement was increasing. Finally, I was to go to one of the magnificent schools I had dreamt about for years. And I was going to a good school. Every day and in every lesson I was going to learn something new. Let's see, when school was over how would Keko return to that village? If what teacher Fatih had said was true, I would be a king.

"The feudal period is over. We are in the age of science. Whoever has knowledge they are the hero. The armed heroes of the past are now farm labourers, who don't know for whom or for what they are working."

When I went to bed at night I tried to imagine the school I was to attend. I knew that every class had its own classroom. There might even be a gym and library in the school. Furthermore, in the middle school there would not be just one teacher, but many.

I was sure that I would be successful in Istanbul, as I enjoyed studying. Those children who got bad marks must be stupid. If there was a school, and there were books and a teacher, how could a child get bad marks?

I felt that everything would be wonderful. Istanbul was just my kind of city. Even if my uncle didn't love me, everyone else would. On finishing middle school I would go to high school and then on to university. I couldn't contain myself. I wanted the years to pass as soon as possible and for child Keko to move forward as student Keko.

University, even the name was different. Who knew what kind of world it was?

My return would be legendary. I was going to enter the village with those who worked under me. Just like that commander. But I wouldn't be a bad man like him. On the contrary I would be a good man, a public servant who was needed. Villagers wouldn't flee when they saw me, wouldn't be afraid, wouldn't curse and would even watch out for me and miss me. Everyone, including the gendarme commander, would show me respect.

My uncle Rahmi had gone out early. After taking the children to the nursery he was going to come back and pick me up. I had had my breakfast, got dressed and was waiting. Although I wasn't showing it, my heart was thumping. Keko, the chosen student of the famous school, was finally to wear the uniform. Everything, just everything, was going to be wonderful. The big city, a new school, new friends, a new teacher… My father had said: "The grass is always greener on the other side of the fence. Go and see! There are all kinds of people in Istanbul." Of course, he was mistaken.

My grandfather was in front of the window, awaiting my uncle's return. He was also counting his prayer beads and murmuring a prayer. As soon as he heard my uncle's voice he clenched the beads in his palm and got up.

"Come on Keko, the time has come."

We went out the door. My grandfather stroked my head.

"May God make your mind clear. Godspeed. May you acquit yourself well, grandson."

We were accustomed to my grandfather's prayers. We assumed it was a custom and that it was the same whether they were said or not. Years later when I lost my grandfather I was to realise how those prayers had nourished me, protected me and strengthened the resistance in my heart.

As my grandfather said, not everyone could understand the secret and science of prayers. He would explain at length the mystery of the forty gates in the sky, saying: "If you have not experienced real pain, your prayer and your curse will not be effective."

I kissed my grandfather's hand. Then I got in the minibus. We once again went onto the broad roads I had seen on the day I had arrived. On the asphalt road my uncle was flying along. I was taking care to keep my distance from him, just in case. When my grandfather wasn't present my uncle assumed his true identity.

He leaned out of the window and cleared his throat, spitting onto the street. Then he swore at a driver that passed him. The driver responded by making an obscene movement with his hand. My uncle stopped the vehicle. The man put his head out of the window and shouted: "If you're a man, get out of the car, homo!"

My uncle shook his head as if to say: "I'll show you!" and drove off.

My uncle was a man who could change quickly according to the situation. He reached over and put on the tape, as if to forget his exchange of curses with the other driver and his backing down.

Shoes on your feet
Shoes on your feet
Your darling arrives hesitantly
Your darling arrives hesitantly
I will die, I will die
I have ruined my young life
Beating my chest

Beating my breast I will die, die
Wherever she goes I will follow

My uncle accompanied the Turkish song in Kurdish. The poignant voice that I heard for the first time that day, and would listen to often, was very nice. The song ended. My uncle had one hand on the steering wheel while he thumped his chest with the other.

"Ah, ah! Blame the innocent! Blame Rahmi! Rahmi the damned stepson!"

My uncle picked up the students one by one. They were all older than me and well dressed. They were talking amongst themselves. I didn't want them to realise that I was listening to them. I was looking out the window as if I was not aware they were in the vehicle. We had come to the end of the smart asphalt roads. We entered a spotless road laid with cobbles with trees on both sides. The road was on a slight slope leading to a building surrounded by high walls.

We halted in front of an inlaid iron gate resembling palace gates. The children quickly got out. A man with a hat came over. My uncle greeted him and got out of the vehicle. He signalled for me to get out. My excitement was mounting. Then we saw two more watchmen. Mown lawns, colourful flowers in military straight lines, trees of the same type… It was a magnificent school, even better than I'd expected. My mouth was dry and as I walked my legs seemed to be trembling.

The watchmen approached my uncle.

"What's up, Rahmi?"

"Nothing, the headmistress asked for my nephew."

We went onto a narrow path between pruned round fir trees resembling large balloons. At the end of the path were marble steps that were shining as if they had been washed with soapy water. How could a place like this that was trodden on be so clean? Suddenly I recoiled on hearing my uncle's voice.

"Walk! You're stuck there with your mouth open like a jackass."

We passed the lions' heads on both sides of the steps and

went through a glass door. The interior was cleaner than the garden. There was nothing worn out, broken, bent or with its paint flaking off. Everything was brand new and shining as if it had been varnished. The air smelt of soap and eau de cologne.

Underneath a huge Atatürk photograph on the wall were the words: 'Science is the truest guide in life' in his handwriting.

We went into a corridor with pictures of Ottoman sultans on the walls. The second corridor began with a photo of Albert Einstein and continued with photos of Louis Pasteur, Thomas Edison and other scientists. There were lots I didn't know, but it didn't matter. In any case I would have time to learn them all.

On seeing those pictures something teacher Fatih had told us came into my mind. The amusing but real life stories of Alfred Nobel, who had regretted discovering dynamite, of Albert Einstein, whose own family had doubted his intelligence, and of numerous other scientists.

We suddenly stopped in front of a door. My uncle cleared his throat, straightened out his clothes and knocked on the door.

"Come in!"

My uncle took off his hat and gestured to me. We went in together.

We entered a wide room. A fair-haired woman of about 50 was sitting at a carved table. I looked down, as wherever I looked I could not conceal my amazement. As my uncle had said it was necessary not to look like an idiot.

We were waiting on a red carpet to attention.

While the headmistress put on her glasses she looked me up and down.

"Come closer, boy!"

I took a timid step forward. The headmistress, with red lipstick and blue make-up on her eye lids, was looking at me. I blinked several times so that she wouldn't understand my confusion.

"Come closer, boy. Why are you standing so far away?"

My uncle took me by the arm and while pulling me forward, said in a low voice: "Walk, boy, why are you hesitating?" The dryness in my mouth was getting worse. And on entering the room I had felt slightly queasy and held it back.

"You have received a diploma, haven't you?"

I opened my mouth to speak, but no sound came out. I nodded.

"What was your average grade?"

With difficulty I was able to say: "All excellent, my teacher." My uncle butted in.

"Headmistress, he was top of his class. He is probably embarrassed to say so. As you asked, I'm saying," he said, smiling.

"Good, good. Now the child will need a uniform. A bag and shoes are also necessary."

"Uniform?"

"Why are you surprised, Rahmi? Have you seen a child without a uniform?"

"Honestly, headmistress. Thank you. You have accepted my nephew at the school. Otherwise the poor boy was not going to go to school. But I cannot tell a lie, I cannot get him a uniform."

"I'm not surprised, Rahmi."

"You know the situation, headmistress."

The headmistress raised her hand to silence my uncle. "Okay, Rahmi, okay. We as a school will provide the uniform. If we order it today it will come within two days. But the child is already late. In my opinion he should start straight away."

"Your wish is my command."

Inside I was repeating what I had heard. The headmistress had said: "Let him start school today." How was I to start? I had no bag, books, exercise book or pen. Fortunately my aunt had dressed me in clean clothes. What if I had come wearing the clothes I had on when I left the village?

The headmistress looked me up and down for a while, then turned to my uncle.

"Okay, Rahmi. You may go."

As my uncle went out the door my excitement increased. I was alone in the large and grandiose room with the headmistress. She stood up and came over to me. The intense smell that we had encountered on entering the room became even more intense. It was a fragrance I had not come across before. She put a hand on my shoulder.

"Look, my boy. You are not aware of it yet, but this is a great opportunity for you. Receiving a diploma from this school is very important in this country."

What could I say?

"Your aunt explained that you had recently come from the village. You will of course understand urban realities."

I had never heard the term before. Urban realities... They would definitely be different from Heredile realities.

We left the room. I was walking along long, broad corridors with the headmistress. Every so often I read some sentences from notices on the walls that caught my attention.

At the end of the long corridors we stopped in front of a door. The headmistress went inside and I stayed outside. The door opened again. The headmistress raised her voice a little, saying: "Why are you outside, come on in!"

We had presumably arrived at the class I was to attend. Now I was to go inside and who knew which row I was to sit in, next to what kind of boy? I took two steps. There were no pupils inside. There were around thirty men and women wearing uniforms the colour of the lettering on my uncle's minibus.

The headmistress put a hand on my shoulder and began to speak.

"Colleagues, this is the scholarship pupil I told you about."

"Headmistress, is this the child you mentioned would come from the orphanage?"

"No, this is service driver Rahmi's nephew."

"Hmmm... "

Why had they thought I was from an orphanage? Even if my mother and father died I would not be abandoned as I had my clan.

"If we look at the place he has come from we may accept he has come from an orphanage. Or perhaps even worse… "

"I understand."

"Is there anything you wish to say?"

No one answered the headmistress. On the faces of the teachers who were looking me up and down was an expression that I could not at that time understand. A white-haired man shook his head.

"Ma'am, I am aware of what you want to do. I hope your good intentions do not harm the child."

"Vehbi, what are you saying? Can our school do harm to a child? I am proud that we are offering an opportunity to such children. He is a poor child from the lowest class in our country. We are gaining a child who would not be able to study if we did not assist him. Please think in this way and be proud. To be a student and a teacher at this school is a privilege."

Most of the teachers nodded as if to say 'you're right', agreeing with the headmistress. One of those sitting down was not wearing a uniform. He was a man of about forty-five, wearing a dark blue tracksuit. Our eyes met, he smiled and greeted me: "Welcome to Istanbul and welcome to our school."

Someone had smiled at me, and not only that, had said 'welcome' to me. It was not possible for me to forget this. I suddenly felt more comfortable. My fear, shyness and even my excitement had subsided a bit.

The headmistress said: "Açelya, I want you to take the boy to your class." Açelya, who had long fair hair, stood up and came over to me. "Certainly, head!"

I went out into the corridor with teacher Açelya. Cemal, my blood brother I had left in the village, came into my mind. In the last days he had been resentful.

"Why are you behaving like this? Aren't we blood brothers? Why have you got such a long face?"

"What difference does it make? Soon you'll have a lot of blood brothers. Don't pretend to be upset."

"I thought we were going to be confidants until death. If one of us was in trouble the other would come to his aid. What happened?"

"If that was the case you wouldn't have left the village."

"You mean studying? If you had such a chance, wouldn't you go?"

He thought for a moment, then bowed his head.

I didn't see him again after that day. He didn't come on the last day. I looked for him until we left the village, but I didn't dare leave my grandfather and go to his house as I feared my father would send my grandfather alone.

As I was pondering these things a door opened. Teacher Açelya signalled with her head that I should go in. This time it was certain that I had arrived at the class in which I was to study and my excitement reached a peak. I looked at teacher Açelya. She shook her head to both sides as if to say: "Why are you waiting?"

I went in and halted. My eye had been drawn to the large blackboard. The words written on it were not Turkish. When I saw the word 'yes' I realised the words were in English. Teacher Fatih had had us memorise one hundred words and twenty sentences in English, although it was not part of the curriculum.

A woman teacher with curly white hair was holding a piece of chalk. Trying to smile, she looked at us as if to say: "Why have you come?" Some of the pupils were writing the words on the board in their exercise books. As I went in I gradually became the centre of attention. They looked me up and down.

I was waiting with teacher Açelya next to the door. The teacher indicated one minute with her hand and turned to the class.

"When she took the book, he had already finished it."

Then she put one hand on her waist and moved the other over

the formula on the board. "Just write down the rule. You have examples in your books."

The children began one by one to raise their heads from their exercise books. Most of them had a faint smile on their faces. When our eyes met they averted their gaze. I lowered my head again. Teacher Açelya said: "Mehpare, I have brought the new pupil the headmistress mentioned. The teacher replied: "I see," and turned to me.

"What's your name?"

I was very excited. Teacher Açelya left the class and closed the door behind her. Everyone was waiting for me to answer. The teacher repeated her question: "What's your name, child?"

I gulped. Then suddenly, in a loud voice, I said: "Keko!"

There was immediately a wave of laughter.

"Did you hear?"

"What did he say?"

"He said Keko, didn't he?"

"What a name!"

"Like Fido!"

"Human landscapes from my country." [a reference to a poem by Nazim Hikmet]

It had come out of my mouth suddenly. On my identity card my name was Ali Kemal but in the village everyone, including my teacher, my mother, father and headman, called me Keko. Until that time no one had called me Ali Kemal. That was why I had been confused. I had made the first mistake that would make my school life a misery.

My grandfather's name was also Ali Kemal. Boys born in the village would receive the names of their grandfathers and uncles. For this reason the same name would be used in a family several times. In order to prevent confusion the younger person's name would be shortened. Hasan would become Haso; Ali Kemal, Keko; Ali, Aliş; Mehmet, Memo. Those who came after me received my uncles' names.

On just the first day, at the first moment I had stupidly uttered my nickname instead of the name on my identity card, thereby enabling the whole class to laugh at me.

"Great, yeah!"

"That's it!"

"Wow, pretending to be naïve and taking the mickey!"

"There's no place for such tricks in this school, mate."

"This is good, we've been really stressed out since this morning."

The teacher raised her ruler and everyone fell silent. I didn't know what to do. I needed to correct my mistake. I should apologise and say my real name, but at that moment I didn't know how to do it. My mouth was even drier. The teacher turned to me. She looked annoyed.

"Is this your real name, my boy?"

"No."

"So why don't you tell us your real name?"

What could I say?

"I'm listening to you. What's your real name?"

With difficulty I said: "Ali Kemal Karadağ".

"So your name is Ali Kemal, is that right?"

I nodded.

"So why did you say Keko?"

I couldn't answer.

If I had said: "it just slipped out of my mouth," perhaps the teacher would have forgiven me, but I didn't have the courage to say it. My cheeks and ears were burning.

"Miss, it's no problem for us. We'll say Keko, so as not to offend him."

"Kekoooo!"

"Kekoş, hey Kekoş!"

The class was rocking with laughter. The teacher was looking at me as if to say: "This is your fault". She banged the ruler against the board with a crack and shouted:

"No, it's not on! There is no place in this school for such non-sense."

My ears had started to hum. It was the first time I had felt so stupid and incompetent. The day I had entered the school I had dreamt about for years I had become a figure of fun. Perhaps the whole school would hear about it, even the teachers, and their first impression would be of 'a naughty boy'. Everyone would point at me and say: "Look. There's the halfwit who can't say his own name."

"Have you heard, a complete imbecile has come to the school?"

"Like a baby just learning to speak."

"No!"

"He can't even say his name."

"Really?"

"His name is Keko. Can you imagine?"

"Retard!"

"Imbecile!"

The teacher raised her ruler again and this time brought it down on the desk with a crack.

"Quiet! Be quiet, I say! I attribute this to the boy's first-day nerves. I'm sure it won't happen again. He will also learn the school rules."

"Miss, is it possible for a person to forget their name? If you ask me our friend is acting. I propose he join the drama group."

What was drama? Why were they proposing me for it?

At that moment I didn't know that Levent, who was proposing me for the drama club, would play a significant role in my life. This was how I met Levent, who would leave no stone unturned in efforts to make my life a misery. At the beginning he had presented me with a new word: drama.

"Miss, aren't we going to continue the lesson? I don't understand the last formula you put on the board."

This was Aycan. She was the most hardworking, irritable girl in the class. She was a girl who on setting eyes on her set something off in my stomach. She had sparkling eyes and looked like an angel in fairy tales.

I would get to know my classmates gradually, but that day they demonstrated to me plainly what kind of friendship they would offer. Although it was difficult for me to understand and accept, the reality was as clear as day.

For me to find the wonderful friends of my dreams in a big school in the big city was as difficult as finding a phoenix. But it is easier to believe in dreams than in truths. Especially if those truths are painful.

As the days passed, I would get to know every pupil in the class one by one, and would flounder between the pain they had caused and my dreams. The moments we met that were full of surprises would take their place amongst my unforgettable moments and would be a reason for me to smile in future years.

Teacher Fatih at every opportunity used to explain stories that emphasised the importance of communication between people. That first day, what kind of model of communication was my introduction to my classmates? It was akin to blows raining down on my face.

I had entered a long period of shock. I was stumbling and falling, then on every occasion demonstrating the maximum effort to get to my feet. I was not in a state to analyse my own feelings, let alone theirs. I hadn't expected any of the incidents that took place. Every stone from the external gate to the interior, all the teachers and pupils, were against me. They didn't want Keko. I wasn't suitable for them. What was I? Was I a plaything given to them for their amusement?

The first thing I did in the evenings when I returned as if from a battle, tired and demoralised, was to run to my grandfather. Even if I didn't say anything I would sit next to him quietly and try to get over the shock I had suffered that day.

There were two paths in front of me: to stay in Istanbul and go to the school where every day I was an object of derision, or return to the village and marry Hatun and live a life I didn't want. Both options were terrible. I was in a dead-end street without any hope.

There was no one I could share my pain with. At night I would secretly pour out my feelings into my diary. The subject was always the same. Lack of success in my lessons, the mickey-taking at school and the dozens of curses I couldn't utter to their faces. If it hadn't been for those glances that relieved me I don't know what I would have done.

Their conversations, like themselves, were alien to me.

"Hey men!"

In the first days I couldn't work out what 'men' meant. Then I learnt that it was used to mean 'my mate'. Those who addressed each other in this way were good friends. It was as if they were unaware of my existence, let alone admitting me to their circle. They behaved as if I was a monkey they could make fun of when they got bored.

"Hey Keko!"

"Are you lost in thought? Have you remembered your time in the village?"

"You've been here a month and your mouth is still wide open."

Some nights I would write nicknames I had made up for all the children in the class, including the teachers.

For Levent, itchy, for Aycan, nymph, for Sude, nettle tree, for Burak, fatty, for Can, cauliflower ears. The list went on and on. In the class of twenty three I sat at the back on my own. When they wanted to remember me they would turn their heads and laugh sarcastically at me. If it were possible I would have gone to the other side of the wall and have them forget me completely.

As the Keko in the village I could have called them to account, but I had to control myself. My uncle had cautioned me frequently. Otherwise I could have beaten up three of them at once.

"If I hear the slightest thing I'll have your guts for garters. If they get angry with you, I'll lose my job. Don't forget this! And don't rely on my father! I'll break your bones. It's thanks to me they accepted a bumpkin like you. Be thankful to me! You don't realise it, but they love and appreciate me there. Not everyone is like your grandfather. He is the only one who doesn't appreciate me."

I knew my uncle couldn't break my bones, but I didn't want him to lose his job on my account.

At dawn we would leave the house. My uncle feared they would find out he was using the school vehicle to secretly run a service for the kindergarten. He had told the nursery owner that the vehicle was his, and that the school allowed him to also work for the nursery. As the children were small, they had to be put in the vehicle and unloaded, which took time. Both schools did not like him to be late, and often warned my uncle. With me alongside him he had it easy. In the morning I assisted him. We would collect the children from their homes and drop them off at the nursery. Then we would speed off to do the school run. The pupils we picked up were from the high school section, which suited me. None of them knew me or took any notice of me. So on the route I was comfortable. Most of the time I would listen to their conversations, learning their lifestyles, ideas, aspirations and, sometimes, their attitudes to us villagers. They called some girls 'Kezban'. Some time later I learnt that the nickname Kezban meant 'like a village girl'.

Girls who were daring towards boys were called 'kaşar' [strumpet], which was really a kind of cheese. It was shameful to use this term for girls and women. If someone in our village used the word in this way about a girl or woman from another family, the matter could only be dealt with by shedding blood. But here there were even girls who smiled when they heard the word. They didn't care about lots of things we would shed blood over. There were other phrases.

"*Gecekondu* bastard!"

"Dork!"

"Snotty nosed!"

"Dickless!"

Almost all the boys in the minibus had girlfriends. Most of them were from the same school. A boy named Halil had a silver identity bracelet on his wrist bearing the name Şule. Şule was Halil's girlfriend. Despite warnings from teachers, Halil continued to wear the bracelet. A bracelet with his name on it was on Şule's wrist. I saw Şule come to the minibus one day and take a book from Halil. Were the pair engaged? Fortunately, no one knew I was engaged to Hatun. On the way to school I would take off my ring and put it in my pocket. When I left I would put it on again. I had sworn an oath, I could not take it off permanently. But as rings were not allowed in school it was normal for me to take it off.

There was a fair-haired boy called Alican who always sat in the back corner seat. He never joined in conversations. He would stare vacantly out of the minibus window and take no interest in those around him. No one would show an interest in him, either.

Then one day Alican didn't turn up. My uncle sent me to the door of a luxury villa to ask after him. A maid in a white apron said: "The little master is not well today." When the maid opened the door I looked inside for a few seconds. It was a huge house like a mosque. There were carpets on the floor and chairs like in palaces. In the corners there were huge vases and pictures on the walls.

I returned to the minibus and said: "Apparently he's ill." His classmates said: "Hopefully he won't go to hospital this time."

At that time I didn't know what Alican's illness was. Throughout the journey I thought about what it would be like to live in such a mansion. It was a huge house like a field. Everyone must have had their own room. Comfortable beds you could bury yourself in, all kinds of food, lots of books, nice, ironed clothes, a bicycle, several footballs, newspapers coming every morning, radio, TV, tape, *saz*, perhaps even a guitar.

On that first day when I was beaten by my uncle I wanted to immediately return to the village. Gradually I had begun to say: "Just as well I didn't go back." But sometimes such incidents happened at school that I said to myself: "Keko, get up, even if your grandfather doesn't come, return to the village. Or at least leave this school."

When there was silence in the class my heart would come into my mouth. I was afraid that someone would get bored and find some reason to make fun of me, but I didn't let on. Most of the time something would occur. It was mostly Levent who would taunt me.

One day the teacher said she was going to see the headmistress for a short while and left the classroom. After the teacher left, Levent began to sniff the air.

"There's a smell in the class."

Everyone looked at Levent, who was continuing to sniff the air seriously. I was trying to scribble something in my exercise book without taking any notice of him. It was as if I felt he would soon target me. I was not wrong. Levent turned towards me and said: "The smell is coming from there." I heard him but pretended not to and tried to continue writing. Then he got up and headed towards me as if he was tracking the smell. He was a good actor. Anyone who saw him could not have known he had planned it. His classmates, who knew him, began to laugh. I lifted my head and looked at Levent. I didn't want him to think I was frightened of him.

Levent, who was standing right next to me, turned up his nose in disgust and said: "Have you farted?"

I was startled. In the village it was shameful to let off gas in a crowd. There was a story my grandfather often told:

"Years ago a man left his village and went to town. While he was there he farted in public. For this reason the people of the town changed the name of the man's village to Farter's Village. Out of shame the man left the village where he had been born and went far away. When he was an old man he returned, wanting to see his relatives and those he'd left behind. As he approached the village he saw a young man and asked him where he had come from. The young man replied: 'From Farter's Village.' The man turned round and never went to his village again."

Now Levent was saying: "A fart smell is coming from you."

This was too much. I looked him in the eyes. Either he would retract what he'd said or I would teach him a lesson he deserved.

"What's this? Aren't you ashamed at stinking out the whole classroom?"

I got up slowly. Levent was still continuing.

"This is Istanbul, mate. There's no place like it. In public…"

I remember leaping at Levent, and then our falling to the floor. Levent was underneath. Then he was on top, but I immediately got on top of him again. I apparently punched him. When I came round Aycan was both crying and shouting.

"What's going on? Did you leave your stress balls at home?"

At that time I didn't know what a stress ball was. When I learned what it was I realised how accurate Aycan had been. I should write Stress Ball as my nickname on my list.

In the end it had been Levent who had been the last straw and made me lose control. When I got up, Levent was lying flat out at my feet. His face was covered in blood. There was no longer any laughter, or if there was I was in no state to see it. I walked out of the class.

Chapter Ten

WELCOME TO HELL

Nothing was as I had hoped in the school I had begun with such great dreams. From the very first day, this school, which I had watched like an unattainable princess, from its garden to its walls, to is splendid iron gate, its classrooms and its toilets, that I had approached with love and care and that had raised my hopes to a peak, hadn't wanted me.

My teachers included, almost the entire class had become separate nightmares that descended upon me at every opportunity. Anyone who wanted to relax, laugh or humiliate someone would directly attack me. Furthermore, none of the teachers did anything about it. And as if I deserved it most of the time they would ignore me, behaving towards me as if I was surplus to requirements. If I had at least been able to gain the support of one or two teachers things might have been different.

The pressure on me, the psychological assaults, abuse and isolation got worse. I didn't know how I was going to gain acceptance from my classmates with whom I hadn't even had the chance to become properly acquainted. All I could do was work until morning to be better in class. The teachers belatedly appreciated my efforts, but it was still not possible for me to compete with the others, most of whom received private tuition.

My grandfather had noticed my unease. "Don't give up something you have started. Even if you think you have given it up, it will pursue you for your whole life. The best thing to do is finish this school, whatever it takes."

It was easy to say, but difficult to do.

I had realised how important my friends in the village were to me. Loneliness, rejection and constantly being made fun of were the worst feelings in the world.

All the children in my class had succeeded in opening up wounds of various sizes in my heart, as if they had reached an agreement. There were very few pupils who didn't humiliate me. The wounds sometimes turned into new feelings and new thoughts, rarely leading to me being strengthened. Like an acrobat walking on a tightrope near the clouds, I was trying not to fall.

In fact, in those first days I was so confused I was unable to analyse my feelings. If I had been comfortable, if I had been able to lift my head and look everyone in the face one by one, if I had been able to pluck up the courage to discuss with them, who knows, I might have had friendly hands extended towards me. Like being in an extended period of shock, as my dreams and hopes moved further away from me, the emptiness filling my insides was wiping all meaning from my life.

Sometimes they stole my exam papers from the teachers' room and passed them around. I pretended not to know or care. Umut threw my exam paper, which he had folded into a paper plane, towards my desk. I caught it, trying to appear calm. I was just about to open it when the teacher came into the room. Aycan ran over, took the exam paper made into a plane and complained about Umut to the teacher. The teacher opened the paper plane and looked at it. Then she straightened out the paper, put it on the desk and started the lesson as if nothing had happened.

That day, at that moment, I made my decision. I was going to return to the village. Even if my grandfather didn't come, I was going to return. I couldn't put up with this torture much longer. I was not going to allow the big city to swallow me up, as my father had feared. For now I was between the teeth of the big city. At every chew, although it was as if thousands of needles plunged into my body, I was still intact. I would not become like Tahir.

The one thing I had to do was save money. The day I had saved up the money for a return ticket I was going to head for the bus station. I had begun to miss all my friends, Bera, my mother, my father, my siblings, the mill and everything I had left behind. I was longing for Heredile. I had no other way out but to return.

I had no option but to live that life that I had previously belittled and resisted. I was to repeat the past of my father that I found meaningless. Like the others, I was to live and die in the village where I had been born. I should marry whoever my mother and father wanted, have a lot of children, like everybody else, and work in the mill. Who knows, maybe one day a road, water and even electricity would come. The day electricity arrived we could get a television set. A television means being able to watch the whole world. We would not need to leave the village.

I didn't say anything to those in the house. For a few days I awaited the summons from the headmistress. I was ready for it. I was expecting to have to account for beating up Levent. Perhaps as I went through the gate a janitor would say: "The headmistress is waiting for you," or as I went into the class they would say, "Stop! You've been expelled. You beat up the richest boy in the school. How dare you?"

None of these things happened. Why hadn't Levent informed the school authorities? Perhaps he had been unable to accept he had been beaten up by me.

What they thought or did no longer interested me. I was going to leave the school anyway. I wasn't talking to them. In order that our eyes wouldn't meet I constantly pretended to be busy with something. After the fight, fewer people were taking the mickey out of me. At least they shied away from openly mocking me. They were a bit more underhand about it.

Preparations for 19 May had begun. Despite the insistence of the teacher, I said I didn't want to take part in the demonstration group.

One afternoon during break I was as usual strolling around on my own. Suddenly I saw that children were shouting and bawling and throwing stones at the roof of the neighbouring building. They were trying to make a crow back away. The girls were screaming at the crow: "No! No! Please don't do it!"

A large crow had grasped a small kitten in its claws and after flying off a little had dropped the kitten on the next roof. It had now gone up to the kitten to catch it again. The children were trying to save the kitten by throwing stones at the crow.

"Let's call the fire brigade. Only they can bring it down."

"By the time the fire brigade comes the crow will have taken the kitten."

In a moment I had climbed up a plane tree and leapt onto the roof.

Levent pointed at me and shouted.

"Look at the monkey. Chiquita!"

The voices of Sude and the other girls drowned out Levent's voice.

"Well done, Ali Kemal!"

"You're a hero!"

"Be careful, Ali Kemal!"

I had got close to the kitten when the crow acted more agilely than me and grabbed the kitten between its claws and took off. At the same moment I grabbed the crow. It began to peck me to force me to let it go. It had no intention of giving up its prey and I couldn't loosen its grip. The crow was screeching horribly as if it was saying: 'This is my food.' I shook it hard and squeezed. Its claws opened and as the kitten fell I caught it in mid-air. Just at that moment I heard Aycan scream:

"Look out, Ali Kemal! It's going to attack again!"

The angry crow landed on my head. I knew what it wanted to do but Aycan's scream that made clear she was thinking of me had dispelled all my fear. I closed my eyes tightly and pushed the crow away with a rapid movement of my hand. It must have realised it couldn't beat me and it flew away.

I needed to go back to the plane tree and descend with the kitten. I was thinking of Aycan. She had shouted at the top of her voice for me. It was obvious that she would be upset if anything happened to me. It was going to be difficult to get down, but I had a pleasant feeling inside me. I was trying not to hurt the kitten I was holding carefully in my bloodied hands. I was praying it wasn't dead. There weren't many branches on the tree. To climb such a tree you had to be a monkey, as Levent had said. Whatever happened I should make sure I didn't fall.

Just at that moment the headmistress arrived. As soon as she saw me she shouted.

"Ali Kemal!"

I turned my head towards her but couldn't say anything.

"What are you doing up there?"

Lying on a branch looking at the kitten I stopped for a moment.

"My boy, I said what are you doing up there?"

Levent answered in my place.

"Miss, our classmate has missed his days in the village. He says he cannot do without climbing a tree."

Aycan said: "That's enough, Levent! Stop mocking Ali Kemal." Then she turned to the headmistress.

"Miss, Ali Kemal climbed the tree to rescue a kitten."

The headmistress shouted at me in her shrill voice.

"Oh my God! Ali Kemal! I want you to come down very carefully."

I quickly descended.

"Look at that, like a cat."

"What cat, more like a squirrel."

Levent did not look happy at what he was hearing.

"They don't call him a villager for nothing."

Aycan ran over and took the unconscious kitten from my hand. That day for the first time Aycan's hands touched mine. I pulled my hands away as if I hadn't felt it.

The headmistress was very tense.

"That's enough! Everyone back to their classes! You're coming with me, Ali Kemal!"

The rules were clear. They couldn't be ignored just because of good intentions. Those who broke the rules had to appear before the disciplinary board.

"Go and see the nurse immediately and get your hands dressed. Then you can go to class, Ali Kemal. I will inform the board. I'm sure they will want to see you very soon."

I had not been up before the disciplinary board before, but I didn't care. As I was returning to the village soon any penalty was of no importance.

Just at that moment Sude's father, a vet, came in. He said he had spoken to his daughter on the phone. He smiled when he heard what had happened. Then looking at my hands he turned to the headmistress.

"What happened here?"

When I went into the class for the first time I saw smiling faces. Sude, Aycan and Murat were looking at me in a friendly way. It was really nice to see friendly faces, which I'd longed for. Yes, I could have cried like a girl. It was a strange feeling. I had never felt so relieved.

I didn't reply to Murat, who said: "Wow, man.! You saved the cat's life. You're a hero!" But inside I hugged him.

I was doing my best to avoid Aycan's glances, as whenever I looked at her I forgot everything.

As I sat down, Sude congratulated me in a meaningful tone of voice.

"Ali Kemal, you did a great job. I thank you. If you hadn't saved the cat I wouldn't have been able to study today. You're wonderful!"

What a good turn that crow that wanted to gouge my eyes out had unknowingly done me.

Chapter Eleven

BEING A KURD

Of course, Levent was not happy at this unexpected incident and my sudden hero status. The animosity that had begun on the first day was steadily growing. If it hadn't been for him perhaps I wouldn't have recalled my first days at that school as a nightmare for the rest of my life. The anger and resentment I felt towards him was changing me with every passing day.

"Speak for yourself, girl! You might not study, but not everyone in this class is a cry baby like you."

Sude gave Levent a withering look and did not reply. Following the last lesson I was again called to the headmistress's room. The disciplinary board had assembled. Hayrettin Bey, the PE teacher who had greeted me with a nod on my first day, was there. He again greeted me with a smile. There was another, elderly, tall man wearing a suit. He was sitting in the headmistress's chair. Hamza, the janitor, first offered tea to him, then to the headmistress and the other teachers. The look on the face of the man in the headmistress's chair was cold. He nodded and the headmistress began to speak.

"I welcome Cevdet Bey and my dear colleagues. The reason we are here is that one of our pupils broke the rules. Ali Kemal climbed onto the roof of the next building in a dangerous way in order to rescue a kitten. Of course, love for animals is laudable, but just as he was a bad example to his classmates, he also put his own life in danger. Now, here we are all going to talk about this together."

Our English teacher, Mehpare Hanim, asked the first question:

"Ali Kemal, did one of your classmates ask you to climb up to the roof, I mean was there anyone directing you?"

"No."

"Did you decide yourself?

"Yes."

"What was your purpose?"

"My purpose?"

Mehpare Hanim smiled and repeated her question.

"What was your reason for going up there?"

"To save the cat."

Just as Mehpare Hanim was going to allow other colleagues to speak, Cevdet Bey interjected.

"Could it have been to make a show for your classmates?"

"Show?"

"Yes, might it have been a show?"

I shrugged my shoulders.

"I don't know what show means."

There was silence for a moment.

Cevdet Bey asked in a louder voice: "Are you Kurdish?"

"Yes."

Some of the teachers lowered their heads. No one was talking. Only the PE teacher Hayrettin Bey was clearly looking at me and smiling. Cevdet Bey shook his head and turned to the headmistress. She didn't know what to say.

"I don't think so, sir. The boy didn't mean that."

"Didn't you hear?"

"He might be excited, I mean..."

Cevdet Bey turned again to me.

"You, are you a Kurd or a Turk?"

I was really surprised.

"I'm a Kurd."

Cevdet Bey smiled meaningfully and looked again at the headmistress. She began wringing her hands.

"Cevdet Bey, believe me, I didn't know. It didn't occur to me."

"I gave all responsibility for the school to you. This is why you receive a salary."

"You're right, but his uncle has been a service driver for the school for three years. We haven't seen any transgression."

The other teachers supported the headmistress.

"Yes, he's a bit irresponsible, but we haven't seen any rebelliousness. I mean, he never said he was Kurdish."

"That's incorrect, it's wrong! They call themselves Kurds. In fact there is no such thing."

When Cevdet Bey began to speak, everyone went silent. Now his voice was louder.

"If you had carried out your duties properly all this would not have happened."

"It was an error..."

"It was not an error! Everything is clear. Don't you see?"

"Sir..."

"I'm holding all teachers responsible for this."

Teacher Hayrettin turned to the headmistress and said:

"Shouldn't we be talking about what the boy did, rather than his ethnic identity?" Cevdet Bey got more annoyed, going bright red.

"Keep going, Hayrettin Bey. I'm really curious as to what you're going to say."

Teacher Hayrettin turned to me. There was a friendly expression on his face. It was as if he wanted to rescue me from the situation I was in.

"Ali Kemal, if a similar thing happened to you again, you wouldn't act in the same way, would you?"

I wasn't expecting such a question. I thought for a minute or two. Then I slowly said: "I'd do it." The headmistress's eyes bulged, as if to say: "What have you done". There was a look of sarcastic pleasure on Cevdet Bey's face, as a result of being proved right.

"Ha! He says: 'I would do it.' He says: 'I won't stop behaving rebelliously and subverting order.' You'd have to be stupid not to understand this."

Hayrettin Bey again interjected. Pointing to me, he said: "I don't think the boy did it to be rebellious."

Cevdet Bey turned to me. His voice was decisive and sure. "Tell me, why would you do it again?"

"In order to save the cat."

"You're saying you'd do it again, knowing full well that it is contrary to school rules to climb a tree and get on the neighbouring roof?"

I wasn't going to stay in the school. If I broke the school rules what could they do to me. At most I would be expelled. But if I could save that kitten why shouldn't I? I nodded my head in assent.

Cevdet Bey clapped his hands together.

"Is there still someone amongst you who objects? Hayrettin Bey, I wonder if you have understood what a thing it is to be Kurdish?"

"But sir, you are acting as if none of the school rules have ever been broken. Please!!"

Cevdet Bey raised his voice again.

"Do you recall a student who defended the offence he had committed?"

There was not a sound from anyone.

"Or anyone who said: 'I'd do it again'?"

Hayrettin Bey was about to say 'But, sir,' when Cevdet Bey, whose face was red, stood up.

"Do you realise what you are defending?"

"Sir, you have misunderstood me."

"I think it is not beneficial for you to remain at the school."

A lot later I was to learn that Cevdet Bey was the owner of the school. That day I realised that Hayrettin Bey could be sacked because of me. I needed to prevent that. I raised my hand.

Teacher Açelya said warily: "I think Ali Kemal is going to express regret. Aren't you, Ali Kemal? Could we let him speak?" Cevdet Bey sat down again.

"An apology now after all that has gone on is of no account for me."

The headmistress looked at me as if to say "Apologise", saying: "Come on, Ali Kemal, whatever you're going to say, say it now!"

"I found out this school was fee-paying after I started. I thank you for accepting me without payment. I wouldn't have wanted to break the rules, but there was no other way to save the cat. I accept the punishment you will give. I have decided to leave your school."

The headmistress looked at me as if to say: "What have you done?" slapping her hand on her knee. Cevdet Bey shook his head and looked at the teachers.

"You see? What cockiness. He's saying 'Who are you?' to us. 'You are of no importance for me'.

"He's really not like that at all, Cevdet Bey."

"To be honest, as a very quiet pupil..."

"Is this your silence? Don't you see, he's not a normal boy. Look how rebellious he is. He is rejecting our good intentions with the back of his hand like an adult. Are there any amongst you who haven't noticed this?"

The headmistress did not want to annoy Cevdet Bey further.

"Sir, I will carry out the necessary procedures. I will do my utmost to ensure the boy is transferred to a state school within two days. The child said he didn't want to stay at this school. This may be sufficient reason for the Ministry of Education."

Cevdet Bey left the room without speaking. He was followed by the headmistress. Teacher Hayrettin came over and stroked my head. The teachers took a deep breath, but they still looked bemused.

"That's all we needed."

"My boy, wouldn't it have been better if you hadn't talked big?"

"And all over saving a kitten."

"I've never heard anything like it in my life."

"Look at what we were talking about"

"Something we're not accustomed to."

"A pity!"

When everyone had left, Hamza, the janitor, came back in to collect the glasses. He looked around and when he was sure no one was listening, said: "Boy, are you mad? What did you think you were doing, saying: 'I'm a Kurd'?"

"Hamza, aren't you a Kurd, too?"

"No, you're the only one who's a Kurd! Do you say you're a Kurd everywhere?"

Uncle Rahmi swore at me all the way home.

"Thanks to you I almost lost my bread and butter, Keko! If

only my father wasn't here, how I would separate your bones from your flesh. You bumpkin! You told Cevdet Bey you were a Kurd, huh! You've got bandit blood in your veins. They're right. You're going back to the village, boy! My father came and took up residence. When are you going to leave? Didn't your grandfather tell your father when he left the village?"

In the evening I told Tahir what had happened. He was not at all surprised. He smiled and said: "Welcome to Istanbul."

The person I really feared was my grandfather. He had never been angry with me before. I was fretting that he would be cross with me for saying I was Kurdish in school. I didn't know how I would explain. After dinner my aunt brought the tea.

Uncle Rahmi began to explain while slurping his tea.

"Dad, an important thing happened today."

My grandfather acted as if he hadn't heard my uncle.

"If you hear what your grandson Keko did, you won't believe it."

My grandfather suddenly looked at me.

"I was going to punish him but I've left it to you."

I lowered my head. My grandfather looked at my uncle as if to say "What are you on about?". My uncle was enjoying himself. I had not seen him slurp his tea with such gusto before.

"I was really surprised, dad. Your grandson, this Keko, stood up in the school and said: 'Ah, I'm a Kurd.' What do you have to say about that?"

I was silently praying that my grandfather would not be angry with me.

Uncle Rahmi was frothing at the mouth as he explained. For a short time my grandfather did not speak. Then he picked up the glass of tea on the stool and turned to my uncle. For the first time he was speaking to my uncle while looking him in the face.

"What should he have said, Rahmi? Should he have shouted: 'I'm not Kurdish, I'm Turkish'?"

Uncle Rahmi, like me, was not expecting this. "But dad, this is Istanbul," he stuttered.

There was mirth in my grandfather's voice.

"What about Istanbul, Rahmi?"

"You know, Dad, that the word Kurd is not popular."

"Does our Kurdishness disappear just because they don't want to hear the word Kurd?"

"No, but…"

"For instance, Rahmi, you've been in Istanbul for years. So are you now a Turk?"

"For a moment Uncle Rahmi hesitated. "No, Dad, no way! I certainly haven't become a Turk, but…"

"But you're saying you don't admit to being a Kurd."

Uncle Rahmi nodded.

"That is, you're denying your origin."

"No dad. Is that possible?"

"You're concealing it."

Uncle Rahmi hung his head. He looked dispirited. My grandfather turned to Tahir.

"Tell me grandson. What are you?"

Tahir shrugged his shoulders as if he didn't know what to say. My grandfather turned again to my uncle.

"You see, Rahmi. This is what hiding your origin and denying it is. First you get confused, then those who are born later are born dead. Look, your son doesn't know if he is a Kurd or a Turk."

"He's stupid, what can I do?"

"Have you ever told your son he's Kurdish, Rahmi?"

***

The next day when I went into class, Sude came over to me. They had heard I had been in front of the disciplinary board.

Most of them didn't care that I had received a punishment. Levent was prominent among those who were secretly pleased I had been punished, but a few people did not approve of my being punished. Sude made her point in front of the whole class and asked for others' support.

"Ali Kemal saved that kitten, friends. Should saving the life of a living thing be punished? No! We should support our classmate on this issue."

Sude had called me a classmate. It was a wonderful feeling to know that there were people who supported me. If I hadn't been embarrassed I would have asked Sude to repeat what she had said. I shrugged my shoulders as if going in front of the disciplinary board was nothing exceptional.

"It's not important."

Sude looked around.

"Meanwhile, I have some good news for you guys. My dad says the kitten will get better."

Then she turned to me. All my life I have not forgotten the look of gratitude and affection in her eyes. Who cared about being expelled from school? Even if they'd put a noose round my neck I wouldn't have cared.

Just at that moment Aycan came in. When she heard I had been in front of the disciplinary board she shouted angrily:

"They must have gone mad! Are they going to punish you when they should be thanking you?"

Sude was calmer, but more determined.

"Definitely not. We will tell the disciplinary board what we think of them."

Levent, as usual, was not happy with Aycan and Sude's interest in me.

"Girls, aren't you getting carried away? The guy climbed up to the roof so he could be a hero, and you want to give him a medal."

Sude squared up to him as if she was going to take out all her anger on him.

"What did you say?"

"Isn't that the case?"

"What's the case? Are you so cold-hearted? Would you have been happier if the kitten had died? Or is that just how I understand it?"

"What's up? Do you want to organise an awards ceremony because this monkey saved a cat?"

Sude interrupted Levent.

"I don't understand. Who are you calling a monkey?"

Later I learned that the word monkey was English.

"Aagh! I don't want to argue with you. Do what the hell you want."

Levent's face was bright red and he seemed to be trying hard not to cry. During the break, Sude came up to me and said: "My father says the kitten will survive, but I'm sorry you were in front of the disciplinary board. You don't deserve this."

At that moment Sude could not have understood what a good thing I had done for myself by saving the kitten.

"Don't worry. It's not important. I don't care about the disciplinary board. Really."

"But they can do you harm."

"Nothing will happen, never fear!"

"No, we should do something by backing you all together."

The reality was that I no longer liked the school. Many things at the school seemed to reject me. I was fed up at having to hold my breath when I passed the canteen so as not to smell the odours coming from inside. And encountering new words in almost every lesson gave me headaches.

When in the village I knew that being a Kurd was not a good thing, but at least there no one ostracised anyone for being a

Kurd, as we were all the same. However, being a Kurd in Istanbul was like being a black sheep in a flock. I had got tired of standing up to people who looked at me as if I was a sick black sheep.

No one yet knew I had decided to leave the school. Perhaps it was better this way. When the English teacher came in, Levent had turned the volume on his radio in the shape of a watch up to full and was listening to an English song, the name of which I didn't know.

"I have been a human so damn long

But the monkey won't set me freeeee…"

Most of the boys were laughing, but the girls didn't seem happy. Aycan had gone red in the face.

"Turn that off!"

"What?"

"I'm saying turn off that rubbish you're playing!"

"Why?"

There was an expression on Aycan's face that was both sad and angry. Levent's behaviour was upsetting her.

"I'm giving you three seconds."

Levent was very annoyed at Aycan's reactions to me, as he was also in love with her. It wasn't possible for him to love her as much as me, but there was something between them that I had not been able to work out. "What three seconds?"

"One, two…"

Levent raised his fist into the air and brought it down on the small radio on the desk, which must have cost who knows how much, smashing the expensive thing into pieces. He threw the pieces onto the floor and stood up.

"Are you happy now?"

Aycan stared at him without replying. Levent was really annoyed.

"You've really rated this bumpkin…."

He slammed the door and left the classroom. Bumpkin… Levent had called me a bumpkin. This was the slang word that city people most used for men who came from villages.

The teacher didn't understand what had happened, but couldn't say anything to Levent. None of the students gave a damn about the teachers; some of the teachers even fawned on the students. It seemed the rules were only there for me. It was as if teachers who did not hesitate to reproach me for the slightest mistake were taking great efforts so as not to upset the other students.

English was the hardest class for me, as I didn't understand anything that was said. The teacher had given me words to memorise. Although I repeated the words dozens of times a day I confused them. I didn't even understand words I knew the first time they were said. And when it came to songs, I didn't understand a thing.

Our English teacher, Mehpare Hanim, was a middle-aged woman who attached importance to discipline. As she walked towards her desk she suddenly stopped and turned to the class.

"Now, I'm giving you a task."

"We've only just started the class, Miss."

"You're going to do it now. Composition in English. Write down the words of the song you've just been listening to. And then explain what they mean."

I didn't know the meaning of any of them. What could I write? The teacher walked to her desk and sat down. Then she brought over a piece of paper and placed it on my desk. The words of the English song were written on the sheet of paper.

"You may use a dictionary, Ali Kemal."

I nodded.

I was very young. A friend had come from Damascus to visit my grandfather. With him he brought a baby hawk, by the name of Adopted, that did not want to descend from Granddad Abdul's shoulder.

Abdul's son had found Adopted on the mountain when he went to cut wood. It was still a baby, at the most two months old. It was beside its mother that had been shot by hunters. When it arrived at his house, granddad Abdul had fed it and after that it never left his side. He had said: "if one day you are attacked by a wild animal, try to catch its eye. If you can explain what you are feeling through your gaze it may spare you."

Sometimes those in the class frightened me more than all wild animals. But even if I knew I was to die, I was not going to try to catch their eye. I would rather die. And what would I say to them? Was I to say: Please don't humiliate me. I was created from flesh and bone like you. And you don't know, but I'm a good footballer.

Sometimes I felt like shouting: "You can all go to hell. Bastards!"

Levent, who never missed an opportunity to hurt me, had not been supported by the class on this occasion. When he hadn't been able to repeat his entertainment he had gone home. When the bell rang to indicate break-time, Hamza came in. He said: 'The headmistress is waiting for you."

I felt the time to leave school was approaching. I turned and looked at Aycan. Our eyes met. It was difficult to believe, but every day she was looking at me more beautifully. How bitter it would be to no longer see those pure glances?

Let it be. I didn't care about leaving school. I had seen Aycan look at me in that way, so even if I died I wouldn't feel sorrow. If only I was able to beat up Levent once before leaving school. The fact he was going to get away with what he had done was driving me crazy, but my hands were tied. If I hadn't promised my grandfather I wouldn't care about my uncle.

When I entered the room the headmistress was talking on the phone.

"Certainly sir, however you wish. I will do the necessary. Absolutely, sir. Our PE teacher is very experienced in this matter, as you know. He's a former footballer."

My favourite teacher, or in fact the only teacher I liked, was Hayrettin. He had behaved in a friendly way to me from the first day. As soon as he had seen me he had smiled. Istanbul had taught me what to smile at someone or to look down on someone meant.

When teacher Fatih had come to the village on the first day he had smiled at all of us, at all the villagers. He had smiled in such a sincere way that none of us had found it strange. Even adults who didn't like the school were affected by his sincerity. Whereas almost all the commanders who came to our village were very angry. They always looked at us as if we were criminals.

Most of the teachers in that school were like those commanders. When they encountered me they ignored me as if they didn't know what to do. Some nights I wondered why they behaved like that, but I couldn't find a reason. Was the problem just that I was a Kurd, or was the fact I was poor have something to do with it?

History teacher Melih Hodja was the worst of the lot. He made it so obvious that he didn't respect me to the extent that when he spoke to me the tone of his voice changed automatically. Melih Hodja didn't like Hamza either. He behaved towards him as if he was a clumsy, stupid person who shouldn't be in the school, rather than as a janitor. Perhaps he sensed he was a Kurd. Watchman Haydar never went into his hut when Cevdet Bey and Melih Bey were in the school. He would walk up and down, ready for anything, as if someone was going to enter the school at any moment and mess it up.

When the headmistress put down the phone she turned to me.

"Ali Kemal, I need to ask you something. Do you want to go to an ordinary high school or a vocational one?"

I didn't understand anything.

"I don't know."

"What do you mean, my boy? Which one do you want?"

Was I going to be able to go to school again?

"Are you thinking of going to a vocational high school in the future?"

I shrugged my shoulders. I wasn't going to stay in Istanbul, so it didn't matter. As soon as I left this school I was going to look for ways to return to the village. In those days I thought all schools in Istanbul were like Ilim College. The only problem was to prevail upon my grandfather. I didn't want to return without him. Then again, if I had to, I would return by myself.

"It's all one to me."

The headmistress took a deep breath. "Ali Kemal, haven't you discussed this matter with your mother and father? What do they think? I don't want to do something that you don't want. Rather than asking your uncle, who is your guardian, I'm asking you."

"My mother and father are in the village."

"When you arrived your lessons were very bad, but your teachers say you have endeavoured to rapidly close the gap. Your maths teacher in particular says you have ability."

I didn't reply. The headmistress wanted me to choose a school. As for me, I didn't know which schools taught what lessons, the difference between them or how it would influence my life.

I had closed the gap a little, but I was still bottom of the class. In the first days I had made mistakes that had the class rocking with laughter. While they were amusing themselves, I felt as if a knife was going into my stomach. Although the teacher explained my errors I didn't understand anything.

I pretended not to hear the jeers, but it didn't help as I felt my cheeks redden. Then a horrible hum would fill my brain. As soon as I got home I would bury myself in my text books. I would read them again and again in order to understand. I learned some pages by heart, right down to the last comma. But however hard I tried, I could not make up for the missing knowledge from earlier years. It was very difficult for me to catch up with my classmates who received private tuition from the best teachers.

In particular, Levent constantly being on my case and the insensitivity and impatience of teachers was causing me to become increasingly unhappy.

Who knew how surprised they would be to see me dashing back to the village I had left without a backward glance and had dreamt of returning to years later? My father would say: "I said so! This is what happens to those who don't listen to good advice."

The first thing I would do on returning to the village would be to see Sülo. I would embrace him and apologise. Sülo had written a single sentence as a composition for teacher Fatih on the subject of "What profession will you choose?" "I will be a shepherd until the end of my life." After teacher Fatih had read Sülo's single-sentence essay he looked at him and smiled. As his eyes filled with tears he said nothing and shook his head.

After the lesson we gathered around Sülo and began to judge him.

"Hey Sülo, teacher Fatih was left tongue-tied."

"You could at least have said: 'I'll be a farmer.'"

"Yeah, but why didn't teacher Fatih say anything?"

"Then he had tears in his eyes."

"Why?"

"What do you mean 'Why'? When he saw his efforts were going to waste he found it hard to stop himself crying."

This last sentence was mine. Sülo looked at me without saying anything and left. At the time I hadn't realised I'd upset him. Later, when I thought about it, I realised what I'd done. Sülo was sincere. He loved his animals so much that he couldn't imagine being separated from them.

All my friends who heard I had returned would come running. It would be like before, we would be poor but happy.

The worst thing would be not being able to take them the presents I'd promised.

While I was in Istanbul my brothers had been working at the mill. Perhaps my father would have understood my worth and wouldn't behave badly towards me as he had previously. Could we be a good father and son? I really wanted that. I had even tried to imagine happy times with him, but hadn't been successful. It was really difficult to imagine my father loving me.

The reality was clear. There was no future in the village. I would have a boring and primitive life, but at least it wouldn't be humiliating like life in the city. No one, but no one could talk down to me in the village. And no one would accuse me just because I was a Kurd. No one would make fun of me, except the commanders and soldiers who came to the village from time to time.

I had begun to think about the events that would make me very unhappy in the village. Even marrying Gülistan would be better than being in Istanbul. In any case, I was engaged to Hatun. Really, what kind of girl was Hatun? What was I going to do when I married her? I didn't feel anything at all for her, on the contrary, when I thought of her my chest tightened. Or was I not going to be a real man? According to uncle Ekber, a man was someone who fulfilled all his duties to the woman who was his wife. If he couldn't do that it meant there was something wrong. Matters of love were not appropriate for Kurdish men, but men's duties were different. If you didn't want to be a woman's plaything, you should never fall in love.

On returning I should tell Gülistan about Istanbul. Perhaps if she heard what sort of place it was she would abandon the idea of coming here. After all, I didn't want her to experience the painful problems I had been through.

I would also tell my friends about the big schools here. Big cities were like hell for village children like us. There was no need for them to be upset because they couldn't come here.

I had understood what Tahir had meant when he told me that "Schools are hard" on my first day and why he hadn't been able to study. Perhaps his unhappiness was linked to this to a great degree. As if it wasn't bad enough to be humiliated outside, he was also constantly humiliated by his own father at home.

The headmistress shook her head as I remained silent.

"My boy, if you're going to a vocational high school there's no need to go to a prestigious middle school. Perhaps choosing an easy school would suit you. What do you think?"

In fact, what the headmistress meant was this: "You're stupid, it's not possible for you to succeed in prestigious schools. Select an easy school and easily get a diploma."

It would have been really nice to have said: "Damn all schools, teachers and especially headmistresses" while slamming the door on the way out, but as always I controlled myself, as if I did that they would think I was mad as well as stupid and perhaps they would sack my uncle. Everything would be blamed on me. I wanted to leave the school as soon as possible. Even seconds seemed long.

When I returned to the class the lesson had begun. I knocked on the door and went in. When the music teacher saw me she smiled. I wanted to explain I was late because I had been in the headmistress's office. The music teacher was still smiling.

"Come here, Ali Kemal, to my side."

I thought she was going to ask me about the notes from the previous lesson. My back was sweating. It was easy to memorise the notes, but when I started saying: "do, re, mi," my classmates mimicked my accent and laughed.

"I congratulate you. When they explained how you had put your life in danger to rescue a kitten tears came to my eyes."

In order to see whether the teacher was sincere I looked her in the eye. She was sincere and definitely wasn't taking the mickey. She couldn't yet have heard I was being kicked out of school.

"It was not something everyone could have done."

Levent, without raising his head, said: "Miss, I thought the same thing. We call him a yokel, but he climbed up the tree like a monkey."

The music teacher turned towards Levent.

"Levent, even if you're joking, you shouldn't speak to your friend like that."

"Miss, heroes are always alone, do you know that?"

"Levent, that's enough!"

"For this reason Keko is not our friend."

At night I was creating more and more fantasies about Levent. In one, I had encountered Levent on a piece of waste ground. There was no one else there. I gave him such a hiding that I felt relieved as though it had really happened. Sometimes I would hit him, arms and legs flailing. Sometimes I knocked him unconscious with one blow and then jumped on his prostrate body for minutes at a time. He was bigger than me, but I was still sure I would beat him more easily than a small boy.

Aycan looked at Levent with a mocking look on her face and said:

"Levent, are you still in the same place?"

"Eh, what's up?"

"Do you know, you're like a broken record."

"And you should give up being this yokel's bodyguard."

The music teacher stood up and rapped her ruler on the desk.

"Silence! You can discuss this outside the class."

The class fell silent. Aycan and Levent continued to look daggers at each other for a while.

While the teacher sang the song she had taught us the previous week, she walked between the rows of desks:

'I drank milk, my tongue was burnt, oh, oh

It spilt and the rug was burnt, oh, oh

I am not on the rug, oh, oh

My rose in my garden burned oh, oh'

Then we began to repeat the notes along with the teacher.

"La, la, sol, do, re, re, re…"

The lesson ended. The teacher picked up her bag and left the classroom. I felt like going out to get some fresh air. As I put my books in my bag I heard Levent whistle.

"Psssstt!"

At first I ignored him.

"Hey, yokel, I'm talking to you."

I didn't know how to answer. He continued.

"While listening to the song did you think of the yellow cow? Did you remember how five times a day you used to milk your sister, sorry, your cow, before you came here?"

I thought of my grandfather.

"When someone tries to annoy you, don't show your anger. The best response to him is to take no notice and be as calm as possible. If he understands you are angry he will realise he has achieved his goal."

As I put my book in my bag I straightened up calmly. Trying to suppress the anger rising inside me I went up to Levent. As I approached him I sensed his fear. Frightening him increased my self-confidence. He thought I was going to attack him, but he was mistaken.

"You're very ignorant. You know nothing about even the simplest things. Cows are milked twice a day, not five times. And in general women do it."

Without waiting for an answer I turned and walked slowly out of the classroom. Levent didn't reply. Now I was sure he was scared of me. He had realised I would beat him if we came to blows. That was why he was tense when insulting me.

I went into the woods behind the school. I didn't care about leaving the school, it was only the thought of not seeing Aycan again that pained me. It was no longer the end of the world not to study, it was not being able to see Aycan again. When I was sure there was no one around I punched the trunk of a tree as hard as

I could. It was as if my fingers were broken. While I blew on my fingers I looked up and my eyes met those of teacher Hayrettin who was watching me from a window on the second floor. He nodded to me and I returned the greeting with a smile. There was nothing to be done. Everyone would go their own way. The good ones like Hayrettin Hodja were not sufficient to counter the many bad ones.

When I got home my aunt was in the kitchen. She was about to prepare pickles. My grandfather was craving the village cabbage pickle and my aunt had rolled up her sleeves. When she said my grandfather had gone to the market to buy cabbage, I put down my bag, saying: "I will go and take them from him," and went out.

My grandfather had bought two cabbages and some fruit and had stopped and was looking around. I ran up to him.

He was pleased to see me. "Come here, Keko. I was wondering how I would get these home. Hold one end of these!"

"I won't, granddad."

"Why not?"

"Leave them, granddad, I will carry the lot."

"No way! Do as I say."

I shrugged my shoulders. "It's up to you, granddad. In that case, I'll sit down and you carry them."

He laughed in a way I really liked.

"Either I'll carry them by myself or you'll carry them. I don't like two people carrying them."

After we had brought back the cabbages, I began to help my aunt with making the pickles. When we had finished she got up to make my grandfather a coffee. He said: "Today I'm going to drink coffee with Keko. Make one for him, too." My aunt had understood why. She nodded and smiled.

"Of course, dad. I hadn't suggested it as I know you think children shouldn't drink coffee."

My grandfather raised a finger and said: "Of course children shouldn't drink coffee, but Keko did a great thing today, so he will drink coffee like a grown up."

Chapter Twelve

A TRICK OF FATE

Every morning I went to school thinking "Today is the last", but somehow the news I was waiting for just didn't come. When would they call me and say: "Right, off you go,"? If it had been up to me I wouldn't have gone to school at all, but my uncle insisted. "They took you on a scholarship. It would be disrespectful to leave before they tell you to go."

In fact, my uncle wanted me to be removed from school as soon as possible. When we returned to the village he would be king again. As soon as my grandfather was on the bus my uncle would remind my aunt who he was. Then it would be Tahir's turn. He would learn what it meant to oppose his father. I knew that my grandfather really missed Heredile, but he would not leave either my aunt or Tahir to my uncle's tender mercies.

There was to be a run in our PE class. We were to run around the school three times.

In the changing room Levent was as usual trying to demoralise me by drawing attention to me with his jokes.

"Keko, I hear there is a family of lizards on the roof. Shoot up there and let's see how many there are."

At such moments my hands tightened into fists beyond my control and moved towards Levent. I tried to calm myself down by hitting my fists softly against my legs. Having to put up with his stupid jokes was painful. If I stayed much longer at the school I would not be able to control myself. I needed to leave without getting in a fight. As for Levent, he was doing his utmost to pick a fight.

As we went out of the changing room he confronted me.

"Chicken! You're a chicken!"

To stop me going out of the door he leaned on the doorframe and smirked at me. I stopped and without replying to him pondered what to do. There could not be a better opportunity to plant one on his nose.

Just at that moment Hayrettin Hodja came in.

"Boys, are you still not ready?"

Levent answered the teacher without taking his eyes off me.

"We're ready sir, but some of our classmates don't know how to put on shorts."

Hayrettin Hodja turned and looked at us. Levent was still in the same position.

"Because they're used to wearing baggy trousers."

Hayrettin Hodja came over and grabbed Levent's wrist, separating it from the doorframe. He then indicated that I should leave.

"I don't want you to disrupt the lesson. You know I'm going to take an important decision. It'll be good if you stop squabbling like nursery school children."

Levent was not wary of any of the teachers. So he didn't care about Hayrettin Hodja's warnings. When I went into the hall, the girls were already lined up. Aycan looked at me and smiled. I smiled shyly back. The others came behind Hayrettin Hodja. We lined up, the boys facing the girls.

The teacher raised his hand and called for silence.

"First the girls will run. You will run around the school three times on the track."

Everyone was ready. For me it was the first time, but the others had done it before.

"Ready, steady, go!"

As soon as he blew the whistle nine girls shot off. Hayrettin Hodja was watching them. Then he turned to us.

"In today's race you are more important for me. We still haven't selected the players for the school football team. This race will help my evaluation. So I want you to be careful and not to waste this opportunity."

When I heard the word football my heart missed a beat. There was a bittersweet excitement inside me that I could not suppress. How I had convinced myself as I left the village that I would play football in Istanbul. As soon as I arrived I intended to tell my uncle to take me to the Beşiktaş youth team. Then I was to train day and night and make progress. If Beşiktaş had been too far I could have gone to Fenerbahçe. But I definitely had to play for Beşiktaş. The whole of Turkey, even the world, would hear my name.

"Ali Kemal Karadağ! Beşiktaş's most successful goal scorer!"

The girls came in one after the other and wrote their names on the list.

When the boys lined up, Levent's arrogant smiles were still aimed at me. When teacher Hayrettin blew his whistle we all went off together. Levent was leading the way. Behind him were Berk and Okan, and behind them, me. As we began the second lap I was running alongside Levent. It would not have been that difficult for me to win the race, but it had little meaning. In all probability Levent was going to win the race, as he had apparently grown up in a sports club. He had received special tuition in many disciplines, such as long jump, gymnastics, basketball, volleyball and karate. He had achieved success and was registered with various clubs. He had lots of cups at home.

As I ran I thought of Bera. The races I'd run with him in the village were such fun. He had never learned to race with me. For him it was a greater pleasure to run alongside me than pass me. Most of the time I ran as hard as I could and tried to pass him to get him into the mood for a race, but he would easily catch me up.

For a moment it wasn't Levent alongside me, but Bera, and I forgot Istanbul and the Ilim College that didn't accept me and began to run. Saying: "Come on, Bera!" to myself, I ran as fast as I could. I don't remember when I left Levent behind, but at that moment as I imagined running with Bera I felt the anger that had built up inside me ever since arriving in Istanbul dribbling out. Why hadn't I run at previous moments when I had been driven mad by anger and when I couldn't sleep at nights? When I saw the teacher raise his hand at the finishing line I wasn't immediately able to stop. I passed him and sat down under the trees. Aycan and Sude came over.

Sude looked surprised.

"What was that, yaah!"

While we were talking, Levent crossed the finishing line. Selim and Murat looked at each other, laughing. Levent kicked at a stone in anger and spat. Murat said: "Hey man, what are you doing? There's a first for everything."

That day I broke Levent's record. No one had thought it possible that I could finish in front of Levent, who was being specially prepared for the Olympics and had been to America for that purpose. Hayrettin Hodja smiled and put his arm on my shoulder.

"I will definitely put you in the team."

It was nice to hear that even if I wouldn't be able to play. Hayrettin Hodja must have forgotten I'd been expelled.

Levent was nowhere to be seen. The noise that jarred on my ear had also gone.

I overheard people saying he had left without permission. I ignored it as if I wasn't interested, but it was really comforting to know he wasn't in the school. Taking deep breaths I headed for the changing room.

That afternoon there was a trial match for team selection. Being selected for the team was not important for me as I was returning to the village, but it would be wonderful to play a match with a real football before I went.

There were boys from four classes, including ours. I didn't take any notice of them so as not to show my excitement. They were talking amongst themselves.

"Let's have Sedat and Kadir."

"You control the midfield, that'll be enough."

"Don't trust Cem too much. He gives up easily."

"This time we'll be in the team."

"We'll show them what teamwork is."

As far as I could make out they had split up into three groups. They wanted to get into the team as a group, not as good players.

When Hayrettin Hodja arrived they fell silent. Some of them couldn't keep still. They were doing warm-up exercises like running on the spot.

With the sound of the whistle we all started running. After two laps we went on to obstacles. Hayrettin Hodja and trainer Necdet, who I was seeing for the first time, were earnestly taking notes, and sometimes talking amongst themselves. Then they stopped. They had noticed Levent's absence. Hayrettin Hodja was angry, but Necdet was tense.

"As he's not here we'll do the selection without him."

"But you know what the school administration is like. If it was up to me I would agree with you, but…"

We waited for two hours for Levent to be collected from home. He behaved as if nothing had happened and didn't look in my direction. I was doing my utmost to avoid him. I didn't want to argue with him before the match.

As for him, he was taking out his anger at not being able to needle me on those around him. He was rude to everyone, including Hayrettin Hodja.

"When are we going to start the match?"

"Be patient like everybody else, Levent."

When Necdet came over and began to put us in groups of four, the tension increased further.

"Necdet, please don't separate me from my group."

"Necdet, let Ender stay with us."

Hayrettin Hodja was the one who had the final say in all disputes.

"Those who oppose Necdet will be left out. People who show a lack of harmony here will not be able to play as a team in big matches."

We played five-minute matches in groups of four. As I expected, no one passed to me. Once Murat was about to pass to me when from amongst the spectators Levent shouted: "Muraaat!"

"I pretended not to hear, but I didn't touch the ball once. We had a break and everyone went to the canteen. I went to the lounge as I didn't have any money. Then teacher Hayrettin came over holding a toasted cheese sandwich and an *ayran* in his hand. He offered them to me. I was so ashamed and my face went red right up to my ears.

"Sir, I don't feel hungry, otherwise I'd have got something."

"Don't object! After you've eaten come back to the lounge."

I was ravenous. As soon as teacher Hayrettin had left I ate the sandwich with relish. It was the first time I'd eaten anything at the school. And when I drank the *ayran* I began to feel stronger.

Before the second stage had begun there was a quarrel between Levent's group and boys in another class.

"You don't know anything about football!"

"Levent, I'm sorry for your father. He believes you will become a sportsman. I think you should tell him the truth."

"It's not that easy, not everyone with money can be a footballer, mate."

Burak, who always assisted Levent, pushed a boy called Sadık. Then Sadık and his friends got together and squared up to the others. I noticed that Levent withdrew when he realised they weren't going to get the upper hand. In this way in the fight that had been started by Levent, it was Burak, Ender and Alican who were roughed up. Levent wasn't even touched.

Hayrettin Hodja came over and broke up the fight. Burak and Alican were crying. Levent acted as if he'd had nothing to do with it. Burak left the selections in tears. No one took any interest in him.

It was the last match. I think teacher Hayrettin deliberately put me in a team with boys from another class. I scored three goals and surprised everybody.

"Look at the villager!"

"I told you he was a monkey, guys, but you didn't believe me."

"He's a bumpkin, but he's a good player."

"He's got a good shot on him!"

Levent and his gang were trying to demoralise me and undermine my performance, but as I scored the goals it was as if I was above the clouds.

We were all really tired and dripping with sweat. Barış from the opposing team came over.

"Ali Kemal, you're a really good player. Where did you learn?"

I shrugged my shoulders. I was worried that they would laugh when I said: "I learned in the village", but for the first time it was a friendly conversation. I didn't want to let it slip. "I learned, playing with friends…"

"You're very talented. In my opinion the teacher should pick you."

I again shrugged my shoulders. I was acting as if it wasn't important. At the end of the day I was really happy to have shown them I could play. What else could I wish for? At that moment those trials and the team to be selected were the most important things in the world. If an angel had descended from the heavens and said: "you will be selected for the team, play just one match and no one will humiliate you," I could willingly have given up five years of my life.

The 'Wow!' sound that rose from those watching when I scored the first goal was still in my ears as I trudged towards the dressing room. Levent had been shown a red card twice. In the changing room the boys in the other class surrounded me.

"Hey Keko, don't forget to pass to me!"

"You've got a great shot on you, mate."

Had someone called me 'mate'? No, I shouldn't get carried away. It wasn't possible for someone in this school to call me 'mate'.

"You were running like the wind, yaah!"

"What wind, more like a hurricane!"

If Bera heard that, who knew how pleased he would be?

Levent came towards me holding the ends of the towel on his shoulder. He looked at me as if he was going to spit in my face. Then he began to taunt me in a sarcastic tone.

"Of course, every bad thing has a good side. Being a villager is something like that, isn't it, Keko?"

I tried not to take any notice, as usual, but he went on.

"Lots of sun, fresh air… In time you turn into a monkey. It's normal for a monkey to be faster than a human."

The boys in the other class seemed to be surprised.

"Keko?"

"What do you mean, villager? What villager?"

"Haa… You don't know. Our friend Keko is a real yokel. And from the lowest end of the village."

Sadık was not happy with Levent's sarcastic comments.

"I think you should think of yourself, not Ali Kemal."

"He's right, you were very slow, Levent."

Levent had started snorting.

"In my opinion you should find another excuse for your failure. This is not convincing."

Levent suddenly lost control. He threw the towel off his

shoulder and punched Sadık hard in the face. Sadık staggered and fell. As Levent moved forward to continue his assault he bumped into me. The genie was out of the bottle. I couldn't allow him to attack someone else on my account.

"Don't bring others into your problem with me. Look, I'm here."

He was looking at me in such an evil way it was as if he would have tried to kill me if he'd had the chance. But he couldn't pluck up the courage to attack me. I felt I had started out on a road of no return.

Hayrettin Hodja came in and stopped when he saw Sadık lying on the floor, bleeding.

"What's happened again? Aren't I able to leave you alone for a minute?"

This time no one defended Levent. Sadık was the headmistress's nephew. His father was an inspector at the Ministry of National Education and his mother was a lecturer.

As I returned home in the service vehicle I relived the matches we had played, second by second. The roar of "Goal!" when I scored the first goal was still in my ears. My uncle had noticed the difference in me.

"What's up, why are you grinning like that?"

"Me?"

"No, me!"

"Nothing."

"Don't I know you? Both you and Tahir. I know your number. Don't try to hide it from me. I'm a good judge of character. I'm also the man, but no one appreciates me."

I hadn't understood what my uncle meant.

"Ah, I understand, you're happy because you're leaving school, aren't you? Of course it's been difficult. You haven't got the guts. You haven't got the brains, you can only work in a mill."

"No, uncle, it's not like that."

"I'm just wasting my breath! If only I was in the village working at that mill. I would have revived it if my cruel father hadn't driven me away. I wouldn't have been alone in exile. Fate is cruel."

My uncle blew his nose and started to cry. Sometimes he cried like this when he listened to Müslüm Gürses. He always said he had suffered an injustice and that a small mistake had been blown out of all proportion, but he seemed to avoid explaining what that small mistake was.

"Is it a crime to fall in love? Is it a crime to love someone? What did I do? What happened? Should someone be driven away from the place he was born? You wouldn't do that to your stepson. My own father kicked me out like a dog. If my father heard I had died he would celebrate."

My uncle was both crying and shouting curses about my grandfather. Previously this had frightened me, but by now I was used to it.

"Ah, ah! Heredile dogs! You tore my heart out, you godless ones!"

I was not in a state to take any notice of my uncle. I felt pleasantly tired. I had shown them that a village boy could be a good footballer. When I went to school the next day Levent came over to me as if nothing had happened and said: "Don't get spoiled. If I'd wanted to I'd have passed you. I felt sorry for you as you were wandering about sorrowfully."

I took my books out of my bag and put them on my desk without speaking. When he saw I wasn't answering he went back to his place. I restrained myself from shouting at him with difficulty. My God, one day grant me the opportunity to give him a good hiding.

The first lesson was English. A short story was to be read. Levent whispered something in Selim's ear. After Selim had nodded he said: "Sir, let Keko read it."

While I read it they would laugh and make fun of me. There was no escape, but still, I tensed all my nerves so as not to give myself away.

The teacher nodded as if he agreed and turned to Selim.

"It's not a bad idea, Selim, but you look keener. Today you will read."

Selim looked as if he regretted what he had done, but he didn't object.

At the end of the lesson the English teacher called me over and said: "Bring your workbook, Ali Kemal." He indicated three passages and said: "Work on these, I'll get you to read them out," then left the classroom.

Why didn't the headmistress call me and tell me: "You don't need to come any more."? Why were they delaying things if I wasn't going to continue at the school? And how was I to work at English by myself? I didn't understand anything. Nearly everyone had left the classroom. I was sitting at my desk pondering my gloomy situation. The door opened and Aycan came in. As soon as I saw her my heart started beating faster. It was always like this. My heart would beat faster and my face would redden up to and including my ears. Again my face was hot. I pretended to look for something in my bag so as not to show it. She came over and sat next to me. I took no notice and continued my search. Why had she sat down next to me? My cheeks were on fire. In the village they would say: "You're like a girl", to men whose cheeks reddened. A faint scent of eau de cologne wafted over from Aycan's direction. I raised my head as if I had just noticed her presence.

"I heard the teacher, Ali Kemal."

"Yes?"

"If you like, I can help."

As if I had forgotten the teacher, I said: "On what subject?"

"With the English lesson."

"Ah, why bother?"

"I want to help you. You need help. That's right, isn't it?"

"Who, me?"

"Yes, you."

Just at that moment, I remembered something my grandfather had said.

"If someone tells the person he loves a lie, be sure he will tell everyone lies."

But again, I couldn't say to Aycan: "I don't understand most of the lessons. I read them like an idiot, but answer most of them wrong."

"Anyway, I'll soon be leaving this school."

"Why?"

"Because I broke the rules."

For the first time we had spoken this much. The subject was terrible, but it was wonderful to sit next to her and hear her voice so close and to sense her perfume. Moreover, I was sharing a secret with her.

"But that's unfair."

I said: "I'm pleased," as if I was unaffected by being with her and left the class without waiting for her answer, sniffing at her excited glances. Although in reality at that moment my heart was beating so fast it was almost coming out of my chest. My biggest fear was that if she understood I ached for her she would tell her friends that: "The stupid villager instantly fell in love with me."

Everyone was in the garden, the corridors were completely empty. I only just managed to stop myself from jumping with joy. Aycan was worried about me. What could be better than that? To feel that she thought about me, if only for a second, was enough to make me happy for days. She liked me. Perhaps I was exaggerating a little, as there was no reason for her to like me. At the end of the day I was a confused, unsuccessful Kurdish village boy. But to imagine that, especially to think that I might be her sweetheart one day, was fantastic.

In my imagination, Aycan was to be my only sweetheart throughout my life. I had sworn this to myself. Even if I married ten times, she was going to be my real sweetheart.

On the way home I didn't speak. I appeared to be listening to what my uncle said, but none of it remained in my mind. I always felt relieved to be going home. At the end of a day spent with city children it was pleasant to go back to the house and be with my own people. But on that day it was as if I didn't want to enter the house. Now school meant Aycan. To leave school meant to leave Aycan. So what was to happen when I left school? Thinking that after leaving the school I wouldn't be able to see her again made me want to cry and shout to the sky. How would I bear being without Aycan? What would my darling, who resembled a fairy godmother in fairy stories, do if she knew how much in love with her I was? She had such a bewitching beauty. When I recalled the meaningful glances between her and Levent, it tore my heart out. No way did Levent deserve her. And they didn't suit each other. While Levent was coarse and mean, she was elegant, graceful and good. Aycan was the most beautiful girl in the world. I loved the most beautiful, nicest, most intelligent girl in the world.

My grandfather sensed something strange.

"What's up, Keko?"

"Nothing, granddad."

"Nothing?"

My voice began to tremble.

I feared that if I hugged my grandfather and cried, then told him what had happened, he would say he had come here for my uncle and that my problems were endless.

"What can happen, granddad?"

"Keko, did someone say something to you?"

It seemed that the tears welling up in my eyes were concerning my grandfather.

"What if they say something, Granddad?"

"What does anyone have the right to say to you, my son?"

Separating from Aycan was worse than everything.

"Keko, has someone said something about you being Kurdish again?"

I shook my head.

My uncle took advantage of the situation to butt in.

"I hope you're not going to cause more trouble at school at the last moment."

I hadn't caused trouble, but trouble had come and found me. Levent was the biggest trouble. The most beautiful thing was Aycan. My whole life was a mess. First my dreams had crumbled, then I had lost control of my life. When I returned it would not be possible for me to be the same as before. How was I to explain this to my fiancée, Hatun? She would not want to believe that I could not love another girl until the end of my life.

It was not for nothing that they said in Heredile that love ruined a man. So was I slowly being ruined? I was obsessed with Aycan. Could a man think so much about women? Why should an honourable man become involved in an unrequited love?

My uncle butted in again. I didn't hear him. He prodded my arm and repeated his question.

"I'm talking to you. Hayrettin Hodja said about you 'Your nephew is really good'. I didn't understand what he meant."

"If only you'd asked the teacher instead of pressurising the boy."

My uncle looked daggers at my aunt.

"Should I have been disrespectful? I said: 'Thanks to you, sir.'"

What could Hayrettin Hodja have been referring to?

"Tell us, nephew. As Hayrettin Hodja said you were good you must have done something."

"I don't know. The trials took place."

"The trials? Ah, for the school team. They hold them every year. But it's Cevdet Bey and the headmistress who really make the decisions in that school. Even if that's why Hayrettin Hodja said what he did, don't get your hopes up. If they've decided to expel you, even if the teacher wants he can't do anything."

"Anyway, I don't want that school. Even if they tell me to stay, I won't."

Tahir was listening to us and smiling. My uncle shook his head.

"I thought you were smarter than Tahir, but you take after him. You're as thick as two short planks."

My grandfather glared at my uncle and he fell silent. While my uncle topped up my grandfather's tea, my grandfather turned to Tahir and said: "Tahir, come and sit next to me."

Tahir got up and sat down next to my grandfather. In the evenings, my grandfather would get Tahir to read the old newspapers he had brought from the tea house. Tahir would first read out the headlines. My grandfather would think for a couple of seconds, then, if he indicated with his hand that he wanted Tahir to continue reading, Tahir would read out the details of the story. If my grandfather indicated 'pass', Tahir would move on to another headline.

My grandfather would listen carefully to every news item, from time to time shaking his head meaningfully and occasionally muttering:

"What's the world coming to?"

"May God let things end well."

"That's all we needed!"

"At the Presidency Cup match Mr Kenan Evren drew attention to the disaster in the Aegean."

"The baby-faced member of the bloody terror organisation."

When my grandfather heard the word 'organisation' he would become flustered. He knew that organisation meant those in the mountains. The number of those who had joined from Heredile was not small.

"Ah, stop! Read that one, let's hear what they have to say about the organisation."

On a few occasions I heard my grandfather pray for those in the mountains after he had performed his prayers, saying: "God, when will this end," in a tearful voice.

"All the leading members of Turkey's strongest terror organisation, MLSPB, were captured by the security forces. The members of the organisation clashed with the security forces, resisting for two and a half hours, but most of them were killed. Seven bodies, amongst them theoretician militants, were taken to the state hospital morgue.

Amongst those arrested is innocent-faced Meryem Çarıkçıoglu, who made innocent youths into terrorists by deceiving them…"

After such articles my grandfather would become preoccupied and at such moments would sometimes talk to himself.

"My God, when will this bloodshed end? How much longer will this oppression continue? Hey, owner of the universe, bring this to an end!"

I was curious about the organisation of the innocent-faced terrorist girl. I went over to my grandfather.

"Granddad, I thought there was no stronger gang than those in the mountains?"

My uncle suddenly flared up. "What are you saying? Those in the mountains etc. What's it got to do with you?"

My grandfather lifted his head and looked at my uncle. In general when the newspapers began to be read, Uncle Rahmi would go to his room, where he would smoke and wait until it was time to go to bed. For some reason he had stayed that day. If it hadn't been for my grandfather I could have suffered a beating like on the first day.

With my grandfather's glare, Uncle Rahmi left the room. When he had gone my grandfather sat Tahir and I opposite him. He did this when he was going to say something important. He would call us, get us to sit down opposite him and wait for a while without saying anything. We would be very curious about what he might say. Sometimes when we were about to say: "Come on Granddad!" he would say: "First learn to be patient. Then to listen. Open your ears. Prepare your minds." Then he would take off his hat, put it beside him, and start. He again did that. "You're children. In fact you're no longer children, you're young people. Keep your distance from things that might get you into trouble."

I had understood what my granddad meant. Tahir was not as knowledgeable on the subject of those in the mountains as me. For that reason he was curious about them.

"Granddad, who are those in the mountains?"

"If I live long enough I will explain to you, but now is not the time. And don't ask or think about them."

Tahir was really excited. He didn't want to wait. That night I had to explain to him. As he listened his eyes shone as if he was watching an action-packed American film.

"If only I had been born in the village and gone up to the mountains," he said.

"Why?"

"My father wouldn't be there. I'd have been a fighter."

* * *

The next day when I went into class my eyes met Aycan's. She smiled. I greeted her with a nod of the head. When the bell went for the first break she came over to me and sat down as she had the previous day, opening my bag and putting something inside it. Surprised, I looked at her. It was as if she didn't want anyone else to see. "Come on, let's go out in the garden," she said.

Was I going to go out into the garden with Aycan? I must have misunderstood. Aycan wanted to go out with me in the break. For a while I couldn't get up. I wanted to believe what I had heard. She was standing waiting for me.

"Oh, come on!"

I stood up straight away. I didn't want anyone to stop this moment. As we walked side by side along the corridor, we began to talk.

"I have read all the reading passages in the book onto cassettes. You can study by listening to them."

I could not have said to her: "We don't have a cassette player in the house". I also couldn't have said that when she came over to me my head had spun and that she had made me happy.

We went out into the garden and sat on benches around a wooden table. Every time I looked I immersed myself in her eyes that I was afraid I would get lost in.

"What happened, why are you silent?"

"Me?"

"It's as if you don't want to study and I'm forcing you to."

"Nooo…"

"Or are you angry?"

How could I be angry with her? When she took an interest in Levent or another boy it was like a knife going into me, but I could never be angry with her.

I didn't care about the class. Just to listen to Aycan's voice I needed to find a cassette player. When I told Tahir he said it was easy. He could ask his supervisor, but only bring it the next day.

"That's no good," I said. "Tomorrow will be too late. I have to study."

"I thought you were leaving school?"

I shrugged my shoulders.

"I don't want to disgrace myself at the last moment."

I went to the tea house with my grandfather. The uncle who ran it, Kamil, was very understanding.

"Of course, come and sit down over there. Listen as much as you like! May those in the tea house not listen to songs this evening."

I was alone with Aycan's voice in the small section separated by glass where Kamil did his accounts. I was experiencing my happiest moment in Istanbul. If I listened to Aycan's soft silky voice a million times I wouldn't be fed up. It was as if the hundreds of words I was hearing for the first time, and didn't know the meaning of, were entering my ears with Aycan's voice and penetrating my whole body.

"Once upon a time there was a little darling damsel, whom everybody loved that looked upon her, but her old granny loved her best of all, and didn't know what to give the dear child for love."

I had left the class and begun to roam around a primeval forest. Aycan was Little Red Riding Hood, Levent was the Wolf and I was the hunter who saved Little Red Riding Hood.

Was it possible for people to be made happy solely by fairy

tales? In those years it was as if I only survived by holding on to my fantasies. Consequently, my fantasies were my most pleasant realities.

When the tea house emptied my grandfather came over.

"Come on Keko, the tea house is closing."

"No way!" I shouted.

"Grandson, it's late."

"But I haven't finished my lesson."

Perhaps Aycan would ask for her cassettes back the next day. Maybe when she wasn't by my side I wouldn't be able to hear her voice again. Uncle Kamil turned to my grandfather and said: "Uncle Ali Kemal, this boy will study. Make sure he gets an education."

Kamil closed the tea house and carried the cassette player to our house. After my aunt had opened the door she went back to bed. As soon as my grandfather had gone to bed he fell asleep. I returned to Aycan.

I never tired of listening to her. It was so nice of her to prepare such a thing. I prayed that she wouldn't ask for the cassettes back. When I returned to the village I would take part of Aycan back with me. Listening to her voice I would keep her with me for a lifetime. No one would be able to take Aycan and this secret love away from me. When I heard the sound of a cock crowing far off, my eyelids slowly closed.

When I went into the classroom in the morning I was unable to contain myself. I was doing my utmost not to look at Aycan. I could see her feet and her skirt, but not her face. I was afraid she would hear the sound of my heart beating as she approached me. I sat down at my desk and began to play with my pen as if I was unaware of what was going on. She came right up to me. I didn't know what to say. I hurriedly took my books out of my bag. She sat down next to me. I acted as if I hadn't noticed her.

"Good morning."

"Ah, good morning."

For a moment we looked at each other. I immediately averted my eyes.

"What's up?"

"Nothing…"

"You look fed up."

"Nooo, it just seems like that to you."

"You look tired."

"I don't know."

"I understand. You're annoyed with me. You feel offended because I prepared cassettes for you."

I was alarmed. I was afraid she wouldn't want to talk to me again.

"No, why should I be annoyed? Where did you get that idea? You want to help. How nice. Could one be offended? No, that wouldn't befit me."

When she began to laugh I fell silent so as not to utter more nonsense.

"Anyway, so should I say the cassettes were useful?"

As if I had just remembered, I said: "Ah, the cassettes. No, I haven't listened to them yet, but I've glanced at the passages in the book."

She looked at me in a concerned way, as if to say "Why aren't you studying?" She thought it was necessary for me to work really hard, but she didn't know that however hard I worked it was not possible for me to succeed in that school. The fact I was top of the class in the village school meant nothing here. If I stayed there was no doubt I would go down in history as the weakest student ever to attend Ilim College.

When the teacher came in Aycan went to her desk. In order not to show my excitement I turned the pages of the book rapidly. Then I heard Levent's voice.

"Psstt!"

When he was going to say something to me he generally called out in that way. When I didn't reply he would whistle as if he was calling a dog. As he had whistled this meant he was about to say something.

"Keko, is it true?"

I was dying to jump on him and punch him until I broke his nose, punch him some more and finally head butt him and knock him out. I controlled myself.

"They say you have learned to read and write. Is it true?"

I pretended not to hear him, but I took it to heart. When laughing started I clenched my fists. Aycan was taking an interest in me because she felt sorry for me. I should keep away from her. Since she wouldn't love a half-wit like me, I shouldn't allow her to feel sorry for me. Her feeling sorry for me was worse than all the mickey-taking.

In my fantasy I swore at Levent in the middle of the class.

"Dirty bastard, if your father didn't have money you wouldn't amount to anything." After that I broke all the desks on Levent. Not being able to do any of these things was really frustrating.

"Levent, stop making the same wisecracks. And why do you keep mocking Ali Kemal?"

That was Selma's voice. She was a close friend of Aycan. Was she sorry for me, too?

"Do you want me to take the mickey out of you?"

"That's not funny. And you can't do that anyway."

"Look who's talking!"

"In my opinion your power only suffices for Ali Kemal."

That really hurt. In that way I was declared to be the weakest pupil in the class.

"What did I say to our friend Keko? I just wanted to congratulate him, didn't I?"

Suddenly Aycan spoke up.

"Yes, Levent, Have you congratulated Ali Kemal for winning the race? He finished it in front, you know. Ah, but of course, at that time you were shouting and bawling like a baby and running off."

"It's true, Keko broke Levent's record, didn't he?"

Levent fell silent.

"That's true. What will you do in this situation? For years you were the best."

"Or is that why you are angry with Keko?"

They had also realised that at every opportunity he made fun of me and even created opportunities most of the time.

Levent could not bear the fact that Aycan protected me. Like a crazy man he got up, went over towards her and slammed his hand down on the desk.

"Why do you protect this dirty villager every time?"

Until that moment I had not moved a muscle, as if the conversation was not about me, but feeling he was approaching her I couldn't wait, and turned. Aycan looked scared and was staring at Levent with her large eyes. His aggression had silenced the others. Even if I knew I was going to die I couldn't allow this.

At that moment there was at most two paces between Aycan and Levent. I got up, went over to them and moved between them. I was trying to appear calm and self-assured facing the anger and aggression of Levent. In a calm but determined tone I told Levent: "Leave her alone!"

"Whee! Look at the villager!"

Without saying a word I continued to look him in the eyes. He stepped back a pace.

"Chivalry, uh?"

I wanted to get him away from Aycan and break his face. The most suitable place for that was the area in front of the blackboard. I was still looking at him, challenging him, as if I had not been affected by his mockery.

They had sensed a fight was about to break out. The desks next to us emptied.

Murat went to the classroom door and shouted: "The corridor is clear!" This meant: "You can fight". There was now no going back for either of us. I clenched my fists.

Levent laughed angrily. "Fuck off! Do you think I'm going to fight with someone like you?" He turned round and walked away. What a sneaky character. I was just about to return to my place when he suddenly returned and attacked me. I wasn't expecting it and in a moment I was against the wall and doubled up by a punch in the stomach. I wasn't able to remember the rest. Years later Aycan explained:

"When you were bent double by the wall, Levent was shaking his head and swearing at you. Then in a moment you jumped up and got on top of him. Even when the teacher came you were pummelling him. A janitor and two teachers had a real struggle to take Levent away from you."

When I was sitting in the headmistress's office, looking at my bloodstained hands, I tried to recall what had happened. Then I realised that what I had feared had happened. This time I had really given Levent a good hiding. I felt really relieved, but knowing my uncle would lose his job was worrying mc.

Teacher Hayrettin arrived. He dressed my burst eyebrow and split lip. The headmistress was very angry.

"My boy, I gather that if they hadn't taken your classmate away from you, you would have killed him. What is this?"

I didn't answer. Whatever I said I knew they wouldn't forgive me. It was not necessary to apologise. The best thing to do was to accept the punishment and leave the school as soon as possible.

"Moreover, just as we were trying to enable you to remain at the school…"

I was startled. They were saying they were trying to enable me to stay at the school, but I had no idea about that. And why were such efforts being made? I didn't want to stay at the school. I looked at teacher Hayrettin. He nodded as if to say: "The headmistress is right."

I said: "I don't want to stay at this school." The headmistress got up and came over to me.

"What you're doing is disrespectful! Do you realise that? You have been given an opportunity. You are rejecting this blessing presented on a golden plate."

What was it that was being presented on a golden plate?

Didn't they realise they were assuaging their egos by taking a poor child on a scholarship? Nothing, including the school, now had any meaning for me. "Thank you, but I don't want it," I said, shrugging my shoulders. The headmistress and teacher Hayrettin looked at each other. The headmistress left the room. Teacher Hayrettin sat down opposite me.

"Ali Kemal, I have made great efforts in order for you to remain at the school. Or, more precisely, we have tried to persuade Cevdet Bey."

"Why sir? Why have you made such efforts?"

"I've selected you for the football team. I have high hopes for you. I told them you would make the school's name known. But if you beat up a privileged pupil our task will become more difficult, or impossible."

"Have you selected me for the team?"

"Yes."

I didn't know that either, but it wouldn't change anything now.

"I can't stay at the school, sir."

"Of course you'll stay."

My lip was very painful, but when I thought about how I had been selected for the football team I smiled. When I told them in the village no one would believe me. I would swear an oath. In Heredile nobody swore a false oath. Only to the soldiers could you swear falsely about those in the mountains. And you had to atone for it.

I was not convinced as regards staying at the school. I couldn't bear the daily mickey-taking, especially in front of Aycan.

"Sir, I didn't know about your efforts on my behalf. Thank you. Today…"

"You couldn't control yourself."

"No, I couldn't control myself."

"Never mind, you did well."

For a moment I couldn't believe what teacher Hayrettin had said. Even if it was a joke, a teacher had said: "You did well," to me for beating up Levent. As we looked at each other in surprise we started to laugh. When the headmistress came in we fell silent as if we had been caught red- handed.

"I gather it happened exactly as I thought, headmistress."

"How did it happen?"

"Apparently Levent threw the first punch."

The headmistress looked at Hayrettin Hodja without replying.

"No, no! It wasn't Ali Kemal. This is what I've heard from the pupils."

"Ehhh?"

"You can also ask them."

The headmistress laughed meaningfully. Then, in a half whisper, said: "What will this change, Hayrettin Hodja?"

Hayrettin Hodja shook his head, as if to say he didn't know. Then he turned his back on the headmistress and winked at me. Just then there was the sound of shouting outside.

"I want to see him! Who's this boy, I want to see him! How can my boy be beaten up in this school? Where were the teachers?"

The headmistress went outside agitatedly.

"Will you please listen to me, Sezgin Bey? Believe me, we have given the boy an appropriate punishment. He is being expelled."

"That is not enough, madam, not enough!"

The door opened and a heavily-built man of about 40 – 45 came in.

Hayrettin Bey got up and greeted the man.

"Welcome."

"The reason for my visit is not welcome or pleasant."

"Please sit down. Calm down, we will deal with it."

"Calm down? Don't talk nonsense, Hayrettin Bey! I said I want to see that boy immediately. Let's see who the animal was who beat up my son so badly he was hospitalised."

"The boy is not here. He also suffered."

I got out of the chair I was sitting in and walked towards Levent's father. I had taken out all my rage on Levent, I had hospitalised him and I was now at ease. What happened subsequently could not hurt me.

"I'm here," I said.

The man looked at me in amazement and frowned.

"What does this mean?"

Hayrettin Bey interjected.

"Ali Kemal, go to your class and don't interfere in the conversations of adults!"

"I'm the boy you're looking for."

"Who are you?"

"I'm the one who had a fight with your son, Levent."

The man looked at Hayrettin Hodja as if to say: "Is this true?"

"What is this boy saying? Did this kid beat up my son?"

Hayrettin Hodja was constantly trying to move me away from the man as if to prevent a possible attack.

"Sezgin Bey, please calm down!"

Sezgin Bey nodded as if to say he had understood and looked at us one by one.

"It is apparent that not one boy, but several, ganged up and beat up my son and you teachers turned a blind eye. You will be called to account for this."

At that moment I felt that Levent resembled his father and particularly that he had got his aggressiveness from him. It was as if there was an old Levent facing me. I was enjoying it. I had made both the son and the father angry. It was like beating up two Levents.

Hayrettin Bey was indicating with his eyes that I should sit down, but it looked like Sezgin Bey had no intention of letting me sit down.

"Come on, admit it! You ganged up on him, didn't you?"

"I don't know if there was anyone else apart from the two of us. I only remember the two of us."

"And the others?"

"The others watched."

Hayrettin Bey shook his head. The man looked first at me, then at Hayrettin Bey. Then he pointed at me and said:

"A puny kid like you couldn't get the better of Levent. I arranged fight classes for him. He would have you as a snack, so you must have tricked him."

Without meaning to I smiled. In fact he had played the trick. He had deceived me by pretending to go, then suddenly turning and descending on me.

"And now are you grinning?"

What could I say?

"There can't be cheating in fights."

"No cheating in fights? In real fights you get cheating."

"It would be shameful."

Hayrettin Bey couldn't help but smile. The man looked at Hayrettin Hodja as if to say: "What is this kid saying?"

"Sir, Ali Kemal comes from a village. As you know, traditions and customs are stronger there. I think he means: "If a man cheats in a fight it is shameful."

Sezgin Bey halted abruptly. There was a strange expression on his face. He looked at Hayrettin Bey, then at the headmistress.

"Or is this boy, that boy?"

Hayrettin Bey gulped.

"Which boy?"

He shook his head: "You're the boy that Cevdet Bey mentioned. Now it's clear."

The headmistress was flustered.

"No, no, believe me…"

"Yes, that boy is me," I said. Hayrettin Hodja and the head-mistress looked at each other as if they sensed what was going to happen. The man shouted:

"Look, look! The boy is admitting it."

"Sir, please stay calm."

"Now you'll see! Call the police! And straightaway!"

The headmistress and Hayrettin Hodja were doing their utmost to calm Sezgin Bey down, but he was very obstinate.

"Sezgin Bey, these things happen between boys. They're both young. It was an unfortunate incident. They went a bit too far, that's all."

Sezgin Bey was looking at me as if things were in a different dimension.

"They are very insidious. Look at him. How innocent he looks. If after that fight he can look so innocent he must be a good actor. Come on, admit it, you attacked him from behind, didn't you?"

His father was more horrible than Levent.

"No, attacking from behind is not on."

His voice was gradually getting louder.

"Tell me how the fight started!"

"He was shouting at Aycan, because of me. I told him to leave her alone. Then he punched me and I started to hit him."

"And then?"

"That's it."

The man came towards me as if he was going to hit me. I couldn't hit a man of that age, but I also couldn't allow Levent's father to hit me.

"You hospitalise my son, then you don't remember it, is that so?"

I didn't answer.

Hayrettin Bey looked at the headmistress as if asking for help.

She said: "We're throwing Ali Kemal out of the school. As you will appreciate this is a severe punishment."

"I said call the police. Of course he will be kicked out, but that is not enough."

The headmistress looked demoralised. Hayrettin Hodja interjected in a determined tone:

"We can't call the police, Sezgin Bey. The involvement in such a thing would be a slur on us."

The headmistress nodded as if to approve what Hayrettin Bey had said.

"Let him be expelled immediately! He will be expelled for what he did to my son. And everyone will know it."

"They're not expelling me, I'm going," I said and left the room.

When I entered the classroom, heads turned in my direction. The classroom was silent. Fortunately, Aycan was not there. I began to organise my bag. My uncle would probably lose his job.

Selma came over to me and asked if I was in pain. I shook my head. Where could Aycan have gone? I took my bag and left the classroom without looking back. I didn't know what expression I would see on their faces if I returned. As I walked swiftly along the corridor I felt teachers and pupils from other classes turn and look at me. I continued to walk as if I hadn't seen them. I was trying to make sure our eyes didn't meet.

"He maimed Levent."

"He really gave him a hiding!"

"He deserved it."

"How he hit him!"

In fact I was in pain. Behind the stern expression on my face was a Keko who was finding it hard to stop himself crying.

Leaving behind the magnificent iron gate, I began to walk into the breeze.

Chapter Thirteen

AH ISTANBUL!

I was wandering the streets of Istanbul, a city I was not at all familiar with. At the end of every street another street began. I looked up at the sky: I was heading east.

I didn't have any money in my pocket, but I felt relieved as if I'd come out of a mangle. Having a long walk was good. I was moving amongst thousands of people under high buildings. Behind some huge windows there were people eating meals and drinking tea and coffee. I felt embarrassed to look at them in case they understood I was hungry and thirsty. When it began to get dark I thought: it's time to go home.

My uncle's small *gecekondu* in the 19 May neighbourhood was waiting for me, but I didn't know how to get there.

The nursery we took the vehicle to every morning came to mind. If I went there I could meet my uncle. I didn't know how to get to the nursery, either. I continued walking, pondering what to do. It was as if the mannequins in the shop windows, all looking alike, were quietly following me. When I saw some blonde-haired dolls in a row in a shop window, I stopped. If my sisters in the village saw them they would adore them. When I saw a football, shin pads, football boots and shirts of various teams I felt strange. It must have been a sports shop. It was not befitting to look in a shop window like a cat looking at liver, so I hurriedly moved on. But it had been good, it had cleared my head.

I approached an elderly man and asked him: "Which way is the Ana Kucağı Yuvası?"

"Where's that my son? I've never heard of it."

No one I asked had heard of it. To find an address in Istanbul you needed to know the name of the neighbourhood and the street.

I was lost. In this crowded city I was like a grain of bulgur in a cooker. Wherever the bubbling sound took me, that was the way I went. Years later, when I understood that life was just like that, I recalled the day I had got lost for the first time in Istanbul. There was no point in fleeing the sound of bubbles. The point was to put out the fire under the saucepan. That was what was best for everyone. There was no alternative but to find the one who had set it alight and stop them.

A plump woman said: "There's a nursery on the next street. Perhaps they'll be able to help you."

I walked quickly in that direction. The nursery watchman had never heard of the nursery my uncle provided the service for. He must have understood my despair as he said "wait," and went inside. A short while later he came out and said: "They don't know it either."

It was gradually getting dark. I sat down on a bench by the shore and began to watch the sea. The sound of the gulls descending to the sea and then flying up again reminded me of lullabies. I was so tired that, had I allowed myself, I might have fallen into a deep sleep.

Just then a scruffy man with unkempt hair and a beard approached me.

"Hey, kid!"

His teeth were yellow and his eyes were sunk so deep into his eye sockets I couldn't see where he was looking. I turned my head.

"Have you got any money?"

"What, me?"

"No, me! Of course, you."

I found it strange that a grown man, however poor he was, should openly ask me for money.

"No."

Ignoring my answer he sat down next to me.

"You have, you have. Just check your pockets."

"Uncle, I said no!"

"Go on, just a few coins!"

I got up and walked quickly away, but he didn't seem to be giving up. He stood up and followed me. I began to run. He also began to run. Then, suddenly, a police car stopped right next to us. When the man saw the police he started to run away. As a policeman approached me he shouted at the man:

"Kahraman, you've lost it again!"

"Kahraman, you've taken shoes from the mosque again."

One of the policemen turned to me.

"Young fellow, what are you doing here? Why was he chasing you?"

"I was on my way home and got lost."

The policeman indicated that I should get in the vehicle and I didn't object. After my uncle's vehicle this was the second vehicle I had been in. I had never got in a car in the village. If my father had given permission, I would have got on a bus to go to the free scholarship exams with my teacher, and in Ankara we would have got in a taxi. In fact, if I counted the coach we had travelled in to Istanbul, this was the third vehicle I had been in. Coach, midi-bus and minibus; I had not yet been in a car. And I was curious about the municipal buses. After returning to the village, perhaps I would never see a vehicle again until I died.

By the time we got to the police station it was dark. Who knew how those at home were wondering about me. The superintendent looked like a nice, friendly man. For some reason I had always thought of the police as being similar to soldiers, just with different uniforms. However, the police in Istanbul were very different to the soldiers in Heredile. It was as big a difference as between villager and city dweller.

As the superintendent stirred his tea he said: "I gather you're lost." I nodded. He called out to a man standing to attention at the door:

"Bring him a tea! He's feeling cold."

To the policeman who brought the tea he said: "Take him home and hand him over to his family."

I only told them my uncle's name and surname and the name of the neighbourhood, I wasn't sure they would be able to find it. I noticed another thing. Like the superintendent, the policemen were very cheerful. They were nothing like soldiers. If I told those in the village that they had treated me to a tea at the police station, would they believe me? Keko apparently sat in a police station in Istanbul and drank a tea facing the superintendent. And the superintendent ordered the tea. Whoever heard that would say: "You're making it up. Aren't you ashamed to tell lies?"

When we got home my grandfather, uncle, aunt and Tahir were outside the front door. As soon as I got out of the vehicle my grandfather hugged me.

The police officer said to my uncle: "We found him on the shore."

Tahir nodded towards his father, indicating with his hand that I should be careful as: "He will kill you." I wasn't frightened. I knew my uncle by now. I could guess what he would do and when. We went in and my aunt immediately prepared dinner. They hadn't eaten while waiting for me. My uncle was very angry.

"Dad, it's not on! Without considering where he was from, he hospitalised the son of a factory owner. If the guy wants, he can crush us like a fly. Then he tells the headmistress: 'I don't want to study in your school.' Wouldn't you think: 'My uncle earns his bread here'?"

My grandfather didn't reply. As he didn't answer, my uncle's voice got louder. At one point he was nearly crying.

"I work day and night, Dad. Otherwise you can't survive in Istanbul."

My grandfather didn't reply. My uncle's voice gradually became more pitiful. Then he blew his nose and started to cry.

"And I've got nowhere else to go. Should I have begged on the streets of Istanbul?"

After my uncle had said this, he started sobbing. My grandfather raised his hand and said: "Enough, Rahmi! Don't be ungrateful for this blessing as we eat."

My uncle Rahmi fell silent. My aunt, Tahir and the girls were pleased to see me again. As for Uncle Rahmi, he wanted my grandfather to punish me, or even give the punishment duty to him.

In a strange way Uncle Rahmi resembled Levent. In fact he wasn't as bad as him. Both threw their weight about when faced with people weaker than them, while looking for a place to hide when things got difficult.

When the meal was over, my grandfather began the prayer of thanks, as always. But in this case he added sentences.

"Oh, God! May you give us the strength to forgive our loved ones, and them to forgive us. Grant us devotion and protect us from the traps of Satan."

"Amen," we all said together.

My aunt got up and brought in the tea. My grandfather sat on the couch and signalled to me. I quickly went over and sat next to him. Tahir was getting to like him more with every passing day. Whenever he called him over he ran to his side and when he was going to perform his prayers, Tahir would hold his towel for him. Whereas when he heard his father's voice he would scowl. It was as if Tahir was jealous of the deep relationship between my grandfather and I and his fondness for me. No grandchild could be as close to my grandfather as me.

"Explain!" he said in a loud voice. "Now you explain, grandson. What happened that you should go crazy?"

I was familiar with this voice of my grandfather. He was saying: "Tell me the truth of everything." There were very few things my grandfather wouldn't forgive. One of those was lies. Mistakes were possible and could be forgiven, but deceit was something else. God disliked it and so did His creatures. And lies in particular did not befit a Kurdish man, for he who said: "I am a Kurd," would be fearless and know how to stand up straight.

What could I tell my grandfather? In fact for me there was no bigger thing than me being in love with Aycan, but it was not possible for me to admit this.

"Granddad, they don't want me at school. And I don't want them."

"Did you come from the village because they asked for you?"

I stopped. What could I say?

"I don't know."

Of course I didn't know that they would not want me in Istanbul, look down on me and even attempt to beat me up. Why didn't my classmates like me? Well, they didn't like me, but what about the teachers? What had I done to them? How could I study at that school if they didn't want me?

Tahir butted in.

"If you're Kurdish, a villager and poor, of course they won't want you."

Uncle Rahmi got up as if he was going to hit Tahir, saying: "Don't say you're a Kurd just like that!"

My grandfather turned to my uncle. It was as if his eyes were on fire.

"There's no need for you to say you're a Kurd, Rahmi. There's no need for anyone to say it. Just as it's evident that you're a man, it's apparent that you're a Kurd."

"Dad, you always misunderstand me. I'm saying this so that they stay clear of trouble."

"Look at who's handing out advice!"

My uncle lowered his head. I understood that my grandfather was alluding to uncle Rahmi's mistake to do with his being thrown out of the village. I didn't know what that mistake was. All I knew was that Uncle Rahmi did not seem happy for us to be there.

Years later I learned that my uncle had made signs to both my aunt and another girl, leading to the girls getting a bad reputation. My grandfather paid a hefty bride price for my aunt to avoid bloodshed and sent my uncle to Istanbul. The other girl hanged herself in a barn and my grandfather banned the use of Uncle Rahmi's name in the house. Although my uncle sounded off about it behind my grandfather's back, it was obvious that he felt guilty in front of my grandfather and could not accept that he had been driven away from the place where he had been born.

After everyone had gone to bed I explained what had happened in detail to Tahir. The only thing I could not say was that I loved Aycan.

The next day I didn't go to school. My uncle was very irritable. Now the nursery director might cause problems.

When my uncle left my aunt prepared the breakfast spread again. She toasted bread on the stove and spread butter on it. There was molasses we had brought from the village. I had missed it and ate it with gusto. The girls were looking at me like a hero.

After breakfast I decided to go to the waste ground and play football. I began practising shooting with our punctured plastic ball. This was something we had taught each other when we played in the village. I don't know how long had passed when my aunt brought out some biscuits she had made. Meanwhile, neighbourhood boys had congregated around us. A boy with muddy, patched trousers came over and said:

"What's your name?"

"Keko."

"Mine's Haydar. Shall we have a match?"

We immediately sorted out teams. It was as if I had been born in that neighbourhood. I have never forgotten that day and that moment. The feeling of happiness I experienced on that small piece of waste ground has remained with me throughout my life.

All the boys from the neighbourhood were there. No one tried to oppress anyone else. Although we were competing against each other our joy, excitement and pride were undivided. I had forgotten that I was in Istanbul, that I had been expelled from school, that my uncle didn't want me and that my dreams would not be realised. This was a moment when for the first time since coming to Istanbul I was accepted for who I was.

When my uncle came home in the evening he was smiling. Looking like he wanted to win favour with my grandfather, he said: "Nephew, I have good news for you."

My uncle was going to give me good news!

"Congratulations! The headmistress summoned me and said: 'Rahmi, we will accept your nephew back at the school out of regard for you.'"

It was as if a needle had been sunk into my body. "I won't return!" I shouted.

Uncle Rahmi looked first at me then at my grandfather. Then he shouted angrily:

"What, what are you saying?"

"I can't study at that school. I can't go there again. I don't want to."

"You'll go. Such disrespect is not on. It's a big school."

I looked at my grandfather. His head was lowered, he was thoughtful. He wasn't saying anything.

"I don't want to, yah!"

My uncle again flared up like straw on fire. As if he had forgotten my grandfather he stamped his foot and shouted, frothing at the mouth: "What are you saying? Of course you'll return. I'll say, go back, and then you won't you go back?"

My aunt was also not as she had been before. Like me, she trusted my grandfather and was no longer frightened of the husband who had beaten her for years.

"Rahmi, tell us the truth of this matter. Why does the headmistress want him to return to school? Anyhow, when I go in to do cleaning she will tell me. Better for you to explain now."

My uncle turned to my aunt. There was a mischievous smile on Tahir's face. He was looking at his father as if to say; "You can't beat us anymore." My uncle took two steps towards my aunt, then stopped. He was like a big, confused child.

In fact, my uncle was someone to pity, not fear. He was like a tetchy cat, scratching at anything that treads on its foot, but at the same time, helpless. He said: "God damn you," and slammed the door on his way out.

My grandfather wanted me to go to school. Going to that school which rich children went to was perhaps a mistake, but there were state schools. The state allocated people to schools without discriminating. It educated everyone. I was also going to be amongst that everyone. Whatever I explained to my grandfather he would not change his mind. He accepted my leaving Ilim College, but I must go to a state school. I was so sure that whatever school I went to in Istanbul they would make fun of me and not accept me that I would have preferred to die rather than go to school.

A week had passed. I went to the local school with my grandfather. The headmaster sat my grandfather down facing him and called for coffee.

My grandfather said: "You're a civil servant, this school's headmaster, and I'm a citizen from a village. I've brought my grandson. I don't understand this enrolment business, but I want my grandson Keko to study here. Tell us the way to do it."

The grey-haired, smiling head looked like a good man. "Welcome granddad. Of course we'll enrol him. Would it do for us to give offence?"

On the one hand I was afraid, but on the other there was new hope growing inside me. Could this school be different to the other one? The headmaster looked different to the headmistress at Ilim College. When he heard the word villager there was not a disdainful look on his face. He even behaved in a respectful way to my grandfather, and smiled at me.

The headmaster asked my grandfather what the village produced. When he heard we had a mill his eyes sparkled. "The water flows so nicely at a mill."

"Where have you seen a mill, young man?"

The headmaster was from a village in Kırşehir province. There was also a mill in his village. In his childhood he had often gone to watch the wheels turn.

When my grandfather had finished his tea we got up. The head took us to the door. I had not been mistaken, this school was different.

"Don't worry, granddad, I will write and ask for the boy's registration to be sent here."

When we got home my aunt met us at the door. She was very pleased when she heard about the head's friendly reception. She didn't want us to go to the village. "Thanks be to God! Calm has come to our home," she would often repeat. What would she have done if she had heard Uncle Rahmi saying: "I don't know how much more I can take of my father," which he did on certain days.

Three days later we heard from the school. I got ready and went there with my grandfather.

The head looked thoughtful.

"Ali Kemal uncle, the registration looks difficult."

"Why young man, what's the excuse?"

"There is no excuse, uncle. Ilim College doesn't want to give up your grandson. Apparently he's been selected for the football team. Actually, if the parent wants they can take the child to the school they wish, but… the headmistress rang specially."

We came home. It was as if I was back to square one. I was annoyed when my grandfather said: "Every cloud has a silver lining. If you like, return."

"Granddad, how many times will I say, I don't want that school."

My grandfather was sniggering, which annoyed me. It was as if he was enjoying the fact I was being made fun of.

"Keko, if they don't want to let you leave the school, they must know something. You always liked playing football. Show them how you can play."

Even the idea of being with them, especially with Levent, in the same place, was driving me mad.

In the evening Uncle Rahmi came home. His attitude to me had changed.

"My lion nephew! Hamza told me. You destroyed them at the trials. Why didn't you tell me?"

Tahir was also excited.

"I wish I was at that school, too. What a lot of goals we would score together, wouldn't we? If it doesn't happen there, we'll set up a team in the neighbourhood. Is that not possible?"

He picked up a pen and paper. He had always dreamed of such a team, but his father had not allowed him to do it. Now my grandfather was here. I was here. We could establish a great team. The team we had in the village had excited him. He wanted to go to the village just to see the team, but his father would never take him. I had promised that we would go to the village together. We would go to the village and play a match every day.

They had slapped my uncle on the back and said: "Come on, bring your nephew back." And he had enjoyed their appreciation and was sure he could persuade me.

"Tomorrow morning we will set out early."

Once again what I feared had materialised.

"Uncle, I don't want to go to that school."

My uncle suddenly stood up and said:

"What do you mean, son? They told me to bring my nephew and I said: 'Your wish is my command'. How can I now say: 'I couldn't bring him'?"

My uncle was determined to take me in spite of my grandfather. He did not want to lose his job and it was obvious that he was proud I had been selected for the team.

The next morning I was back in the headmistress's office.

The headmistress looked me in the eyes and said: "Tell me, Ali Kemal, what are we going to do with you?" My old shyness had gone. "Don't do anything, Miss."

"Ali Kemal, what do you want?"

"To leave the school."

The headmistress looked at me and raised her eyebrows as if to say: "Is that right?"

"Now look!"

My grandfather had been proved right once more, but I didn't know how I could stay at the school. In an environment where whatever I did I drew attention to myself, how could I be comfortable?

"We don't want you to leave this school, Ali Kemal."

Without meaning to I said a little louder: "I don't want to stay."

"My boy, are you shouting?"

I lowered my head. The headmistress came over to me and raised my head by lifting my chin.

"I want you to promise me something."

"……"

"You won't fight anyone from now on."

"I can't promise, Miss. Someone may want to fight me and if I run away I'll be considered a coward."

The headmistress laughed involuntarily, then grew serious.

"So what shall we do?"

What could I say? The headmistress would not understand if I said it would be a torture for me to continue at the school. Just at that moment Hayrettin Hodja came in. He winked at me and sat down in one of the black leather armchairs.

The headmistress swivelled in her chair and, indicating me with her head, said:

"Ali Kemal doesn't want to remain here."

Teacher Hayrettin did not look surprised.

"If you will allow it, let us speak one to one for a while."

"To tell you the truth, I am really surprised. As you know, we persuaded Cevdet Bey with great difficulty. Even when we accept fee-paying pupils, we screen them. As for Ali Kemal, he is rejecting this chance we have offered him. I see this as greatly disrespectful."

Since I had started there, this was the sentence I had most often heard from the headmistress:

"You've been disrespectful, Ali Kemal!"

As Hayrettin Hodja got out of the armchair he nodded to me and we went out into the garden together. Some children who saw us together stopped their conversations and looked at us. They must have heard about the fight. When Hayrettin Hodja realised I was uncomfortable, he headed for the sports section. We went in and sat down. Hayrettin Hodja began to speak in a deep voice.

"When my father died I was only five. We had a small cottage on one side of town. The school was on the other side. I was such a puny little boy that it was impossible for me to walk that far. We didn't have a single coin to pay for the dolmuş, either. Winter was approaching and we hadn't even been able to buy wood to fill the stove. One morning my mother wrapped an old mattress tightly in a quilt and strapped it to her back. She took me by the hand and we left the house. We walked, but not a short distance, quite a long way. It was difficult to understand what my mother was thinking. She was a quiet, but brave woman. We came to a large road, then got in the back of a lorry and left our hometown on an icy night."

"Did you come to Istanbul in that lorry?"

"If only we had. We changed vehicle seven times before we got to Istanbul."

"How long did it take?"

"I still don't know. I mean, I don't remember. It was a very eventful journey. By the time we arrived in Istanbul it was as if we had been in a war. We were so hungry I cannot explain. As always we were broke. My mother rummaged through rubbish to find bread for me. I don't know how many days passed like that. Still when I recall those days my heart sinks. I feel sorry for my mother rather than myself."

"Then what happened?"

"Later my mother managed to find a job washing up in a restaurant. Every day I went to work with her, I didn't leave her side. My mother was happy, but the bosses didn't like me. There was no one at home to look after me. We slowly got used to it. Sometimes I dried the plates. Later we moved to another restaurant. When that closed my mother became an assistant chef in a bigger restaurant. I was still with her. Then when the chef left she replaced him. With the increase in pay, the first thing we did was move to a place only two streets away from the restaurant. She enrolled me in a school. I was a year younger than the other children, so would often get beaten. It was as if our entire existence was built on hardship. Time passed quickly. The first day I saw you I remembered little Hayrettin setting out for Istanbul holding his mother's hand."

I was really surprised. I wondered if there were other teachers like Hayrettin Hodja, who were from small towns and were poor, at Ilim College. I had thought that only the janitor, Hamza, might be from our region.

We fell silent. Teacher Hayrettin's eyes seemed to have filled with tears. Then he became serious.

"Look Keko! Now listen to me well!"

For the first time a teacher was calling me Keko.

"Life is more difficult than it appears for everyone."

I wanted to ask who was made fun of more than me at that school, but remained silent.

"Sir, I can't stay at this school."

"Because your friends here are different to your friends in the village."

"They are not my friends."

"Sometimes you have to be with people who are different to

you. You even become friends with them. Actually, this is not a very bad thing."

They were bad. They looked for opportunities to make fun of me. Furthermore, the teachers, the headmistress, everybody publicly blamed me; on every occasion they found the others in the right.

"I know. It's unfair on you. It annoys you, and, to be honest, it used to annoy me."

He suddenly started to laugh.

"You know, Keko, there is a nice thing that you are not aware of."

I looked at him in surprise.

"Life is like this. When you struggle and win against those who try to crush you and ostracise you, your power will increase. Every day you will get a bit stronger. If you throw in the towel, you will feel the pain of the defeat for the rest of your life."

"I can't be together with them."

"Don't you want to play football?"

What could I say? I couldn't say this was one of my biggest dreams since I was a small child. I took a deep breath. What was really causing me pain was not being able to see Aycan again.

"Think again, Ali Kemal. From now on everything can be different."

"How so?"

"Because I have great hopes for you."

Teacher Hayrettin had smiled at me from the first day.

"You could be a star."

"Me?"

"The football team needs a hare like you."

"Hare?"

"I'm looking for a player who can run like a hare. You are exactly the hare I am looking for."

Hare? I had never thought that one day I would be so pleased with the word hare.

"You're saying this."

"The others think like me, too."

I looked disbelievingly.

"Why do you think the headmistress is so insistent?"

But the headmistress had told me other things.

"Don't worry. When Cevdet Bey heard that the football team could do well in the inter high school matches he forgot everything else."

The school team needed me. It was difficult to believe this. It was a nice feeling. Even if Hayrettin Hodja hadn't said it to boost my pride, it had done so anyway. But I still didn't want to lose the relief that I felt on account of the idea of leaving the school.

"Sir, please don't insist. Even for football I can't stay at this school."

"Because…"

"Because it is very difficult for me to succeed in this school. Impossible, even."

"You're right. They're more successful than you because they all have private tuition. They also received good education at their previous schools."

"There you are, you know."

"And you're afraid of this. You beat Levent up once. If you do it again, your uncle will lose his job. If it wasn't for your uncle you might have tried a bit more to stay, wouldn't you?"

I had not thought like that. Yes, if my uncle hadn't been there, beating up Levent again would have been a great pleasure. I had no intention of putting up with Levent for my uncle's sake. And there was no way I could permit Aycan to see me being subdued by Levent again. I would rather die. I wanted to leave the school as soon as possible. I had given Levent a hiding, let Aycan remember me like that.

Just as I was about to get up, Hayrettin Hodja grabbed me by the arm and made me sit down again.

"There are things you don't know, Ali Kemal."

What could they be? If I stayed at that school any longer, the only thing they could do was put up a bust of me as a problem pupil. In everyone's eyes I was a villager and a bad-tempered aggressive boy. As if that wasn't enough, I had also become meek in the eyes of Aycan, which was the worst thing of all.

"Cevdet Bey believes that thanks to you we will make the school famous. From now on no one will touch you, you can be sure of that."

I shrugged my shoulders as if to demonstrate that I didn't believe it.

"I can give you a guarantee. I promise you. If the team is amongst the leading teams it will be an influential advert for the school. And it will also be good for you, for sure. You will demonstrate what Keko is capable of."

"Advert?"

"You run really well. You surprised us all in the trial match. If we work a bit, with some concerted training you could win us more than one match. And that could really enchant the school administration, that is, Cevdet Bey."

"The headmistress didn't say that."

"What did she say?"

"You heard her too."

"What?"

"That the school had done me a good turn and that I had been most disrespectful in not accepting it."

Hayrettin Hodja began to laugh.

"Bravo Ali Kemal! You are smarter than I thought. You understood the headmistress's attitude easily."

"No, I don't understand it."

"Don't expect the headmistress to tell you: 'The PE teacher has discovered a gem in you, and Cevdet Bey is pleased that the school therefore has a chance to win such a competition.' She thinks you might get too big for your boots if she said such a thing."

The headmistress had been unable to tell me the truth, for it did not suit her to say: "We threw you out of the school a day ago and now we are taking you back for our own benefit." I had to swallow this. The headmistress could not say anything that would shake her authority, even if it was true.

Istanbul was demanding unconditional obedience from me. What they called respect was obedience. Even my playing in the school team was tied to this. First I was to accept being a slave. I had been selected for a football team, which had been a dream of mine for years. Cevdet Bey, who had treated me like a street dog because I was a Kurd, wanted me to stay at the school. In fact he didn't want it, he was ordering it. For me to reject this wish was, of course, disrespectful. Even if they needed me, they would give the order.

I don't know why I capitulated. What was the real reason? To study? Aycan? Football? Or all of them?

Despite my teammates who didn't want to pass to me, it was great playing in the school team.

In the early days I had imagined playing in a competitive match on a big pitch with Levent in the opposing team. My teammates were constantly passing to me wherever the ball went. I was moving slowly towards Levent. The spectators were shouting "Goal, goal, goal." I hit a shot with all my might and the ball went like a missile towards Levent. And boooom! Levent with the ball in his lap was dragged all the way along the ground and into the net.

With a shout from Tamer from the garden our conversation was disrupted.

"Teacher!"

Hamza came in.

"Hodja, your pupils are waiting for you in the garden."

"What are they waiting for?"

"For you to look out of the window."

Teacher Hayrettin and I went over to the window. As soon as I saw those below I drew back.

Levent, Ersin, Tamer and the others were waiting for Hayrettin Hodja with their team shirts, balls, shin pads and football boots. I didn't want them to see me looking at them enviously.

Everyone had heard that I had joined the team unwillingly and that I had accepted with difficulty on the insistence of Hayrettin Hodja.

"Look at the villager, mate, apparently he doesn't want to be in the team."

"Hayrettin Hodja calls him a hare."

"It's appropriate, the guy really runs like a hare."

However much I hated the word villager, I loved the nickname hare to the same extent.

The next day I got in my uncle's service vehicle, my legs trying to go backwards. There was nothing to be done. They had got their way. I was still, if not as much as before, the village boy amongst them. But I had gained the nickname 'hare'.

In the words of teacher Hayrettin: "The team's lifesaver will be Keko the hare!"

Keko the hare!

Chapter Fourteen

GULISTAN IN ISTANBUL

Every month one letter, sometimes two, would arrive from the village. Their curiosity mixed with longing and our disappointment at not finding what we sought coalesced into one. Being a family was like this. Emotions were chasing each other. Even if we were apart physically, our hearts were as one. Wherever you went in the world, your past and your memories did not leave you. Even if sometimes they caused you to stumble, the way to become a human being in this world was through your loved ones. Perhaps it was Heredile, which I had fled without looking back, that I most loved in this world. My loyalty to Heredile, and to the love I felt inside me for Aycan, never waned.

In every letter we received from the village was the line: "Don't forget us", but in the letter that arrived that evening there was a surprise.

In addition to the yearning they had felt for years, longing for my grandfather had been added, a void which was not possible to fill. When I wasn't there it was clear. My grandmother would not let anyone sit in my grandfather's place next to the stove. That empty cushion remained there in the corner. It seems that death under the ground is easy, but real death is separation. Anyway, even if we were far away, their only consolation was to know we were alive. Everyone wished for nothing more than to kiss my grandfather's hands and for his benediction. May God grant long life to my grandfather, and may he enjoy seeing all his grandchildren. May stones not touch my feet and my mind stay clear. I should not allow myself to be tempted by Satan to allow the big city to change me. Whatever I was, I should stay that way. To become spoiled, brash or naughty did not befit a child of the clan. I was not to ruin my essence. And especially I should never ever disobey my grandfather. I should also respect all adults in the house (they meant Uncle Rahmi and my aunt).

My friends always asked after me. Celil had also written a letter. It was in the envelope. And Celil had also cautioned me to read that letter when I was alone.

For the first time there was a sentence about Uncle Rahmi. Although he was only indirectly mentioned, it pleased him so much that for ages there was a smile on his face and a vacant expression. He didn't speak, as if he feared breaking the spell.

I took Celil's letter and sat down on the couch excitedly. My aunt had made halva and while I ate it I read the letter.

My dear friend Keko.

I greet you and kiss you on both cheeks. I want to tell you about a match we played at school. There was a poem technique the teacher taught us? Acrostic. Do you remember? Words within a poem. Read the poem I have written below well. I have lots to say, but for the moment know this.

We played the match at night in the moonlight:

Acrostic poem:

Goals, I conceded three

Uttered constantly you did

Like, what do you want?

It was a yellow ball we played with

Sadly, it was punctured

The air escaped from it with a hiss when we kicked it

Anyhow, what did we have?

Now you're in Istanbul, don't get too excited

It was confusing for us all when you left

See, there's a gap in our team

Can we fill it?

Our national service awaits

Military duty we're waiting to do

In limbo

Not unhappy

Getting lost for words

The end will be bad

Our place you have forgotten

I'm not saying it just for the sake of it

Sad to say

Time is running out

A little is left

Night time, when the person you don't want to mention

Before you suddenly appears

Unsaid, but not impossible

Lastly, you won't be comfortable

Celil had written me a poem, using the acrostic technique, as he didn't want anyone to understand what he had written. I read the first word in every line from top to bottom and it read: "Gülistan is coming to Istanbul." What an absurd sentence. How was Gülistan coming to Istanbul and with whom? Why was she coming? And what would she do here? As Celil had written it secretly, it meant no one knew yet. Ah Gülistan! You always had a mad side. As my uncle said, if only Allah had created you as a man then your madness would not have stuck out like a sore thumb. I wondered what had happened. She had not been betrothed to Fevzi. Something had happened but we still didn't know it. For sure, they had not written about it so that my grandfather would not get upset. I was not able to think too much about it as I had enough on my plate.

I tried my hardest at my lessons. Sometimes Aycan would lend me her notes. In exams when she looked at me, seeing the worry on her face deflated me. I just wanted to be successful for her. I hated looking like a stupid boy in front of her, and wanted to beat myself.

When she came over to me during the breaks I would keep our conversations brief so that she didn't realise I was excited. Sometimes while she spoke I would suddenly return to the class as if I had forgotten something. I was afraid of dropping a clanger, of losing face before her or of wearying her.

In training sessions I was like the wind. I ran so fast that even other schools in the area began to talk about the speed of 'Keko the Hare'. For me even the slightest praise was worth as much as the Spoonmaker's Diamond, but I looked unaffected by such praise and appreciation as if that was the way it should be.

Levent had been in hospital with a severe case of 'flu, and was off school for ten days. While he was absent the other pupils began to treat me better. It was as if he had distanced everyone around me and prevented those who wanted to get closer. I knew that Levent had incited those who treated me badly, but this was not sufficient reason for me to forgive them. This time it was me ignoring their invitations to friendship. I continued to spend the breaks alone. Aycan, sometimes other girls and boys, came over on a pretext and tried to engage me in conversation.

When Aycan came my heart immediately started beating faster, but despite that I behaved the coldest towards her.

I was still the loneliest pupil in the school, but I was upright. Everyone was agreed that I preferred it this way. They were the only reason for this solitude, but they were not even aware of it.

I used to go mainly to the back garden. Most of the time I would have a text book with me.

When the bell rang for the third break, I was about to sit down under a tree when I heard a voice from behind the wall.

"Keko!"

Thinking someone was messing about I pretended not to hear.

"Hey Keko!"

I couldn't believe my ears, but that was her voice. I leapt onto the wall. I was not mistaken. The voice was Gülistan's, but she was nowhere to be seen.

"Keko, are you deaf? You've made me shout!"

It was her. After not seeing her for months she was scolding me as if we had only just parted.

"Gülistan, what are you doing here?"

"Nothing, I've missed you so I came here."

"Gülistan, what are you looking for here?"

"Didn't you get Celil's letter?"

"I got it, but I didn't believe it. How did they allow you to leave?"

"Forget all that. Since last night I've been on the streets. We got off the bus in the middle of the night. I've been wandering all day to find the school."

"So what will we do now?"

"You tell me."

"What do you want?"

"Idiot! What do I want? I'm starving."

The bell was about to ring. If I didn't return to class everyone would look for me. Gülistan gripped the ivy and climbed up the wall, then jumped into the school garden. I was afraid someone would see her.

"Gülistan, are you mad? You can't come into the school. It's forbidden."

"What are you saying? If I don't come into the school where will I hide?"

"Gülistan, there's nowhere to hide here. This is not the village school. It's dangerous."

"I will find me a place. Don't interfere. So it's dangerous, huh? The places I've come from, you think this school will frighten me?"

By the time I arrived in class the lesson had been underway for some time.

"Why are you so late, Ali Kemal?"

"I had an upset stomach, sir."

"Are you alright now?"

"I'm fine."

Throughout the lesson I thought about Gülistan. The door leading to the basement was locked. I had left her on the stairs and returned to the class. What if someone saw her? I didn't know what she would do.

When the bell rang Aycan immediately came over.

"You look strange. Are you alright?"

"I'm fine," I said as I hurried to the back garden.

There was no one in front of the basement door. It was still locked. I climbed up onto the wall and looked at the road. Gülistan was nowhere to be seen. Just as I was about to walk away she shouted loudly. She was on the other side of a window looking onto the heating boiler. I approached excitedly. She opened the window.

"Gülistan, how did you get in there?"

"Quick, bring me something to eat!"

"From where, how will I bring it?"

"Hurry up, Keko!"

I had loose change in my pocket that my grandfather had given me. I hurried to the canteen and bought a toasted sandwich. I wanted to buy *ayran* too, but I didn't have enough money. I ran back to the back garden. The headmistress was wandering around with teacher Açelya. They were looking at the empty fruit juice bottles strewn on the ground, complaining, and picking them up and throwing them in the bin.

I sat down on a bench as if I was going to eat my sandwich and waited for them to go. Before they had gone the bell rang. I wrapped the sandwich in paper, put it in my pocket and ran to class. This time I entered the classroom with the teacher. Aycan smiled and with a movement of her head asked 'How are you?' I smiled as if to say I was fine.

When the bell rang I was out of the classroom before the teacher.

Levent shouted behind me:

"Hare, what's up, where are you running? Have you found a carrot in the back garden?"

Gülistan was waiting in front of the window. As soon as she saw the sandwich she grabbed it and bit off half of it.

"Keko, you rogue, is this all you could bring? I'm dying of hunger, I tell you."

"That's all the money I had, Gülistan. There was none left."

She took a lira out of her pocket and gave it to me. "Get two more of those, and a water and an *ayran*."

I put the money in my pocket and ran back to class. I sat down at my desk. It was our last lesson. How was Gülistan to spend the night in that boiler house? How was I to get what she wanted? My uncle only just made it in time for the nursery service.

As soon as I left the classroom I dashed to the canteen. They had closed it. I went out into the garden.

My uncle had put the last pupil in the vehicle and was looking at me.

"If you'd been any later, I would have broken your bones."

The next day I got up early and prepared bread and olives for Gülistan. I also took an apple.

It was like a dream, but Gülistan had done what she'd said she'd do. She had come from the village to Istanbul. How had she got here? How was it that those in the village were not looking for her? How come news had not reached us yet? I didn't know the answer to any of these question. Who knows how she had passed the night in the boiler house?

As soon as I got out of the vehicle I went to the back garden before entering school. As I had guessed, Gülistan was still in the boiler house. When I said: "I've brought you these," she paid no attention at all.

"Imbecile! Do you think I've gone hungry until now?"

"Did you go out and find something to eat?"

"There was no need for me to go out."

I had to urgently find her a place and get her out of the school. Where could I take her? There was no option but to tell my aunt. It was not possible for her to stay another night in the school. While I was thinking about this, Erdem came into class.

"Hey folks, have you heard? A thief has been in the canteen."

"Did they take the safe?

"No, the thief apparently broke the door and got in. But they don't seem to have liked our canteen as they said: 'One or two biscuits are missing.' The headmistress didn't believe it. She suspects the canteen man's helper."

I felt as though I had been punched in the stomach. Gülistan recognised no boundaries. My God, if it became known that I had hidden my cousin at the school and that she had broken the door of the canteen and stolen food, they would remember me all my life as a thief.

I hadn't even noticed that Aycan had sat down next to me.

"Ali Kemal, for two days you've been very subdued."

Aycan was perhaps the last person I could tell, but when she put her hand on my shoulder, I said: "I have to find a place urgently."

"What place?"

"Never mind!"

The teacher came into class. As soon as he came in he said: "Those who have articles for the wall newspaper should bring them in." Aycan raised her hand straight away.

"Sir, I left the article I prepared in one of the books I was reading in the library. May I fetch it?"

"Of course, but don't be long."

"Could Ali Kemal help me? Looking inside all the books might take time."

We left the classroom together. I regretted telling her.

"Explain this thing properly."

We went down to the boiler house together. We passed along the corridors and came to the iron door. We went in and it was empty.

"She was here, but isn't now."

"Are you sure?"

"Yes."

Suddenly, Gülistan emerged from behind the boiler. Her face and hands were black. "Who's this girl?"

"Aycan, she's a classmate."

"What if she tells my uncle?"

"Gülistan, don't talk nonsense! You can't stay here."

"As if I'm enjoying staying with the mice. There's nowhere to go."

"You can come to us."

I got flustered. I turned to Aycan.

"To you? No way! Your mother and father?"

Gülistan was determined.

"Don't listen to him, tell me! Your house must be better than here."

"Look, listen to me."

Aycan's mother was looking for a cleaner. They had put an ad in the newspaper. Several people had enquired. Gülistan was to go to the house like one of those who had seen the ad. But first she had to get cleaned up.

I couldn't sleep that night thinking about what to do. Gülistan had to leave the school. I had given her the address, but it would be difficult for her to find. I couldn't do my homework, thinking "What if she gets lost or something happens to her?"

Just as I was dropping off to sleep I heard a sound. I looked out the window. In the pitch black Gülistan was signalling for me to open the door. I got up quietly and opened it. Everyone was asleep. Gülistan went to the bathroom. Just then my uncle got up. He was sure to be needing the toilet. I went into the bathroom. The two of us began to wait in the bathroom, holding our breath.

My uncle turned the locked door handle.

"Who's in there?"

"It's me, uncle."

"You've chosen a great time to go. Hurry up."

Gülistan pointed to my stomach. "Uncle, I've got a stomach ache, I can't come out straight away."

My uncle went out into the garden, muttering. When she heard him go outside she gestured for me to turn my back and sat on the toilet. She too obviously needed to relieve herself. Then she got up and whispered to me: "I have to wash, but there's no hot water."

"You can't wash now, anyway. Let's wait until morning."

Once we were sure my uncle had gone back to bed, we left the bathroom. We went to the room I shared with my grandfather. We prepared a concealed place under the bed my grandfather slept on and she immediately lay down. I returned to my bed.

In the morning my uncle called out to me.

"Uncle, I don't feel at all well."

"What's wrong?"

"I have a stomach ache. I can't go to school today."

My uncle grumbled and got dressed. My aunt was going to the headmistress's house. They left together. The girls were at school. My grandfather had woken up and was listening to the news on the radio. Every once in a while I looked at Gülistan. She had woken up. She couldn't emerge from under the bed. She gestured to me to heat up water.

I went into the kitchen and put water on the stove. Tahir woke up and hurried out. He was late for work. Only my grandfather was left in the house. When he went to the bathroom, Gülistan came out from under the bed and went to my aunt's room. When my grandfather came back I took the water to the bathroom and told Gülistan. She had already found suitable clothes in my aunt's wardrobe. She went into the bathroom with a towel. While she was in the bathroom I hid in my aunt's room so that my grandfather would think I was in the bathroom.

In no time she had freshened up and got dressed. She was ready to go to Aycan's house. I didn't know how I was going to evade my grandfather and take her.

We managed to get out of the house without my grandfather noticing and ran to the main road. We jumped in the first minibus that came along. Suddenly Gülistan shouted at the man sitting next to her.

"Who do you think you are?"

"What's it to you?"

Gülistan pushed the man away.

"So you think you can touch me and then say what's it to you, huh?"

The driver, who had a large moustache, pulled in to the side of the road. He took the cigarette out of his mouth and said: "Get out, you!" The man made as if to stand up to the driver, but one of the other passengers pushed him out of the vehicle. Another passenger offered Gülistan his seat and the minibus moved off.

After we had got out of the minibus we took a bus, then began to walk. At the address given us by Aycan there was a large mansion at the top of a hill. The watchman at the gate conveyed our message inside, then came back and said: "A worker has been hired."

We began to walk back. There was nothing we could do. We now had to find another place for Gülistan. Suddenly, we heard Aycan's voice and halted. "Ali Kemal! Come back!"

We turned round and went back. We again walked towards the big iron gate. They admitted Gülistan. Aycan gestured for me to go. I wanted to wait, thinking they would throw her out on the street again.

A little later the watchman called me over. "Okay. I gather Miss Gülistan is going to stay here."

I ran to the minibus stop. By the time I got home my uncle had returned. Moreover, my grandfather was still at the mosque.

As soon as he saw me, he confronted me. "You liar! I thought you had a stomach ache?"

I went into the back garden to avoid my uncle. The dirty clothes Gülistan had taken off were under the wall. I picked them up and took them indoors so that no one would see them.

Just as my uncle had raised his hand and was about to strike me, we heard a voice say: "Rahmi!!" At first we thought it was my grandfather, but when we turned round we saw Tahir smiling at us. He had played a trick on his father and stopped him by imitating my grandfather's voice. But my uncle was not a man who could tolerate such jokes.

He squared up to his son, saying: "You haven't had a beating from me for a long time." Tahir bounded out into the garden. He still had a sarcastic look on his face.

"I'll wait here until my grandfather returns."

* * *

The next day Aycan was waiting for me. She was very excited at being part of the game.

"I didn't know my mother had taken on a cleaner. When she didn't want to see Gülistan, I insisted, saying: 'Mum, I called her by phone. I didn't know you had found someone. She's come from her village. We summoned her here, we can't send her away.' Then Gülistan said she had called from the village, and had come because she thought she had been accepted. My mother decided to take her, too. If she likes her, she will stay on. So at the moment she has a place."

However much I'd thanked her, it would have been insufficient.

Ah Gülistan, ah. Who knows how distraught the people in the village were? Who knows what else she had done that I was not aware of?

I didn't know what she would do next, but I was still frightened. In the village there was no punishment for going into the mountains, for that meant going willingly to die. But the punishment for girls who ran away to Istanbul was death. Gülistan had begun a brand new life in Aycan's family's mansion. I had called her and cautioned her firmly against saying that I was engaged.

No one else apart from me knew where Gülistan was. I was sure that Aycan would also keep our secret.

The days passed quickly. This incident had brought Aycan and me closer. Of course, she didn't know that I was in love with her.

The first year of the school where I frequently fled to the toilet to cry, was nearly over. We were to receive our reports. My marks, most of which had been low, had improved. But I was still sure I would have to retake the exams.

First the successful students received their reports. Aycan was top of the class. Erdem and Murat received commendations and after them five students received certificates of achievement.

Levent, who constantly didn't complete his homework, only had to retake exams in one subject. He complained:

"They're doling out notes to everyone, but when it comes to me, they've skimped."

"Ali Kemal Karadağ!"

As I heard my name, I got up with my heart thumping and walked towards the front of the class. What would the teacher say, I wondered.

"Ali Kemal, nearly all your marks are average."

I was so excited that I couldn't make out whether the teacher was being sarcastic or praising me.

"Someone who doesn't know you would think you were an average student if they looked at this report, but when we consider your lack of knowledge in the first days all we teachers consider you have achieved great success."

I stopped myself from cheering. Not having to retake exams was a great success for me.

"Well done Ali Kemal! Keep it up. I am sure that next year you will be higher up. Here's your report."

I took my report and returned to my desk. I sat down and pretended to glance at the report without attaching importance to it. The section on retaking exams was blank.

As always, Levent had something to say:

"Hodja, while you praised the monkey, why did you punish me?"

The teacher merely smiled at him.

I had passed the first class. I was now a second year student at middle school. A great weight had been taken from my shoulders. I had succeeded. No one could have understood the importance of it more than me.

Just at that moment the door opened and Hayrettin Hodja came in with the headmistress. He was holding a box. He smiled, greeted the teacher and turned to us.

"As you know guys, we have left another year behind. After a busy year you have received your reports. You are all successful. We know this. Now we are going to give another one of your classmates an award. Ali Kemal Karadağ, who didn't miss one training session, has earned this year's medal for scoring the most goals in the matches we took part in."

In the previous few days every morning when I woke up I had had a pain in my stomach from thinking that I would have to retake exams and would be a figure of fun. But now, just as I had passed all the classes, I was also to receive an award.

When Hayrettin Hodja put the medal with a red ribbon around my neck and congratulated me, I could have flown out of happiness. Despite this, no one else apart from me realised this, as I did my utmost to be calm as if nothing had happened. Levent's mocking voice did not affect me as much as it had before.

"Aahh! The hare is smiling!"

"Yeah, that's right. We've never seen him smile before."

They weren't wrong. For the first time I had lost control. I immediately gathered myself up and returned to the old, stern-looking Ali Kemal. The whole class applauded me. At one stage I looked at Aycan. Her eyes full of affection shone as if she had received the medal. That was the best part of the medal, the happiness I saw in Aycan's eyes as she looked at me.

The worst thing about breaking up for the holidays was not being able to see Aycan for three months. While talking to Sude I had heard her say: "We're going to Silivri." I didn't know where Silivri was. In the evening I asked Tahir and found out. They must have been going to their summer house by the sea.

Could I use Gülistan as a pretext to go and see Aycan, I wondered.

Chapter Fifteen

I FELL IN LOVE

Despite having had a really bad year, I was happy. I had come through with flying colours. I still had the chance to study. I still felt pressure at school, but it was as if my hopes had revived. Istanbul had taught me a hard reality at a tender age. It was very difficult being a villager, poor, and, moreover, a Kurd, amongst wealthy city people.

I was doing my utmost so that the pride I felt in my success in the team would not be apparent. I behaved as if I had no part in the team's victories. It had to be unimportant, like passing a subject without retaking exams.

The best thing was breathing the same air as Aycan. It was incredible to feel her presence, look at each other from time to time, see her smile, hear her voice, take her scent into my lungs and watch her cascading hair. She was the most beautiful girl in this world. I could have laid down my life for her without a second thought. I knew that I had absolutely no chance of a future with her. She would become a young woman and one day fall in love with an appropriate person and probably marry him. As for me, I would take consolation in my small recollections. I had no right to even profess my love for her.

With the onset of the school holidays, my days without Aycan began. I realised that I had gained most of my powers of endurance at school from her.

One Sunday morning I got up and timidly went to her house. I knew they weren't there, but at least I could get some news. The watchman at the gate recognised me straight away. "That's lucky. I was just now looking for your address. Miss Aycan left a letter for you."

My heart started beating as though it would leap out of my chest. Aycan had written me a letter.

"The lesson notes were with me."

Aycan had been so considerate as to write me a letter. I took the envelope and walked off at pace. I wasn't even aware of passers-by. I went down to the shore and sat on one of the benches under a tree. I opened the envelope. It was as if Aycan's hands were in mine at that moment.

"Ali Kemal, we need to speak. About Gülistan. Call me on this number or come here. We'll also have seen each other."

I don't know why I had expected a longer letter. At the bottom of the letter were her telephone number and the address of their summer house. I didn't care a jot about Gülistan. I was to hear Aycan's voice or even see her. The last sentence was really meaningful. She said: "We'll also have seen each other." 'Come for Gülistan and we'll have seen each other, too.' Wasn't life wonderful!

I could no longer conceive of a world without Aycan. I was both very happy and very melancholy as if I couldn't live without her.

What had happened to my ideals and my dreams? I was going to be the hero of Heredile? I was going to become a public servant and return to straighten everything out? I was going to be at the centre of the world?

When I had fantasised so much I had forgotten love. Or, more correctly, love had never occurred to me. Now I was wallowing in a torrent of emotions that held me tightly. Even when I felt pain I lost myself in a mass of feelings from which I delighted.

I returned home. My aunt had made *dövme*. It was one of the best foods prepared at weddings. It would be pounded so much in the pestle that the meat and bulgur would be thoroughly mixed. Perhaps that was why it was called *dövme*. I wondered if Aycan had ever eaten *dövme*. If she had, would she have loved it as much as me? What was her favourite dish? What a lot of things I didn't know about her.

My grandfather was silent. My aunt, Tahir and my uncle were also quieter than usual. Something must have upset them, but as my mind was on Aycan I wasn't even curious. When everyone had gone to bed Tahir came over to me and said: "What's a village guard?"

"I don't know. There were none in our village."

"Have you ever seen one?"

"I haven't. It was said there were some in nearby villages."

Tahir shook his head.

"Why did you ask?"

"My uncle has become a village guard."

"Which uncle?"

"Your father."

I was startled. My father couldn't be a village guard. He had always hated them.

"You must be mistaken. My father couldn't be a village guard. No way!"

"The commander forced him. He apparently said: 'See what happens if you don't.'"

"Who told you this?"

"My father heard it in our villagers' tea house."

We went to bed.

My mind was still on Aycan, but I was disturbed. My father was not someone who would become a village guard. I couldn't think of one man in Heredile who would accept becoming a village guard.

The next morning at breakfast I timidly asked my grandfather.

"Granddad, is it true what I've heard?"

"……"

"Has my father become such a thing?"

"Apparently they picked 5 men. One was your father."

I felt a strange wish to cry. While I was struggling with people at school, my father was there grappling with soldiers. I wondered how they had forced him to accept. For the first time I felt on the same side as my father.

"Granddad, you know, my father would never have become a village guard."

My uncle growled:

"Well, it's happened!"

My grandfather peered out of the window with a defeated, melancholy look on his face.

The despairing look on his face stimulated my anger at my uncle and for the first time I glowered at him.

"My father wouldn't become a village guard, Uncle! They must have forced him to take a guard's gun. He would never oppose his people, his clan. There is no one in Heredile who would draw a gun on one of his own."

Perhaps my uncle would have attacked me if my grandfather hadn't been there, but on this occasion he didn't overreact. It was even as if he had regretted what he'd said.

"God knows."

It was as if the problems I'd wrestled with all these years had lost their importance. While thinking my father had accepted the guard weapon in great pain, I also felt guilty. In Heredile, a man could willingly give his life for the clan. Even if you skinned him alive he wouldn't or couldn't give away his fellow villager.

How was my father to be a village guard? When the commander realised my father was not carrying out his duties what would they do to him?

When my grandfather went to the bathroom my uncle crossed his legs.

"Eh, nephew, it'll soon be time to go. My father will follow this up. It's a stain on our reputation."

My aunt was flustered.

"What will he do if he goes?"

When my uncle realised my aunt didn't want my grandfather to go he got annoyed.

"Don't interfere in men's business. Of course they'll go."

My fear and discomfort were increasing. In such a situation I couldn't say to my grandfather: "I can't leave the school; especially I can't do without Aycan."

Early the next morning I borrowed some money from Tahir and set off for Silivri. I had received detailed directions so as not to get lost.

At 10 I was in front of Aycan's family house. It was a smart two-storey marble-mosaic villa set amongst oleaster trees. On the garden gate was a red creeper rose. For a while I watched the balconies. Her mother and father got in a car and left. Perhaps it was better if they weren't there. Still I timidly approached the front door and rang the bell. My heart was beating as if it would leap out of my chest.

Before I had rung the bell again, Aycan's smiling face appeared. It was abundantly clear from the way her eyes were shining and her smile showing a mouthful of teeth that she was happy to see me.

"Was it easy to find?"

"Of course."

In fact it had not been at all easy.

"Come inside."

"I won't come in, if you like."

"Don't talk nonsense, please come in."

All the furniture was brand new, it looked as if the walls had been newly painted. A smell of cooking came from the kitchen.

"Sit down."

"You'll be wanting me to find a place for Gülistan, won't you? You're right, of course, I also…"

"Ask if Gülistan is able to go anywhere."

"Is she ill?"

"On the contrary, she is frightfully healthy according to the doctor."

"Why did she go to the doctor?"

"Before Aycan could reply Gülistan arrived wearing a bathrobe with her hair swathed in a towel. She looked calm and happy. It was as if she had lived in that house for years.

"Keko, is that you?"

"Gülistan, are you alright?"

"Thanks be to God."

Gülistan had yet to marry, so she couldn't be pregnant, but her belly looked just as though she was expecting.

She smiled when she saw me looking at her stomach. "Soon you will have a nephew or a niece."

"What?"

I couldn't believe my ears.

Aycan winked at me and called me to the balcony.

"Gülistan, are you joking?"

"Go away, do I have to explain to you?"

I didn't want to argue with Gülistan in front of Aycan.

Aycan gestured again with her hand for me to come. "Don't get flustered. It's no problem. We just need to talk a little, that's all. I think you also need to know."

"What's going on?"

"Gülistan, could you bring us some *börek*, and some tea with it. Ali Kemal must be hungry."

"No, no, I'm not hungry."

In fact, I was as ravenous as a wolf.

We went out onto the balcony, which was amongst flowers, and sat down at a round, glass table.

Gülistan brought out two trays of *börek* and tea and left them on the table. "Don't take any notice of him. He's always shy. And grouchy. And he's going to be a man."

Gülistan was bold enough to go out onto the balcony wearing a bathrobe.

"Okay, I'm going indoors. Enjoy yourselves."

As Aycan explained I didn't know what to say. When Gülistan came from the village she was apparently pregnant. She had left a letter for those in the village saying: "I'm going up to the mountains," then fled to Istanbul. When she started work it became obvious in the first month that she was pregnant. Just as she was about to be dismissed, Aycan's aunt heard about it. The aunt, who had not managed to have a child, decided to adopt the illegitimate baby that Gülistan was going to have. Since that day it had been prohibited for Gülistan to work. She needed to look after herself and the baby very well. She was being waited on hand and foot and was very happy. Aycan's mother was a little uneasy. What if someone came from the village? Mightn't they harm Gülistan, the baby and them?

I couldn't believe what I had heard.

"Come on, let's go to the sea. We'll continue talking on the beach."

"To the sea?"

"Why are you surprised? Didn't you bring your swimming costume?"

"No, I didn't bring it."

In fact I was embarrassed about undressing in front of Aycan.

"Are you going to come all this way and not go in the sea?"

"Anyway, I'll return soon."

"Aww, I thought you would stay until the evening."

Aycan wanted me to stay with her. And I was very grouchy, as Gülistan had said. I just couldn't sum up courage when I was with Aycan.

"Until evening? Your mother and father will come."

"They already knew you were coming."

"I mean, maybe you have work to do."

"Ali Kemal, how strange you are. What work could I have to do?"

Her voice was annoyed, as if she had been offended. I smiled.

"Okay, don't get angry. Let's not go in the sea, but we can walk if you like."

"Okay, I'll just get ready, then I'm coming."

When Aycan went inside Gülistan came out. She was wearing shorts down to her knees, and a short sleeved red t-shirt. Her long hair had been cut to shoulder length.

"Keko, have you news of our family?"

"Gülistan, what have you done, yah?"

"You asking as well is all I need."

"What's going to happen now?"

"Don't worry about me. From now on no one can touch me."

"How so?"

"They are going to adopt my child and I will live with them in Istanbul. I will do whatever I want. What more could I want from God?"

"What if my father and uncles hear about it?"

"If they hear, let them hear. I don't care."

"Don't you care?"

"Filiz Hanım's husband is a police chief."

"What?"

"Yeah… Cihan Bey is a chief of police. He will be the father of my child. Who can approach them? He said: 'If someone gets near you, I will throw them all inside."

"You know, don't you, our lot are not frightened of going to jail for killing someone for honour."

"For God's sake, sod all that! How is my grandfather, talk about him. He's the only one I miss, you know."

When Gülistan asked about my grandfather she seemed sad.

I went outside with Aycan. We walked together through the development between magnificent villas. The smell of the various kinds of multi-coloured flowers hanging from gardens, the immaculate paths, children running about, cats and dogs, all living things seemed happy there.

We went down to the shore. Aycan suddenly turned and said: "Or don't you know how to swim?"

"I know," I said. I was not happy that she thought I was an idiot who didn't know how to swim. We walked on a bit further. Then a ball which children were playing with fell into the sea. There wouldn't be a better opportunity. I jumped into the sea after the ball. For years I had swum under the waterfall at the mill, but the sea was different. Where we swam at the waterfall we were not out of our depth. Here, the water was at least as deep as two men. I caught the ball and threw it back to the children. Then I swam back to the shore.

Aycan looked surprised.

"You've got all your clothes wet just for a ball."

"So be it."

"And you didn't bring your swimming costume. We'll have to dry your clothes."

"They'll dry on me."

"Ali Kemal, you're talking nonsense. Okay, we're heading back home."

We reluctantly returned to the house. When Gülistan saw me she burst out laughing. Then she took me into her room and forcibly stripped off my clothes. She then gave me her pyjamas to wear. Whatever happened I couldn't go out into the sitting room in women's pyjamas. While we argued about this the door opened. Aycan's mother was smiling at us. Immediately behind her was her father.

"You should have thought about that before you jumped in the sea, young man. Come into the sitting room, sit down and wait for me."

I had disgraced myself. I didn't want to say no and upset them. Aycan put a film on the video and we began to watch it. Gülistan brought us some food. They had made chicken stew. It was delicious. I broke off small pieces and ate slowly so that it wouldn't be understood that I was hungry, whereas if they had allowed me I would have polished off the lot in five minutes. When we had finished eating, Aycan's father came over carrying bags. He had brought me some clothes. I was really embarrassed. And what would I tell my uncle and the others?

"No, I don't want these."

"Are you going to go home in these pyjamas?"

"I'll wear my own clothes."

Gülistan laughed, saying: "I put them in the machine ages ago. It'll take two hours for them to come out. Put these on. You can say: 'A benefactor gave them to me.' You're in luck." Whenever Gülistan opened her mouth, she embarrassed me. What a relaxed person she was, as if she had created the world.

I left with my brand new clothes and shiny shoes. Aycan wanted to see me to the gate. We walked side by side. That moment was the only reality for me. Neither the baby in Gülistan's belly nor my father who was a village guard were important. Aycan and I were side by side. There was ten centimetres between us. She was not tired of spending time with me.

Just as we were about to part, she looked me in the eyes and said: "Come again, Ali Kemal."

"If I'm not busy, I'll come."

She looked at me sulkily. I didn't want to leave her like that. I suddenly became excited. I actually wanted to say: "I'm dying for you. What have you done to me?"

Chapter Sixteen

MY FATHER, A REAL VILLAGE GUARD

That day in Silivri, as soon as I had left the housing development I began to feel a burning desire to go back. Aycan was constantly with me. She was walking, talking, laughing; sometimes, too, she was stretching out her hand to me. Even in my imagination I didn't have the courage to hold her hand.

How could Aycan possible be my sweetheart? I could have had the world's greatest romance with her, of course, but only realised in my dreams! To think anything else would be deemed madness or even a crime. Was Aycan going to love the school's poorest, village boy, moreover a Kurd? What could I give her? I had even managed to find Gülistan somewhere to live with her assistance. What would have happened without her, who knows?

On such a day when I was arguing with myself, an unexpected letter arrived. Even if my father, mother and siblings had all arrived I wouldn't have been that delighted. For a few minutes I couldn't open the envelope. I sat down on the couch and moved my fingers over the address as if I was stroking it. At last I had found a friendly hand that would understand me.

"Dear Keko, when I heard you had gone to Istanbul and enrolled at a school I was delighted. I'm sure you will be successful. All you have to do is try hard. I have confidence in you. Oh, and meanwhile, don't neglect to go to the public library. Write and tell me what books you read."

The letter was very short, it was as if I had come round. Yes, I was a villager. Yes, I was a Kurdish boy. Yes, I was poor. But at the same time I was a man. I was a boy of the clan. I had come to Istanbul to study. Despite it being very hard, I had passed the first year without needing to retake exams. That strength I had built up when wishing to leave the village had partially returned.

Love was beautiful; Aycan was more beautiful than love. It was not possible for me to get either without deserving them. I should work really hard for Aycan. There was no point in crying like a girl or fantasising. I went out into the street and started walking. I don't know how long had passed. A young man two or three years older than me was approaching. I stopped him and asked him if he knew the public library. He didn't know where it was, nor did others I asked.

Finally, a policeman said it was quite a distance and that I could get there on the number 124 bus. No way was I going to offend teacher Fatih. Whatever he said for me was definitely right. I should go.

When I got to the Aziz Berker library in Kadıköy it had already closed. I looked in through the window. There were books on all the walls, on shelves reaching up to the ceiling. As always, teacher Fatih had indicated the right place. Moreover, this time he had extended his hand from afar. I laughed to myself. Then I sat down on one of the wooden benches under the pine trees.

Early the next morning I was at the door of the library. It had not yet opened. I sat down on the same bench and began to wait. The weather was lovely. The sound of a radio coming from an unclear location mingled with birdsong:

'Everything that happens to me is because of you

What did you want from my love

Everything that happens to me is because of you

What did you want from my love

I've been ruined, I cannot love again

Everything that happens to me is because of you.'

Soon a plump woman in her fifties with short, ginger hair arrived. I waited a short time then entered the library.

I stopped in the middle of the library and looked at shelves holding hundreds of books. The smell of the books mingled with the woody smell of the old shelves. There were things that offered people tranquillity.

"Yes?"

The woman on duty who had just opened the door was probably surprised I had arrived so early.

"I've come to the library."

"Is there a particular book you're looking for?"

There was no title in my mind.

"What is the entrance fee?"

"Entrance to where?"

"The library."

The ginger-haired woman smiled.

"It's free to go into libraries."

"Oh, really?"

"Yes, is it the first time you've come here?"

"Yes."

"So, let's see, is there a book you'd like?"

What was I going to say? I was an ignorant student who didn't even know that libraries were free.

"Look, young man. If you like, sit down at one of those tables and take books you like from the shelves and have a look at them. Then don't forget to put them back in the same place, of course."

I felt embarrassed. Thanking her I moved towards the shelves. There was such a variety of books. Different colours, sizes, old, new, it was as if there were a whole lot of books waiting for me.

For the last year I had not been able to look at any books apart from text books. Whereas reading poems, short stories and novels was really pleasant.

I don't know how long had passed. The ginger-haired woman came over and said: "Young man, have a break, if you like. Go out into the garden for some fresh air, for instance. Normally, we would close for lunch, but seeing you so engrossed I didn't close today."

Again I was embarrassed. I didn't even know they closed for lunch there.

"I'd better go home."

"It will be closing soon, anyway. By the way, do you know you can take books home?"

To take books home might involve paying money.

"……"

"As a rule, we don't lend books to people before they become members, but if you want, choose a book and bring it back tomorrow. We'll make you a member then. Borrowing a book is also free."

So there were also good things about Istanbul. It was free to go into libraries and even take books home. I would read all these books. Schools were on holiday. In this way I would be able to forget Aycan a little. Still, I was reluctant to borrow a book without paying as if it was shameful.

"I don't know… borrowing a book…"

"Take one, don't be shy."

"Thank you."

"Look, this time I'll pick one. Tomorrow, once you have become a member you will choose a book."

"Okay."

"Have you read Khayyam before?"

I hadn't. With the book in my hand I got on the bus and went home. My grandfather and aunt had wondered about me. I told them about the library.

My grandfather nodded. "Can reading ever be bad, grandson? The Creator's first instruction to his creatures was 'read'."

"There are lots of books there, Granddad. You would be surprised if you saw it."

"If only it was closer, I would have gone to see it."

"I'll take you there, Granddad. It has a garden, too. It has trees like in our village."

My aunt had not heard of the library. Nor had my uncle. He drove a service for schools, but he still hadn't heard of it. In his opinion, any place in Istanbul that was free was suspicious.

"Don't try to teach me about Istanbul, nephew. If it's free there must be a catch. Who are they cheating?"

My grandfather didn't reply to my uncle but it was obvious he was annoyed. That night I showed the Omar Khayyam book to my grandfather. He smiled.

"Of course I know him. You say Khayyam, we say Tentmaker."

"Tentmaker?"

"Just enough to keep me alive, and half a loaf is needful; And then, that I and thou should sit in a desolate place Is better than the kingdom of a sultan."

"Granddad, where did you hear of Khayyam?"

My grandfather laughed.

Early the next morning I went to the bus stop with my grandfather, and from there to the library. Once again we were there before it opened. We sat in the garden. My grandfather was affected by the large pine trees, recalling the village.

"Can a world containing such magnificent things be evil, my grandson? The Creator has given us such blessings... However, people do not appreciate them."

"Granddad, have you remembered the mill?"

He had tears in his eyes and did not reply.

After the ginger-haired woman had arrived we waited a short time, then went in.

"You're early again, young man?"

I was a bit nervous as I had come with my grandfather.

My grandfather answered for me:

"A very good morning to you."

"Good morning to you, too."

"My grandson came here yesterday. Thanks, you lent him a book to read. He said it was free so I thought I'd come and see."

"Welcome. This is a state-owned library, so of course we lend books for free. If only all young people would come here."

I sat down next to my grandfather. Just as I had done the previous day, my grandfather was staring at the shelves full of books in surprise.

"Grandson, is a lifetime long enough to read this many books?"

"I don't know, granddad, there are very nice books. Time flies by."

"From now on you have permission from me. Come here every day. Read as much as you can. Where else will you find free books, grandson?"

From that day onwards I began to go to the library every day early in the morning. My aunt prepared sandwiches for me to eat when I got hungry at lunchtime. Mahmure, the ginger-haired woman who worked at the library, sometimes treated me to tea when I ate my sandwiches in the garden. Meanwhile, we would chat. She recommended certain books to me. I enjoyed and read all the books she recommended more quickly. I had become a member. Almost every evening I borrowed a book to take home. In the evenings I would read to my grandfather. My uncle didn't like this as the television would be off.

I most liked the novels of Orhan Kemal. I read them until after midnight.

Without realising it, I had begun to change. In the novels I read I was introduced to dozens of heroes who fell in love at my age. In this way I learned that the love I felt for Aycan was not deviant, and I decided it was actually normal. Furthermore, the first love was deemed in some way sacred.

I had a small notebook that I wrote for Aycan and kept, as if I was going to give it to her. Everything I wrote about her had love in it.

Your eyes are sea-green. There is not a boat, nor an island, nor a shore. I'm drowning.

Quiet my heart! I know you have yearned. Quiet, may she not know she is yearned.

Ozdemir Asaf

'Perhaps the sun will one day rise for the two of us.

A human being will not die in an ocean, but go and drown in a spoonful of longing.

God, show me a path that leads to her.

There is one, every day I fall more in love with her.

To love is not to be together with the person you love, don't forget!

Because love is not to live with her, in fact, but to live her.

I am at the last place of living, that is I am with you.

Have you ever fallen in love with someone you have never seen, touched or kissed?

If you had done you would know what love is.

Do not leave me to others. If you see, you could not bear it.

To look in someone's eyes means to run the risk of entering her dreams. If you are not capable of loving, you won't look.

"I've forgotten", you say to those around you, but only you know that you haven't forgotten. Love is such a thing, even if it goes you still can't forget it.

I loved you in the chorus of a song that is not ours.'

After beginning to go to the library, I had other note books. I wrote down everything I liked. Sometimes I wrote selections to teacher Fatih. In frequent letters I sometimes talked about books I had read. Was it only possible in novels to study at a school where there were close friendships like in *Hababam Sınıfı*, I wondered.

Presumably, city people didn't like the saying: "The villager is lord of the nation", a saying teacher Fatih often repeated.

One evening the doorbell rang. When I opened it facing me was Aycan's family chauffeur. My uncle was sitting indoors. I was afraid that he would hear Gülistan's name.

"What's happened?"

"Miss Aycan has sent you a note."

When he thrust a crumpled envelope into my hand I opened it excitedly. Inside was a torn, creased piece of paper. The scrawled handwriting was not Aycan's.

"Dirty Keko, where are you? Come here, I have things to tell you."

This must have been Gülistan's handwriting. My uncle, who was right behind me, was startled to see the note. Thank God Gülistan had not written her name.

"What's this? Has the rich girl written you a letter?"

"There was homework we were going to prepare together."

"In the summer holidays?"

"Of course. There is also homework in the holidays."

The next morning I set out early. My aunt thought I was going to the library. I was going to Silivri.

When Aycan saw me she was delighted.

"Welcome."

"Thanks."

Gülistan was tactless, as usual.

"Hey, Keko, you've grown up and you're still acting coy? I'm like your big sister. If you're not going to show concern for me, who are you going to show it for?"

When Aycan went inside I whispered in Gülistan's ear.

"If you were in the village you couldn't talk like this. You're in the club and you're trying to manipulate me?"

Suddenly I had become Keko from Heredile. Gülistan stepped back a little as she saw the look on my face. Sadness spread across her face.

"I know that if I was in Heredile I would be long dead. If there had been someone else apart from you, I would be dead in Istanbul, too. But you're different, Keko. If that weren't the case do you think I'd have come?"

"……"

"Why are you staring at me like that?"

Even if she was angry there was an expression on her face pleading for pity.

"Don't overdo it!"

She smiled cheekily again.

"Okay, I won't make jokes in front of this rich girl again."

When Aycan came back she was holding two glasses of fruit juice.

"You must be tired. It's hot," she said as she handed me one of the glasses.

After looking daggers at me, Gülistan went inside.

"Have you brought your swimming costume?"

I raised two hands in the air to show I hadn't.

"What are you up to?"

"Nothing, I'm reading books."

Her eyes suddenly brightened.

"Really? What are you reading?"

"I'm reading lots of things."

She also read and there was so much to talk about. Aycan was a real bookworm. She read mostly in English and had read most of the famous Turkish writers. She took me by the hand and led me inside. I followed her without letting on I was excited. We went into her room. One wall was books from end to end.

"You can take whichever one you like."

I shrugged my shoulders.

"There's no need. I've become a member of the library, all the books are there."

"The school library?"

"No, the public library."

I was talking as though I had already known about public libraries and had gone and found it myself. Aycan had never been to a public library, as her mother and father immediately bought her the books she wanted. In the house they lived in during the winter she had a special reading room. All her books were there. Now she insistently wanted to give me the books she loved.

This was a miracle. We had something in common. We both liked to read and there were lots of things we could talk about. Aycan's mother was a fan of Kerime Nadir, as she loved romantic novels. She also liked novels about old Istanbul. Her father preferred books about history and politics.

The books Aycan liked had gained importance in my eyes. I felt that if I read them I would get to know her better.

When her mother called us to lunch I was telling her about Orhan Kemal's novel, Hanım'ın Ciftligi [Lady's Farm]. Our conversation about books continued at the meal table.

As we got up from the table her mother smiled.

"Aycan, for the first time I've seen you talking about books with a friend. How nice!"

"I didn't know, Mum. Ali Kemal never told me. It seems that he also loves reading. He's become a member of the local library. He borrows books from there. His favourite is Orhan Kemal."

When leaving Silivri, Aycan prepared a bag of books she'd chosen and thrust it into my hand. Just as I was putting on my shoes Gülistan leapt out.

"I'll see Keko off. And we'll have a chat."

I thus had to say goodbye to Aycan in front of the house.

"Don't forget your swimming costume the next time you come, okay?"

Her mother smiled as if she also wanted to see me again. We

left them and walked towards the exit of the development.

"Hey Keko, don't you get letters from the village?"

"We get them."

"Do they mention me?"

"Nooo…"

"So they haven't heard yet."

"What?"

"That I didn't stay in the mountains."

"But they who go to the mountains never come down."

"My name's Gülistan."

"So you went up to the mountains and then came down, is that so, Gülistan?"

"Yeah, Keko. Why are you surprised?"

"Okay, but why did you go up and why did you come down?"

"Ah, look, that's a sensible question. Why did I go up the mountain? And why did I come back down again?"

"Why?"

"Never mind."

"Gülistan, tell me!"

"I said never mind. Now listen well. If you get any news pass it on to me."

I stopped. There was a question that had been gnawing at me for a while. There was no one else but Gülistan that I could share it with.

"Gülistan, I heard something."

"What did you hear?"

"They say that my father has become a village guard."

"My uncle?"

"Yeah."

"Uncle Ajar?"

"I said yes, Gülistan."

"I think not, no. No way. I don't like him, but there's no way Uncle Ajar would become a village guard."

"That's what I said. It's like the flow of letters from the village has slowed. And they only write very short letters now. There's something strange going on."

"Has my grandfather heard?"

"He's heard."

"If only you hadn't told me."

"Maybe it's not true, Gülistan. What do you think?"

"Don't worry. I will find out."

"From whom will you find out?"

"From Cihan Bey. He's a very high up chief of police. He's bound to know."

"And if it's true?"

"I said, I doubt it, Keko. And what would my uncle do? Is he going to surrender his clan to the soldiers? Even if he knew he would die he wouldn't do it."

The summer holiday had been good for me. Like a tired warrior I was both resting and renewing myself. From time to time I would go with Tahir and gather the local boys for a match on the waste ground. My aunt was gradually smiling more. My uncle was not as tense as he had been. It was as if he had got used to my grandfather and me. The possibility of my father being a village guard also seemed to be on his mind, but he was not as uneasy as us. He looked at us as if to say: "See, apparently my big brother can also make a mistake."

My grandfather was melancholy, as if he had lost Heredile. He said he wouldn't go back. It would be better for all his sons to die than for him to be the father of a village guard.

In the evenings I read him books. His favourite was *rubai* [Persian verses]. Tahir read out the newspaper headlines. My grandfather told Tahir about Kurdish history in colloquial language. As I had already learned it by heart I didn't pay much attention.

It was the end of August. I had read all the books Aycan had given me. I wanted to give them back to her before something happened to them. I set off early for Silivri. I also had a surprise for her.

Aycan was delighted to see me at the door when she least expected it. With her joy I was also filled with happiness. They were about to sit down to breakfast.

"I've had breakfast. I'll wait inside."

It was as if her mother hadn't heard me.

"Come here and sit down."

Gülistan's belly was really pronounced. She was wearing a maternity dress with a ribbon.

"It's really lively. It wakes me up at night with its kicks. I wonder if it will be a boy?"

I was embarrassed for Gülistan. In Heredile even married women wouldn't talk openly about their pregnancies. Gülistan was as relaxed as a city woman.

"I hope it will be a boy. Cihan would be in seventh heaven."

"Hopefully he will be a successful man like his father."

As Aycan put an omelette on my plate she said: "You've brought the books back. How quickly you read them."

"There's nothing else to do."

"Which one was your favourite?"

"I'll show you after breakfast."

Anton Chekhov's short stories were incredible. I had put red rose petals between the pages. Would Aycan notice, I wondered? I had hesitated, thinking she might be angry, but I couldn't help myself.

Aycan's father also liked Anton Chekhov. According to him he was the best story teller there had ever been.

For a moment I became flustered, thinking her father might find the rose petals, but there was nothing I could do. Aycan had already put the books back on the shelves.

Her mother had a surprise for me. She had bought me a swimming costume, plastic shoes, goggles and a cap.

"No, I don't want them. I already have some."

"I won't accept objections. Come on, straight to the sea!"

My cheeks had reddened as I didn't know what to do. It was as if once again the fact I was a poor villager had been displayed on my face.

Aycan took me by the hand and said:

"Come on! How many times have you been here and you haven't even been in the sea once."

Going in the sea with goggles, watching crabs in the sand under the water side by side with Aycan was wonderful. Gülistan brought *börek* and *ayran* and shouted to us from the shore. I was so hungry that I was unable to conceal my hunger.

Aycan ran towards the house.

Gülistan looked thoughtful. "Keko!"

"Hmmm?"

"Wait, listen to me. You can eat later."

"What's up?"

"Uncle Ajar has really become a village guard, apparently."

"My father?"

"Yeah."

The attraction of the *börek* had gone. We didn't speak for a while.

Aycan returned with a bottle of cold fruit juice. She gave one glass to me and filled another for herself.

"I don't like *ayran*. My mother always sends *ayran*. Doesn't she, Gülistan?"

"I'd better not stay too late."

"What's happened?"

"Nothing. It's getting late."

"I thought we were going to have a swimming race?"

I went back to the house and changed.

Her mother put my wet swimming costume, shoes and goggles in a bag and gave it to me. "Don't take off your cap."

"It would be better if I didn't take them."

"Shame. Can presents be given back, Ali Kemal?"

Aycan took me to the gate of the development.

"What's happened, Ali Kemal, are you angry about something? We were having such a good time, then you sulked."

"No offence. It just happened like that…"

"What just happened?"

"Don't ask. Perhaps I'll explain one day."

"Are you angry with me?"

I was flustered. I was afraid that if she thought I was angry with her she wouldn't want to speak to me again.

"No, no. How could I be angry with you? You're very good."

She smiled.

"In fact, you're even too good."

"What do you mean, too good?"

We laughed together. We were close. If I had raised my arms I could have embraced her.

"You're always very good. Who could be angry with you? Also…"

"Also what?"

"You see…"

"Oh, Ali Kemal. Are you always going to leave your sentences unfinished?

"For me you are the most important thing in Istanbul."

"What?"

I ran off.

Chapter Seventeen

HIGH SCHOOL STUDENT KEKO

The first day we began high school I went through that iron gate proudly. Now I was Ali Kemal who had beaten the odds at ilim College, and was the football club's star player.

In our middle school yearbook there was a paragraph that described each pupil:

"Ali Kemal, that is, Keko, that is, Hare. The first day he went into class he made us laugh. When he began to run we said; 'Ah….' When he hit the ball we said: 'Wow!' He doesn't say much. He doesn't want buddies. The guy is cool from birth. When it came to copying, he didn't even attempt to. His fists are also very strong. Does the school give him a bursary or the other way round, it's not clear. Thanks to him the whole of Istanbul has heard the school's name."

No one knew about the storms breaking out inside me. No one knew that I was madly in love with Aycan, including her. Moreover, this love was like weeds growing between rows of crops. The more I urged it on it would stick its head out somewhere and grow a bit more each day. I had convinced the whole school that I didn't need buddies, but it was not true. From time to time I really missed my friends in the village. I had such a need to sit down with them and pour out my heart to them. If I could just have explained what was inside me to someone, I would have been really relieved.

My uncle did not want to send Berivan, who had completed primary school, to middle school. My aunt told the headmistress. The headmistress took my uncle to one side and reprimanded him severely. Out of fear he would lose his job, my uncle enrolled Berivan at a local middle school. Berivan studied hard and asked me about everything she didn't know. When my uncle went to the parents' meetings he would come back very cheerful. He also regretted Tahir not continuing his studies.

With Tahir I had an up and down cousin relationship. Even if we argued, we would immediately make it up. Most of all he was jealous of my closeness to my grandfather. One day I said: "He also loves you, why are you like this?"

After he had looked at me for a long time, he lowered his head and said: "I know he loves me, too, but he loves you more. If we are both his grandsons, why does he discriminate?"

The main things we had in common were our fathers and football. Neither of us liked our fathers and we both loved to play football. If my uncle hadn't harped on to Tahir so much about my success at school we would have quarrelled less.

"He came from the village, from the village! You were born in Istanbul. Feel ashamed! Curl up and die! He's become the favourite of that great college. Teachers point to me, saying: 'That's Ali Kemal's uncle.' But I can't take pride in that. Why? Because I can't say: 'I've got a lazy good-for-nothing, stupid son back at home. A disgrace.'"

"Uncle, you've gone too far. Which teacher said that when he saw you?"

One day Tahir was tearful. He couldn't bear it any longer and shouted at his father:

"And you're a disgrace to my grandfather."

At that moment my uncle lost it. He picked up the tongs from the stove and squared up to Tahir, who didn't attempt to flee. He didn't move a muscle. He stared at his father. It was sudden. I went between them and the tongs caught me on the top of my head. Blood came out in streams. My grandfather was sitting in the garden. Hearing my aunt's scream he came in.

When he saw me, he staggered and came over and put the huge palm of his hand that I so loved over the wound. "This blood is not good, daughter-in-law. A doctor's needed," he said, and collapsed next to me.

Tahir ran to the neighbours. My aunt was thumping her knees and turning around us not knowing what to do.

"Rahmi! Rahmi! I swear to God, may your hands and feet break so that you can't hit anyone again!"

My uncle was crying by my grandfather's head.

The neighbour's son, who had just come back from his military service, came in and took my grandfather in his arms, carrying him to my uncle's vehicle, shouting: "Open the door!"

My uncle ran to open the door of the vehicle he so fussed over. They laid my grandfather down in the back seat. Holding a towel on my head I followed my grandfather. Tahir was in front of the door looking at us. I signalled for him to sit next to my grandfather.

I sat next to my uncle. I was no longer frightened of him. He also knew he could not hit me. In fact, he could not easily hit Tahir either, but that day he had lost it. The minibus moved off. At the last minute my aunt jumped in the minibus barefoot. She was crying her eyes out, and grumbling. "Ah, father, if you weren't here, what would we do? Wouldn't we be at the mercy of people unfit to grovel at your feet?"

My aunt's provocative words hurt my uncle.

"Shut up, woman! Or I'll take out my anger on you!"

"Have you still got anger left, Rahmi? It will consume you. Just wait a while, you'll see."

We arrived at the hospital. They put both of us on stretchers.

The blood was still coming from my head. I was feeling faint. I was looking at my grandfather and I apparently passed out.

When I came round the two of us were in the same room at the hospital in beds facing one another. My aunt was sitting between us reading the Quran. She was still barefoot. My grandfather was looking at me with tired eyes. When he saw I had woken up he smiled.

"Granddad, how are you?"

He laughed.

"Grandson, you're asking me? You tell me how you are."

"I'm fine, granddad. Don't worry about me."

After my aunt had finished reading the Quran she closed it, kissed it and put in on top of a cupboard. Then she came over to me.

"My God has saved you."

They had put stitches in my head and put a drip on my arm. I smiled at my aunt so that she would relax. "Where's Tahir?" I asked.

My aunt nodded towards the door. He was waiting for us, embarrassed because he was the cause of what had occurred.

"Go and call him, auntie! Let him come here and sit down."

My aunt brought Tahir in. For a while he waited by the door with an expression on his face that was a mixture of fear, worry and sadness. Then he went tearfully over to my grandfather and grasped his hands. My grandfather lifted his head and gestured for my aunt to leave the room. She went out.

He said firmly to Tahir: "Go and close the door and come and sit next to me!" He pulled himself up and sat upright on the bed. "Sit facing me," he said to Tahir.

Tahir perched on the end of my bed. Neither of us could guess what my grandfather was going to say. He would not easily get angry with us, but there seemed to be a look on his face that would scold us.

"Now listen well. Let this be my legacy to the two of you.

You're not alone. You are children of the clan. Wherever you go in the world, you have a clan. Tahir, your mother is not a girl of the clan, but brides from outside have been entrusted to us and we have to behave attentively towards them. For breach of trust is unacceptable. It is our duty to look after them with honour. If harm comes to them, I will not give my blessing to the one responsible, know this. You will protect this woman, who is the mother of one of you and the aunt of the other. If anything happens to me, this is your duty. And where I am absent it is yours. If Rahmi lifts his hand, you will hold him. However much I am angry with him, he is your elder. I won't say; 'Hit him', but grasp his hand. Hold it well and don't allow yourselves to be beaten."

Tahir started to cry more. His shoulders were shaking as he sobbed. My grandfather seemed to be angry at Tahir's weeping.

"Quiet! What am I saying to you? Keko did the right thing. Of course he will intervene. He did well, but he was unable to protect himself."

In the evening the police came to the hospital.

"We gather there's been a wounding."

My grandfather said: "Yes, my grandson."

"Who injured you, young man?"

Pointing to my grandfather, I said: "I can't talk."

Tahir was laughing quietly.

"Granddad, is this your grandson?"

"They're both my grandsons."

"How was this boy injured? Was there a fight?"

"While they were playing he fell."

"Come on, granddad. Did the boy fall on his head? It's obvious they hit him."

The policeman turned to me and I nodded, as if to say: "They're telling the truth.".

The policeman left and Tahir and I started to laugh. Tahir said: "Granddad, isn't this a clan matter?"

My grandfather nodded.

"Don't let it go any further, grandson. With God's help our business will not rest with the state. Of course, I will punish that oaf. I will not let him get away with it."

After that day Tahir and I became a little closer. Tahir was not as jealous of me as he had been before. As for my uncle, he seemed quieter and more subdued. Whenever he started to menace my aunt, we would stand up and look at him. And he would not continue as he had previously.

I was corresponding constantly with teacher Fatih. I told him about the books I read, the library, the football team, my grandfather and even Tahir. Somehow I couldn't bring myself to mention Aycan. I needed his opinions about the future. It was as if I found my way thanks to him. There were two options as regards university: either I was going to read politics or law. These two departments would be more helpful for me to move up the ladder towards my goals than other departments. In one or two years' time I would be at university. If I didn't get a scholarship it would be hard, but teacher Fatih had said: "Don't think about that now."

One day when I told Aycan I wanted to study law, she said: "Perhaps I will study in the same department as you."

"Really? Do you want to study law, too?"

She shook her head and looked at me with those beautiful eyes.

"No, but I don't want to go to a different place to you."

I didn't know what to say. For me it was so important to be in the same environment that she could never have guessed. But I could never have told her that. I still thought I didn't deserve her.

When we got our half-year reports Aycan invited me to her house. Her father had heard I wanted to study politics or law. Both her mother and her father wanted her to study politics, but Aycan had always turned her nose up, saying she wanted to study the history of art at Mimar Sinan. Was she now going to opt for law because of me?

Gülistan had come too. Her son was two, but she was still breastfeeding. Filiz Hanım only gave the child to Gülistan when she breastfed him. Otherwise she didn't allow her to touch him.

Gülistan didn't seem to care. Her eyebrows were thinner than the last time I had seen her. Her hair had been dyed a lighter colour. She now wore trousers. With every passing day she was adapting to Istanbul. The clan and Heredile were far in the past for her.

Who knows, perhaps those in the village assumed she had died in the mountains. Even if someone suspected something different, they wouldn't share it with anyone else. For it to be heard that she was in Istanbul would be a catastrophe for the clan. If they knew she had had a child, uncovered her head and wore trousers, who knows what would have happened? I didn't care. I wasn't angry. Some clan traditions were very nice, but some of them were nonsense. It was obvious that regarding women in particular they were unjust.

The worst thing was my father being a village guard. It was as unacceptable as Gülistan having an illegitimate child. My grandfather had decided not to return to the village because of it. According to letters written by Celil, no one in the village spoke to our family any more. My father no longer went to the mill. My uncle was running it by himself, helped by the children, who had now grown up. My father would get up early, take up the weapon given by the state and set out. All the village guards were under a commander. My father didn't speak to anyone. When he had heard that my grandfather had said: "I won't return to the village," he had sent word, saying: "What could I do? If Ankara has selected me, is it my fault? The sword of justice has no scabbard." But my grandfather had not forgiven him.

It was difficult for us to change certain things. My father, like me, was passing through an inevitable tunnel. It was difficult for me to understand what he was experiencing, but I could guess.

For me there was a single light at the end of the tunnel: university. I had no choice other than to finish university. For all I knew, one day I might work and pay back Ilim College for accepting me without a fee. For all this I had to finish university. For this reason I was studying day and night. I was one of the top five students in the class. I was telling myself: "Not long to go. In two years' time you'll be at university. When you've graduated you'll be able to call everyone to account. But for now your hands are tied, your tongue is silent, your eye is blind and your ear is deaf."

I passed the difficult days and my problems by reading the books I loved and corresponding with teacher Fatih. And clinging to my grandfather. My grandfather was really good for both Tahir and me. I was no longer a child, but sitting on the floor next to him listening to his tales was a limitless pleasure.

Tahir was preparing an 'April Fool's Day' prank for his mother. He was going to tell his mother he had eloped with his friend's sister from the upper neighbourhood. He was moreover going to tell her he had 'Coerced her'. For this reason he was busy messing up her hair. Just then the postman came. I immediately recognised the handwriting on the envelope. Celil had written it. I said: "So my father got Celil to write."

Every letter we received was like a copy of the previous one. They seldom wrote anything new. So I opened the letter without any great enthusiasm. But this time it was very brief:

"Father, Ajar has been shot. Condolences. May you live long. It's not clear who shot him. We don't know whether the soldiers or those in the mountains shot him. It is fate."

My grandfather was stunned. Then he said: "Read it again!"

For the first time I didn't do what my grandfather had told me. I looked at Tahir. He came over and embraced my grandfather. We told my aunt. She came running. It was as if life had stopped for all of us at that moment. My grandfather's tears trickled slowly and silently onto his cheeks. He was elegising as if he was talking to himself.

"Ajar, you've caused your own death. Didn't you know there was a suitable way to die? Did you surrender with the village guard weapon on your back? How were you caught unawares? Hey Ajar, who tricked you? Was it appropriate to go to the ground besmirched, Ajar?"

So as not to upset him we didn't shout or holler. The next day

I didn't go to school. Tahir didn't go to work.

My uncle had to go, but he also had a heaviness, a sadness about him.

"So will I never be able to see my elder brother Ajar again? I always wondered what kind of man he was."

My father had died. Even if I didn't love him an emptiness had grown inside me. When I heard he had become a village guard I was very angry, but with his death that anger had been replaced by a dull ache.

My aunt was crying in the kitchen and wailing a lament:

[in Kurdish]

Mother, my darling

Tell me, how are you

I kiss your hands father

Greetings to sister and brother

Mother, being far away is hard

I don't forget the cause of the homeland

The heart wants to return

What can I do, I can't

I couldn't say in school that my father had died. Only Aycan noticed the difference in me. Despite her insistence, I couldn't tell her. I just said: "I'm fine."

Then Gülistan came to the school. Cihan Bey had told her that my father had died. I don't know how Cihan Bey could be informed about my father so easily.

"Don't be sad, Keko. He lived by the sword and died by the sword."

"What are you saying, Gülistan. He was my father."

"And wasn't he my uncle?"

I sat down and wrote my mother a long letter. I told her not to be sad and that as her son I would be at her side, and would look after my siblings. I couldn't neglect my lessons. It was now very important for my family that I went to university.

I had received acknowledgement in the second and third years of middle school. For the first time I was to receive a commendation. When the teacher read out my name I walked to the lectern. I received my report and acknowledgement but there was not a trace of joy inside me.

As I sat down, Murat said: "Laugh man, or at least smile a little!"

I sat down as if I hadn't heard him and opened the buttons of my jacket. I had done my duty but I was in no state to be pleased. My father had died. It was just as well there was the clan. My mother and siblings were to stay in the same house and my uncle would look after them.

That summer my grandfather fell ill. Tahir and I decided to take him to the village, but my grandfather was determined not to go. "It is my testament. If I die, bury me here. I won't allow anyone to say: 'the village guard's father has come,'" he said.

Chapter Eighteen

APPRENTICE KEKO

At weekends I was working as an apprentice at the neighbourhood butcher's. Remzi the butcher considered butchery, his family trade, to be a sacred profession. Meat from animals that were killed in a cruel way was not auspicious. A lamb that was less than a year old was not considered halal. A butcher had to be clean and know the rules. He would not touch meat without washing his hands. Letting meat go off was a sin. If it hadn't been sold, it should be given to a poor person or an animal before it went off.

Remzi would not throw out the bones, either. When women who could not afford to buy meat came cap in hand and asked for bones he would wrap them in newspaper and give them to them.

Most of our customers were our neighbours and I was only just getting to know them. It appeared that the 19 May neighbourhood was a really friendly place. What great romances, great adventures and trivial quarrels took place there on the outskirts of Istanbul, in a neighbourhood consisting of houses with no title deeds belonging to people who had pulled themselves up by their own efforts.

It was a nice area, where children played in the street, where everyone addressed each other by the informal 'you', where secrets were shared, where, when necessary, there were fights and people knew how to make up. Like at school, I also had a nickname in the neighbourhood: Scribe, because they always saw me with a book in my hand. If not as much as Hare, I also liked my nickname of Scribe.

Sometimes I would answer those who asked: "Hey, Scribe, what's going to happen to this country?" with a mere shrug of my shoulders and a smile. How could I know about the state of the country when I couldn't figure out what would happen to little Heredile. One of the most important things I had learnt in Istanbul, in fact, was that Istanbul was not a city without worries and cares as we had imagined it. There was even more misery in big cities than in villages. Those who said: "Istanbul's streets are paved with gold," were lying. Someone who was hungry could find food for years in Heredile, but in Istanbul it was impossible to survive without money.

Remzi really liked me. Some days he would give me bones that had not been completely scraped. In this way my aunt began to put meat in almost all our meals.

That summer I suddenly shot up in height. My shoulders had also broadened. I had had a moustache for some time. In the mirror I began to see a man who was not like the Keko in Heredile. I was a worried young man obsessed with Aycan, dreaming at night of going to university. I was no longer a child. No one could easily make me cry.

With the death of my father I had for a moment been scared of life. While he was alive I didn't think of my mother and siblings. There was someone looking after them. But now they were at the mercy of my uncles and the clan. My aunt had said: "From now on nothing will be like it was previously for your mother." When I heard that I didn't dwell on it.

I didn't want to leave school and return. And, anyway, no one expected me to do that.

Tahir had heard about our villagers' tea house in Tarlabaşı. He said he went there frequently, listening like a stranger, and had met men from Heredile. He felt comfortable with them. He said getting a glass of tea and sitting quietly amongst them was good for him.

As for me, I wasn't at all interested. I had no time to spare for them. If Tahir wanted, he could go there. He wanted to meet the clan, which was his right.

One evening after everyone had gone to bed he came over to me and said: "I'm going to tell you a secret."

"What's happened?"

"I'm going to the mountain."

"Which mountain?"

"Kato."

"What?"

"I'm leaving tomorrow."

I jumped out of bed and grabbed him. "You don't know. Those who go there can't come back. Only your corpse will come down."

"I know. Don't forget, I'm a Kurd. I'm going to go there and fight. I asked for Kato mountain in particular. I also want to see the village. While there I will definitely go down once and see it. My uncles, my aunts, the whole village, your friends… Don't look at me like that. I'm curious. And what's happened to you? Do you think you're from Istanbul just because you go to a private school?"

"Don't talk nonsense, Tahir! What is there in the village? Can you go up to the mountain for that reason?"

"Yes, I want to see the mountain, too. I'm going to fight. I'm going to fight for my people, for my cause."

"What cause?"

When I woke up in the morning Tahir had already left the

house. That evening I had intended to speak to him and make him give up his stupid plan. But he didn't come back in the evening. Towards midnight my uncle and aunt began to worry. I was afraid my grandfather would be sad.

Tahir hadn't come back by morning. My uncle got up intending to go to the police.

"Wait uncle! I know where he's gone."

"If you know, why did you let us get in this state?"

Anxious and frightened, my uncle and aunt sat down on the couch.

My grandfather stared at me. I didn't know how I would tell them. I was more worried about my uncle's reaction. I was just about to speak when my grandfather asked: "Has he gone to the mountain?" I nodded.

My aunt put her head in her hands and began to sob. Uncle Rahmi's eyes were also moist.

"My father knows, you know, why don't I know, eh!" said my uncle, as he confronted me. My grandfather stopped him, saying: "Rahmi!"

"Dad, why are you doing this? Am I a scarecrow in this house?"

"Ask that to yourself, Rahmi?"

My uncle sat down next to my aunt and began to cry. My grandfather went over to the window, pulled the curtain and looked out at the sky. He no longer heard us.

I went over and took my aunt's hands in mine.

"Don't be sad. I will go and bring him back."

A glimmer of hope appeared in my aunt's tear-filled eyes.

"Really, Keko?"

My uncle started to cry more intensely.

"Forget him, he won't be able to come back."

"I promise, uncle. I won't come back without him."

There was a pleading look on my uncle and aunt's faces.

"You look after my grandfather well. May bringing him back be my duty."

I got dressed and prepared. I had a week's wages in my pocket. It would just about pay the fare of the bus to the village.

My aunt came over, took a purse from her bosom and stuffed it into my hand.

"Keko, bring him back. I beg of you!"

I went into the sitting room and embraced my grandfather.

"Give me your blessing, Granddad!"

He looked at me. He didn't say: "Where are you going? Why are you asking for my blessing?"

With tearful eyes he said: "Well done. May God speed, grandson."

I put on my shoes and left the house. My anger at Tahir was increasing. As if it wasn't bad enough that he had upset his family and my grandfather, he was also dragging me after him. He had jumped willingly into death's embrace. For adventure he was going to the mountains.

Throughout the journey I pondered how I would bring Tahir back. No solution occurred to me. What would I say? Was I to go up to Kato and say: "I've come to take my uncle's stupid son?" In that case I would definitely at least get a beating. First it was necessary to go to the village and find some people who were going up to the mountain.

The bus stopped for a break. I got out and began to walk. I bought a bread ring and sat down. The bus company was giving out free tea. I took one and suppressed my hunger.

Just as I was about to get back on the bus I saw books on a stand. I bought Ince Memed [Memed, my Hawk] by Yashar Kemal and hurriedly bought it and dashed onto the bus. I sat down in my seat.

Thanks to the book my thoughts were diverted and the journey passed quickly. It was the middle of the night by the time we got to the terminal. There was no vehicle going to the village. I set out along the road. An old truck stopped. I was able to get as far as the road below the village. I jumped in the back of the lorry. I was entering the village where I had been born like a thief. I felt tension rather than joy. My father had died as a village guard. I didn't want anyone to see me.

I was to ascend Kato mountain. It wouldn't do for me to enter the village in the daytime and draw attention to myself. I got out of the truck and set off on a narrow path. In the moonlight I noticed that the trees had got denser. There was the sound of barking dogs in the distance.

At the entrance to the village two dogs came over barking. I stretched out my hands and they sniffed them and went away. I entered the street and there was Bera, he ran towards me and jumped on me. Ah Bera! My faithful friend! I'm here, but look, I'm like a fugitive.

I hugged him and kissed him. Then we began to walk side by side. Bera was limping. A wall of the threshing room seemed to have collapsed. I went in quietly and crept in through the upper door.

Everyone was asleep. I tiptoed into my mother's room. She was sleeping with Sumra. I sat down and watched them for a while. Sumra was nearly a young woman. My mother had creases on her face. My dear mother! Who knows what pain she had suffered? There was the sound of a cock crowing in the distance. I was lucky to have come without being seen by anybody.

When my mother opened her eyes and saw me she shrunk back.

"Bismillah! [In the name of God]"

"Don't be frightened, Mum, it's me."

"Keko! My Keko! Is it really you, my brave boy?"

"Quiet Mum, they'll hear."

My mother got up and hugged me. With tears in her eyes she kissed my cheeks and head. A little later Sumra, too, woke up. They were both bewildered.

"Let no one hear I've come."

"Why, son?"

"I'll explain, Mum. Now I haven't got much time."

I turned to Sumra. "Sumra, go and tell teacher Fatih that I've come. He shouldn't tell anybody."

When Sumra left I told my mother what had happened. I had to find a way to get to Kato. Ascending was not a problem. It was necessary to get to the camp and speak to a commander without being shot.

My mother was on the one hand examining me and on the other sobbing. "My Keko! My brave boy! What a handsome young man you've become. Is it you? You're like a lion. And you've studied, eh? You're the rose of my bosom, Keko. If only your father had seen you!"

"Mum, don't cry. I'll come again, but now I have to find Tahir and return."

"My son, how many years have you been gone? I've died longing for you. And now you're going straight back?"

"Mum, I have to come back for you and for my siblings. I will take you to be with me, don't worry. My father has died but I am here. You are not alone."

My mother started to cry even more.

"Ah Keko, if only you knew…"

"Don't cry, Mum. Look, you'll make me cry too."

"Keko, you should know that you are the only one I trust. You are my only support."

That day there, if I had known what had befallen her, would I have left her in the village? I would have brought her and my siblings to Istanbul and not listened to anyone. Whatever it cost, I would have got them out of there. But I didn't know. It just didn't occur to me.

My mother brought teacher Fatih upstairs without anyone realising. He was waiting for me in my grandfather's room. My uncle and his sons had long before headed off to the mill. The children had gone downstairs to drink soup.

I embraced teacher Fatih. I was now taller than him, but I was still his little pupil.

"Tell me, this visit does not seem auspicious."

When he heard what had happened he nodded.

"Just as well you consulted me before going to the mountains."

"I have to go up, hodja. I can't return without him. I promised."

"They've probably not got off the bus yet. I'll find them. If we can get to them before they go up, we'll take him. If we can't, then there's no point going up. You won't be able to get him back easily. Those who go to the camp cannot return to their old lives."

Teacher Fatih changed my clothes and gave me a pair of glasses to wear. "Let's go together," he said.

He had told the village head man that: "A guest has come from the Ministry of National Education. I'm going to the city with him."

I said farewell to my mother and Sumra and went out. We walked through the fields and no one saw us.

We walked swiftly to a hamlet two villages distant. We were both out of breath. Out of fear I couldn't look around me. We went into one of the barns that was on the verge of falling down. We pulled away a pile of straw and passed into a neighbouring house. It was empty. In one of the rooms there were weapons. If soldiers had found me here I probably would have spent the rest of my life in prison.

"I assumed they would not pass by without coming here."

"Where shall we look now?"

"I hope they haven't gone up. I don't know."

We went back the same way and pushed the pile of straw against the door.

Seeing my questioning glances, teacher Fatih shook his head. "No, I'm not one of them, but in Heredile teaching is like this. You get to meet everybody."

Just as we came out of the barn, we heard voices. Seeing Tahir with four villagers I restrained myself from jumping up in the air with difficulty. The men a little while later emerged from the house they had entered without Tahir.

Teacher Fatih was concerned. "I don't know any of them. They probably don't know me either. They definitely won't give Tahir back."

The men had gone outside the hamlet. I went silently into the house. Tahir was sat in the corner, looking left and right. When he saw me he jumped to his feet in surprise.

"Hey Keko, what are you doing here? Or are you, too, going to Kato?"

I went up to him and pushed him in the chest. I was very angry.

"Idiot!"

"What's going on?"

"You're not thinking of your mother and father. Don't you think of my grandfather, either? Now how will we evade these guys and return?"

"I won't go back!"

"You'll go back! And immediately!"

He lowered his head. It was obvious that after setting out on the road he had felt regret. Just then teacher Fatih came in.

"The guys are coming back. They've got two sacks with them."

There were two sickles by the wall. I took one and quickly scratched Tahir's leg.

"Aagh!" He shouted.

Teacher Fatih was looking on, bewildered.

"Hide hodja!"

Then I turned to Tahir. "After the men left you climbed on the wall and fell. You can't go up, you need to see a doctor."

I quickly hid between some cupboards next to the wall.

Hearing Tahir's 'aagh!' the men came running in.

"What's happened?"

Tahir extended his leg. Exaggerating the pain on his face, he began to groan: "I think it's broken. I need a doctor."

"What doctor?"

"Before you've gone up the mountain are you going to cause trouble for the organisation?"

"Who's going to carry me?"

"Look, trouble!"

"And you were meant to be sturdy?"

"I'm still sturdy. What can I do if my leg is broken?"

"Piss off!"

"The fault is not yours, it's that of the one who thought you were a man and brought you here!"

"We're going to take these sacks up. You wait here. We'll come back for you. If soldiers come don't tell them anything."

"I won't."

"If you like, tell them, and I'll cut out your tongue."

After the men left we waited a little longer. Then I went out and looked after them. They were moving swiftly. Teacher Fatih said: "Let's wait a little. Just in case, we need to be sure."

We crossed the fields and went down a slope onto the road. We said farewell to teacher Fatih and hugged each other.

When we got to the bus station it was nearly dark. I went to the toilet with Tahir. "Wait here. Don't come out until I get the tickets. I will come and collect you."

If my aunt hadn't given me money I don't know how I would have bought the tickets. There were soldiers everywhere. It was best not to get off the bus. I wanted to take Tahir back to Istanbul in one piece and stick him in front of my grandfather.

For a time we didn't speak on the bus. I hadn't slept and wanted to sleep, but I was worried about Tahir doing something crazy. At the first break I sat him in the window seat and plonked myself down in the aisle seat. If I dropped off he wouldn't be able to get off the bus without waking me up. A little later Tahir went into a deep sleep. It was obvious that he, too, was very tired.

When we reached Istanbul I relaxed. We got off the bus. Tahir didn't want to go home. I dragged him to the bus stop. We got on the bus going to the 19 May neighbourhood. When we got to the neighbourhood our pace quickened. I wanted to see my grandfather as soon as possible. As we neared the house we saw a crowd. Crying: "Granddad!!" we both ran. We were not mistaken. My grandfather had been taken ill. Uncle Fevzi, a former health worker who lived nearby, had checked my grandfather's blood pressure. Seeing it was high he had given him medication. When my grandfather saw us he started to cry. Tahir ran and kissed his hands. It was as if he was apologising. My grandfather hugged him.

My aunt smothered Tahir with kisses. The she turned and kissed me.

"Keko, thank God for you. My God protect you."

When my uncle saw Tahir, a smile spread across his face. For the first time I felt he loved Tahir.

My aunt was joyful, as if she had given birth to Tahir again. Everyone, including my uncle, was surprised that he had returned so soon. My aunt kept saying: "Keko. How did you bring this madman back?"

"Aunt, you won't believe it, but it was easy. Even I was surprised. I won't lie. I had no hope of finding Tahir before he went up to Kato, and if I found him, of being able to bring him back."

My uncle shook his head and said: "Of course it was easy. You had your grandfather's prayers with you. What trouble could you get into?"

For the first time I was hearing my uncle say something positive about my grandfather. Even when he spoke well, he would reproach him. Now he was saying that we had avoided trouble on account of my grandfather's prayers.

My aunt had made potato *köfte*. She knew that Tahir, me, the children and my aunt all liked it. She gave the first plate to my grandfather and the second plate to me. I passed the steaming plate to my uncle. Another time my uncle would have looked askance at my aunt for not serving according to age. He took the plate and began to eat.

We were a family. If one of our finger nails was broken, we all felt the pain.

Chapter Nineteen

GULISTAN'S LOVE

In the 19 May neighbourhood there was drama in almost every house. There was hardly a single house that did not have problems with money, debts or illness. In winter conversations about rheumatism increased. According to Granny Çakır, the wild cucumbers that grew on the side of the road were just the job for rheumatism. Even small children had learned that garlic and lemon were good for blood pressure. Doctors could not cure epilepsy. The only remedy was to go to the traditional healer in the neighbourhood, who would banish spirits. Stutters were also not doctors' work. It was necessary to make a cut below the tongue. The circumciser Cemşir Efendi was the man for this. He had a light hand.

Those who had health insurance would ignore this and go to the hospital. They would wait in long queues and return with bags of medicines prescribed by doctors they saw for five or ten minutes. Those who didn't have health insurance would sometimes seek treatment at hospital by using a relative or friend's name. Most of the time they would seek out their neighbours' unused antibiotics or painkillers.

My grandfather did not like to use medicines. Whenever our tonsils swelled up he would rub warm olive oil into our necks and shoulders, immediately followed by giving us linden tea with clove and lemon.

I had no time to be ill. I was working day and night as if I was memorising all the lessons in year two.

I had an increasingly angry ambition inside me. It was as if I was getting my own back for the early days. No question that teachers asked would remain unanswered. I was working like mad so that I would get ten out of ten in my report.

So that none of my classmates had a part in my success, I didn't want to borrow lesson notes from anyone, even Aycan. I kept the best, most legible notes in the class. For this reason, everyone borrowed notes from me. I lent them without attaching importance to it.

"Mate, do the teachers tip you off beforehand or something?"

"Whichever paragraph you underline, the questions come from that one."

"You make a really good summary."

Everything had gradually fallen into place. I was the brightest student at the school. I had encountered Cevdet Bey a few times in the corridors. I had ignored him and passed him without greeting him. I thought he would discipline me, but he didn't mention it to anyone. Even if I knew I would be kicked out of the school, I wasn't going to greet him.

My uncle didn't even raise his voice to me anymore, let alone beat me. My aunt didn't let me leave Tahir's side. My grandfather was alongside me. The nicest was Aycan. She loved me. To know this was an indescribable happiness. If she knew about the poems I wrote about her, who knows what she would have done?

In all probability she would have opened her eyes wide and exclaimed: "Ali Kemal, you and poetry!... No, I'd never believe it. You are not the person to write a poem for love."

Perhaps she would have said something I didn't expect. Judging from Sude's significant glances, Aycan had told her something. Had she said: "I like Ali Kemal," I wondered. As for me, I was still not bold enough to confess my love. How love cast a spell on you. If I hadn't read dozens of novels I would have had doubts about myself. Could a man suffer the pain of love like a woman? Moreover, a man of the clan. Only men who had gone off the rails would cry over a woman. I knew that many of the things I had learnt in Heredile were nonsense, but I still couldn't get them out of my head.

However, heroes of novels explained wonderfully what a beautiful feeling love was, how it seared hearts, without discriminating between men and women. Someone who was not in love could not be aware of what it was to be a human being… But I still couldn't pluck up the courage to confess my love, and when I was alone I would shout to the sky: "I love Aycan! I'm in love with her. She is my everything! No one can take her from me!"

Despite all that I had experienced and the past, I was now happier.

I was returning home from the market with my aunt. We were both carrying bags.

My aunt was talking about the prices of everything we had bought.

"Even onions are expensive."

"Are there dishes without onion, aunt?"

"There are vegetables here that no one eats in the village that we cannot afford. If only they tasted like they do in the village."

Suddenly I stopped dead. Gülistan was there smiling at me.

"Hey Keko!"

My aunt didn't understand who it was. She looked at her and then at me.

"Keko, who is this woman?"

Gülistan wanted to take my aunt's bags from her. She resisted.

"Wait a minute. I recognise you from somewhere."

"You can't, aunt. I'm Gülistan. When you left the village I was still apparently drinking milk from my mother's breast."

"Aaaah! Bismillah!"

Gülistan's eyes resembled her mother's eyes. My aunt was flabbergasted. She assumed, as everyone did, that Gülistan had died.

"Bismillah! Oh my God!"

"Aunt, you don't seem to be pleased."

"Didn't you go up to the mountains?"

"I went up and descended as I had gone up."

"How was that?"

"Are we going to talk in the middle of the road? Let's go home."

"Yes, you're right. Let's go."

When we entered the house my grandfather was asleep. When Gülistan saw him she started to cry silently. Then she slowly approached him and kissed the hem of his jacket.

My aunt, Gülistan and I sat in the kitchen. My aunt was dumbfounded. I put the kettle on and went outside. When I returned with two packets of biscuits from the grocer's both of them were crying. Gülistan looked comfortable, as though she lived with us in that house. She began to prepare the glasses and tea tray.

"Keko, you never told me."

"If I had told you, what would you have done, aunt?"

"That's true, but is it right to fool everybody?"

"Gülistan always gave as good as she got and said:

"If they hadn't coerced me, I wouldn't have done it like that, for sure."

"Now stop, explain from the beginning."

As they talked, I looked at my grandfather. He was still asleep. I wanted to leave Gülistan and my aunt to talk privately, but my aunt said: "No way. You stay here. Now let Gülistan explain how it happened and how she got down from the mountain on her own."

"How did it happen, aunt? His name is not necessary, that bastard and me fell in love. His mother didn't want me. We were supposed to elope together. We had agreed to meet at midnight so I went past the cemetery to the edge of the village. We were to meet there and flee to Istanbul. I waited there until dawn. He didn't turn up. I went back home. Meanwhile my mother had noticed I had gone and told my father. When I got home my mother was being beaten by my father. They hadn't even bothered to go looking for me. They were only concerned about: 'What will we tell the villagers and how will we cleanse our honour.' When my father saw me he was delighted as if news had come from heaven, but he still gave me a good hiding. Then that lying dog sent me a message. 'Don't wait for me. I'm going up the mountain. Marriage is forbidden for me, I'm going to fight.' I still believed him. I missed him, as I thought he loved me. I left a note for those at home saying: 'I'm going to the mountain'. To reach the camp I walked for three days and three nights. All by myself, aunt. God knows how I managed it. When I think about it even now, I feel faint. Is it easy? Anyway, I reached the camp. I thought I was going to please that bastard. I was going to say: 'Look, I've come. If we're going to die, let's die together.' I thought he would be thrilled to see me, but what do I see? It seemed that he had also gone up the mountain after his love. He was really in love with someone else, but I hadn't realised. That is, he was stringing me along. Then when the girl he loved, the headman's daughter, went up to Kato, he followed her. When he saw me he couldn't hide it any longer. 'Forgive me, I love her. She doesn't love me, but I can't do without her,' he said. God damn him, even when he was enjoying himself with me, he was carrying a torch for someone else. Would I put up with that? I kicked up a row. I told everyone in the camp what he'd said to me. First the commanders were angry with both of us. Then one was kindly. 'You're wrong. Both of them are our women, our sisters. If you have deceived them you are deemed to have betrayed us, too.' They gave him a good telling off. He said to me: 'Don't stay here. You won't be any use to us. Don't waste yourself. Go back to your village.' I said okay, but was I going to return to the village? Straight off to Istanbul. I had already sent news to this one through Celil."

"Where have you been all this time in Istanbul, girl?"

"Don't go there!"

"Oh, woe is me! Or did bad things happen to you, Gülistan?"

"They didn't, but were going to. I made them regret being born. They intended to lead me astray and make money."

"My God! What did you do to escape, Gülistan?"

"What would I do, aunt? I'll hang the guy from the ceiling by his dick!"

"Then?"

"Thankfully, I met nice people."

"And how is everything now?"

"I'm really well. It's just as well I left Heredile."

"What do you mean, girl? Is there anywhere like the village? I miss it so much."

"No, no. I don't miss it. This is my home now."

"All by yourself?"

"Why should I be all on my tod? I'm getting married soon."

Until that moment I had been quietly listening to Gülistan, but on hearing the words: 'I'm getting married', I leapt to my feet. "Who are you marrying?"

"Ozan."

"Who's Ozan?"

"Cihan Bey's guard. He's been after me for a while. I was afraid of him, but now I love him, too. We're in love. He's a gentleman. He has a job and a salary. What else could I want?"

My aunt was embarrassed. "Enough, girl! What kind of talk is that, about love and romance?"

"Why, what's the problem?"

"Okay Gülistan, but why have you come here now?"

"Why do you think, to invite you to the wedding."

She stopped, then looked at my aunt, me and the house sadly.

"And I've missed my people. I wanted to see my grandfather… I would really like to see him and ask for his blessing, Keko."

"No way! If he sees you his blood pressure will rise."

My aunt didn't know what to say. Gülistan left an invitation and departed.

The next day while talking to Aycan in the break I raised the subject of Gülistan.

"Did you know?"

"Of course."

"You didn't tell me."

"Because she didn't want me to."

"You even hid it from me, you mean."

"Would it have been right, in your opinion? If she trusts me and shares a secret, would it be right for me to disclose it?"

She spoke so beautifully that when she spoke I forgot everything.

"Have you other secrets you haven't told me?"

She stopped and bashfully averted her gaze.

"Yes."

"What is it?"

"I said it's a secret, yeah."

"So you're not going to tell me."

"Actually, I want to tell you, but…"

"Eh, tell me in that case."

"I don't know."

"Come on, don't leave me in suspense, tell me."

She looked around, then took her marker pen out of her pocket. She reached out and took my hand. She opened my palm and said: "Close your eyes!" She wrote something on my hand with her pink marker pen. When she'd finished she closed my palm.

"Don't look now. When I go you can look."

I was really excited. I smiled and nodded. She ran off. As she left I opened my palm. "I've fallen in love," was written there.

I couldn't concentrate on listening to the teacher during the lesson. I was afraid someone else would see the writing on my hand. I didn't want to wash it. At least I wanted to examine each letter one by one that night and watch my palm.

As soon as the bell went I left the classroom. When Aycan saw me she scampered off to the upper corridor. A chase began that no one else was aware of. I eventually caught her at the bottom of the stairs leading to the attic floor. Without speaking I grabbed her hand and wrote: "With whom?" on her palm.

The next day we again ran into each other in the corridor. She was smiling like a mischievous child. It was her turn. In the canteen she came over in the crowd and swiftly wrote: "With an idiot," on my palm.

Was I stupid? I had a slight doubt about myself. If she meant someone else and I was assuming it was me, wouldn't I really be in a stupid situation?

As the queue moved forward we got closer to each other. Quietly, I said: "What is this idiot like?"

"He's very handsome. His eyes are beautiful."

"Is there such a handsome person in this school?"

"Do you want to meet him?"

The suspicion inside me began to increase.

"Perhaps."

"Okay, in the second period I'll introduce you, I promise."

I went into the classroom, but my mind was still on Aycan. I couldn't relax until I was sure. What if she was really in love with someone else? How would I forget her?

When the bell went I left the classroom. I felt uneasy. I was seriously afraid I was going to meet an unexpected person. Sude came over.

"I gather Aycan is going to introduce you to someone, yeah. I'm going to take you. She is waiting in the top corridor."

"Isn't that the teachers' section?"

"We've chosen it specially so that no one sees."

We went up the stairs together. On the one hand I was angry at myself. Why had I asked Aycan? When had she fallen in love with someone else? So why had she acted so warmly towards me? Whenever I looked at her she was smiling at me.

When we reached the corridor it was empty. Sude took a black band from her pocket. She said: "Put this over your eyes."

"What nonsense!"

"Ah! Are you scared?"

"Why should I be scared?"

"Quick, hurry up! If one of the teachers comes your meeting won't take place."

I put the black band over my eyes. Sude took my arm and guided me. I was just angry at myself. I was a fool who had become a plaything of the girls. We went through a door.

Sude said: "Now look. When I go out you'll take off the blindfold. The boy Aycan is in love with will have arrived."

"Where will he come?"

"To where you are. Don't move."

Sude left and closed the door and I removed the blindfold. I was in the teachers' toilet facing the mirror. I looked at my face in the mirror in bewilderment. It was me. The idiot Aycan was in love with was facing me. I smiled at my face in the mirror. For the first time I looked closely at my eyes. Aycan had said: "His eyes are really beautiful."

Just then the physics teacher came in.

"Ali Kemal, don't you know that students are not allowed in here?"

Even if all the teachers had come and been angry with me they could not have ruined my pleasure at that moment. I smiled and greeted the teacher.

"You're right, hodja, I'm leaving now."

"It's not on, breaking the rules doesn't befit a student like you."

****

I went to Gülistan's wedding secretly with my aunt. The groom, Ozan, was from Bursa. All his family showered Gülistan with bracelets, necklaces and earrings. Gülistan, with her bright red lipstick and blue eyelids, looked like a film star. What would the people of Heredile done if they had seen her like this, I wondered?

Just then Aycan came over and joined us. After that day she had avoided me. I turned. We looked at each other for a time.

"Why are you laughing?"

"Can't idiots be happy, too?"

"Are you happy?"

"Very."

As Gülistan and Ozan signed the register Aycan held my hand. For those few seconds it was as if the world had stopped.

Chapter Twenty

THE SPELL IS BROKEN

Sitting in the hospital room at the bedside of that slender, motionless body moving a little closer to death with every passing second I could not stop myself crying.

If it's necessary to own up, I'm not sure if I was crying for Keko or for other things.

From the photocopies of his journal that I had with difficulty obtained from the fat police superintendent in Stoke Newington Police Station on the pretext I might find a clue, I had learned of his adventures as far as Istanbul. How had he come to London, got mixed up with the Tottenham Boys and what had he experienced in that organisation? It was still a mystery. Perhaps the police had deliberately not given me those sections.

Whatever he had experienced, what had this young man wanted that life had deemed a noose to be appropriate for him?

What had he done apart from struggling at a risk to his life to leave his village to go to a state school?

Neither Istanbul nor London were his choice.

"Ah Keko! Ah Ali Kemal! Ah Hare! Ah Scribe! Ah apprentice butcher! The scholarship student at Ilim College. As if this were not enough, you also fell in love. Just as well you fell in love and loved that pretty girl. While everything was good why didn't you stay there, Keko? As fate loves such episodes of love, why didn't it leave you there? Okay, so you left your love behind and came after your mother, but how did you fall into the clutches of that gang? Why did you attempt suicide? Who is the boy who committed suicide alongside you? Why did you both do it at the same time in the same place? He died, you survived. Don't do it, Keko! Get up! Please come back! Don't leave Aycan."

I spent days at Keko's bedside. From time to time the Moroccan boy would come and after watching him for a minute or two would leave. Whenever I approached him to speak to him he would quickly flee like a frightened bird.

The information I had gathered was not at all encouraging. Keko had worked for drug dealers. According to police records he was in the gang. The fat superintendent replied to all my objections with sarcastic looks. The last sentence I managed to get out of him was mocking.

"Look at pictures of serial killers, you'll see that most of them look innocent."

He meant that Keko was one of the innocent-looking criminals.

I was frightened to talk to Keko's mother. It would be inhuman to make the poor woman's wound bleed more. Anyway, she had moved and I could not find her new address. If I managed to find her perhaps she would explain the whole story of her own accord.

Whatever happened something had to be done for Keko. He must recover and go to the university of his dreams with his sweetheart.

Habibe turned up. As soon as she saw me she said: "Your eyes are puffed up again."

I told her what I had read in Keko's journal. She asked for the fat superintendent's name and telephone number. As she stood up she said: "Go home and rest a bit. Tomorrow we'll go and speak to his mother."

I had no hope of that. I shook my head and said it wouldn't be possible. When she left the Moroccan boy came back. Approaching me timidly.

"What do the doctors say? Will he wake up?"

There was a sad despair on the boy's face? He must have been a good friend of Keko. I embraced him and put my head on his chest. He was probably caught up in the same swamp as Keko and was really the one who needed consoling, but I was in no state to console anyone.

"He'll get up. Pray!" I said.

The boy looked at me. "Even if he gets up he has no chance. Aziz will not allow him to live."

"Aziz?"

He looked at me quietly.

"Who's Aziz?"

"The big boss."

"Tell me, who is this boss?"

The boy acted as if he hadn't heard me, took my hands and kissed them and left. I called the fat superintendent and asked him: "Do you know anyone called Aziz?"

He didn't reply.

"Who is this guy? What's his connection to Ali Kemal?"

"Where did you learn this?"

The previous month I had laughed when the doctor told me: "You're on the verge of a depression," but I think I really had depression. Otherwise would it have been possible to cry over a boy I had only seen once on a bus?

The next day Habibe came by. "Come on, let's go," she said.

"Where?"

"To see his mother."

"What?"

For days I had been ringing around trying to find Keko's mother.

"Please don't tell me you got the address from the fat superintendent?"

"Of course I got it from him."

"Bastard! Why didn't he give it to me?"

"Could you look at him like I do?"

"How did you look at him?"

"Pig! He almost had an orgasm."

We went out. I was in no state to wait for a bus. "Let's get a taxi. I'll pay," I said.

Keko's mother was in a women's refuge. The police had told her: "You'll only be safe here." When she saw us she was initially excited, then wasn't sure whether to talk or not.

"I promise you. I'm going to help both Keko and you. But I need to know what happened to you."

She explained at length, crying as she did so.

When Keko's father, Ajar, became a village guard the whole family was ostracised. As she was a woman she couldn't do anything. She continued to work and look after her children. Their lives, that were already hard, became harder still. Her only hope was her son Keko in Istanbul. He was going to study, become something and then take them all to Istanbul.

It was fate. When they had brought her husband's dead body and left it in the threshing room she thought it was a prank. He was there just lying in the threshing room. She went to his side and waited there for a few minutes. It was unclear who had shot him. Was it soldiers or those in the mountains who had killed him? Perhaps they would never find out. She had hugged her children and cried for days.

For a woman whose husband died in Heredile there were two possibilities. Widowed women either had to marry a brother of their dead husband and continue to live in the same house, or leave their children and return to their father's house. She hadn't wanted any of her brothers-in-law. Was she to sleep with men she had known for years as brothers? She also couldn't leave her children. She had wanted to take her children to her father's house and continue her life there.

But it appeared that the traditions favoured men. No woman could take her children to their father's house. And widows on their own were not looked on favourably in the village. Whatever happened, she had to find a husband.

Thankfully, her brothers-in-law were fine, but the villagers were putting on pressure. It was as if they were taking revenge on her dead husband.

It was as if they were saying: "As you became a village guard, look, now we're going to force your wife to marry."

She had no choice. She was going to flee to Istanbul, to her son, Keko. Then he would take in the other children, too.

She had left the house after midnight and got a bus first thing in the morning. Two days later she had been locked in an articulated lorry with close to a hundred people she didn't know, mostly men. Crammed together in the dark they had begun their journey. They got out occasionally for some fresh air. People wet themselves, vomited, cried… the driver took no notice. A few days later they were deposited on the side of a mountain and told by the driver as he got back in the cab: "This is England." However, it was a lie. They had dumped dozens of people in Italy and cleared off. They then boarded a bus, then a train, then a ship. Finally, there were some who cried as they said they'd come to London. As they'd signed documents without thinking they were made to start work in a factory. As soon as they received their wages, most of the money was taken away from them. They were told: "First pay your debt, then bring over your children."

Months later she had been able to send news to Keko. Within a month he had arrived. But then he was different. He was always like that, even when he was a small child.

He had told her: "Don't be sad, mum, we'll return to Istanbul and bring my brothers and sisters there."

Men had confronted him and shown him the documents. They had told him: "These need to be paid."

Keko had made a calculation. "Mum, we will only be able to pay this in three years if we both work day and night."

Keko worked as a waiter during the day and a watchman at night. She worked in a factory. Keko's friend had got mixed up with a gang. One night he arrived suddenly. He was in a real mess. It appeared he had hidden the stuff in his bag under the bed. Then the gang had met Keko. Their leader wanted Keko, but Keko didn't want them.

The leader of the gang paid off her debts without asking them. At first they hadn't understood. They had been bewildered when the men had come and said: "We'll no longer ask for money from you. Aziz has paid your debt. From now on you'll pay him."

They hadn't realised it was a trap. But even if they had, what could they have done? Apparently the man called Aziz wanted to leave Keko with no choice. Then Keko's friend, who had come late at night, and had lost the packet he had taken to sell, had said: "It's with Keko". In fact, the boss knew it wasn't, but it was done to force Keko to join the gang.

Then, when Keko resisted, they had sent a message, saying: "We'll kill your mother."

In order to save his mother from the clutches of the gang he had attempted suicide with his friend.

The message they'd wanted to send had been: "Our mothers are no longer of use to you. Leave them alone."

This was what had happened. If Keko died could his mother still live?

I couldn't bear it any longer and clutched Habibe's hands.

"Please, find this Aziz for me. Just find him!"

"Are you crazy! The guy's obviously mafia. Those guys are dangerous."

I cried long and hard with Keko's mother until we were exhausted. Habibe left us. I went back to the hospital. When I saw the doctor I approached him.

"Is there no hope?"

"He's a tough boy. His body is very resilient."

I asked for permission to go in and see him. He was sleeping so beautifully I believed he wouldn't die.

In the evening Habibe arrived. She thrust Aziz's address into my hand and left, saying: "You're going to get me into trouble as well."

It was ten o'clock. I left the house and took a bus to Tottenham.

A little while later I was in a street with an underground disco. I went down the steps and took a deep breath in front of an iron door. There was a long queue. Nearly a hundred young people were waiting to get in. The substance users were obvious from their faces.

I rang the bell. A black man with gold front teeth opened the door. He realised straight away that I wasn't a customer. He looked at me as if to say: "What do you want?" A strong smell of smoke and the sound of strange music came from inside.

"I would like to see Mr Aziz."

"Who's Aziz?"

"I know he's here."

"Who are you?"

"I'm Aziz's aunt."

As if I had said something very strange he indicated for me to wait and went inside. A few minutes later he came back and let me in. The smell of grass was everywhere. There was no room on the dance floor. Moving between young people who had passed out on the floor we went upstairs to the second floor. We then went through a narrow corridor. The smell of marijuana and thick smoke had been left behind. The music could also no longer be heard. We went down stairs at the back into the garden. Walking along an ivy-covered path we passed a small wooden door virtually hidden behind two pine trees. We entered an imposing building made of long redbrick. The African left me at the door. A well-dressed Englishman in his fifties opened the door. In a calm voice he said: "Good evening madam," as he ushered me in.

We walked towards the stairs. Everything was clean and plush. We entered a dimly lit room contained large leather armchairs. One wall consisted of a large aquarium in which small piranha fish swam. There were soft red carpets on the floor. On a table was a jug of water and as yet unused glasses.

A tall man observed me then stood up. Before he asked, I answered: "I would like to see Mr Aziz."

He raised his eyebrows slightly and with a smile on his face looked at me.

"You said you were his aunt. You must recognise your nephew."

"Yes."

"I'm Aziz."

This man, who from the hair on his head to his very toes was the spitting image of an Englishman, was saying: "I'm Aziz."

I sat down in a plush armchair and rested my head. The blond-haired, blue-eyed, well-built Aziz sat in the opposite chair.

He was waiting for me to speak with a curious, impatient gaze.

I wasn't feeling the slightest fear. It was also apparent that he wasn't afraid.

Our eyes met. He looked more like a bank manager than a mafia boss.

"Why have you come?"

Rather than speak to him I felt like crying out to Keko.

"Die, Keko, die!

Die, child with beautiful eyes, die immediately!

This world does not deserve you.

Die!"

THE END